Mienthe tur[...]

them. A stranger. He was much older than Mienthe—older than Bertaud, she thought, though she did not understand why she thought so. His black hair was not streaked with gray and his eyes were ageless, but Mienthe was sure that he was actually much older than he looked. He had an austere, proud face and powerful deep-set black eyes. His clothing was all of black and a red as dark as dying coals.

And there was something strange about his shadow. It wasn't just the flickering light of the lamps: The shadow itself flickered with fire; it was *made* of fire, but with eyes as black as those of the man who cast it. And it was the wrong shape—not the shape of a man at all, but Mienthe could not have said what form could have cast it. She took an involuntary step back, expecting the rugs and drapes and polished wood of the solar to blaze up in flames. But the shadow seemed to contain its fire, and nothing else burned. Then the man turned his head, glancing at her with a strange kind of indifferent curiosity. Mienthe saw that although his eyes were black, they, too, were filled with fire. She stared back, feeling pinned in place with shock and terror, like a hare under the shadow of a falcon.

LAW OF THE BROKEN EARTH

THE GRIFFIN MAGE TRILOGY: BOOK THREE

RACHEL NEUMEIER

www.orbitbooks.net

This book is a work of fiction. Names, characters, places, and incidents are the product of the author's imagination or are used fictitiously. Any resemblance to actual events, locales, or persons, living or dead, is coincidental.

Copyright © 2010 by Rachel Neumeier
Excerpt from *House of Shadows* copyright © 2010 by Rachel Neumeier
All rights reserved. Except as permitted under the U.S. Copyright Act of 1976, no part of this publication may be reproduced, distributed, or transmitted in any form or by any means, or stored in a database or retrieval system, without the prior written permission of the publisher.

Orbit
Hachette Book Group
237 Park Avenue
New York, NY 10017
Visit our website at www.orbitbooks.net.

Orbit is an imprint of Hachette Book Group. The Orbit name and logo are trademarks of Little, Brown Book Group Limited.

Printed in the United States of America

First mass market edition: December 2010

10 9 8 7 6 5 4 3 2 1

This one's for Dad, who makes sure all the hardware in my life keeps running so that I don't have to be distracted by leaking pipes, oil changes, clogged filters, or any of the myriad nuisances that beset everyone not so lucky in their relatives. Thanks, Dad!

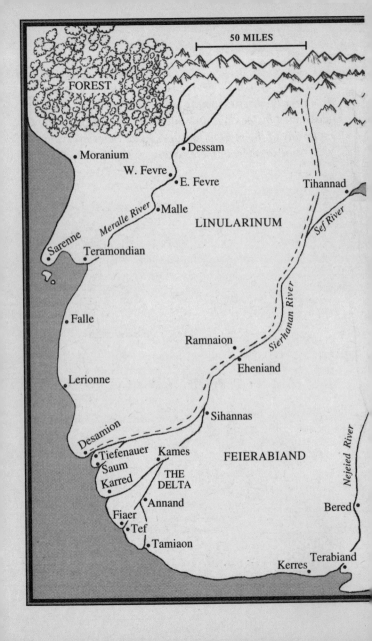

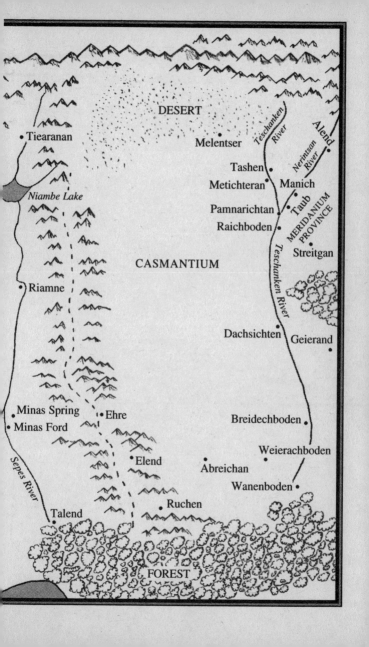

LAW OF THE
BROKEN EARTH

PROLOGUE

Mienthe did not remember her mother, and she was afraid of her father—a cold, harsh-voiced man with a scathing turn of phrase when his children displeased him. He favored his son, already almost a young man when Mienthe was born, and left Mienthe largely to the care of a succession of nurses—a succession because servants rarely stayed long in that house. If Mienthe had had no one but the nurses, her childhood might have been bleak indeed. But she had Tef.

Tef was the gardener and a man of general work. He had been a soldier for many years and lost a foot in a long-ago dispute with Casmantium. Tef was no longer young and he walked with a crutch, but he was not afraid of Mienthe's father. It never crossed Mienthe's mind that *he* might give notice.

Despite the lack of a foot, Tef carried Mienthe through the gardens on his shoulders. He also let her eat her lunches with him in the kitchen, showed her how to cut flowers so they would stay fresh longer, and gave her a kitten that grew into an enormous slit-eyed gray cat. Tef could speak to cats and so there were always cats about the garden and his cottage, but none of them were as huge or as dignified as the gray cat he gave Mienthe.

When Mienthe was seven, one of her nurses started teaching her her letters. But that nurse had only barely shown her how to form each letter and spell her own name before Mienthe's father raged at her about *Good paper left out in the weather* and *When are you going to teach that child to keep in mind what she is about? A sight more valuable than teaching a mere girl how to spell*, and the nurse gave him notice and Mienthe a tearful farewell. After that, Tef got out a tattered old gardener's compendium and taught Mienthe her letters himself. Mienthe could spell Tef's name before her own, and she could spell *bittersweet* and *catbrier* and even *quaking grass* long before she could spell her father's name. As her father did not notice she had learned to write at all, this did not offend him.

Tef could not teach Mienthe embroidery or deportment, but he taught Mienthe to ride by putting her up on her brother's outgrown pony and letting her fall off until she learned to stay on, which, fortunately, her brother never discovered, and he taught her to imitate the purring call of a contented gray jay and the rippling coo of a dove and the friendly little chirp of a sparrow so well she could often coax one bird or another to take seeds or crumbs out of her hand.

"It's good you can keep the cats from eating the birds," Mienthe told Tef earnestly. "But do you mind?" People who could speak to an animal, she knew, never liked constraining the natural desires of that animal.

"I don't mind," said Tef, smiling down at her. He was sitting perfectly still so he wouldn't frighten the purple-shouldered finch perched on Mienthe's finger. "The cats can catch voles and rabbits. That's much more useful than birds. I wonder if you'll find yourself speaking to some of the little birds one day? That would be pretty and charming."

Mienthe gazed down at the finch on her finger and smiled. But she said, "It wouldn't be very useful. Not like speaking to cats is to you."

Tef shrugged, smiling. "You're Lord Beraod's daughter. You don't need to worry about being useful. Anyway, your father would probably be better pleased with an animal that was pretty and charming than one that's only useful."

This was true. Mienthe wished she was pretty and charming herself, like a finch. Maybe her father...But she moved her hand too suddenly then, and the bird flew away with a flash of buff and purple, and she forgot her half-recognized thought.

When Mienthe was nine, a terrible storm came pounding out of the sea into the Delta. The storm uprooted trees, tore the roofs off houses, flooded fields, and drowned dozens of people who happened to be in the path of its greatest fury. Among those who died were Mienthe's brother and, trying to rescue him from the racing flood, her father.

Mienthe was her father's sole heir. Tef explained this to her. He explained why three uncles and five cousins—none of whom Mienthe knew, but all with young sons—suddenly appeared and began to quarrel over which of them might best give her a home. Mienthe tried to understand what Tef told her, but everything was suddenly so confusing. The quarrel had something to do with the sons, and with her. "I'm...to go live with one of them? Somewhere else?" she asked anxiously. "Can't you come, too?"

"No, Mie," Tef said, stroking her hair with his big hand. "No, I can't. Not one of your uncles or cousins would permit that. But you'll do well, do you see? I'm sure you'll like living with your uncle Talenes." Tef thought Uncle Talenes was going to win the quarrel. "You'll have his sons to play with and a nurse who will stay longer than a season and an aunt to be fond of you."

Tef was right about one thing: In the end, Uncle Talenes vanquished the rest of the uncles and cousins. Uncle Talenes finally resorted to the simple expedient of using his thirty men-at-arms—no one else had brought so many—to appropriate Mienthe and carry her away, leaving the rest to continue their suddenly pointless argument without her.

But Tef was wrong about everything else.

Uncle Talenes lived several days' journey from Kames, where Mienthe's father's house was, in a large high-walled house outside Tiefenauer. Uncle Talenes's house had mosaic floors and colored glass in the windows and a beautiful fountain in the courtyard. All around the fountain were flower beds, vivid blooms tumbling over their edges. Three great oaks in the courtyard held cages of fluttering, sweet-voiced birds. Mienthe was not allowed to splash in the fountain no matter how hot the weather. She was allowed to sit on the raked gravel under the trees as long as she was careful not to tear her clothing, but she could not listen to the birds without being sorry for the cages.

Nor, aside from the courtyard, were there any gardens. The wild Delta marshes began almost directly outside the gate and ran from the house all the way to the sea. The tough salt grasses would cut your fingers if you swung your hand through them, and mosquitoes whined in the heavy shade.

"Stay out of the marsh," Aunt Eren warned Mienthe. "There are snakes and poisonous frogs, and quicksand if you put a foot wrong. Snakes, do you hear? Stay close to the house. *Close to the house.* Do you understand me?" That was how she usually spoke to Mienthe: as though Mienthe were too young and stupid to understand anything unless it was very simple and emphatically repeated.

Aunt Eren was not fond of Mienthe. She was not fond of children generally, but her sons did not much regard their mother's temper. Mienthe did not know what she could safely disregard and what she must take care for. She wanted to please her aunt, only she was too careless and not clever enough and could not seem to learn how.

Nor did Aunt Eren hire a nurse for Mienthe. She said Mienthe was too old to need a nurse and should have a proper maid instead, but then she did not hire one. Two of Aunt Eren's own maids took turns looking after Mienthe instead, but she could see they did not like to. Mienthe tried to be quiet and give them no bother.

Mienthe's half cousins had pursuits and friends of their own. They were not in the least interested in the little girl so suddenly thrust into their family, but they left her alone. Uncle Talenes was worse than either Aunt Eren or the boys. He had a sharp, whining voice that made her think of the mosquitoes, and he was dismayed, *dismayed* to find her awkward and inarticulate in front of him and in front of the guests to whom he wanted to show her off. Was Mienthe perhaps not very clever? Then it was certainly a shame she was not prettier, wasn't it? How fortunate for her that her future was safe in his hands...

Mienthe tried to be grateful to her uncle for giving her a home, but she missed Tef.

Then, late in the year after Mienthe turned twelve, her cousin Bertaud came back to the Delta from the royal court. For days no one spoke of anything else. Mienthe knew that Bertaud was another cousin, much older than she was. He had grown up in the Delta, but he had gone away and no one had thought he would come back. Only recently something had happened, some trouble with Casmantium, or with griffins, or somehow with both, and now he seemed to have come back to stay. Mienthe wondered why her cousin had left the Delta, but she wondered even more why he had returned. She thought that if *she* ever left the Delta, she never would come back.

But her cousin Bertaud even took up his inheritance as Lord of the Delta. This seemed to shock and offend Uncle Talenes, though Mienthe was not sure why, if it was his rightful inheritance. He took over the great house in Tiefenauer, sending Mienthe's uncle Bodoranes back to his personal estate, and he dismissed all the staff. His dismissal of the staff seemed to shock and offend Aunt Eren as much as his mere return had Uncle Talenes. Both agreed that Bertaud must be high-handed and arrogant and vicious. Yes, it was vicious, uprooting poor Bodoranes like that after all his years and *years* of service, while Bertaud had lived high in the court and ignored the Delta. And flinging out all those people into the cold!

But, well, yes, he *was* by blood Lord of the Delta, and perhaps there were ways to make the best of it…One might even have to note that Bodoranes had been regrettably obstinate in some respects…

Since the weather in the Delta was warm even this late in the fall, Mienthe wondered what her aunt could mean about flinging people into the cold. And how exactly did Uncle Talenes mean to "make the best" of the new lord's arrival?

"We need to see him, see what he's like," Uncle Talenes explained to his elder son, now seventeen and very interested in girls, as long as they weren't Mienthe. "He's Lord of the Delta, for good or ill, and we need to get an idea of him. And we need to be polite. Very, very polite. If he's clever, he'll see how much to everyone's advantage raising the tariffs on Linularinan glass would be"—Uncle Talenes was heavily invested in Delta glass and ceramics—"and if he's less clever, then maybe he could use someone cleverer to point out these things."

Karre nodded, puffed up with importance because his father was explaining this to him. Mienthe, tucked forgotten in a chair in the corner, understood finally that her uncle meant to bully or bribe the new Lord of the Delta if he could. She thought he probably could. Uncle Talenes almost always got his own way.

And Uncle Talenes seemed likely to get his own way this time, too. Not many days after he'd returned to the Delta, Lord Bertaud wrote accepting Talenes's invitation to dine and expressing a hope that two days hence would be convenient, if he were to call.

Aunt Eren stood over the servants while they scrubbed the mosaic floors and put flowers in every room and raked the gravel smooth in the drive. Uncle Talenes made sure his sons and Mienthe were well turned out, and that Aunt Eren was wearing her most expensive jewelry, and he explained several times to the whole household, in ever more vivid terms, how important it was to impress Lord Bertaud.

And precisely at noon on the day arranged, Lord Bertaud arrived.

The family resemblance was clear. He was dark, as all Mienthe's uncles and cousins were dark; he was tall, as they all were tall; and he had the heavy bones that made him look sturdy rather than handsome. He did not speak quickly and laugh often, as Uncle Talenes did; indeed, his manner was so restrained he seemed severe. Mienthe thought he looked both edgy and stern, and she thought there was an odd kind of depth to his eyes, a depth that somehow seemed familiar, although she could not put a name to it.

Lord Bertaud accepted Uncle Talenes's effusive congratulations on his return with an abstracted nod, and nodded again as Uncle Talenes introduced his wife and sons. He did not seem to be paying very close attention, but he frowned when Uncle Talenes introduced Mienthe.

"Beraod's daughter?" he asked. "Why is she here with you?"

Smiling down at Mienthe possessively, Talenes explained about the storm and how he had offered poor Mienthe a home. He brought her forward to greet her lord cousin, but Lord Bertaud's sternness frightened her, so after she whispered her proper greeting she could not think of anything to say to him.

"*Manners*, Mienthe," Aunt Eren sighed reproachfully,

and Uncle Talenes confided to Lord Bertaud that Mienthe was not, perhaps, very clever. Terre and Karre rolled their eyes and nudged each other. Mienthe longed to flee out to the courtyard. She flushed and looked fixedly at the mosaics underfoot.

Lord Bertaud frowned.

The meal was awful. The food was good, but Aunt Eren snapped at the maids and sent one dish back to the kitchens because it was too spicy and she was sure, as she repeated several times, that Lord Bertaud must have lost his taste for spicy food away in the north. Uncle Talenes worked smooth comments into the conversation about the brilliance with which Bertaud had handled the recent problems with Casmantium. And with the griffins, so there *had* been something to do with griffins. Mienthe gathered that Feierabiand had been at war with the griffins, or maybe with Casmantium, or maybe with both at the same time, or else one right after the other. And then maybe there had been something about griffins again, and a wall.

It was all very confusing. Mienthe knew nothing about griffins and couldn't imagine what a wall had to do with anything, but she wondered why her uncle, usually so clever, did not see that Lord Bertaud did not want to talk about the recent problems, whatever they had exactly involved. Lord Bertaud grew more and more remote. Mienthe fixed her eyes on her plate and moved food around so it might seem she had eaten part of it.

Lord Bertaud said little himself. Uncle Talenes gave complicated, assured explanations of why the tariffs between the Delta and Linularinum should be raised. Aunt Eren told him at great length about the shortcomings of the Tiefenauer markets and assured him that the Desamion markets on the other side of the river were no better. When Uncle Talenes and Aunt Eren left pauses in the flow of words, Lord Bertaud asked Terre about hunting in the marshes and Karre about the best places in Tiefenauer to buy bows and horses, and listened to their enthusiastic answers with as much attention as he'd given to their parents' discourse.

And he told Mienthe he was sorry to hear about her loss and asked whether she liked living in Tiefenauer with Uncle Talenes.

The question froze Mienthe in her seat. She could not answer truthfully, but she had not expected her lord cousin to speak to her at all and was too confused to lie. The silence that stretched out was horribly uncomfortable.

Then Uncle Talenes sharply assured Lord Bertaud that of course Mienthe was perfectly happy, didn't he provide everything she needed? She was great friends with his son Terre; the two would assuredly wed in two years, as soon as Mienthe was old enough. Terre glanced sidelong at his father's face, swallowed, and tried to sound enthusiastic as he agreed. Karre leaned his elbow on the table and grinned at his brother. Aunt Eren scolded Mienthe for her discourtesy in failing to answer her lord cousin's question.

"I am happy," Mienthe whispered dutifully, but something made her add, risking a quick glance up at her lord cousin, "Only sometimes I miss Tef."

"Who is Tef?" Lord Bertaud asked her gently.

Mienthe flinched under Aunt Eren's cold glare and opened her mouth, but she did not know how to answer this question and in the end only looked helplessly at

Lord Bertaud. Tef was Tef; it seemed impossible to explain him.

"Who is Tef?" Lord Bertaud asked Uncle Talenes.

Uncle Talenes shook his head, baffled. "A childhood friend?" he guessed.

Mienthe stared down at her plate and wished passionately that she was free to run out to the courtyard and hide under the great oaks. Then Uncle Talenes began to talk about tariffs and trade again, and the discomfort was covered over. But to Mienthe the rest of the meal seemed to last for hours and hours, even though in fact her lord cousin departed the house long before dusk.

Once he was gone, Aunt Eren scolded Mienthe again for clumsiness and discourtesy—Any well-bred girl should be able to respond gracefully to a simple question, and why ever had Mienthe thought Lord Bertaud would want to hear about some little friend from years past? Anyone would have thought Mienthe had *no* sense of gratitude for anything Talenes had done for her, and no one liked an ungrateful child. Look up, Mienthe, and say, "Yes, Aunt Eren," properly. She was much too old to sulk like a spoiled toddler, and Aunt Eren wouldn't have it.

Mienthe said *Yes, Aunt Eren*, and *No, Aunt Eren*, and looked up when she was bidden to, and down when she could, and at last her aunt allowed her to escape to the courtyard. Mienthe tucked herself up next to the largest of the oaks and wished desperately for Tef. Speaking his name to her cousin had made her remember him too clearly.

Six days after Lord Bertaud's visit, not long after dawn, a four-horse coach with the king's badge in gold scrollwork

on one door and the Delta's in silver on the other arrived
at the house unannounced. It swished around the drive
and pulled up by the front entrance. The driver, a grim-
looking older man with the king's badge on his shoulder,
set the brake, leaped down from his high seat, opened
the coach door, and placed a step so his passenger could
step down.

The man who descended from the coach, Mienthe saw,
did not fit the image implied by its elegance. He looked
to be a soldier or a guardsman, not a nobleman. By his
bearing, he was well enough bred, but no one extraordinary. But he wore the king's badge on one shoulder and
the Delta's on the other. Mienthe did not move from the
window seat of her room. She was curious about the visitor, but not enough to put herself in her uncle's way.

She was surprised when Karre put his head through
her door a moment later and said, "Father wants you. In
his study. Hurry up, can't you?"

Mienthe stared after Karre when he had vanished.
Her heart sank, for whatever Uncle Talenes wanted, she
already knew she would not be able to do it, or at least
would not be able to do it properly, or would not want to
do it. Probably he wanted to show her off to the visitor.
Mienthe knew she would look stiff and slow and that
Uncle Talenes would regretfully tell his visitor that she
was not very clever. But Karre called impatiently from
out in the hall, so she reluctantly got to her feet.

She was not surprised to find the visitor with Uncle
Talenes when she came into the study, but she *was* surprised at Uncle Talenes's expression and manner. Her
uncle liked to show her to his friends and talk about what
he would do with her father's estate when she married

Terre, but this time he did not look like he had brought her in to show her off. He looked angry, but stifled, as though he was afraid to show his anger too clearly.

In contrast, the visitor looked...not quite oblivious of Uncle Talenes's anger, Mienthe thought. No, he looked like he knew Uncle Talenes was angry, but also like he did not mind his anger in the least. Mienthe admired him at once: *She* never felt anything but afraid and ashamed when Uncle Talenes was angry with *her*.

"Mienthe? Daughter of Beraod?" asked the visitor, but not as though he had any doubt as to who she was. He regarded Mienthe with lively interest. He was not smiling, but his wide expressive mouth looked like it would smile easily. She nodded uncertainly.

"Mienthe—" began Uncle Talenes.

The visitor held up a hand, and he stopped.

Mienthe gazed at this oddly powerful stranger with nervous amazement, waiting to hear what he wanted with her. She felt suspended in the moment, as in the eye of a soundless storm; she felt that her whole life had narrowed to this one point and that in a moment, when the man spoke, the storm would break. But she could not have said whether she was terrified of the storm or longed for it to come.

"I am Enned son of Lakas, king's man and servant of the Lord of the Delta," declared the young man. "Your cousin Bertaud son of Boudan, Lord of the Delta by right of blood and let of His Majesty Iaor Safiad, bids me bring you to him. He has decided that henceforward you will live with him in his house. You are to make ready at once and come back with me this very day." Looking at Uncle Talenes, he added warningly, "And you are not to fail of this command, on pain of Lord Bertaud's great displeasure."

"This is outrageous—" Uncle Talenes began.

The young man held up a hand again. "I merely do as I'm bid," he said, so sternly that Uncle Talenes stopped midprotest. "If you wish to contend with this order, Lord Talenes, you must carry your protest to the Lord of the Delta."

Mienthe looked at the stranger—Enned son of Lakas—for a long moment, trying to understand what he had said. She faltered at last, "I am to go with you?"

"Yes," said Enned, and he did smile then.

"I am not to come back?"

"No," agreed the young man. He looked at Uncle Talenes. "It will not take long to gather Mienthe's things," he said. The way he said it, it was not a question but a command.

"I—" said Uncle Talenes. "My wife—"

"The lord's house is not so far away that you will not be able to visit, if it pleases you to do so," Enned said. He did not say that Mienthe would visit Uncle Talenes's house.

"But—" said Uncle Talenes.

"I am to return before noon. We will need to depart in less than an hour," said the young man inflexibly. "I am quite certain it will not take long to gather Mienthe's things."

Uncle Talenes stared at the young man, then at Mienthe. He said to Mienthe, within his voice a note of conciliation she had never before heard, "Mienthe, this is outrageous—it is insupportable! You must tell the esteemed, ah, the esteemed Enned son of Lakas, you will certainly stay here, among people who know you and have your best interests close at heart—"

Mienthe gazed into her uncle's face for a moment. Then she lowered her gaze and stared fixedly at the floor.

Uncle Talenes flung up his hands and went out. Mienthe heard him shouting for Aunt Eren and for the servants. She lifted her head, giving the esteemed Enned son of Lakas a cautious glance out of the corner of her eye.

The young man smiled at her. "We shall leave them to it. Where shall we wait where we will be out of the way?"

Mienthe led the way to the courtyard.

Enned son of Lakas admired the huge oaks and trailed his hand in the fountain. Mienthe stood uncertainly, looking at him, and he turned his head and smiled at her again.

His smile lit his eyes and made Mienthe want to smile back, though she did not, in case he might find it impudent. But the smile gave her the courage to ask again, "I am not to come back?"

"That's as my lord wills," Enned said seriously. "But I think it most unlikely."

Mienthe thought about this. Then she turned and, going from one of the great oaks to the next, she stood on her toes, reached up as high as she could, and opened the doors to all the cages one after another.

The birds swirled out and swept around the courtyard in a flurry of sky blue and delicate green, soft primrose yellow and pure white. The palest blue one landed for a moment on Mienthe's upraised hand, and then all the birds darted up and over the walls and out into the broad sky.

Mienthe lowered her hand slowly once all of the birds were gone. When she nervously looked at Enned, she found that although he was looking at her intently and no longer smiling, his expression was only resigned rather than angry.

"Well," he said, "I suppose I can pay for those, if Lord Talenes asks."

Uncle Talenes did not ask. He was too busy trying to persuade Mienthe that she really wanted to stay with his family. Aunt Eren tried, too, though not very hard. Mienthe looked steadfastly at the floor of Uncle Talenes's study, and then at the mosaic floor of the entry hall, and then at the gravel of the drive. When Enned asked her if everything was packed that should be, she nodded without even glancing up.

"Well, you can send back if anything is missing," Enned told her, and to Uncle Talenes, "Thank you, Lord Talenes, and my lord sends his thanks as well." Then he handed Mienthe formally into the coach and signaled the driver, and the horses tossed up their heads and trotted smartly around the sweep of the drive and out onto the raised road that led through the deep marshlands into Tiefenauer.

Mienthe settled herself on the cushioned bench and fixed her gaze out the window. A bird called in the marshes—not the little brightly colored ones from the cages, but something that sounded larger and much wilder.

"You will like the great house," Enned said to her, but not quite confidently.

"Yes," Mienthe answered obediently, dropping her eyes to her folded hands in her lap.

"You cannot have been happy living with your uncle,

surely?" Enned asked, but he sounded uncertain. "Now we are away, will you not speak plainly to me? My lord did not mean to take you away from a house where you were happy. He will send you back if you ask him."

Mienthe turned her head and stared at the man. "But you said he would not send me back?" Then, as Enned began to answer, she declared passionately, "I will never go back—I will run into the marshes first, even if there *are* snakes and poisonous frogs!"

"Good for you!" answered Enned, smiling again. "But I think that will not be necessary."

He sounded cheerful once more. Mienthe looked at her hands and did not reply.

The great house was not what she had expected, though she had not realized she expected anything until she found herself surprised. It was not neatly self-contained, but rather long and rambling. It occupied all the top of a long, low hill near the center of town. It had one wing sweeping out *this* way and another angled back *this* way and a third spilling down the hill *that* way, as though whoever had built it had never paused to think what the whole would look like when he had designed the parts. It was made of red brick and gray stone and pale cypress wood, and it was surrounded by sweeping gardens—not formal gardens such as at her father's house, but wild-looking shrubberies with walks winding away into them.

The house was huge, but nearly all the windows were tight-shuttered, and there was nothing of the crowded clamor that should have occupied so great a dwelling. Mienthe remembered that her lord cousin was supposed to have dismissed all the staff. She would have liked to ask Enned about this, but she did not quite dare. The coach swept around the wide drive and drew to a halt, and the driver jumped down to put the step in place. Enned descended and turned to offer Mienthe his hand.

Lord Bertaud came out of the house before they quite reached it. He looked tired and distracted. Behind the tiredness and distraction was that other, darker depth that Mienthe could not quite recognize. But his expression lightened when he saw her, and he came down the steps and took Mienthe's hands in his.

"Cousin!" he said. "Welcome!" He smiled down at her with every evidence of pleased satisfaction. The darkness in his eyes, if it had been there at all, was hidden by his smile. Mienthe blushed with confusion and nervousness, but her cousin did not seem to mind, or even notice. He said to Enned, "There was no trouble?"

"Not at all," Enned replied cheerfully. "I enjoyed myself. What a pity all your orders cannot be such a pleasure to carry out, my lord."

"Indeed." Lord Bertaud released one of Mienthe's hands so he could clap the young man on the shoulder. "Go help Ansed put the coach away, if you will, and settle the horses, and then come report to me."

"My lord," Enned answered, with a small bow for his lord and another for Mienthe, and turned to hail the coach's driver.

Lord Bertaud drew Mienthe after him toward the house. "You will be hungry after your journey. I had my men wait the noon meal—I am afraid we do not have a cook as yet. Indeed, as yet we have few servants of any description," he added apologetically. "Of course you must have a maid, and I have arranged interviews for tomorrow, but for the moment you must make do with

Ansed's wife. Edlis is her name. I am sure she will not be what you are accustomed to, cousin, but I hope you will be patient with her."

Mienthe, who was not accustomed to any but the most grudging help with anything, did not know how to answer.

Lord Bertaud did not seem to mind her silence, but led her into the house and down a long floor. The floor was not decorated with any mosaic tiles. It was plain wood. Though the boards were clean, they were not even painted, and they creaked underfoot. He told her, "You may explore the house after we eat, or whenever you like. I have put you in a room near mine for now—all the house save part of this wing is shut up at the moment, but later you may certainly choose any room that pleases you."

They turned a corner and entered the kitchens, which were wide and sprawling, with three ovens and four work counters and a long table in front of two large windows. The windows were shaded by the branches of overhanging trees, but open to catch any breeze. The door to an ice cellar stood open, with a cool draft rising from it, and only one of the ovens glowed with heat. It was immediately obvious that there was no proper kitchen staff, for the meal was being prepared by a man who looked like a soldier.

"Yes," said Lord Bertaud, evidently amused by Mienthe's expression. "I did not want to hire a cook you did not like, cousin; the cook is almost as important as your maids. So it's camp cooking for us today, I fear."

"Well, my lord, I think we've managed something better than camp fare," the man said cheerfully. "Nothing fancy, I own, but a roast is easy enough, and you can always tuck potatoes in the drippings. And I sent Daued into town for pastries." The man nodded to Mienthe politely. "My lady."

Mienthe hesitantly nodded back.

"We will all eat in the staff hall today, with perfect informality," declared her cousin.

"Yes, my lord," agreed the man, and poked the roast with a long-handled fork. "This is so tender it's near melted, lord, so we can serve as you please."

"Half an hour," said Lord Bertaud, and to Mienthe, "I think you will like to meet my new gardener. I hired him just two days past, but I'm quite pleased. Just step out through that door and I think you will find him working in the kitchen gardens, just here by the house."

Mienthe stared at her cousin.

"Go on," Lord Bertaud said, smiling at her. "Tell him that everyone will be eating in the staff hall, please, cousin. In half an hour, but if you are a little delayed, no one will mind."

This all seemed strange to Mienthe, but then everything about her cousin seemed strange to her. When Lord Bertaud nodded firmly toward the kitchen door, she took a cautious step toward it. When he nodded to her again, she turned and pushed open the door.

The gardener was sitting on a short-legged stool, carefully setting new ruby-stemmed chard seedlings into a bed to replace long-bolted lettuces. Though his back was toward Mienthe, she knew him at once. She stopped and stared, for though she knew him, she did not believe she could be right. But he heard the kitchen door close behind her and turned. His broad, grizzled face had not changed at all.

"Mie!" Tef said and reached down for the crutch lying beside his stool.

Mienthe did not run to him. She walked, slowly and carefully, feeling that with any step he might suddenly turn into someone else, a stranger, someone she did not know; perhaps she only imagined she knew him because the smell of herbs and turned earth had overwhelmed her with memory. But when she reached the gardener and put a cautious hand out to his, he was still Tef. He rubbed dirt off his hands and put a hand on her shoulder, and pulled her into an embrace, and Mienthe tucked herself close to his chest and burst into tears.

"Well, now, it was an odd thing," Tef told her a little later, when the brief storm had passed and Mienthe had washed her face with water out of his watering jug. "This man rode up to my house four days ago. He asked me was I the Tef who'd used to be a gardener for Lord Beraod. I said yes, and he asked me all about the old household."

"And about me," Mienthe said. Four days ago, so Lord Bertaud must have sent a man to Kames almost as soon as he had left Uncle Talenes's house. So he must have been thinking even then about bringing her to live with him in the great house. That decisiveness frightened Mienthe a little because she still had no idea why her cousin had brought her to live with him.

"Yes, Mie, and about you, though not right at first. I could see he'd been working around to something, but I didn't rightly know what, and then after I knew what, I'd no idea of why. But I couldn't see what harm it would do to answer his questions, so I told him."

"Yes, but what did you tell him?"

"Well, the truth! That your mama died when you were

three and your father barely noticed you except when you got in his way; that Lord Beraod had a temper with a bite to it and couldn't keep staff no matter he paid high; that you had twenty-seven nurses in six years and hardly a one worth a barley groat, much less a copper coin; and that—" He paused.

Mienthe looked at Tef wonderingly. "What?"

"Well, that I'd let you follow me about, I suppose," Tef said gruffly. "So this man, he said Lord Bertaud, Boudan's son, had come back to the Delta and meant to be lord here, only he needed staff, and would I want to come be a gardener at the great house? I said I wasn't any younger now than I was then, but he said Lord Bertaud wouldn't mind about that. And then he said the lord would be sending for you, Mie, so I gave my house to my nephew's daughter and packed up my things, and, well, here we are."

Mienthe thought about this. Then she asked, "But *why* did he send for me?" and waited confidently for the answer. It never occurred to her that Tef might not know.

Nor was she disappointed. Tef said briskly, "Well, that's simple enough, I expect. You know the old lord, Lord Berdoen that was your grandfather, you know he was a terror, I suppose, and rode his twelve sons with a hard hand on the rein and whip, as they say."

Everyone knew that. Mienthe nodded.

"Well, Lord Boudan, your cousin's father, he had just the same cold heart and heavy hand as the old lord, so they say. Anyway, Lord Boudan, he sent his son to serve at court—that was while the old king was alive, but by all accounts, Prince Iaor liked Bertaud well and kept him close. So even after Lord Boudan and then the old king died, Lord Bertaud didn't come home—not but for flying visits, do you see. He'd hated his father so much he couldn't stand any part of the Delta, is what I'd guess, and so he stayed on at court. And he still is close to the king, from what they say about this past summer: They say Iaor sent your cousin as his envoy to Casmantium after that trouble this summer, did you hear about that?"

Mienthe shook her head uncertainly, meaning that if her uncle had said anything about it at the time, either he hadn't said it to her or she hadn't been paying attention.

"Well, I don't know much about it, either, but there's been talk about it around and about the Delta because of your cousin's being our right lord, do you see? And some folk say one thing and some another, but I guess there was some kind of problem with griffins coming over the mountains into Feierabiand early in the summer, but it all had to do with Casmantium somehow, which *that* part makes sense, I guess, since everybody knows that's where griffins live, up there north of Casmantium. And Lord Bertaud was important in getting it all to come out right, somehow, and then the king sent him to Casmantium after it was all over, to escort the young Casmantian prince to our court as a hostage—"

"Oh!" said Mienthe, startled, and then put a hand over her mouth to show she was sorry for interrupting.

"Well, that's what they say, though how our king made Casmantium's king send him, I'm sure I don't know. He must be about your age, I guess. The young prince, I mean."

"Oh," Mienthe said again, feeling intensely sorry for the displaced Casmantian prince. "I suppose he was sad to leave his home and go somewhere to live with strangers?" She supposed he might even have been sorry to leave his father, too, though that required some imagination.

Tef patted her hands. "Oh, well, Mie, a boy that age might be ready for an adventure, maybe. And you know, our Safiad king's a decent sort by all accounts. Anyway, I've barely seen your cousin to speak to, you know, but somehow I don't think he'd be the sort to lend himself to anything that wasn't right and proper."

"He seems kind," Mienthe whispered.

"He does that. Anyway, besides about the young prince, I heard tell of something about a wall in Casmantium, but I can't rightly say I know what that was about, except it was about the griffins again and likely needed some kind of mageworking to build. They say the Wall is a hundred miles long and was built in a single night, but I don't know as I believe even the greatest Casmantian makers and builders could do that. Not even with mages to help."

Mienthe nodded.

"Well, your cousin's no mage, but I guess he built that Wall, or maybe had it built, somehow. Whatever he did, he came out of it with honors from both the Casmantian king and our king, which you can maybe guess or else our king wouldn't hardly have sent his own men to serve Lord Bertaud here in the Delta, would he?"

Mienthe wondered again why her cousin had come back.

"Oh, well," said Tef, when she asked him. He paused, picking up a clump of dark earth and crumbling it thoughtfully in his fingers. "You know, Mie, I think maybe Lord Bertaud was hurt somehow in all that mess this summer, and don't fool yourself, if there was any kind of battle, I'm sure it was a right mess. They always are. Or maybe he was just tired out. I wonder if maybe he...well. What I think is, when it came right to it, when he found he needed a place to shut himself away from everything and just rest, somehow he found himself thinking of the Delta. It's in his blood, after all, however hard a man his father was."

Mienthe nodded doubtfully. "But—" she began, and then exclaimed, "Oh!" as she suddenly understood something else. "*That's* why he dismissed all the staff here— because he'd hated his father's house so much and didn't want anyone here who'd been here when he was a boy! Is that why?"

"I should think so. He's allowing the staff to reapply, but the word is, only the younger staff have a chance to come back—it's just what you said, he doesn't want anyone here who reminds him of those bad years. And that's why he sent for you, do you see, Mie? Because he saw you in your uncle Talenes's house and you reminded him of himself, that's what I expect happened, and he decided to rescue you just as the king once rescued him."

"Yes..." Mienthe said softly. She could see this was true, that it must be true. Her heart tried to rise up and sink both at once. From being afraid that she would not be able to please her cousin and that he would send her back, she found herself afraid that she would not be able to please him and that he would be disappointed in her. Her famous, important cousin might not be sorry he had rescued her, but he would be sorry he had rescued *her*. That he had not found a girl who was clever and pretty and graceful—someone he could be proud of having rescued. Tears welled up in her eyes, and she rubbed her sleeve fiercely across her eyes—she never cried, and here she was weeping twice in an hour!

In an hour. Mienthe jumped to her feet and said, "He said half an hour!" and then she *really* wanted to cry, because here she had barely arrived at the great house and already she was letting her cousin see how careless and stupid she was—

"Hush, Mie, it'll all be well," Tef promised her, patting her foot because he couldn't reach her shoulder. "Do you think he didn't know we'd get to talking? Hand me my crutch, there's a sweet girl, and don't cry."

If you are a little delayed, no one will mind, her cousin had said, Mienthe remembered, so maybe Tef was right. She tried to smile, but still said anxiously, "But we should hurry. To the—to the staff hall, he said."

"The staff hall it is, then," Tef agreed, climbing laboriously to his feet.

CHAPTER 1

Six years later

Tiefenauer, largest town of all the wide Delta, was a place of broad streets and ancient cypresses and swamp oaks. Wooden boardwalks lay beside all the important streets, allowing passersby to keep out of the winter mud that sometimes flooded even over the cobbles. Deep drainage channels ran underneath the boardwalks, so that only the greatest storms of spring and fall would flood the town. Even so, winter and spring and fall were the seasons when Tiefenauer bustled with energy and life.

In the summer, when the days grew long and the air hung motionless and heavy, the town became as somnolent as the air. Flowers of purple and red tumbled from every balcony, and it seemed that every house in Tiefenauer had at least one balcony. Fat bumblebees hummed placidly among the flowers, and all the people of Tiefenauer hung out little pots of sugar water to attract the large purple-backed hummingbirds, and the little red-throated ones, to their balconies. Larger birds darted among the branches of the great trees and nested in the streamers of moss that festooned them.

Years ago, Tan had lived in Tiefenauer for one long, lazy summer that stood out, jewel-bright, in his memory. He wished fervently that it was summer now. The Delta was seldom so terribly cold, but it surely seemed cold enough. He knelt, shaking and half frozen, in the dirty straw of his cell, and tried not to laugh. There was nothing the least amusing in his situation, except that it was so utterly, perfectly ludicrous.

He said to the prison guard—a brawny young man with broad shoulders, big hands, and, currently, an expression of grim distaste, "I suppose everyone begs you to carry messages to their friends and promises rewards for the favor. But does everyone ask you to take a message to the lord himself? Not even a message. Just a name. I swear to you, he'll know that name. I swear to you, he'll want to see me. He *must* see me. It's—"

"Desperately important, I know," interrupted the young guard. He gave a scornful, uneasy jerk of his head. "Of course it is. But they're busy up in the great house. Anyway, it's against the rules. That's enough for me! Do you think I want to be stuck down in this pit forever? I'll warn you, though, don't trouble offering a bribe to Jer when he comes on duty. He'll take your money and give you nothing for it."

"If I had anything to bribe either of you with, I'd risk it," Tan assured the young man. "Unfortunately, all I can offer is a promise that if you take my name up to the great house, you'll not remain a prison guard."

"Because I'll be a prisoner myself?" the guard said, not quite as naive as he looked. "Indeed, I would be in your debt, esteemed sir. I said, it's against the rules." He half turned, preparing to go on with his rounds.

Tan longed to pound his hands against the floor and shout. But it wouldn't help, and anyway he was too tired. He made himself speak softly instead. "Well, I'm sure that's a comfort to you. When I'm found murdered in this cell, I hope you will wonder how far you are responsible. But you won't need to reproach yourself, will you? You'll know you followed the *rules*."

The guard turned back, frowning. "I think you're safe enough in our keeping."

Tan laughed out loud. "You think, what? That I'm some thief or common thug? I'm asking you, begging you, to take my name to the Lord of the Delta himself, and you think I'm a *thief*? Is that what you think?"

The young guard opened his mouth, shut it again, turned his back, gave Tan an unsettled look over his shoulder, and walked out. The door slammed behind him with disheartening finality, leaving Tan alone in the dark and cold. Tan pressed his hands over his eyes. Perhaps a little less sarcasm, a little more humility? If he had not learned a measure of humility tonight, he surely never would.

He eased himself back to sit against the wall. The stone was dry enough, but cold. It seemed to suck the warmth right out of his bones. After a moment he hunched away from it and huddled into the straw. The window of his cell admitted, at the moment, nothing past its bars more alarming than the chill air of earliest spring and little curls of mist. Tan wondered how long it would take for Linularinan agents to track him to this cell. How they would laugh, to find him so stupidly trapped, and by his own people! And then someone would throw a poison dart through that window or, much worse, bribe the prison guards to release him into their hands. And after that...

It was appalling that only the basic integrity of a young prison guard who didn't break the rules might protect him from his enemies. He knew, of course, that no such integrity could possibly protect him well enough.

The outer door swung back suddenly, letting in the bright swinging light of lanterns and the heavy tread of boots. Tan straightened, then got to his feet and tried to look intelligent and at least somewhat respectable. The young guard had come back, and with him was the officer of the watch: a powerful man with a harsh, brutal face.

"Well?" he said to Tan.

"Esteemed Captain," Tan said immediately, and bowed.

"You don't consider our protection here adequate, is that right? You've got *special* enemies, that's what I hear. You think you'll fare better if your name goes up the hill, do you?"

"If you please to send it, esteemed sir, and I swear to you it will be recognized."

The captain looked Tan up and down with obvious distaste. "You're safe enough here, I assure you, so you may set your heart at rest on that account."

Tan bowed his head and said nothing.

"Huh. A prodigal cousin, are you? Got in bad company and came dragging home to beg pardon and payment of your debts from the lord?"

"If you like," Tan agreed obligingly. He tried to look dissolute and repentant.

"You think Lord Bertaud will be happy to hear your name, do you? Not likely! Theft, brawling, murder: What else do you drag at your heel? You think the lord will pardon all that for whatever blood you might have in common?" The captain sounded like he doubted this. He said with grim satisfaction, "You think he wants some bastard half cousin up at the great house *now*, with the king's household in residence? If you had the sense of a turnip, you'd hope no judge had time for you until next month, after the king's gone back to Tihannad, if you hope for mercy from Lord Bertaud."

Tan gazed at the captain. He said slowly, "King Iaor is here?"

"You didn't know?" This time, the captain sounded honestly astonished. "Earth and sea, man, where have you been the past six years? It's that long since His Majesty began breaking his annual progress in the Delta for a month or more! Ever since Lord Bertaud came home." He looked grimly pleased to crush Tan's hopes.

"If Bertaud doesn't know my name, Iaor will," Tan declared at once, hoping it was true.

The captain scowled. "*Lord* Bertaud, man, and *King* Iaor, man! Let us have some respect!"

Tan bowed apology. "I beg your pardon, esteemed Captain. I meant no disrespect." He tried to remember a name that both Bertaud and the king might recognize.

"Well," the captain said, looking at him hard. "And what name is it that they'll know, up at the great house?"

"Teras son of Toharas," Tan said, hoping that this was true.

"Huh." The captain turned his head and fixed the young guard with a cold eye. The young man straightened his back and swallowed. "Since you and the prisoner are both so concerned for his safety, you can stay on after your shift and keep an eye on him," said the captain. "Without extra pay, of course." He walked out.

The young guard looked morosely at Tan. "Thank you so much. I ought to beat you bloody."

"Your captain may yet send my name up the hill," Tan said softly. "That chance is worth any beating. So is your watchful presence here. Did you think I did not mean my warning to you? You may well have saved my life tonight." He bowed his head, adding formally, "I am in your debt, and you may call upon me." He looked up again, smiling, and added, "For all you may not find such a promise very impressive just at this moment. What is your name, if I may be so bold as to inquire?"

The guard seemed warily impressed, and not very inclined to carry out his threat. He hesitated for a moment and then said, "Tenned. Son of Tenned."

"Tenned son of Tenned. I thank you." Tan bowed. Then, as the young man did not seem likely to carry out his threat, Tan sat down in the straw, wrapped his arms around his body, and tried not to shiver the last of his strength away. Tenned's presence was indeed a comfort and a safeguard. Tan might even dare to rest, if he were not so cold.

Tenned regarded him for a long moment. Then he set his jaw, hooked his lantern to a hook high up in the wall, and left the room.

But he came back in mere moments with a threadbare blanket and a hard roll stuffed with sausage, both of which he tossed wordlessly through the bars to Tan.

Despite his surprise, Tan caught the food and the blanket. A flush crept up the guard's face when Tan stared at him, making him seem younger still. Tan shook his head. "Truly, you need a place in some other company. You are too kind to be"—he gestured at the walls of his cell and, by extension, at the prison entire—"here."

The guard crossed his arms uneasily across his chest and glanced away. But he said in a low voice, "Maybe, if the captain doesn't send word up the hill... maybe I'll go after all. At noon." He gave Tan a hard look. "If the captain lets me off duty at noon. That's a double watch. He'll set up to three extra, if he's angry enough. He did that to a new guard last week, when he let a prisoner get his keys."

Tan might have wished Tenned to be careless enough to let Tan get his keys, but this seemed most unlikely. He contented himself with nodding sympathetically.

But at two hours past dawn, the guard captain came back himself, with a pair of extra guards and a set of slender keys. The stamp of their boots woke Tan, who sat up and then got to his feet, laying aside the blanket with a nod of thanks to Tenned.

"I don't know as anyone recalls your name, mind," the captain told Tan. "Maybe they're only interested. But you're to go up and they'll take a look at you, at least. *I* wouldn't care to miss it. I'm taking you up myself."

Tan looked over the two guards the captain had brought with him and shook his head. "You should have more men."

The captain lifted his eyebrows. "What? That tough, are you?"

"Not for me. Six men, at least. Ten would be better. You should detail half to keep their attention outward."

For a long moment, the captain was silent. Tan wondered whether he had at last succeeded in impressing the man with his sincerity, if nothing else. Or, given the captain's harsh, expressionless stare, whether he had at last succeeded in offending the man beyond bearing. The man had shoulders like an ox; he could undoubtedly deliver a ferocious beating if he decided a prisoner was being deliberately insolent. "Not that I'd try to instruct you in your business, esteemed Captain," Tan added, trying his best to look respectful.

But the captain only said at last, to one of his men, "Beras, go round up everyone who's free and tell 'em meet us at the front gate. Tenned. Unlock that cell." He shot Tan an ironic look and threw the young guard a set of manacles. "Chain the prisoner."

Tan put his hands out cooperatively, hoping to get Tenned to chain his hands in front of his body rather than behind. From the deepening irony of the captain's expression, the man recognized that old trick. But he said nothing, and Tenned did indeed allow Tan to keep his hands in front.

The great house stood, in fact, on a long, low hill—low, but the only hill for half a day's travel in any direction, the Delta not being renowned for hills of any kind. The house was itself essentially long and low, though one wing had two stories and one round tower at the edge of the adjoining wing stood two stories higher than that. The tower was windowless. Tan wasn't quite certain what that said about the character of the man who had commanded it built.

The house had been built by a succession of Delta lords, each adding to it primarily by building out into its grounds rather than upward. One wing of the house had originally been stables—but very fine stables—and another had once probably been a mews, from the look of the extremely broad windows. The current stables and mews and kennels were just visible, far around the side of the house. If Tan had seen them earlier, he might have guessed that the king was in residence, both from the general busy atmosphere and from the fineness of the horses. The guard captain appeared to be heading for a door over in that general area.

The captain had, in the end, surrounded Tan with nine guards and had ordered five of them to forget the prisoner and watch the streets. Half a dozen crows flew overhead, cawing harshly. They flew ahead of the little procession and over the rooftops to either side. Another crow perched on the captain's shoulder, tilting its head this way and that, its bright black eyes intelligent and alert. It seemed the captain had an affinity for crows. At the moment, Tan could hardly imagine a more useful affinity, though he'd have preferred to have a larger flock looking for trouble. Though, even so, it didn't seem likely anyone with a bow could stay hidden on a roof with even a few crows flying watchfully near. Even a man who could whisper to his arrows and make them turn to strike their target had to aim somewhere *near* where he wanted them to strike.

The captain followed the flight of his crows with a frowning look, then turned his attention back to his prisoner. Perhaps he suspected some ruse on Tan's part. Tan would have been happy to have a ruse in mind, but he did not. Perhaps it was better so. As his trouble last night had so clearly demonstrated, he might in fact be safer in chains and surrounded by guards than he would have been slipping quietly through the city on his own. Especially with royal guardsmen set all about the great house.

"Here we are," the guard captain said to Tan as they came up to a narrow, plain door set in the side of a plain, windowless building. "I see we had enough crows after all—and two or three guards would have been sufficient, after all."

"Unless the force you displayed deterred my enemies," Tan suggested blandly. "Esteemed Captain."

The captain looked at him fixedly for a moment. But then he merely put out one massive hand and shoved the door open. It was not locked. They shed half the guards and all the crows as they went through it, and through a barren entryway, and at last into an unadorned reception room that contained nothing but a small table and one chair.

The chair was occupied. Bertaud son of Boudan—so Tan supposed—looked up. His gaze was intent and mistrustful, but not, Tan thought, actually hostile. At least, not yet. The young man Tan remembered from the court at Tihannad had grown into a solid, self-assured lord. He'd come to look a good deal like his father, which must surely gall him. But there was an interesting depth in his eyes, and lines around his mouth that Tan did not remember. Tan wondered how he had come by that compelling intensity.

Tan went to one knee before Bertaud's chair, rested his bound hands on his other knee, and bowed his head for a moment. Then he lifted his head and looked Bertaud in the face. Their eyes met. Bertaud's look became searching, then questioning. He drew breath to speak.

Before he could, Tan said quickly, "Hair darker than yours. Longer than yours, tied back with a plain cord. Ten fewer years, forty extra pounds, and no sense of style. A ring on my left hand—"

"A beryl," Bertaud said. He straightened in his chair, frowning. "Set in a heavy iron ring. You were before my time." He meant, before Iaor had made him lord of the king's own guard. "I remember you with Moutres." Lord Moutres had held that post of trust for Iaor's father and then, for some years, for Iaor.

Rising, Bertaud came forward to examine Tan more closely. "How do you come here?"

"Ah…" Tan hesitated. He asked cautiously, "Do you know… what I did for, um, Moutres?"

Bertaud frowned again. "Not in detail."

"The king knows—"

"His Majesty is otherwise occupied."

There wasn't a lot of give in that flat statement. Tan paused. Then he said, "I've just come across the bridge. From Teramondian. I was too closely pursued to get across the river farther north; I was forced to run south and even so I hardly made it out of Linularinum. But now I understand that His Majesty is here after all, so that's well enough. If he'll see me. Or if you will, my lord, but *privately*, I beg you."

Bertaud simply looked at him for a long moment. Tan tried to look like an earnest servant of the king rather than a desperate fool who'd put a foot wrong in the Linularinan court and run home for rescue. After a moment, Bertaud said, "Teras son of Toharas, is it? Is that the name I should give to the king?"

Tan hesitated. Then he surprised himself by saying,

"Tan. You may tell His Majesty it is Tan who has brought him a difficult gift."

"Son of?"

Tan shook his head. "Just Tan." He was prepared for either suspicion or scorn, depending on whether the lord took him for insolently reticent or the son of a careless father. He certainly did not intend to lay out any explanations. Especially as both answers obtained.

But he saw neither suspicion nor scorn. Lord Bertaud only inclined his head gravely. "So I shall inform the king," he said, gave the guard captain a raised-eyebrow look, and left the room.

The captain stared down at Tan and shook his head. "Huh."

Tan bowed his head meekly and composed himself to wait.

After a surprisingly short time, however, the door swung open once more. Bertaud came in first, but stepped aside at once and personally held the door.

Iaor Daveien Behanad Safiad, King of Feierabiand and, more or less, of the Delta, clearly did not keep any great state when he visited Tiefenauer. He had brought no attendants nor guardsmen of his own; he wore no crown and no jewels save for a ruby of moderate size set in a heavy gold ring. But nevertheless, even if Tan had never seen him before, he would have known he was looking at the king.

King Iaor was broad, stocky, not overtall. But he held himself with more than mere assurance, with a presumption of authority that was unquestionably royal. Tan took a breath and waited for the king to speak first. But the king glanced impatiently toward the door, so Tan gathered they were in fact still waiting for someone—perhaps the king was not without attendants after all.

Lord Bertaud was still holding the door, with an air of amusement as well as impatience. A hurried tread was audible, and then a stocky, broad-shouldered young man of perhaps eighteen entered hastily, escorting a girl about his own age, trim-figured and pretty in a straightforward way, wheaten hair caught back with a ribbon.

"I beg your pardon, cousin," the young woman said hastily to Bertaud, then bit her lip and turned to the king. "It's my fault Erich's late—I asked him where he was off to in such a hurry and then I made him bring me. If you—that is, if you don't mind? Please?" She glanced sidelong at Bertaud.

"Mienthe—" began Bertaud, in a tone of exasperated affection.

"The fault was entirely mine," declared the young man, who must be, Tan realized, Erichstaben son of Brechen Glansent. Or, as the Casmantians would have it, Prince Erichstaben Taben Arobern, first and only son of Brechen Glansent Arobern, *the* Arobern, King of Casmantium, currently a hostage at the court of King Iaor. Though the Casmantian prince certainly did not seem to feel his status as a hostage. He said to Iaor, in a deep voice that carried a guttural, clipped accent, "Your Majesty, if you will pardon my forwardness—"

"*If* you please—" began Bertaud sternly.

King Iaor held up a hand and everyone stopped.

A reluctant smile crooked Bertaud's mouth. "You won't permit me to scold them?"

The king said drily, "If Erich is to attend us here, then I can imagine no possible reason your cousin should not."

He gave the pair a long look and added, "Though if I send you away, I shall expect you to go without argument."

Both Erich and Mienthe nodded earnestly.

The king returned a grave nod. Then he looked at Tan for a long moment, his expression impossible to read. Then he said, "Teras son of Toharas?" To Tan's relief, his voice held recognition and a trace of amusement.

"I've gone by that name," Tan said, a little defensively. "Not for some time, I admit."

"No," agreed the king. "Though I recall it. But it is your own name that brought me to hear you." He sat down in the chair and raised his eyebrows. "Well? I understand you meant to come to me in Tihannad? You are far out of your way."

"Fortunately, so is Your Majesty," Tan said smoothly. He glanced around at the clutter of guardsmen. "You'll want to speak to me privately. Or more privately than this, at least." He thought he should ask the king to send away the Casmantian prince and Bertaud's cousin, but he also thought Iaor would refuse. And at least he could be almost entirely certain that neither of them could possibly be a Linularinan agent.

King Iaor tilted his head to one side and glanced at Bertaud. Bertaud nodded to the captain. "You and your men may wait outside." When the captain glowered in disapproval, he added, "If you would be so good, Captain Geroen."

The disapproval became outright mulishness. "No, my lord. With His Majesty right here, *and* your lady cousin?"

"We know this man," Lord Bertaud said patiently.

"You don't, my lord, begging your pardon. You might

have done once, but now he's been in Linularinum, hasn't he? For years, isn't that so? And this is a man my guardsmen took up for mayhem and murder! He had two bodies at his feet when they found him, and him unmarked!"

Bertaud's eyebrows rose. The king sat back in the chair, crooking a finger across his mouth. Erich grinned outright, but Mienthe looked solemn and a little distressed. The guardsmen all stared at their captain in horror.

The guard captain said grimly, "My lord, neither you nor His Majesty nor Lady Mienthe will be left alone with a dangerous prisoner while I'm captain of the prison guard. Nor I won't resign. You can dismiss me, if it please you. But if you do, if you've any sense, my lord, you'll call for someone you trust before you talk to this man. Dessand, maybe, or Eniad. Or some of His Majesty's men." He glared at Bertaud.

"I think," Bertaud said gently, after a brief pause, "that you had better stay with us yourself, Geroen."

Captain Geroen nodded curtly.

"Then, if you will free the prisoner's hands, and dismiss your men—"

"Nor you won't loose those manacles, my lord, not without you keep more than one man by you! No, it won't do him any harm to wear iron a bit longer."

This time the pause stretched out. But at last the lord said, with deliberate patience, "Perhaps you will at least permit me to dismiss your men?"

Geroen set his jaw. His heavy features were not suited to apology, but he said harshly, "I'd flog a man of mine for defiance, my lord, of course I would. I'll willingly take a flogging on your order, just so as you're alive to *give* the order! I beg your pardon, my lord, and beg you again not to take risks that, earth and *iron*, my lord, *are not necessary*."

Tan was impressed. He rather thought the guardsmen had all stopped breathing. He knew they had all gone beyond horror to terror. If he'd meant to try some move of his own, this would surely have been the moment for it, with all attention riveted on the captain. Alas, he had no occasion to profit from the distraction.

"Captain Geroen, you must assuredly dismiss your men, if you are going to corrupt their innocence with so appalling an example," Bertaud said at last, after a fraught pause. "You may do so now."

The captain made a curt gesture. His men fled.

"I think," Bertaud said drily to the king, "that this is all the privacy we will be afforded."

The king was very clearly trying not to smile. "Your captain's loyalty does you credit, my friend." He transferred his gaze from Bertaud to Captain Geroen. "Of course, without discretion, loyalty is strictly limited in value."

There was nothing Geroen could say to that. He set his heavy jaw and bowed his head.

"So," Iaor said to Tan, his tone rather dry, "perhaps you will now tell us the news you've brought out of Linularinum."

Tan glanced deliberately at Prince Erichstaben, at Lady Mienthe.

"I think we need not be concerned with Erich's discretion," King Iaor said.

"Certainly not with Mienthe's," Bertaud said crisply.

Tan sighed, bowed his head, and said, "I'm one of

Moutres's confidential agents, as you no doubt recall, Your Majesty. I don't know whether you knew that I've been in Linularinum, in Teramondian, at the old Fox's court? Been there for years, doing deep work, do you understand? And I won something for it. I got Istierinan's private papers."

"Istierinan Hamoddian?" King Iaor asked sharply.

Tan tried to look modest. "Why, yes. Himself. He was a little upset, as you might imagine. I got out of Teramondian two steps in front of his men. I'd intended to run for Tihannad, but they clung too close to my heel. By the time I got to Falle, they were only half a step behind, and less than that by Desamion." Tan stopped, lifted his chained hands to rub his mouth. After a moment, he went on in a lower voice, "Earth and stone, I thought they had me twice before I made it across the river—" He stopped again. Then he took a hard breath, met the king's eyes, and said, "They came across the river after me."

"*Did* they?" King Iaor leaned forward, gripping the arms of the chair. "How did they *dare*?"

"I don't know, Your Majesty. That surprised me, too, the more as they must have known you were here. Not a mark on me, Captain Geroen says. Earth and stone, every hair I own should be white after the past days. They pressed me hard enough I was barely able to keep upright by the time a brace of earnest guardsmen caught me standing flat over a couple of bodies in an alley. Caught in the street by the city guard! Moutres wouldn't be the only one to laugh himself insensible, if he knew. But," and Tan gave Geroen a little nod, "if they hadn't picked me up, I don't know that I'd have lasted the night. And if Captain Geroen hadn't set an extra guard on me last night, and put half his men around me to bring me up here, the whole effort might have been wasted."

The king slowly leaned back in the chair again. "Well, no surprise that the city had a restless night. What were these papers you stole?"

"Oh, everything," Tan said briskly. "Lists of Istierinan's agents, and lists of men he suspects are ours. Lists of men who aren't agents, but dupes and useful fools, and of men who have been bribed. Comments about Linularinum's own nobility and men of substance, which ones Istierinan is watching and which ones he thinks susceptible to bribes, and which ones are susceptible to blackmail—the notations there made fascinating reading, but the list of *our* people is even better."

The king blinked. The Casmantian prince, young Erichstaben, looked, for the first time, as though he wondered whether he should be present to hear this. Mienthe's gaze was wide and fascinated. Bertaud asked, "He had all that out in plain sight?"

"Locked in a hidden drawer, my lord, and all in cipher, of course. Three different ciphers, in fact. I broke them. Well, two of them. I already had the key for one."

"I see. And where are these papers now?"

"He didn't have them when he was picked up last night," Geroen declared.

"I destroyed them, of course. After I memorized them."

"You memorized them," Bertaud repeated.

"I have a good memory."

"I see."

"I'll give it all to you, now." Tan glanced from Bertaud to the king and back. "Today. Right now, if you'll permit me. I'd suggest at least a dozen copies to be sent north as well, to both the winter court in Tihannad and the summer court in Tiearanan. Any couriers who go openly by the road had better have fast horses and plenty of nerve, but Linularinum must *not* imagine they've stopped that information getting out. It's very good His Majesty is here. Now that I'm in your hands, that should stop Istierinan's agents flat where they stand, no matter their orders."

"Yes," said Bertaud. "I see that." He hesitated, glancing at the king. Iaor made a little gesture inviting him to proceed. Bertaud turned back to Tan, regarding him with narrow intensity. "A secure room," he said aloud. "With a desk and plenty of paper. And at least one clerk to assist you. You will permit a clerk to assist you?"

"Of course, my lord." Though Tan didn't much care for the idea. Nevertheless, he knew he would not have the strength to write out all the copies as swiftly as it had to be done. He said smoothly, "Anyone you see fit to assign the duty."

"We'll want guards," Geroen put in grimly. "All around the house, not just the spy and his clerks. And in the stables. And around the couriers. And the couriers' equipment." He glanced at King Iaor. "I'll ask His Majesty to set his own guardsmen all about his household."

"And I shall see they coordinate with yours," the king said to Bertaud, who nodded thanks.

"I'd ask for Tenned son of Tenned as a guard. And food," Tan put in with prudent emphasis. "And wine. Well watered," he added regretfully. He would have liked to add, *and a bath*, only truly he did not want to take that much time. He was intensely grateful that both Bertaud and Iaor seemed able to grasp the concept of urgency. If not of perfect discretion.

"All of that, yes. Very well. Free his hands, Geroen." The lord's tone brooked no argument. "I want you back with your men and on the job. You may leave this man to me. That *is* an order."

The captain's shoulders straightened. "Yes, my lord."

The paper was crisp and fresh, the quills well-made, and the clerk glum but quick and with a fair hand—no surprise, as he looked to have Linularinan blood. There were no windows in this room. Three guards were posted outside each of its two doors, and Tenned son of Tenned inside the room, looking alert and nervous. Bread and soft cheese occupied a separate table, and wine cut half-and-half with water.

The clerk was horrified at what Tan wrote out for him to copy. "I shouldn't know any of this," he protested. "Earth and stone, I don't *want* to know any of this!"

Tan looked him up and down. "Are you trustworthy? Discreet? You don't babble when you're in your cups, do you? You're loyal to Feierabiand?"

"Yes!" said the clerk hotly. "No! I mean, yes! But—"

"Then you'll do, man. Would you tell Lord Bertaud he should have selected a different man? Did you make these quills?"

"Yes..."

"Good quills. Now be quiet and let me work." Tan let himself fall into the cold legist's stillness that let him bring forth perfect memories. That stillness didn't come quite so easily as he'd expected—well, he was already tired. And distracted—he'd need to write an analysis to accompany these lists—later, later. No thought, no fretting, just memory. He let the quill fly across the paper.

He rose out of that trance of silence and speed much later to find Bertaud himself sitting at the table beside the clerk, writing out a copy in his own hand. He blinked, surprised—and then groaned, aware all at once of his aching hand and wrist. And back. And neck. In fact, he ached all over, far worse than usual. Pain lanced through his head, so sharp that for a moment he was blind. How long *had* he been working? Even his eyes felt gritty and hot. Tan laid the quill aside and pressed his hands over his eyes.

"That's everything?" Bertaud asked.

Tan had very little idea what he'd just flung onto paper. But he shouldn't have stopped unless it was. He opened his eyes and peered blearily down at the stack of pages. "I think so. It should be." He shuffled rapidly through the papers. Everything seemed to be in order. Except— "I need to write a covering analysis. Broken stone and black iron! I don't think I have the wit of a crow left at the moment." He leaned back in his chair, stretching. Every bone and ligament in his body seemed to creak. Well, he'd had the bare bones of an analysis in his head since he'd left Teramondian. And the quill was still flowing with ink. Better still, with ink that resisted smudging. Sighing, he picked up the quill once more. The headache stabbed behind his eyes, and he couldn't keep from flinching. But the analysis still needed to be written. After that he might be able to finally put the quill down and *sleep*.

Bertaud silently passed him more paper and looked through the just-finished lists. His eyebrows rose, and he shook his head. He passed half the lists over to the clerk, taking the other half to copy himself. He could at least work quietly, for he did not harass Tan with questions, but left him alone to try to bludgeon coherent phrases out of his exhausted mind and fair script out of his stiff fingers. The little sleep he'd gotten in the prison seemed days past... He finished at last, tossed down the quill, and blew on the ink to dry it.

Bertaud took the analysis without comment, read it through once quickly, then again more slowly. Then he gave Tan a long look.

"The ink isn't smudged?" Tan asked blearily. "I didn't transpose two phrases or lose half a paragraph?" His gift shouldn't allow such mistakes, but he was so tired...

"No," Bertaud said. He sat down again and began to copy out the document. He said absently, not pausing in his task, "You need rest, I know. I'll send you to your bed shortly. Before I do, take a moment and think. Is there anything else I should tell Iaor when I bring him this?"

Tan rubbed his hands hard across his face. Then he poured himself some watered wine—well, he reached for the decanter, but Tenned was there before him and handed him a glass without a word. Tan nodded to the young guard and tried to collect his thoughts while he waited for Bertaud to finish the copy he was making and give the original to the clerk.

Then he said, "Tell His Majesty the whole lot could be false, deliberately put in my way to mislead us. One always has to remember that other men are also intelligent," he added to Bertaud's startled look. "But I don't think that's the case here, not from the way Istierinan stirred up all Linularinum and not from the feel of the information. Still, you might tell the king...remind him that the politest smile still hides teeth, and that no Linu-larinan smiles without calculating which way fortune is tending. All the rest is"—he waved a hand—"contained there."

"Yes," said the lord. He rose with his set of papers. And, after a moment of thought, gathered up an equal pile of blank pages, which he made into an identical packet. Tan nodded his approval.

"Twelve more full copies, and hand them out as they're finished," Bertaud said to the clerk. He added to Tan, "I've sent half a dozen couriers out already, for Tihannad and Tiearanan, but four of those were carrying blanks and the other two only had partial copies. I'll send some of these with couriers, mostly across country, and some with soldiers. And I've arranged to send a couple out in, hmm, less-conventional hands."

Tan inclined his head again, satisfied with all these arrangements. "And I?"

"You'll stay here in my house. You need time to rest and recover."

Tan nodded.

"My steward here is Dessand. Eniad is captain of the king's soldiers quartered in Tiefenauer. Geroen you have met—"

"What, he's still a captain of the guard?" Tan said in mock astonishment. "You didn't flog the hide off his back?"

The lord smiled. "I did worse than that. He's no longer merely a captain—he's *the* captain now. I made him captain of the whole city guard. I'd been looking for a replacement for the post. Geroen will do well, I believe."

Tan believed it, too. He scrubbed his hands across his face again, then pushed himself to his feet, all his joints complaining, and looked at young Tenned.

"Bath and bed, says my lord," the guard said earnestly, answering all of Tan's hopes. "Or supper first, if you like. Whatever you like, esteemed sir." He gave Tan an uncertain look. "Teras son of Toharas? Or is it, uh, Tan?"

Lord Bertaud lifted an amused eyebrow.

For once, Tan honestly could not think of a single reason to claim a false name. Istierinan's men knew very well who he was and would not care what name he used. And to the people on this side of the river, it should matter even less. "Tan will do," he told the young man. "A bath, bed, supper...I can't think of anything better. You'll attend me?"

"Yes..." Tenned did not quite seem to know whether he thought this was a better assignment than standing guard in the prison or not.

Tan smiled. "Well, you look strong enough to catch me if I collapse on the stairs rather than making it all the way to that promised bath. Good. Hold high the lamp, then, and light well the path!"

The young man nodded uncertainly, clearly missing the reference. Lord Bertaud, however, caught the allusion. He smiled, though a little grimly.

Tan grinned and declared, "Wishing no one any ill in the world, my lord! Or no one who ought properly to be on this side of the river. By now, Istierinan's agents will have realized it's far too late to stop all that"—he waved a vague hand at the growing stack of paper—"from getting out, and away home they'll go, feathers well ruffled and plucked. Then all good little boys will sleep safe in their beds, which is just as well." He paused, suddenly realizing that he was speaking far too freely. "Bed," he muttered. "Yes. Tenned—"

"Esteemed sir," the young man said, baffled but polite, and held open the door for Tan.

He had, later, only the vaguest memories of the bath or of finding a wide bed swathed in linen and lamb's wool, in a warm room lit by the ruddy glow of a banked fire and smelling, oddly enough, of honeysuckle. He must have felt himself safe, or else he was exhausted beyond caring, because he sank into the darkness behind the fire's glow and let the scent of honeysuckle carry him away.

CHAPTER 2

Mienthe had been feeling odd for days: restless and somehow as though she ought to be doing something urgent. But she had no idea what that should be. Before King Iaor had brought his household to Tiefenauer, she had longed to travel north to meet them. She'd *longed* to leave the Delta, which was not a new feeling, but something was different about it this spring. It seemed both stronger and more urgent this year, and she didn't know why. She'd expected the feeling to go away after the king arrived. Yet, even after the great house was filled to the roof tiles with Iaor and Niethe and the little princesses and all their attendants—and Erich—the restlessness had lingered. Mienthe didn't understand it. Usually the best month of the year was the one in which the king and his family and Erich visited the Delta.

Erich had been a stocky, rather small boy of twelve when King Iaor had compelled the King of Casmantium to send him to Feierabiand. As a guarantee of civility

between the two countries, Iaor had said. Erich was supposed to stay in Feierabiand for eight years. Mienthe supposed King Iaor thought that was long enough to make
his point.

Erich had come to the Delta with Iaor every year since
the king had begun making his annual progress through the
south of his country, so he and Mienthe had met when they
were children. Mienthe had been new to the great house,
uncertain of her cousin, shy of strangers, frightened of
King Iaor and all his retinue. Erich had been new to
Feierabiand, awkward with the language, excruciatingly
conscious that he was supposed to honorably represent
his father and country, and glad to find one person in the
great house he didn't need to be wary of. They'd become
friends at once.

The year after that, during the awful period of Tef's
illness, Bertaud had asked Iaor to send Erich to the Delta,
and the king had permitted him to come. Mienthe had
been so grateful. Erich had not been at all shocked at
Mienthe's grief for a man who had not even been kin,
a man who had been only a servant; indeed, it had been
Erich who had persuaded Bertaud to let Mienthe help dig
Tef's grave, even when her hands blistered and bled. She
had been so grateful.

Now the eight years of Erich's residence in Feierabiand
were almost past. He was eighteen now. He'd changed a
great deal since last year's visit. Last year, he'd suddenly
become taller than Mienthe. But though he'd come into
his height, he'd been as angular and ungainly as one of
the storks that nested on the rooftops of the town. His
hands had seemed too big for his bony wrists and his
elbows had stuck out and he banged into the furniture and

dropped plates. But this year he seemed to have turned all his growth into brawn. He'd filled out and got some weight on his bones, and he now looked very much the young man and not a boy at all.

He would be nineteen in midsummer, three weeks before Mienthe's birthday, and the year after that he would turn twenty, and then he would go home. Mienthe didn't like to think about that. She was almost certain his father would never let Erich come back to Feierabiand, and almost as certain that her cousin Bertaud, reluctant as he was to leave the Delta, would never again find it necessary to visit Casmantium.

She could ask Bertaud whether she might accompany the king's household when King Iaor left Tiefenauer. Erich would like that—*she* would like that. Or she thought she would. She ought to. Bertaud might let her go, even if he refused to leave the Delta himself. She wanted to ask him for permission—or at least, she felt as though she *ought* to want to ask him. But somehow the idea of joining the king's progress didn't exactly feel right. Mienthe had wanted so badly to go north just a day or so ago, but now she just didn't. Neither feeling made any sense!

Probably it was just the spring making her so restless. Probably it was watching the swallows dip and whirl through the sky and fly north, toward the higher country where they nested.

She found that she welcomed the distraction that her cousin's astonishing new guest had brought. She even found herself at once disposed to like him—even though she'd seen him only during that first strained interview, and even though he had clearly not wanted her there.

She'd liked him and been glad he'd made it safely to the great house, for all he'd seemed to bring an echo of violence and fear with him. And of course, it had been fortunate he'd come to the Delta, since he'd found the king so much faster than if he'd gone to Tihannad.

Tan had an air of having *lived*, of having been out in the world. She liked that, even given just the little glimpse she'd had of him. She'd liked the slightly mocking quirk to his mouth when he'd said, *I have a good memory*. She had admired the way he'd spoken with such confidence to the king and to her cousin, even though he was clearly exhausted and maybe even a little frightened.

She would never have guessed, if she'd seen him in town, that he was actually Feierabianden. He looked pure Linularinan. No doubt that had been very helpful to him in his...profession. One expected Casmantian people to be broad-boned and clever with their hands; some of the artisans in town were Casmantian and one could spot them a mile away and by torchlight, as the saying went. The folk of Linularinum weren't quite so distinctive, but they were born with contract law and an inclination for poetry in their blood to go along with their straight brown hair and their prim expressions. That was what people said. There were plenty of people with mixed blood along the river, especially in the Delta, but Tan didn't look like he'd been born of mixed blood. In fact, he looked *exactly* like Mienthe's idea of a Linularinan legist, except not as old and stiff as most legists. And friendlier. And, oddly, less secretive.

Well, again, that was probably because he was a spy. He could probably look friendly and openhearted and honest no matter what he was thinking or feeling.

Probably seeming sincere was part of being a confidential agent. You seemed ordinary and normal and people told you things. That wasn't very nice. Probably Mienthe should be cautious of trusting him. But she didn't feel cautious. She felt concerned. They said Tan had written out all the information he'd brought and then collapsed in exhaustion. He'd been either asleep or unconscious for two days now, which could happen when somebody overused his gift. Nevertheless, Mienthe felt strongly that she should go look in on him, make sure he was well. That was foolish. She'd already looked in several times this very day, once this very afternoon. Of course he was perfectly well.

Nevertheless, she found herself wandering restlessly toward his room, even though she had no real business to take her in that direction.

"Mie!" said Erich as she passed the kitchens—of course he had been in the kitchens—and swung out the door to stride along beside her. He handed her a sweet roll, wrapped in paper to keep the honey and butter from dripping onto the floor. "Where are you going?"

Mienthe hesitated.

"To see if the spy is awake," Erich said cheerfully. "Yes, I thought so. You should let me come."

"I ought to ask one of my maids to come," Mienthe muttered. "I meant to, Erich, truly, but Karin wasn't handy just now."

"And Emnis might worry and fuss," Erich said comfortably. "So she might. I will go with you. Wait a little and I will get a plate of sweet rolls. Nobody would be surprised if you brought the spy some rolls." His voice was deeper and somehow grittier than it had been even last year, which was when his voice had finally broken.

His slight accent seemed to have become a little more pronounced with that change.

"He's probably still asleep—"

"If he's woken up, he will no doubt be glad of the rolls," Erich said, shrugging. "I don't mind going to look. If he's still asleep, *I* will be glad of the rolls. You eat that one, Mie. You're too thin." He turned and disappeared back into the kitchens, coming back almost at once with a generous plateful of rolls.

Tan was still asleep, but Captain Geroen, sitting in his room with his legs stretched out and a glower on his coarse-featured face, was glad to see the sweet rolls and didn't question Mienthe's right to look in on the spy.

"I never thought a legist could wear himself out with a quill like a soldier on a forced march," the captain said. "Makes me glad to be a speaker and not a legist. Even aside from liking crows better than just their feathers." He gave the bed a disgusted scowl.

"You think he's all right, though?" Mienthe asked. She trusted her cousin's judgment, but she wasn't certain she liked the guard captain. He frightened her a little. Erich didn't seem frightened, but then he wouldn't. He leaned in the doorway and ate another roll himself.

"I should think so, lady. Just exhausted." The captain gave the bed another disgusted look, but this time Mienthe thought she could see concern hiding behind his grim features. "With more than the effort of lifting a quill, to be fair, from what he said of his past days. No, he'll be up and about—"

Tan shifted, moved a hand, made a wordless mutter of protest, opened his eyes, tried to sit up, and groaned.

Captain Geroen wiped honey off his fingers with the cloth that had been draped over the plate, stalked over to the bed, and put a surprisingly gentle hand under Tan's elbow to help him sit up. Then he poured some water into a glass, set it on the bed table, stepped back and glowered at the spy, fists on his hips. "Stiff, are you?"

Tan glanced past the captain to take in Mienthe's presence, and Erich's beyond her. He seemed half amused and half dismayed to find his room so crowded. But he nodded thanks for the water and said to Geroen, with a deliberate good humor that had more than a slight edge of mockery to it, "Well, I see Bertaud—forgive me, let us by all means be respectful, I mean to say *Lord* Bertaud— didn't flog the flesh off your bones. What astonishing leniency!"

The captain looked embarrassed, an expression that sat oddly on his heavy features. "He's not much for the post and the whip, is our lord. But I did think he might dismiss me."

"After the shocking example you set for your pure-minded naive young guardsmen? I should hardly be astonished he found a more suitable penalty."

"Hah. He told you about that, did he?"

"He did. I admit I'm surprised to find you here watching me sleep. Flattering though it is to be the focus of your personal attention, I should imagine the new captain of the entire city guard might have one or two other matters of almost equal consequence to absorb his attention."

When he put it that way, Mienthe was surprised, too. But Geroen only lifted a heavy eyebrow at Tan. "I have been attending to them, as happens. And then I came back to look in on you. Just how long do you think you've been out?"

Tan leaned back against the pillows, looking faintly disturbed. "I see. How long, then?"

Mienthe said anxiously, "You worked right through that whole day and collapsed well after dark. That was fifty hours ago, more or less."

"So a good morning to you, esteemed sir!" said Captain Geroen drily. "We were beginning to wonder whether you'd ever wake again or just sleep till you turned to stone, and the bed linens around you."

"Ah." Tan seemed slightly stunned. "One would think I'd had to write out all eighteen copies myself. No wonder I'm so—" He turned his head toward the plate of rolls Mienthe still held and finished plaintively, "So close to collapsing a second time for want of sustenance. Lady Mienthe, are any of those, by chance, for me?"

Mienthe laughed. "All of them, if you like! And we can send to the kitchens if you'd like something else." She handed the tray to Captain Geroen to put on the bed table, where Tan could reach them. "We should go—I'm sure you want to eat and wash and dress, and I should tell my cousin you're awake—"

Tan waved a sweet roll at her. "Lady Mienthe, you are a jewel among women. Sit, please, and tell me all that has happened in the past two days—or at least, if anything important has happened, perhaps you might mention it to me? Any official protests from Linularinum? Alarms in the night? Has Istierinan presented himself to Iaor with a demand for my return?"

Mienthe couldn't help but laugh again. "No!"

"Good," said Tan, and bit with enthusiasm into the roll.

"I'll go," Geroen said. "I should report." He gave Erich a significant look.

Erich gestured acknowledgment. "I'll stay," he assured the captain.

"Good to have that settled," Tan said cheerfully.

He wasn't at all as Mienthe had expected. Bertaud had told her that spywork was hard and dangerous, and that good spies saved a lot of soldiers and should be respected. And Erich had pointed out that everyone knew Linularinum had lots of spies in Feierabiand, so really it was only fair that Feierabiand have some in Linularinum.

Mienthe supposed that spywork must be frightening and dangerous and difficult. It must be hard to find out secrets and sneak away with them—Mienthe had a vague idea that spies slipped through darkened rooms and found secret ledgers in locked desks, and thought she would die of fright if she tried to sneak around that way. But worse than that would be making somebody trust you when you knew all the time you were going to betray their trust. *That* would be hard. Unless you really didn't like the person you were betraying, but then pretending you did would be worse still. She had wondered what the kind of man who would do that might be like. Tan wasn't at all what she had imagined.

"Tan..." Mienthe said curiously, wanting to hear him speak again, to see whether she could hear any deceit in his voice.

"Esteemed lady?"

Mienthe asked, "Do you never tell anybody the rest of your name?"

"Not often," Tan said mildly. He didn't seem in the least offended or embarrassed, and there was nothing secretive or deceitful in his manner, even when he was explaining straight out that he kept secrets. He said, "I've offended people, you know. There are plenty of people I'd prefer not know my mother's name."

"Oh. Of course." Mienthe was embarrassed that he'd needed to explain that, and embarrassed again because he'd said he didn't want to give his *mother's* name. She guessed his father must have been careless. She didn't know what to say.

Erich said, rescuing her, "His Majesty said he doesn't think he's ever had a confidential agent bring him such a coup, and for all the difficulty it will cause him, he is glad to have a way to set the Fox of Linularinum at a disadvantage."

Tan gave Erich a thoughtful look. "I'm sure that's so, Prince Erichstaben. Yes, I suppose now he has a considerable advantage over both his neighbors."

That was barbed, but Erich didn't seem offended. He only said mildly, "I don't mind. Anyway, I'm going back to Casmantium in two years."

"Are you?" Tan said, with just the faintest edge of doubt in his tone.

Mienthe started to say something sharp, she didn't know what, but Erich said, his tone still mild, "You've been in Linularinum too long, maybe."

After a moment, Tan laughed. "Perhaps."

Mienthe looked at him, puzzled.

"Ah, well," Tan said to her. "You'd think Feierabiand would be closely allied to Linularinum, wouldn't you? We share a common history and a common language, which you'd think would make us far more like one another than either of us is like Casmantium, and there's quite a lot of

shared blood along the river and down here in the Delta."
He gave Erich a little nod and went on, "But in some
ways, I think Casmantium is far more Feierabiand's natural ally. We're alike in our straightforwardness and love of
honesty, which aren't qualities Linularinum admires."

There was an odd, wistful tone to his voice when he
said that last. Mienthe said, "But you loved Linularinum,
didn't you? And then you had to leave it. I'm sorry."

She seemed to have taken Tan by surprise. For a long
moment, he only gazed wordlessly at her. But then he
said slowly, "I suppose you've heard all your life, living
on the border as you do, about Linularinan haughtiness,
how the people of Linularinum look down on the people
of Feierabiand as so many unlettered peasants. About
how secretive and sly they are, and how they never use
one word when they can fit in several dozen. And there's
some truth to that. They love poetry—"

"Oh, I know!" Mienthe exclaimed, and then blushed
because she had interrupted. But Tan only lifted a curious
eyebrow, so she said, "I think everyone on both sides of
the bridge reads Linularinan epic romances. All the girls
in the great house read them—I read them, too. All we
can get, I mean. They're wonderful fun."

Erich rolled his eyes, but Tan grinned. "All the girls
in Teramondian read them, too: high birth or low, court
ladies or merchants' daughters. Their mothers pretend
indifference, but I've noticed even quite elderly matrons
will correct your smallest errors if you refer to even the
most recent epics."

And Tan had actually tested that, Mienthe guessed,
just to amuse himself or purely out of habit. She didn't
know whether that was entertaining or a bit frightening.

"But anyone from Linularinum will go beyond the popular epics. Especially in the court, people would rather quote something flowery and obscure—especially obscure—than simply say anything right out."

"Oh." Mienthe tried to imagine this.

"It's true they're secretive and love to be clever, but half the time when they're sneaking around trying to out-maneuver someone, they're actually arranging something kind for a friend. They like to surprise people, and they don't brag about it when they've been generous."

He almost made her admire secrecy, though it had never before occurred to her that that might be an admirable quality. "Are they kinder and more generous than we are, then?"

"Oh...no, I don't think so. But much less straightforward about both friendships and enmities. It's true what they say, that no one smiles in Linularinum without first calculating which way fortune is tending. But it's also true—this is a Linularinan saying—that the politest smile still contains teeth. You can't guess whether a man is your friend or not by whether he smiles at you."

"They sound very different from us," Mienthe said doubtfully. She wondered if this could actually be true. Though she'd heard that saying.

"In some ways. And in other ways, that perhaps matter more, they aren't different at all."

Mienthe nodded. She was even more certain now that he had loved Linularinum. She looked for something to say that might ease his sense of loss, but couldn't think of anything. Probably a Linularinan woman would be able to think of something subtle and obscure and, what had he said? Flowery. Something subtle and obscure and flowery to make him feel better. She didn't seem to be as clever as a Linularinan woman. She said merely, which was true but neither subtle nor clever, "I'm sorry for your loss. I don't suppose you'll have a chance to go back to Teramondian now."

Tan said after a moment, "It was bound to come to this eventually. That it was *that* day, right then, when all the pieces suddenly fell into order... Well, the years do shatter in our hands, and cut us to the bone if we try to hold them."

Mienthe could not imagine wanting to hold on to the past. Then she thought of Tef, and after all understood exactly what Tan meant. Erich, too, nodded.

"So tell me how I came to be so fortunate as to find Iaor here before me," Tan said to him, deliberately breaking the moment.

Erich shrugged. "*His Majesty*," he said with some emphasis, "likes to see his country. And he likes to leave the cold heights and come down to the Delta before the heat of summer."

"Eminently sensible," murmured Tan, with a quirk of one eyebrow.

"I've always thought so," Erich agreed with a grin. "We chase the spring, and by the time we reach Tiearanan, we find the ice gone from the mountains and the flowers blooming."

"Yes, but it's more than that," Mienthe put in, "because they say His Majesty never guested in the Delta until Bertaud came back. Everything—" She stopped abruptly, having come surprisingly close to adding, *Everything changed when my cousin came home.* How strange that she should have begun to say something so personal.

"The Fox never leaves Teramondian, I think. I think perhaps I prefer His Majesty's"—and here Tan lifted a wry eyebrow at Erich, who grinned back—"inclination to see the whole of his country."

Mienthe nodded. "From here, King Iaor takes his household along the coast to Terabiand, then back north along the Nejeied River to the summer court in Tiearanan."

"Lingering in Terabiand if there are any reports of late snows in the mountains," put in Erich.

"Yes, so the whole progress takes about two months, sometimes more, doesn't it, Erich? I've always wanted to go along…My cousin doesn't want to spend so long away from the Delta, I suppose," Mienthe added a little doubtfully.

"He doesn't care to travel?"

"Oh, before, he went everywhere in Feierabiand, I think," she said. "And to—" *Casmantium*, she had meant to say, but that had been after Casmantium had tried to annex part of Feierabiand, when her cousin had escorted Erich from his father's court to Iaor's and she didn't want to say that. She said instead, "I think he likes to stay closer to home, now."

"Of course," Tan murmured.

Mienthe realized suddenly that Tan really had known about the progress, but had simply wanted to get them talking freely. And she had—much more than usual. She gave him a narrow look, wondering whether to laugh or be angry. "You're very good at that, aren't you? I think I understand why you're such a good spy. Confidential agent, I mean."

Tan looked surprised. Then he laughed and opened his

hands in a gesture of contrition. "Habit," he said apologetically. "One I'll have to break, now I'm no longer an agent—certainly not confidential. Forgive me, esteemed lady."

Mienthe thought it would be very difficult to break a habit of getting people to talk to you, and doubted Tan really meant to try. And the other half of that habit must be not talking too much yourself, at least not about anything important. That must be hard, learning to say things, but nothing that mattered. She'd certainly been carrying more than her share of the conversation so far, which wasn't at all usual for her, and hadn't been her intention, either.

Perhaps guessing her thoughts, Tan said lightly, "I do know some north Linularinan poetry, including a couple of romantic epics you might not have heard this far south. I could write them out for you, if you like."

Mienthe straightened, excited and happy at this generous offer, even though he'd obviously made it partly to turn the subject and partly to flatter her because she was Bertaud's cousin. But she hardly meant to turn the offer down, no matter why he'd made it. She said quickly, "Oh, could you? Of course you could—you have a legist's memory. That would be wonderful, truly! And it would be something quiet you could do, when I know you're still tired." She hesitated, remembering that he was a guest, and still recovering from injury or exhaustion. "If you're sure you don't mind?"

"Not in the least," Tan said cheerfully. "Whom should I ask for paper and quills?"

"Oh, I'll send you all the things you'd need," Mienthe assured him. She jumped up, but then hesitated. "I know you only just came out of a legist's trance. Of course you need to rest. I'd understand if you've worn your gift out for the next little while—I didn't mean to ask you to write things for me if you're too tired or anything—"

"Not at all," Tan assured her with perfect good cheer. "An unhurried little task like this is just what I need to limber my gift and memory and fingers all up again."

"If you're sure," Mienthe said. But he did look tired now, she thought. "But *I'm* sure you should rest. I'll tell the kitchens to send up a real tray, shall I?" There were only crumbs on the plate that had held the rolls.

"A wonderful idea," Tan agreed, and let his head rest against the pillows.

"Though I should go find Bertaud first," Mienthe added doubtfully, once she and Erich were in the hall. There were two guardsmen in the hall, which she found did not surprise her.

"Go," agreed Erich. "I'm sure Geroen passed the word along, but yes, go. I do not mind to go back by the kitchens."

Mienthe grinned and let him go. But once she was alone, her steps slowed. She was, she decided, thinking back on it, not quite as pleased at Tan's offer as she ought to have been. How strange it was, to be a little bit suspicious of every single thing a man said! She found herself wondering if Tan was trying to make a good impression on her, and then wondering if asking herself that question meant he wasn't succeeding, and then asking herself whether it was fair to be suspicious of a man who had, after all, risked his life to bring Feierabiand important information. Or fair to worry about whether Tan was being altogether honest with her, when, after all, she never did know whether *anyone* ever was. Except her cousin, of course.

Her steps quickened as she suddenly found herself eager to talk to Bertaud. She wanted to ask him whether he liked Tan, whether he thought he ought to like him, whether he trusted him—was it possible to like somebody you didn't trust? Was it *proper* to allow yourself to like somebody you didn't trust?

Though the great house had hardly been built to loom over the town, some parts of it were set rather high, and then the whole house was on a hill—not a high hill, but the highest Tiefenauer offered. The solar was nearly as high up as the tower room, but in every other way it was the antithesis of that windowless chamber, being long and narrow and very nearly nothing but windows. It was much too hot in high summer for anyone but a particularly determined cat, but it was perfect in the winter and early spring, especially at sunset, for almost all of its windows looked west. One could look right out over the rooftops of Tiefenauer to the flashing ribbon of the river, the bridge leading in a fine and delicate arch over to Linularinum. Away to the north, the marshes were a dusky emerald with occasional glints of diamond brilliance where the sunlight struck through the dense trees to the still waters beneath. To the south, visible on clear days, the infinite sea stretched away, muddy and opaque where the Sierhanan River emptied, clear sapphire farther out.

Mienthe had expected Bertaud to be in company with King Iaor, with maybe half a dozen attendants besides. But her cousin was quite alone. He was sitting in a high-backed chair drawn up close to the windows. There was a book open on his knee, but he wasn't reading it. He was gazing out over the city, past the city, at the clouds piling up over the sea, purple and gold against a luminous sky, crimson in the west where the setting sun turned the sea to flame.

He did not see Mienthe at once. She watched him in silence for a moment. The brilliant light showed her fine lines at the corners of his eyes, deeper lines at the corners of his mouth. He looked older in this light, only...not exactly older. Her cousin looked, Mienthe thought, as though something had recalled to him some grief or hard memory.

Then, though she was standing motionless, he must have heard her, for he turned his head. The golden light of sunset seemed to fill his eyes with fire, and yet behind the opaque veil of fire, they were dark. Even bleak. Some of the other girls Mienthe knew who also liked epic romances would have instantly spun a tale of love and loss to explain that bleakness. Mienthe didn't think what she saw had any such simple explanation. She didn't understand her cousin's unspoken sorrow, yet somehow she recognized it. She stood mute in the doorway.

Then the setting sun touched the surface of the sea, the angle of the light coming in through the windows changed, and the moment passed.

"Mienthe," Bertaud said, rising to greet her. With the light now at his back, it was impossible to make out his expression at all.

Though Mienthe listened carefully, she could hear neither grief nor loneliness in his tone. She said, "Tan's awake, did Geroen tell you? I went to see him." She'd been a little worried that her cousin might not approve, but he only nodded and invited her, with a gesture, to take a chair near his.

"What did you think of our spy?"

"Oh…" Mienthe tried to think how to answer. "He has enough charm, when he wants to. I think he must have been a good spy."

"Indeed. He's resting now, I suppose? Well enough. I'll want to speak with him tonight. Or possibly Iaor will. Or perhaps both of us."

Poor spy, to have both the king and her cousin looming over him at once.

"I left orders for one of Geroen's men to attend him at all times. I want him to stay close for a few more days, and I don't think I necessarily trust that man to obey any command he'd rather conveniently forget."

Her cousin was smiling a little as he said this last, but Mienthe thought he wasn't really amused. He wasn't used, she decided, to having to doubt whether anybody would obey him, and he didn't like having to wonder.

Mienthe nodded and started to speak, but then stopped. The sun was nearly down, flashing flame-red against the flat horizon where sea met sky. Other than that distant blaze, the world had gone dark. The dark and hidden depths of the marshes rolled out beyond the city; nearer at hand, the earliest stars glimmered into sight to meet the warmer glow of lanterns and lamps in the streets below. Bertaud took a taper from the desk, struck it to life, and stretched up to light the lamps that hung from the ceiling on bronze chains.

And outside the windows of the solar, a sudden blackness moved against the sky. It spread out, bulking enormous—not a bird, no bird would be so large, but certainly not clouds across the sky; it moved too fast and looked all wrong for that. She held her breath, half expecting it to crash against the windows—shattering glass would fly everywhere—she took a step back in fearful anticipation. But then the dark shape, if she'd really ever seen it at all, dwindled and disappeared.

Mienthe took a step closer to the windows, blinking, wondering whether she'd actually seen something or merely imagined it.

Behind her, Bertaud made a wordless sound that held an extraordinary combination of astonishment, longing, intense joy, and anger.

She turned. There was a man in the solar with them. A stranger. He was much older than Mienthe—older than Bertaud, she thought, though she did not understand why she thought so. His black hair was not streaked with gray and his eyes were ageless, but Mienthe was sure that he was actually much older than he looked. He had an austere, proud face and powerful deep-set black eyes. His clothing was all of black and a red as dark as dying coals.

And there was something strange about his shadow. It wasn't just the flickering light of the lamps: The shadow itself flickered with fire; it was *made* of fire, but with eyes as black as those of the man who cast it. And it was the wrong shape—not the shape of a man at all, but Mienthe could not have said what form could have cast it. She took another involuntary step back, expecting the rugs and drapes and polished wood of the solar to blaze up in flames. But the shadow seemed to contain its fire, and nothing else burned. Then the man turned his head, glancing at her with a strange kind of indifferent curiosity. Mienthe saw that although his eyes were black, they, too, were filled with fire. She stared back, feeling pinned in place with shock and terror, like a hare under the shadow of a falcon.

Then Bertaud took a step forward. He said sharply, "Kairaithin. Anasakuse Sipiike Kairaithin. Why have you come here?"

The stranger turned his attention back to him, and the moment passed.

Beneath the sharpness, Bertaud's voice shook. But not, thought Mienthe, in terror. Whatever strong emotion gripped her cousin, it was not fear. Nor had Bertaud moved—say, to step in front of her. He did not pay her any attention at all. Rather than feeling hurt or overlooked, Mienthe found this reassuring. The man—the mage—whoever he was, he had to be a mage, though she had never heard of any mage who cast a shadow of fire—but he could not be so dangerous if her cousin, who clearly knew him, did not think Mienthe needed protection.

Bertaud did not wait for an answer, but said, his tone changing, "You look tired. You look...older. Are you... are you well, then?" His voice had dropped, the anger replaced by...worry? Fear? Mienthe wasn't certain what she heard in his voice. "Did it harm you, crossing the Wall?" Bertaud asked. And then, "But how *did* you cross it?"

The man—the fire mage, Kairaithin—tilted his head, somehow a strange motion that made Mienthe think of the way a bird moved; it had something of that quick, abrupt quality. Mienthe saw that his shadow was a bird's shadow, only too large and feathered with fire, and not altogether the shape of a bird. She blinked and at last recognized what creature cast that kind of shadow—she couldn't believe she'd been so slow to understand. This was not a man at all, not at *all*. He was a griffin. The human shape he wore just barely disguised the fact, and only for a moment.

The griffin said, "The answer to all your questions is the same answer."

His voice was as outrageously inhuman as his shadow: pitiless as fire and with a strange timbre, as though his tongue and throat were not accustomed to shaping the sounds of any ordinary language. He stood very still, watching Bertaud. Not as a falcon watches a hare, Mienthe thought, but she was not sure why she thought it was different, or why she thought the stranger was…not exactly afraid, but wary.

Bertaud, too, stood unmoving. Mienthe thought he had recovered from his astonishment, but she thought he was bracing himself against some message he would not welcome. He said, "What is that answer?"

"The Wall has cracked," the griffin said. Then he was still again, watching Bertaud.

Bertaud clearly understood this very well. "Tehre's Wall?" her cousin said, not a question, but in clear dismay. "How?"

"I do not know. It should have stood for a thousand years, that making," answered the griffin—Kairaithin, Anasakuse Something Kairaithin—and how did her cousin come to know his name? Or the names of any griffins?

Bertaud said, "I thought it would."

"Yes. Something disturbed the balance, which should

have been secure. The Wall has cracked through twice—in the east where the lake lies high in the mountains and then again in the higher mountains of the west, near where the mouth of the lake called Niambe finds its source."

Bertaud took a step forward. "Is it a problem with the wild magic, then? Does that interfere with the mageworking?"

Kairaithin moved a hand in a minimal gesture of bafflement. "Perhaps. The wild magic has lately trembled, yes. Something has troubled it. Or so I felt as I came through the heights. Though why, then, have both the wild magic and the maker's magic woven into the Wall changed this spring, now, at this moment?" He did not attempt to answer his own question, but only stood still again, watching her cousin.

"So you came here to me," said Bertaud, and stopped. There was an expectation in his silence. He was waiting…he expected something from the griffin mage. Something specific. Something, Mienthe thought, that he did not really want to receive, or hear, or know. And the mage expected something from her cousin as well.

"Twice, you have tasked me with my oversight when I did not warn you of an approaching storm," said Kairaithin. "This time I think it best that you know what comes. This wind that approaches now…it will be a savage wind. If the Wall does not hold, as I think it will not, then my people will come down across the country of earth in a storm of fire." There was neither apology nor regret in his tone as he said this. He simply said it. But there was an odd trepidation hidden behind the fierce indifference of his voice. He was afraid of what Bertaud might say or do, Mienthe realized. She blinked, not understanding this at all. She didn't understand why a griffin fire mage—a griffin mage so powerful he could take on human shape and draw himself right out of air and the sunset light—should be afraid of anyone. Certainly not why he should be afraid of her *cousin*.

"Why would they?" asked Bertaud. "How can they? Six years ago, you said that if your people fought mine without quarter, yours would be destroyed. How has that changed? Discounting what—what might prevent them. You have not told them about that?"

"No, nor dare I. Everything I told you six years ago remains true," Kairaithin said sharply. "Save this one thing: My people now count among their treasures the fire mage Kereskiita Keskainiane Raikaisipiike. Kes. My *kiinukaile* Opailikiita Sehanaka Kiistaike remains her first *iskarianere*, but Kes has also taken Tastairiane Apailika as a second *iskarianere*."

"Tastairiane!" Bertaud exclaimed, flinching from a name he evidently recognized.

"Even so. Kes has come entirely into her power. She has become fierce and forgotten the earth from which she was taken. She calls for a wind of fire and a brilliant day of blood, and though I would speak against her, I have no allies among the People of Fire and Air."

Bertaud said, "Even without allies, Sipiike Kairaithin, can you not turn that wind, no matter how strong the storm, and find another for your people to ride?"

"You mistake me," said Kairaithin. And, after a moment, "Do you not understand me, man? When I say I have no allies, I mean I fly alone. The Lord of Fire and Air no longer regards my opinion. He has not since I supported the building of the Wall. He does not understand...none of my people understand…why, on that night of fire, I chose to turn the wind we had brought down against Casmantium. He believes I deliberately caught defeat out of a wind that should have carried us to victory."

There was a pause. Then Bertaud said quietly, "No. I did not know." And, after a moment, "I am sorry, Kairaithin. I would do the same again. But I'm sorry the cost of what we all did that night fell on you."

The griffin mage shrugged off his sympathy. "It has mattered little. While earth and fire were divided, the People of Fire and Air had little need for my strength. Now that the Wall's protection is failing, they still need not regard me." The griffin mage paused. But then he said, his voice not precisely gentle, but so low Mienthe had to strain to hear him, "I would I had found a different wind to call, these six years past, when the cold mages of Casmantium first struck against my people. This one has come about into a different quarter than I ever intended. I see only two directions in which it may lead: the destruction of your people or the destruction of mine. I would choose neither. But I do not see any wind that can carry us in any direction but toward disaster."

"But—" said Bertaud, and stopped.

"Yes," said the griffin. "I am at fault. I am twice at fault. If I had properly judged the wind as I called it up six years ago, I would have guessed what storm it might become. If I had understood that, I would have seen plainly that I should have killed you, there in that desert we made with such bitter cost. Now the chance is gone and I do not know what to do. So I came here to you, though you did not call me. Will you hold me?"

Bertaud did not answer at once. At last he said, "No,"

and hesitated, glancing down. And then looked up once more to meet Kairaithin's fierce gaze. "Not yet. Not if I can avoid it— How long will the Wall stand, can you guess?"

The griffin mage shrugged. "Not long, unless the balance between fire and earth and the wild magic is restored. And, as I do not know what disturbed it, I cannot guess how it might be restored. I have studied the weakness in the Wall over these past days. I have considered the lengthening and branching of the cracks. I do not think it will hold long. Five days?"

"Five!" Bertaud exclaimed.

"Or six. Or ten." Kairaithin lifted a hand and dropped it again in weary uncertainty. "I do not think it will hold longer than ten days, if it holds so long. And what will you do when it breaks, man?"

Bertaud did not answer.

Mienthe had an idea the griffin might have said something else, something more, only she was in the room, listening. His black eyes shifted to consider her. She flinched and tried not to back away, though she couldn't have explained why she thought it would be a bad idea to back away.

Kairaithin turned his gaze back toward Bertaud. "This is…your mate? Your child?"

"My cousin," Bertaud said. Then added, "My *iskarianere*—I think that would do." He moved to stand next to Mienthe, put an arm around her shoulders. Not exactly protectively. Even now, it did not seem to occur to him that she might need protection. Now she had at last drawn the griffin's attention, Mienthe found this extremely reassuring.

"She is yours. I shall not harm her. I have no inclination to harm her. Do you understand me, man?"

"Yes," Bertaud said.

Mienthe wondered what he'd understood that she had missed. This did not seem the moment to ask.

"What will you do?" asked Kairaithin.

"I don't know. Warn Iaor. Go north. Wait to see what happens to the Wall. What will you do?"

"I?" There was a slight pause. "I will seek an alternative wind, though I do not yet perceive any faintest whisper of any breeze I should wish to call up. And I will wait for you to call me. Call me, man, before you call any other. Shall I trust you so far?"

"Just so far," Bertaud said, rather more grimly than seemed reasonable for such an answer.

The griffin mage inclined his proud head. His black eyes blazed with fire and something else less identifiable; even the black eyes of his fiery shadow burned. Then he was gone.

Mienthe took a step away from Bertaud and looked at him incredulously.

"Mienthe—" her cousin began, then dropped into a chair, bowed his head against his hand, and laughed. There was little humor in the sound. He laughed as though he did not know whether he should weep.

Mienthe went to him, put her hand on his shoulder, and bent to rest her cheek against the top of his head. She did not speak.

After a while, Bertaud stopped laughing. He put a hand up to cover hers, where it still rested on his shoulder, and said, "It will be…everything will come right, in the end." He did not say it as though reassuring a young child, nor did he say it with the foolish confidence of a man who believes that a peril must surely be averted simply because he wishes it will be. He said it like a hope. Like an entreaty to the future.

"Yes," said Mienthe, because that was what he needed her to say. She took his hand in hers, tucked her legs up under her skirts, and sat on the floor beside his chair as she had used to do when she was a child. She leaned her cheek against his knee, saying nothing more.

For a long time they sat like that, while the last glimmers of fire-tinged light faded in the west. The lamplight in the solar turned the window glass into an opaque mirror and showed Mienthe her face and her cousin's. She thought she looked shocked, but that Bertaud looked desolate.

"You seem... very calm," Bertaud said at last, his eyes meeting hers in the glass.

Mienthe did not know what to say. She was surprised he thought so.

"Do you know... did you understand..." But her cousin did not seem to know how to finish either sentence.

"He was a griffin," Mienthe said in a small voice. "You knew his name... you knew him. He came to warn you about danger. About a fire mage who is your enemy. About danger to the Wall—the Wall in Casmantium, the one you helped to build."

"Tehre's Wall. Yes. But I didn't help build it. I was only there when it was built." Bertaud paused. He added, reluctantly, Mienthe thought, "Maybe my presence convinced Kairaithin to help build it."

"He is a griffin and a mage," Mienthe said, trying to get this all straight in her mind. "He helped you six years ago when the griffins came into Feierabiand. You stopped us battling them and made them our allies. And then he helped you again when you—when the Casmantian Wall was built. Between fire and earth, he said. Between the... the griffins' desert and the country of men? He is your friend..." She hesitated, feeling strongly that the word did not exactly apply. But she did not know what other word to use. She repeated, "He is your friend, and he has suffered for it."

"I think he has," Bertaud said. He sounded tired and disheartened.

"And now the Wall is going to break? And there will be a...a war between fire and earth? I thought...I never heard anyone say that the griffins were dangerous to us. Only maybe to the northern towns of Casmantium, up close to where the desert lies."

"Yes," said Bertaud. "No. It's a little more complicated than that."

He clearly did not want to explain. Mienthe said cautiously, looking up at him, "And the griffin mage, he thinks you might do something again. As you did six years ago? What *was* it you did?" The lamplight sent golden light and uncertain shadows across her cousin's face, so that his shape seemed to change as she gazed at him: First he seemed wholly a creature of ordinary earth, and then, as the light shifted, half a creature of fire.

"Nothing I ever want to do again," he said succinctly, and got to his feet. Then he just stood for a moment, looking down at her. He asked, "What did you think of Kairaithin?"

Mienthe, too, rose to her feet, not very gracefully from her place on the floor. She wondered what her cousin wanted her to say. That she liked his friend? But she couldn't say she did. That she appreciated what the griffin mage had done for him? But she had no clear idea what that had *been*. She said at last, "He is very...very...He frightened me. But his shadow is beautiful."

Bertaud smiled at her, the weariness she saw in him seeming to lighten a little. "Did you think so? He frightened you, that's reasonable. But he didn't terrify you. Good."

Mienthe nodded uncertainly. "But what will you do now?"

"Now?" He paused, seeming to consider. Then he said, with evident reluctance, "I suppose now I had better speak to Iaor. I suppose we will ride north."

Mienthe felt very young and ignorant. She wanted to ask her cousin about the Wall, about the griffins. She wanted very badly to ask again, *But what was it that you did?* And she wanted to ask again, *What will you do now?* But it was very clear he was evading all questions like those. To protect her? Or because, as Mienthe suspected, he did not know the answers himself? She said instead, humbly, "May I come with you to see the king? I would like—I would like to know what you will do."

Bertaud looked distractedly down at her, half his attention already turning toward what he would tell the king. Or maybe to memories of the past: memories of fire and the Casmantian Wall. But after a moment he nodded. "Yes. Come. If I go north, Mie, you'll stand in my place as the Lady of the Delta."

Mienthe stared at him.

"So you must certainly hear what Iaor and I decide to do," finished her cousin, and touched her shoulder to urge her toward the door.

*   *   *

Niethe daughter of Jereien, known since her marriage as
Niethe Jereien Safiad Nataviad in the most formal, old-
fashioned style, was a lovely and charming woman who
was much younger than King Iaor. Indeed, she was not
so very much older than Mienthe. Queen Niethe enjoyed
being queen, loved her royal husband, doted on her little
daughters, and loathed travel with a deep passion. She
detested the mud of winter and the dusty summer, she
hated rain, and she said the bright sun gave her head-
aches and made her skin freckle. She insisted on wearing
unsuitable clothing and then complained of wrinkles and
stains. She would not ride a horse, but then found fault
with the closeness of her carriage.

But Niethe, who accompanied her husband on his
annual progress only because she hated being parted
from him even more than she hated travel, clearly had
not expected to arrive in Tiefenauer only to have the king
bid her an almost immediate farewell. This taxed even the
queen's good humor, though normally she accepted the
broad demands on her husband's attention with perfect
amiability.

"It can't be helped," King Iaor told her apologetically.
"I'm certain you will be perfectly safe here, and far more
comfortable than possible on a fast ride north."

Even though the queen smiled and nodded, she somehow gave the impression she had turned her back on him.
With a flounce.

Mienthe tried not to laugh. Really it was nothing to
laugh at. If Bertaud and King Iaor thought the breaking of
the Wall was so dangerous they would not even wait for
dawn, but would ride for Tihannad this very night, then

there was nothing at all to laugh at. Niethe knew it, too, or she would really be angry rather than merely teasing Iaor in order to make him think she was not frightened.

What was really odd was that Mienthe felt no desire at all to go north herself. It was just as well, since Bertaud would never have allowed her to come—no more than Iaor would allow Niethe to come—but she was surprised she had no urge to ask for permission whether her cousin would grant it or not.

Erich, of course, *was* going with the king. He came over to Mienthe, leaned his hip against the low table near her, and said lightly, "So now I have at last a chance for swift journeys and brave exploits. I'll cover myself with glory and when next we meet, I will tell you all my tales of bright valor, do you think so?"

"Of course." Mienthe smiled up at him. "I'll expect that of you—brave exploits and bright valor, and only very little exaggeration."

"I never exaggerate!" Erich informed her in lofty tones. "Well, only a very little." He hesitated, lowered his deep voice—it was easier for him to boom than whisper, now—and asked, "You know? Why we—why your lord cousin is going north?"

"The griffins," said Mienthe, deliberately vague. "And the Wall."

"Yes," agreed Erich. He frowned at Mienthe. "My father said—this was years ago, but I remember, Mie. He said your country would regret the alliance it made with the griffins. Creatures of earth should not make common cause with creatures of fire. We are too much...ah. Too much opposed. He said nothing good would come of it."

Mienthe tilted her head. "Well, your father shouldn't

have pushed us to make common cause, then, if he had such strong opinions on the matter."

"No," Erich growled, with rather more force than Mienthe had expected. "He should not have. To be fair, he did not expect any such outcome because no one in Casmantium would think to make that alliance."

"We don't have your bad history with griffins," Mienthe suggested.

Erich nodded. "Yes. The bad history. Your lord cousin, he has a good history with the griffins, is that so?"

"Yes, I think he does," Mienthe said, guardedly, because she could not quite see where the Casmantian prince was going with this.

"He said so. I hope so," Erich said. He looked at Mienthe for a long moment, the expression in his dark eyes very sober. "But you should remember, you should always remember, a creature of earth should not trust a creature of fire. You will remember this, Mie? If the griffin your cousin says is his friend comes here again to speak to you?"

Mienthe was astonished. "I can't imagine why he would. He doesn't know me—he's not *my* friend."

"He made a human girl into a fire mage. Your honored cousin said so. He spoke of it, he and the Safiad."

By *the Safiad* he meant King Iaor, as *the Arobern* meant the King of Casmantium. Even after six years in Feierabiand, Erich liked to use the occasional Casmantian turn of phrase. He might do this to deliberately set himself apart; the prince was not above reminding others that he was Casmantian and royal. But Mienthe thought he simply wished to remind himself of his true heritage and nationality, in moments when he felt himself in danger of forgetting. She wondered what tricks a girl might use to remember her heritage after a griffin turned her into a fire mage. And how well those tricks would work. And for how long.

She said slowly, "I knew that, I think. I had forgotten. And I did not know it was *that* griffin who did it. Bertaud—" She stopped, not wanting to say out loud, *My cousin did not tell me that; he never talks even to me about what happened six years ago.*

"That griffin, he saw you when he came to speak to your honored cousin. Maybe he might come back. He took that other girl, before. Maybe he will come here to look for you."

That seemed very unlikely.

"If he does," Erich said, taking her hand in both of his—her fingers vanished entirely between his enormous hands. He looked intently into her face, "If he does, Mie, remember that a creature of earth should never make common cause with a creature of fire. Never. Promise me you will remember."

"Of course I'll remember," Mienthe assured him, an easy promise to make as she knew very well nothing of the kind would come about. "I'll be careful—truly, Erich. But you'll be the one in danger, which is why you'll get to do all the brave exploits. All I'll get to do here is attend the queen and the little princesses and wait for you to send me news."

The prince's mouth crooked. "Attending those little girls *is* a brave exploit." He stood up and stood for a moment gazing down at her. His eyes held a question, but Mienthe did not know what question she saw there.

But the arrival of the little princesses in person,

brought in quickly to make their farewells to their father, interrupted Erich before he could speak, if he meant to.

The older of the princesses was called Karianes Nataviad Merimne Safiad. She was nearly five years old, plump, pretty, cheerful, and kindhearted; everyone said she was very like Niethe's mother. The littler princess was Anlin Nataviad Merimne Safiad, a child who already, at three, showed her father's strong will and determined temper. Both little girls ran to say good-bye to Erich after speaking to their father. He had been at the Feierabianden court all their lives and, not having a clear idea about just what a hostage was, they thought he was their brother. Erich called them his little sisters once removed and let them tease him into the most impossible mischief.

Erich threw Anlin up into the air and then caught her again, repeating the procedure at once with her older sister. "Oof!" he said, pretending he might not be able to lift the five-year-old. "Have you grown more just over these few days?"

Karianes laughed, but then pouted. "Do you *have* to go?"

"I have to, yes, but Mie will be here."

The little girls gazed at Mienthe with doubtful expressions. A year was a long time to such small children, and they were clearly uncertain whether they should like to trade Erich for Mienthe. Then Anlin said, "You gave me a kitten."

Mienthe smiled, surprised the child had remembered; the last time the princesses had visited the Delta, Anlin had been only just talking. Even surrounded by her nurses and her mother's ladies, she had seemed somehow alone to Mienthe. And one of the stable cats had had kittens the right age. "Yes," she agreed. "A black one with white feet and a white nose."

"He wanted to come," declared Anlin. "But Mama wouldn't let him."

Mienthe had very little idea how to talk to children. "Traveling is hard on cats," she said sympathetically. "I'm sure he'll be waiting for you at home."

"He wanted to come," Anlin repeated, scowling. "He told me he did."

"Maybe she has an affinity to cats, like Tef?" Mienthe said to Erich. She was pleased by the idea, almost like finding such a gift in the child would be a tribute to Tef's memory. But then maybe the child simply had a vivid imagination. She *was* very young for any gift to come out.

Erich shrugged, but looked a little envious. Affinities for particular animals, common as dirt in Feierabiand, were fairly rare in Casmantium—just as the people of Feierabiand usually were smaller and fair, where those of Casmantium were broad and dark. Erich thought the ability to speak to an animal was a very exotic sort of gift, much more interesting than the making and building that were common gifts in his own country. Mienthe thought she wouldn't complain if she had even the most common gift in the world, but both Erich and she were well past the age when gifts usually came out.

The princesses' nurses swept down then to carry them back to their beds, and there was a general movement of the king's party toward departure. Erich pressed Mienthe's hands quickly in his and said, "Remember your promise!" She nodded, and he strode quickly away without looking back.

Bertaud strode over to take Mienthe's shoulders and look down at her in earnest concern.

"You'll be well," Mienthe told him. "You'll find something to do, even if the Wall breaks." Her tone sounded odd even to her own ear, midway between a plea and a command.

Her cousin said swiftly, "Of course I will. And you'll be safe here."

That was a command, to the world if not to Mienthe. She nodded.

"I'll send you news if I can, if there's any to send. And I'll return as swiftly as I may," Bertaud told her. "Mienthe—" He stopped.

Mienthe waited.

"If Kairaithin comes here, if he comes to you," her cousin said, and paused again. Then he said quickly, "If he comes, I think you should probably trust him. Especially if he says he comes from me. If he says so, it will likely be true. Do you understand?"

"No," Mienthe said honestly. "I don't think I understand anything. But I'll remember."

Her cousin barely smiled. "Yes, well. Very well. Remember, then, and that will do. I doubt he'll come. I'm sure he'll have no reason to come here. All the trouble will be in the north." He hesitated another moment, gazing at Mienthe as though he wanted to be certain he'd be able to recall her image perfectly, forever. Then he released her and spun to stride after Iaor.

Mienthe watched him go. If this were a romantic epic, she would disguise herself and sneak along with Bertaud and the king. Of course, if this were a romantic epic, then Erich and she would be certain to have amazing adventures and save Feierabiand—or more likely, both Feierabiand and Casmantium. They would fall in love and part tragically, he to be King of Casmantium and she to be just another Delta lady. They'd never see one another again because, no matter how good the road between the two countries was in the real world, that was how romantic epics ended: tragically.

Mienthe sighed. There was no point in counting over the thousands of reasons it wouldn't work out like that even if she did sneak herself into her cousin's party, which, of course, she couldn't.

Even though it was so late, Mienthe thought she might just slip past Tan's room quickly and assure herself he was safe and well. He would be asleep—she knew that—but she was somehow uneasy and knew she wouldn't be able to sleep herself until she'd glanced in and made certain that he was well. She didn't understand this. But she knew it was true. She didn't even go to the window to watch Bertaud and Erich and the rest ride away. She went straight to Tan's room.

The hallway outside the room was empty, but Mienthe didn't think anything of that; she'd forgotten that Captain Geroen had been told to have his guardsmen attend Tan. It wasn't the absence of the guardsmen that alarmed Mienthe. Yet she abruptly became certain, even as she walked quickly toward the door, that something was wrong. She took hold of the doorknob with a peculiar sense that the door might not open to Tan's room at all—that it might open to anything and any location *except* that room. But when she swung it cautiously back, there was the room after all. The sheets of paper and jars of ink were still laid out in good order on the bed table, but the bed was empty. The whole room was silent and empty.

Or not quite empty. Geroen's young guardsmen were sitting on the floor, against the wall, pale and insensible. But Tan was not there.

Yet Mienthe found she knew where he was, just as surely as she knew, without looking, which way was down or where her own hands were.

She knew Tan was unconscious. She knew he was nearby, but getting rapidly farther away. She knew he was heading west, toward the river and Linularinum. And she knew something else: that she would never manage to persuade Geroen she knew anything at all.

She was right about everything but the last.

CHAPTER 3

Tan, smiling, pulled the bed table nearer to hand and riffled through the stack of paper a servant had brought, along with a very good supper and a passable wine. The supper was now crumbs and the wine was gone, and he had even slept for a while, which he had not expected after so long unconscious. But then, unconsciousness was not quite the same as sleep, he thought, amused. Now, despite so recently wearing himself out with his gift, he found himself rather drawn to the paper and quills that had been provided. The lamplight would be adequate, if he happened to wish to write a little.

It was good paper, thick and heavily textured. Well-made paper like this was a pleasure to work with; it wouldn't let ink smudge or fade. The array of inks was also impressive. The blue was a good, deep color like distilled Casmantian sapphires, the green fresh and bright as springtime, the purple dusky and rich.

He thought that a young woman of the Delta was

unlikely to know, but would probably like, Anariddthen's newest cycle, all sweet love and desperate loss and brave heroism, and an ending that was, contrary to most romantic epics, at least ambiguous rather than tragic. It would please pretty little Mienthe, he decided. He was clear already that anyone who wished Lord Bertaud's goodwill might well give some thought to pleasing his cousin.

The Anariddthen—yes, Tan decided. Not only would young Mienthe probably like it, it also could be taken in pieces of a sensible size. There wasn't much chance he'd fall into the legist's trance and wear his fingers to the bone trying to reach the end in one session. Yes. The Anariddthen would do very well. Green ink, Tan thought, for the beginning. He picked up a green quill—made from a parrot's feather, he presumed, and very handsome it was, if not the sort of quill a professional would care to be seen using for serious work. But perfect for a light romance. He dipped it into the matching ink, and found himself standing alone, chilled half to death, in a cavernous building filled with dim shadows and dusty cobwebs.

There had been no sense of transition at all. Tan's shocked gasp and sharp twitch backward were natural, but ill-advised: He discovered that his ankles were chained together and his wrists chained to his ankles by coming too hard against the limits of the chains, losing his balance, and falling. And then he discovered that another chain was around his neck, this one running high aloft to the distant ceiling of the building. With his hands chained, Tan could not catch himself: The chain about his neck slipped through a steel ring and he was suddenly strangling. It took a terrifying moment of breathless, off-balance struggle to regain his feet, and even then he had to toss his head sharply to get the strangling chain to run back through the slip-ring so he could catch his breath.

His throat felt bruised where the chain had closed around it. For an instant he could not help but picture what would have happened if he'd fallen with a little more force and crushed his windpipe, or if he hadn't been able to get back to his feet and had simply hung there, strangling— The images went beyond vivid to visceral, and he shut his eyes for a long moment and devoted himself to breathing. Slow, steady breaths. He was not going to panic and give himself to his enemies…to Istierinan, to be plain, and what was Istierinan doing with a pet mage running his errands? What mage would it even be? None of the court mages at Teramondian served or worked with or even liked Istierinan, so far as Tan knew. Obviously he had missed something. Evidently something important.

Tan knew very little about magecraft, but obviously Istierinan couldn't have stolen him out of the Delta's great house and tumbled him into this place through a blank moment of time unless he had a Linularinan mage working with him. But, earth and iron, why had the Linularinan spymaster gone to such trouble to do it? Istierinan risked offending not just Feierabiand but *the Lord of the Delta* by stealing Tan out of *his own house*? Even when it was patently too late to stop the stolen information from getting out? It was incredible.

Although, on the other hand, Tan had to credit that Istierinan had clearly managed the trick. Perhaps so silently that Lord Bertaud would not be able to take official offense? At least, so silently that Istierinan could *tell* himself that the Lord of the Delta wouldn't be able to take offense? Tan ran that question backward and

forward in his mind even while he turned most of his
attention toward examining his situation and his prison.
He wasn't injured. Not even bruised, save where the
chain had closed across his throat when he'd fallen. Istierinan and his people had taken some care, then, that he
not be harmed. Yet. But his shirt was gone, and his boots.
No wonder he was cold. His skin prickled with the chill.
Or maybe with fear.

He tried to bury the fear beneath rational thought and
a practical attention toward possible escape. The building
seemed to be a warehouse. Or a barn. A barn, yes. That
loft had probably held bales of hay or straw, and those
rot-riddled boards over there had probably once outlined
neat stalls. Though the table near at hand was new, obviously brought in recently. Like the chains and their bolts.
An old disused barn, then, freshly tricked out for its new
and far more questionable role. Too far from the city, he
was certain, for passersby to hear shouts.

Well, and come to that, why was Istierinan not already
standing at that nice new table, with all the tools he
might require laid out for use? Was he simply waiting
for fear and cold and exhaustion to wear Tan down? The
scene, one had to admit, was quite adequately set for
the purpose. The slip-chain was a nice touch. How long
could a man stay on his feet when collapse would mean
strangling? A long time, Tan thought, but not forever, and
when he died, his death would be, in a way, something
he'd done to himself. Yes, that was the kind of subtlety
that would appeal to Istierinan.

Tan had spent nearly seven years making a place for
himself, or for the man he had pretended to be, in the
old Fox's court in Teramondian. Even before that, he

had spent other, earlier, years living out other false lives in one part or another of Linularinum. He had done it because he loved Feierabiand, and because...well, for many reasons that had seemed good at the time. He had resented Linularinan arrogance and high-handedness; that had been part of it. He had feared what might eventually come about if the Linularinan king and court were allowed to disdain Feierabiand. And he had enjoyed the game of spycraft and his own skill at it. An agent operating in deep cover lived a life of slow, tedious deception that flashed with lightning-lit moments of brilliant terror, and Tan would not have traded those moments for a lifetime of secure prosperity.

Thus, for years Tan had walked the knife's edge of deception, as they said. The knife in that saying was understood to be laid as a bridge across disownment— for spies, if caught, were very seldom owned by their masters—and death. And he had done it even though, in those years, he had learned to love Linularinum as well as Feierabiand.

Every confidential agent struggled with questions about loyalty and treachery. These were questions with which Tan had years ago made his peace. It had helped that he never felt any love for the old Fox, Mariddeier Kohorrian, who paid far too much attention to cleverness and the strictest possible interpretation of the law and not nearly enough to justice. But it had helped even more that in those last years, as he'd gained Istierinan's trust, he'd also learned to hate him. The Linularinan spymaster had seemed to Tan to embody everything he disliked about the Linularinan people while specifically eschewing all their admirable qualities. He was not merely deceitful but falsehearted, not merely justifiably proud of his own skills but contemptuous of those owned by others, and slyly cruel even when he seemed overtly kind.

Maybe silence and cold was exactly the vengeance Istierinan had in mind. Maybe no one would come to question Tan, not even to watch or gloat. An uncomfortable idea, in its way worse than, well, other ideas. Maybe Istierinan was employing time itself as a subtle weapon as well, forcing Tan to suffer from the contradictory fears that someone would come and that no one would. Time to try to escape and fail, to wear out his strength to no avail, with the strangling chain waiting all the while to tighten when he could no longer keep his feet...

At the moment, however, Tan definitely was not desperate enough to wish for the arrival of his enemies. He turned his head, shuffled as far around as the chains would allow, inspecting the warehouse more closely. No windows, no visible door. The slanted golden light of late afternoon filtered in through missing boards high in the roof. The building was not, then, in good shape. He should be able to break a way out, if he could get out of the chains.

Which did not seem likely. The barn might be decrepit, but the chains were new and well-made, and they'd been bolted to a floor that seemed depressingly sturdy. No signs of wood-rot underfoot, no. Above...when Tan tensed the muscles of his neck and cautiously put pressure on the chain around his throat, he could feel no give to the boards above. Nor, when he tried standing on his toes and ducking, could he loosen the slip-chain enough to get his head through. He thought, briefly, about trying to jerk the neck-chain loose. But it would be unfortunate if he accidentally crushed his own windpipe instead of breaking the chain. Istierinan would laugh himself stupid when he finally arrived.

Tan stood quietly for some time, thinking and letting his eyes roam aimlessly about the barn, hoping for inspiration. None came. He found himself shivering and, as he had no other protection, tried to pretend that he wasn't cold. Far too many little breezes and gusts could make their way through the cracks and gaps and the spaces left by missing boards. Spring it might be, but only just, and even in the Delta, it was too cold to go without boots or shirt. The light dimmed...overcast? Tan doubted the roof of this barn would prove tight against wind and rain. A chilly rain would be perfect to complete this situation. Though, as he had no water, he might soon be grateful for even the most bone-chilling rain. Or was it dusk? It seemed too early. But he did not, after all, know how long ago he had been captured. Hours? Days? He surely should be thirstier, if it had been so long.

He tried again to break loose the bolts that held him chained—he'd already decided the chains themselves were hopeless. Nothing. He then tried, briefly, to work his hands out of their shackles. His hands were long, his wrists not overthick. But the steel shackles were too tight. Even if Tan broke the bones of his hands and fingers, there would still be the shackles on his ankles. Hard to deal with those if his fingers were broken. Though if he could only get the slip-chain off, he might count that a net gain. If he was sufficiently desperate. Not yet.

He could try shouting. He knew very well no decent, uninvolved person would be near enough to hear him. On the other hand, if enemies were nearby, *they* would hear him. They might even come. That was an uncomfortable uncertainty. So not yet for shouting, either, then. Though possibly soon...

Then, somewhere out of sight, a door creaked open and thudded closed. Enemies were coming, after all. It was a mark of Istierinan's cleverness that Tan was almost glad to hear them. He straightened his shoulders and turned his head. Boots thumped hollowly across the floor, more than one pair. Dust rose into the air. Someone coughed. Torchlight wavered, red as death.

The Istierinan whom Tan had known, Istierinan Hamoddian, son of Lord Iskiriadde Hamoddian, had passed himself off as a careless court dandy, a man with wit and wealth, but no interest in or connection with serious matters. Dissolute and reckless, though undoubtedly clever. The sort of man admired by younger sons who admired profligacy for its own sake and were likely to die young in some foolish stunt or quarrel.

But Istierinan Hamoddian was showing Tan a very different face now. Not only was he dressed as plainly as any ordinary traveler, but his long, bony face, usually expressive, was blank and still. Very little remained to suggest the self-indulgent courtier Tan remembered. Here, for this role he was playing now, he had not troubled to color the gray out of his hair. No wonder, Tan thought, that he had customarily done so, for the silver at his temples made him look not only older but far more serious. Istierinan's mouth, always ready to crook in ironic humor, was set in a thin line. His wit wasn't hidden, but altered out of all recognition to a kind of grim acuity. His deep-set eyes, though shadowed with weariness, held a cold resolution. Tan wondered, distantly, how many of Istierinan's young admirers would even recognize him now.

Istierinan was carrying nothing. But the two burly men he'd brought with him held cudgels as well as torches, and one of them carried a leather satchel that might contain anything. Tan tried, unsuccessfully, not to imagine the sort of tools it probably held.

Istierinan stopped perhaps six feet from Tan, looking at him without speaking.

Tan stared back, equally wordless. He considered, briefly, pretending innocence and demanding what Istierinan meant by this abduction. But the spymaster did not look in the mood for such pretense, thoroughly ruined in any case by Tan's convoluted flight out of Linularinum to the Delta. No innocent man could have made it, or would have known how to even try, and no clever repartee could possibly disguise the fact.

Nor did Istierinan seem inclined toward any sort of game or indirection. He simply looked at Tan for a moment longer and then asked abruptly, "Where is it? Do you still have it yourself? If you've passed it on, to whom?"

These all seemed odd questions, when Tan had stolen information rather than any object. He said cautiously, "What, it?" Not altogether to his surprise, Istierinan merely glanced impatiently at one of his thugs. The man lifted a muscled arm. Tan kept his gaze on Istierinan, not the thug. He said quickly and sharply, "Well, here we are, very like Redrierre and Moddrisian, and just as unlikely to come to a satisfactory conclusion, do you think? Be sensible, man! I'll answer any question you ask, but if you want answers, you'll have to ask clearly! I swear I don't know what you mean."

The spymaster didn't even blink. The thug stepped

forward, walked around behind Tan, and hit him: a hard, twisting blow to the kidney. Gasping, Tan stumbled and sagged—then found the slip-chain cutting off his air. He tried to straighten and the thug kicked his feet out from under him. Then all of them just stood and waited while Tan struggled, strangling, to get back to his feet. He made it at last, tossing his head hard to loosen the chain and sucking in great lungfuls of precious air.

"Where is it?" Istierinan repeated in a level voice. "Do you still hold it yourself? If you do, then return it, and this can be over swiftly. Or otherwise, if you will not. Or have you given it away? To whom? The Lord of the Delta, likely not." He made a small movement, dismissing this possibility as though he and Tan both knew it was foolish. "But perhaps one of his people might have been able to take it? Well?"

Tan shook his head. "Lord Istierinan, I'm afraid this is going to be a long night. Because I truly do not know what you are talking about! I took nothing returnable. Everything I stole was set down in plain ink and has long since been carried away out of the past into the future—" He stopped as the Linularinan spymaster stepped across to the table and began to take things out of the satchel.

To Tan's astonishment, what he was laying out was bottles of ink and little bundles of quills. Tan almost laughed in sheer surprise. Quills and ink! Whatever Istierinan had in mind, Tan was definitely glad to see legist's tools rather than the other sort. But what did the Linularinan spymaster have in mind?

"Well?" Istierinan said to Tan. Not ominously. He'd taken a quill out of the packet, and ran it now through his fingers. His tone was more one of . . . weary exasperation, if Tan was any judge. The spymaster made a small gesture down toward Tan's feet. "You would have more trouble keeping your feet, I imagine, with broken toes. Or *missing* toes. Or whatever. There are so many possibilities."

"I'm sure you're right," Tan agreed smoothly. "There's surely no need to test the question, if you would only be plain. Lord Istierinan, what is it you *want*?"

"Want?" Istierinan took a small step forward, his calm cracking to show—what? Anger, yes, but not merely anger: There was something else underneath the rage. Fear, even terror, tightly leashed, and something else—desperation? Despair? Istierinan might well lose his position because of what Tan had done to him—probably would, probably should, maybe already had—but Tan had not thought the old Fox of Linularinum would go so far as to torture and destroy a spymaster who failed him. But he could not at the moment imagine what other fear could render Istierinan so desperate now.

Or had the King of Linularinum *not* sent Istierinan after Tan after all? Maybe Istierinan was here on his own, in one last effort to regain the king's favor and his old place in the Fox's court? No, that didn't seem likely— Tan's thoughts were interrupted in their circular flight by Istierinan himself taking a cudgel from one of his thugs and slamming it down toward one of his feet. Tan jerked his foot out of the way and Istierinan changed the strike to a sweeping sideways blow against his knee.

The *crack* of wood against bone was horrifying even before the pain hit, and then the cudgel swept around to threaten the other knee, and Tan tried to get out of the way of the blow, lost his footing completely, and found himself once again strangling helplessly, only this time the agony from his broken knee overwhelmed the terror of suffocation, briefly. Then the lack of air forced even the pain into the background, and at last he made it back to his feet—his foot—but then immediately fell again as some of his weight came onto his bad knee in a red explosion. He made it up once more, somehow, and fought to keep his balance—he dreaded a blow against the other knee, though he told himself, with what rationality remained to him, that surely Istierinan did not mean to kill him, not yet. Though a second blow against the first leg would not be much of an improvement.

But Istierinan did not strike him again, waiting instead for Tan to regain his balance and his breath. When Tan swayed, flinched from the red rolling pain, and nearly fell again, the spymaster put the tip of the cudgel against Tan's chest to steady him. "So," he said softly. "Will you continue to insist that this night be long?"

Tan tried to focus on the question, on Istierinan's face. The haze of sweat and tears and nauseating pain got in the way. He blinked, blinked again, and managed at last to put the pain aside enough to spare some attention to the spymaster. Istierinan was now leaning on the cudgel like a walking stick. If he'd been playing the court dandy, he would have probably looked urbane and sophisticated. Here in this disused barn, no one could have mistaken his ruthlessness.

"Are you listening to me? Are you capable of thought?"

Tan shook his head, not in denial, but trying to clear his mind. Even that motion somehow jarred his leg. Tears of pain came into his eyes; a wave of faintness threatened his balance. At Istierinan's impatient wave, one of the thugs stepped forward to support him.

"Would you care to sit down? Agree to return...what you stole, and you may. One way or the other, you will return it, or at least release it, before dawn. Give it to me now and I will even let you go, no more harmed than you are now. I will sign any binding contract you care to dictate," he added, as Tan's eyebrows rose in wordless incredulity. He took a small but rather fine leather-bound book out of his satchel, gave Tan a significant look, and set the book down on the table, precisely centered. Then he removed the top from one of his bottles of ink, picked up a quill, and gave Tan another look, even more significant. Tan stared at him, hopelessly bewildered.

"Or if you no longer have it, tell me to whom you gave it," Istierinan snapped. "I will at least make this night a short one."

Tan wanted to ask again what *it* was, but was afraid of what Istierinan might do if he seemed to be defiant. The thug, responding to another of Istierinan's gestured commands, released Tan and stepped back, punctuating the spymaster's demand with a clear illustration of what the rest of the night would be like if Tan continued to be obdurate. Tan tensed the muscles of his neck, trying to let the slip-chain carry some of his weight. This was not a successful endeavor. He tried to think. This was also not a very successful endeavor. Istierinan was still waiting. Tan opened his mouth to agree, at least to get Istierinan to release the slip-chain, let him sit down, if only for a moment until the spymaster understood that Tan really could not do as he demanded—even a brief respite would be a very good thing—

There was a shout, and the sound of running steps coming rapidly closer, a lot of men by the sound, and then almost at once the deadly whip of arrows through the cobweb-strewn space under the vaulted roof of the barn and more shouts.

Istierinan whirled, shocked, and then hesitated, taking a step toward Tan. Another shout echoed in the close space, and more arrows flew—better aimed this time, so much better that Tan belatedly realized that the first volley had been meant merely to frighten the spymaster and his men and drive them away from their prisoner. Istierinan realized that, too, and that, chained as Tan was, it was going to be impossible to take him with them in their flight. He snatched up the torches instead and flung them down, shadows whirling and surging as the flames whipped through the air.

Tan expected Istierinan to kill him, since he couldn't keep him. To his surprise, the spymaster spun and reached for the book instead. But an arrow sliced the air not an inch from his hand and then another cut across his forearm, loosing a red spray of blood—Istierinan made a sound between a gasp and a scream, jerking involuntarily away, but even then he did not run. But another arrow struck him in the back. One of his men caught him up as he collapsed, and carried him away at a run, not at all discommoded by the burden.

Then Tan's rescuers were arriving—men in plain clothing without badges or identifying marks, but with very businesslike weapons. Most of them went straight past Tan, hurrying cautiously into the echoing reaches of the barn, but a small group of men stopped to collect the abandoned torches and, very much to Tan's relief, two came to get him free. Tan was not altogether astonished to find Geroen among those who stayed near at hand, but he was speechless to glimpse the slender figure of Mienthe stretching up on her toes to peer over the captain's shoulder.

"Can't you stand?" growled Geroen, coming to look Tan up and down. "Your knee, is it? Sepes, get that chain off from around his neck. Why's that other one still on his hands? What do you mean, you've no key? Earth and iron! What do you need a key for? Didn't anybody ever teach you to pick locks?"

Tan blinked, wondering whether he could have heard this right, but then the captain quite matter-of-factly produced a set of lockpicks and bent to examine the shackles. "Not any locksmith's best work," he added after a moment, straightening as the wristbands snapped open— then caught Tan's arm in a hard grip as Tan swayed and added, "None of that, now! Here, Keier, keep him upright, will you, while I get these other shackles—" He grunted down to one knee to work on the ankle chains.

Tan clung to Keier, but he stared at Mienthe, still baffled by her presence. Like the men, she was wearing plain, sturdy clothing—boy's clothing, in fact, very practical—but no one could have mistaken her for a boy. Her hair hung down her back in a heavy plait, and her delicate bones were much too fine for a boy's. Though admirably composed, she was clearly frightened. She was breathing quickly, her face was pale, and her hands were balled into fists, probably to hide their shaking. On the other hand, she neither babbled nor spooked nervously at every distant sound, the two most common failings of young men on their first assignments in enemy territory. Instead, she walked forward to peer curiously at the things laid out on the table. One of the men guarding her immediately collected a torch and obligingly held it for her. Picking up a quill, she ran the long feather through her fingers. Then she flipped open the book to gaze at its pages. Her brows drew together in puzzlement.

"He can't walk on that," Geroen said to one of his men, oblivious of or indifferent to Mienthe's interest in the things the Linularinan spymaster had abandoned. "You and Sepes, carry him. Jump to it, now, do you think we've got all year for this?"

"Wait—" Tan began, nodding toward the table.

"Shut up!" Geroen ordered curtly. "Do you *know* how much trouble you've caused? I'll give you a hint for free! Not near as much as there'll be if we're caught this side of the river. Keier—"

"Tan, can you..." Mienthe looked at him in concern, her voice trailing off. She closed the book again and tucked it back in the abandoned satchel, so that was all right. And she began to collect the inks and quills as well. The instincts of a spy, Tan thought, to take away anything odd for later perusal at leisure. He was almost amused despite the brutal circumstances, but he was glad to see someone had the right impulse, since Geroen clearly did not.

"I'm well, I'm well," Tan assured Mienthe, through his teeth because he had to choke back a groan of pain as he tried to take a step. The attempt proved ill-advised. "You have that book safe, all those things?"

"Yes—"

"You, and you." Captain Geroen pointed a thick finger at two of his men. "Get him up and out. Lady, if you will, this is not the time to dither about looking at— Did you find anyone?" he interrupted himself to demand as some of his men reemerged from the far gloomy reaches of the barn. And, to the reluctant shakes of their heads, "Too much to expect, I suppose. Lady—"

Mienthe said meekly to Geroen, "Yes, Captain, of course. Is everyone here? Wasn't there any sign of the, um, the men who…"

"Nothing but shadows and starlight as far as we could see," said one of the men who'd gone after Istierinan. He added a little defensively, "Once they were out of this building, there were a thousand places to hide, and there's not much moon tonight."

"It's not likely a lot of Delta guardsmen off the streets will find Istierinan Hamoddian or his men," Tan put in. "Those weren't some petty street-thugs, Geroen. That was the Linularinan spymaster. He might have been struck by an arrow, but those men he had won't be fools. Although you might have taken them by surprise, you aren't likely to take them up now."

Geroen grunted, scowling at any possible excuses. But he didn't order his people after Istierinan, either. He said instead, "Nor I wouldn't want to. Last thing we need here, another spy! You men, get *our* spy out of that chair. Our way's still clear, is it, Jerren?"

Tan wondered, briefly, what kind of animal Jerren bespoke. Something that could see in the dark, presumably. Rats? Owls? But then the two young men the captain had assigned to him lifted him up and he lost all interest in any questions other than *How far to the river?* and *How long till I can lie down?* and, impolite but honest doubt: *So do you have a half-skilled healing mage anywhere in Tiefenauer?*

The barn proved to be set to one side of an abandoned

farmyard, not far from a decrepit house. A stretch of briars and poison ivy and other coarse brush indicated an abandoned pasture, and a timber fence in ill-repair outlined a rutted gravel road. It was not quite raining, but heavily overcast, with a fine mist blowing on the wind.

A lot of horses came up out of the brush. In the dark, the sound of their hooves crunching through the undergrowth took at least a year or two off Tan's life, until he managed at last to make out their riderless state. Strangely, the animals moved all together, not one straying away from the herd—ah. Of course some of Geroen's men would be able to speak to horses; living in Linularinum, Tan had become less accustomed to everyone and his cousin having that sort of gift, but there was a lot of Feierabianden blood in the Delta.

"You can't hardly ride with that leg," Geroen began.

"I'd rather ride than walk, and I'd drag myself along by my teeth to get out of this place," Tan assured him. "Just get me up on a horse and I'll stay there, I promise you."

Though this claim was true in its essentials, getting up into the saddle of even the most patient beast proved even less entertaining in practice than Tan had envisioned. But he was up at last, and they were all moving.

Tan had opted to allow his bad leg to hang loose rather than try to get his foot into the stirrup. Now he rapidly decided that had been a mistake—though he knew any other decision would have been just as agonizing—yes, and falling off would be even worse, though at the moment, *even worse* was something of a theoretical construct. He braced himself against swirling dizziness with a hand on the pommel and tried not to scream or sob or throw up, all bad for his reputation as well as inconvenient when trying to run away.

He'd have liked to sink into blind misery and just endure while Geroen's men got him home. In fact, he rather felt that he deserved to. He could hardly kick his horse to get it up beside Geroen's, but when the captain came past him, he managed to gather enough shards of control and rationality to ask, "How far to the border? What do you figure are the chances of meeting the wrong sort of patrol between here and there? Are these all the men you have?" There were nineteen men, Tan knew, some distant part of his mind having made an automatic count. Nineteen men and Bertaud's little cousin. Not the sort of force he could quite imagine facing down, say, a company of regular Linularinan soldiers under Istierinan's command. Even if they had any right to try, which they arguably didn't, on this side of the river.

"Not far," Geroen said briefly. "But too far, if we run into the wrong sort of trouble. Can you canter?" He gave Tan a close look. "Never mind! Even a trot would have you off in a trice, a blind crow at midnight could see that."

Tan could hardly deny it. He wondered just where Istierinan might have got to, and with whom, and in command of what resources. And just what their chances were of finding out the answers to all those questions. Far too good, he feared.

Mienthe rode over. Even in the dark, anyone could see that she was tense, excited, worried, determined, very young, and, most of all, decidedly female. Why, why, why had Geroen brought her? If they did encounter any regular Linularinan soldiers, it would be blazingly obvious she was somebody important. The Linularinan authorities would have every reason to believe the Delta had deliberately sent her to lend formal authority to some nefarious purpose, and what would Bertaud say if they got his cousin taken up by enemy soldiers on the wrong side of the river?

But she was still self-possessed, and she still had the leather satchel over her shoulder, Tan was relieved to see. She said, to Tan but mostly addressing Geroen, "Tan, I'll get up behind you." Then, as the captain began to protest, "No, it only makes sense! I'm the only one here light enough to let the horse carry two at speed, and I can keep him from falling. Then we can make better time, and if you only have one horse to guard rather than two, won't that simplify everything in case of, well, in case?"

It would, unquestionably. Though Tan also had an uncomfortable vision of the horse stumbling at some unforgiving moment, with both of them falling, to yield twice the disaster they'd otherwise face. Even so...

"Over you get, then," Geroen said gruffly. Tan couldn't tell whether he was also suffering from a too-vivid imagination. He sounded ill-tempered enough either way.

Mienthe slid across from her horse to Tan's without even dismounting. She sat close behind him, her thighs bracing his, her small hands firm on his hips. He immediately felt much more secure in the saddle. The horse's gait smoothed out as it, too, recognized the steadiness of its second rider. Under other circumstances, Tan would have enjoyed having the girl behind him. He tried to think of an appropriate quotation for this sort of situation—he knew there was one—but the agony radiating from his knee not only ruined his memory but also ensured, very decisively, that he'd be thinking no impure thoughts about Lord Bertaud's cousin.

Geroen waved, and the horse lunged forward into a canter along a road they could only barely see; one had to just trust the horses knew where they were putting their feet. "It's not far to the river," Mienthe said to Tan. She didn't quite shout, although nervous excitement made her speak much more loudly than necessary. That was as well, as Tan was tending to lose words and phrases among the waves of pain that beset him.

Tan was certain they would find a company of Linularinan soldiers between them and the river, yet they met no one. This astonished him, until he remembered Istierinan falling with an arrow in his back. They passed half a handful of travelers on the road, so they would be remembered, but Tan could not bring himself to care. They found no one waiting when they finally waded out of the marshes proper and into the mud at the river's edge, which was his sole concern.

"There's a ford?" Tan muttered when he'd realized they'd stopped. He squinted blearily out across the wide expanse of water. For all the sluggish current, the river looked deep here. The water looked like pewter in the dim light, stark angular silhouettes of cypress knees black against the slow-moving glimmer.

Then he watched incredulously as one clumsy but solid-looking rowboat and then another were drawn out of the hidden darkness behind the cypress knees. All that way along the road and then through the marshes, and they'd come out at the riverbank just where the rowboats had been hidden? His opinion of Geroen, already fairly solid, rose another notch.

And he was very, very glad there were boats. Though he was not entirely certain he would be able to make it down from this horse without collapsing into unconsciousness and then into the black swamp mud. Drowning in a foot of water! *There* would be a stupid death. Though, no, of course, he realized muzzily. Mienthe was right behind him. She would drag him out…A guardsman reached up to help Tan down, and he found he'd been right about at least one thing: Black unconsciousness was indeed waiting for him. The last thing he was aware of was Mienthe's sharp exclamation of dismay as she snatched at his arm.

CHAPTER 4

Mienthe had been frightened from the moment she'd
realized that Tan was missing and that, with Bertaud
gone, she was the only one who could possibly order a
raid to get him back. But she had not been utterly *terrified*
until she realized she had actually managed to persuade
Geroen not only to obey that command, but to take her
with him.

Then, once they were committed, Mienthe had been
terrified she'd lose her sense of Tan's position and that
she wouldn't be able to find him after all. She was terrified they'd run into a Linularinan patrol and have to either
run or fight, neither option at all desirable. She was terrified they'd find Tan and be unable to get him back, or find
he'd already been killed. Right at the end, before they'd
found the barn, she'd even thought that she might just be
wrong about what she thought she knew. The conviction
that she knew Tan's position was very strong, but once
that doubt had occurred to her, it had crept persistently

about in the back of her mind no matter how she tried to ignore it.

But then they had found Tan after all, and there hadn't been a lot of Linularinan soldiers, and Tan *had* still been alive—though what had been done to him was brutal, and getting away again was a nightmare.

Then Mienthe had been terrified they'd be caught by Linularinan troops after all, or guardsmen, or spies, or whoever had been in that barn with Tan. But then they'd found the boats, and Tan had fainted, which made getting him across the river much less awful, even though by that time the mist had changed to a cold and very unpleasant drizzle.

And no one had tried to stop them, which amazed Mienthe. She suspected Geroen was also astonished at how lucky they'd been, though he was so gruff it was hard to tell. She was still amazed she'd managed to persuade him that yes, really, she *did* know where Tan was, but no, she *couldn't* explain it to anybody else. But when she'd insisted, instead of ignoring her, Geroen had said, in an extremely neutral tone, "Well, lady, I hadn't heard you'd gone for a mage, but it could be useful now and no mistake."

Mienthe couldn't believe she really might be developing mage power and she was a little ashamed of letting Geroen think she was. But she certainly hadn't tried to stop his arranging the raid. And she'd agreed with him about informing the queen—or at least, she'd agreed with him that the queen shouldn't be informed. Mienthe hadn't wanted to argue with Niethe or her royal guardsmen, and neither, apparently, had Geroen. Instead, they'd agreed that they should move fast. And they had, so fast they'd very nearly got to Tan before his Linularinan enemies had got him across the river. But not quite.

But to Mienthe's intense gratitude, the captain hadn't quit even then, but had instead pulled success right out of the teeth of looming defeat.

Now they were back in Feierabiand and it wasn't even dawn yet, which seemed incredible. She supposed Bertaud and the king must be most of the way to Sihannas by now, and knew nothing at all about what had happened to Tan or what she had done, which seemed in a way even more incredible.

Tan was more or less conscious again, which was unfortunate. Mienthe, riding in the cart next to him, flinched every time the cart jarred across an uneven cobblestone. Tan himself seemed beyond flinching for anything so minor. It had nearly stopped raining, but it was still impossible to tell whether the moisture beading on his face was rain or tears. Mienthe thought Tan was definitely due his share of tears, all things considered.

But there was the great house at last. Unfortunately, the house wasn't waiting for them quietly, as Mienthe had expected and hoped. The lanterns, set high on their tall poles, blazed through the gardens and before every door. Lamps glowed in every window, and the main doors stood wide open to the chill darkness of the streets, and there were Delta guardsmen and royal soldiers everywhere.

Captain Geroen set his jaw, not quite looking at Mienthe where she sat in the cart. "Her Majesty got it out of my officers where we'd gone, I suppose."

Biting her lip, Mienthe nodded. Geroen was right. Queen Niethe must have found out where they'd gone, and even if she approved the result of what they'd done, she might be really angry at their lack of…finesse. Even if she wasn't, she would certainly tell King Iaor all about it. Possibly worse, either Niethe or the king would unquestionably tell Bertaud.

But she said optimistically, trying to sound firm and decisive, "This is the Delta, and her Majesty isn't the Lady of the Delta. With Bertaud gone, I am. He said so." She hesitated. That had *sounded* firm, hadn't it? She wished she felt the truth of the statement with half that firmness. But she continued, "So if I approved our, um, raid, then even the queen hasn't anything to say about it. Or not much." But she couldn't help but add, "I think."

"Huh," said Geroen, clearly not reassured.

"I had hoped she wouldn't find out," Mienthe admitted in a smaller voice. "I suppose she'll tell Iaor. And Bertaud."

"I suppose she will," Geroen agreed glumly, clearly not looking forward to facing her cousin. "Likely your lord cousin will break me right back to prison guard when he finds out about this. If he doesn't toss me in a cell myself."

Mienthe shook her head, though privately she wondered whether Geroen might be right. If they'd been clever and quick enough, they would have recovered Tan *before* the Linularinan spymaster had got him across the bridge. Then they wouldn't have needed to charge off through the marshes and across the river on a wild and completely illegal raid of their own. Bertaud might be really furious, especially with Geroen, because the captain had let her come on the raid.

Mienthe said stubbornly, "Linularinum started it. And I had to go along, or we'd never have managed.

Besides, by the time he finds out, it'll be so long ago, maybe…Anyway, we *did* get Tan back. And we didn't get caught."

"Both matters of the greatest importance," Tan put in from the bottom of the cart, not opening his eyes. His voice was barely audible, but his tone had recovered a thread of mocking humor. "Be a pity to stop here and let all that effort go to waste."

Geroen grunted a laugh, signaled the cart's driver to stop, swung off his horse, and offered Mienthe a hand down from the cart.

The queen, followed by a scattering of staff and servants, came out the open doors at just that moment. She stood for a moment, staring at them. Then she came down the steps and made her way over to the cart. The queen took Mienthe's hand, to her immense relief seeming not so furious after all. Her pretty mouth set as her glance encompassed Tan's pale, pain-drawn face.

"A smashed knee," Geroen said briefly, not quite meeting the queen's eyes.

"I'd never have lived through the night if not for this rescue," Tan managed in his thread of a voice. Mienthe hoped the queen would remember to mention *that* to her husband, as well as the rest.

"I asked for your staff to send for a mage skilled in healing as soon as I understood where you'd gone," Queen Niethe told Mienthe. She touched Tan's throat, then his forehead. She frowned down at him. "Already fevered—well, the mage will see you right, and for that I'm truly grateful." She turned to wave at the hovering servants.

Iriene was the only mage in Tiefenauer skilled in healing, and she was in fact skilled at no other kind of magecraft. But she was a very skillful healer indeed. Folk came from all over the Delta to see her. Mienthe had seen Iriene repair a terribly broken elbow once when one of the upper-house maids' child had fallen out of a window; she could surely fix Tan's knee. And the queen had already sent for her. A tension Mienthe hadn't quite realized she'd felt eased.

Tan, closing his eyes again, whispered, "A mage is better than a miser when health is more valued than gold," which sounded like a quote, though Mienthe didn't recognize the source.

"That's the only injury?" Niethe asked, looking searchingly at Mienthe. "You're well?"

"Yes—"

"Well, good! But there's no credit to your guard captain for that," the queen said, and stared at Geroen, who lowered his eyes wordlessly. Not in the least appeased, Queen Niethe said in an unforgiving tone, "You took *Bertaud's little cousin* across the river into Linularinum, risking who knows what mayhem *and* a cross-border incident? I can't imagine what Iaor will say! And you, Mienthe! What *can* you have been thinking? I would hardly credit it, save you standing here covered in swamp mud!"

Geroen could hardly answer this, so Mienthe did. "Your Majesty, Captain Geroen didn't take me across the river," she said, trying not to let her voice tremble. She made herself meet the queen's eyes. "*I* took *him*. And I'm sorry if His Majesty will be angry, but I'm the Lady of the Delta while my cousin is away, so how could I let Linularinan agents kidnap people right out of the great house? And we did get Tan back."

The queen stared at her, taken very much aback.

Mienthe knew she'd flushed. Her heart was beating too fast. Despite her brave words, she knew the king, and probably Bertaud, would indeed be angry. And she knew she was the one who deserved their anger—she'd taken Bertaud's authority on herself, and whatever he'd *said*, she wasn't at all certain she'd had the right, not really.

She also knew that none of the risks they'd taken would have been necessary if she'd only kept Tan safer to begin with, or moved faster to get him back—she'd known where he was from the moment he'd been taken, and they'd *still* had to go into Linularinum to get him? If she'd only been faster, not only would they have avoided any potential trouble with Linularinum, but Tan wouldn't have gotten hurt.

"Well," Niethe said, now sounding a little doubtful, "if you stopped those sly Linularinan agents from doing their malicious work on this side of the river, that's well done, at least." She smiled suddenly. "I won't scold you, Mienthe. Maybe you're right. I imagine your cousin will have one or two things to say when he returns, however!"

Mienthe imagined so, too, more vividly than Niethe could. She tried to smile.

Behind the queen, the mage Iriene came out onto the porch, took in the crowd with one comprehensive, unimpressed glance, and said sharply, "Why are you all dithering about in the damp? Get this injured man somewhere clean and warm, and everyone else get out of the way, if you please! Do we have a litter? Well, what are we all standing about for, then? You"—she stabbed a finger at some of the queen's attendants—"get a litter and get that man inside. Jump!"

In all the Delta, Iriene daughter of Iriene was not only

the mage most skilled with healing magic but also the one least impressed by rank, wealth, or authority. Only learning impressed her, so Bertaud had told Mienthe, and only if it had to do with healing. She paid so little attention to anything else that Mienthe suspected she might not even know who Niethe was. If she knew, it wasn't stopping her commanding the queen's own guardsmen, who, after only the quickest glance at Niethe, were indeed jumping to obey the mage.

"Gently, there!" exclaimed Iriene, hovering over Tan as he was transferred from cart to litter. She scowled ferociously down at him, waving a sharp hand through the air as though trying to brush away a cloud of gnats. "Well, *that's* strange—" she began, but then her breath puffed out in exasperation as someone staggered and jolted the litter. Instead of finishing her thought, she reached out with one hand and laid her fingers on Tan's leg above the knee. Tan gasped and then sagged all over as the pain abruptly eased.

"So that's in hand," Niethe said as the mage and her party passed indoors. She turned her head, frowning. "Very well. Captain...Geroen, isn't it?"

Geroen ducked his head. "Your Majesty."

"I trust you'll be able to keep hold of him this time? I'm quite certain that Iaor would not approve of a repetition of this night's exercise."

"Yes, Your Majesty. No, indeed. I'll go see to that, then." The guard captain hesitated fractionally, glancing at Mienthe. "If I've your leave to do so."

"Yes," Mienthe said, surprised. "Of course. Go on."

Geroen gave her a curt bow and followed Iriene and her retinue of litter-bearers.

"Mienthe…you're well, truly?" Niethe gave her a searching look. "I see you are. This"—the queen visibly edited any number of phrases such as *harebrained* and *madly foolish* out of her speech—"night's, um, work, was truly your idea? Just what *did* you all do? And how?"

"Captain Geroen would probably explain everything better," Mienthe said humbly. Everything seemed to blur together in her mind. Especially all that horrible ride back toward the river.

The queen smiled. "Well, you can tell me all about it *after* you've cleaned up and warmed up and had a chance to rest, Mienthe, lest you catch the ague and require Iriene's skills on your own account! Perhaps you'll join me for breakfast in the brown room, in, say, an hour? Two hours?"

Appalled at the idea that the queen might wait for *her*, Mienthe assured Niethe that an hour would be wonderful, ample, more than generous. Then she fled hastily to her room. She wanted a long, hot bath with lots of fragrant soap, and she wanted to wash her hair at least twice—she was sure there was swamp mud in it as well as on her clothing, she could smell the reek wafting around her every time she shook her head—and she wanted to wrap herself in warm towels in front of a roaring fire and let her maids comb out her clean hair. Then she wanted her warmest, softest robe and a cup of hot tea and a sweet roll with jam, and *then* she wanted to fall into her bed and sleep for about three days.

She thought she might at least manage a very quick bath and her hair.

"Your clothes! Your hair!" Karin, the youngest of her maids, exclaimed. The girl stared at Mienthe, laughing through her horror. "Let me call Emnis—do you want me to call her?" Emnis was Mienthe's senior maid. Mienthe started to answer, but Karin went on without waiting, "No, of course you don't; if she sees you like that, she'll never help find boy's things for you again *ever*. Did you know the queen was looking for you?"

"I saw her—"

"The *queen* saw you like that?"

Mienthe couldn't help but laugh at Karin's expression. "I think everyone was a little distracted by other things. I'm supposed to go join Her Majesty for a decent breakfast in an hour, or I'd be begging you to run down to the kitchens for me—even the bath could wait. Briefly. Did you hear we got Tan back?"

"Everyone's heard that, and that he's hurt." Karin rolled her eyes, her voice tart on her answer. "Half the household staff has him dying before another nightfall, and the other half thinks he'll be up dancing before dusk, but I don't think even the esteemed Iriene is quite *that* good a healer. But they *all* think he's terribly romantic! The injured hero, right out of an epic. You'd think *he'd* rescued *you* and not the other way around!"

Mienthe laughed again. "Oh, that would fit into an epic much better! What has Iriene said, have you heard?"

"She's still working on him, they say, so I guess he won't be dancing at dusk because she wouldn't take so long for anything simple! Let me help you off with that. There's hot water—I had them bring it as soon as we heard you'd come back—" The girl's voice trembled on that last and she fell abruptly silent.

"I'm sorry you were frightened," Mienthe told her gently.

"I'm never frightened. I'm just jealous because you got to go off on romantic adventures and I didn't." Karin effectively stifled any response Mienthe could make by pulling her shift suddenly over her head.

The water in the copper basin was still hot, for which Mienthe was grateful. Karin helped Mienthe take down her hair and step into the steaming bath.

"What do you want to wear? If Her Majesty will be at breakfast... Do you think the blue dress?"

Mienthe hesitated. "The queen has such lovely things even when she's traveling. And all her ladies... maybe the green?"

Karin laughed. "Oh, the green, then, by all means! I'll lay it out for you. Oh—here's Emnis, after all!" She kicked Mienthe's discarded clothing out of sight behind the door, handed Mienthe the soap, and slipped out toward the wardrobe, adding over her shoulder, "Maybe you could tell me, later, all the parts you leave out for Her Majesty?" She meant, after Emnis was no longer around to be horrified.

Mienthe's senior maid appeared in the doorway, clucking with mild disapproval over the state of Mienthe's hair, looking so perfectly ordinary that Mienthe found she could almost believe that nothing unusual had ever happened or ever would.

Emnis had been Mienthe's maid almost since she'd come to live in the great house. She wasn't especially pretty or at all clever, and she worried if Mienthe got mud on her skirts or under her fingernails, but she was kind and cheerful. She murmured all the time she was helping Mienthe wash her hair, a low-voiced sound as pleasant and almost as meaningless as the babble of a stream. Did

Mienthe want the green dress again, or the white one with the flowers on it, and did she expect to go out in the gardens today, because then certainly not the white. Did she want those new slippers with the pretty stitching on the toes? Here, now, careful stepping out of the bath. Now, couldn't Mienthe please settle down just for a moment so Emnis could dry her hair a bit before she braided it and put it up, and no, there wasn't a trace of swamp-smell left, for a mercy; earth and iron, you'd think Mienthe had been swimming right through the swamps all night. Here, perhaps a touch of this rose oil under her ears, just to be sure.

No, Mienthe thought. Of the whole household, Emnis was probably the one person who had the least curiosity about recent events and the least inclination to gather and pass on rumors. It was restful. She let Karin bring her the slippers with the stitching on the toes, then stood for a moment looking at her maids and at the comfortable rooms around her and thinking, really for the first time, that she might honestly have lost everything on last night's adventure. If there had been a whole troop of Linularinan soldiers at that barn…or if they'd met trouble on the ride home…If there had been a mage with the Linularinan spymaster, as it seemed there must have been, well, they hadn't had a mage of their own—unless Mienthe herself—well, that seemed just silly. But… anything might have happened. She'd known that, but somehow she hadn't really *known* it until this moment after everything was over and everyone was safe. She shivered.

"You're cold?" Emnis asked anxiously and patted Mienthe's hand. "Your hands are cold!" she exclaimed, and went to get a long scarf of dark green and gold that would go with Mienthe's dress.

Mienthe started to explain that she wasn't cold, exactly, only shocked in retrospect by how...well, how thoughtless and, really, she had to admit, how foolish she'd been. But then she didn't try to explain after all. She just accepted the scarf and swirled it around her neck, took a deep breath, and went to find the queen and breakfast.

Breakfast was soft-scrambled eggs and sweet rolls and cold thin-sliced beef and ham and plenty of last fall's cider, hot and spiced and served in enormous earthenware mugs. Mienthe was glad to see all of it, but especially happy to see the cider, which warmed the last of the chill from her bones. Already the long night seemed to have happened a long time ago, or maybe to be the fragile echo of a dream. But the queen was waiting for her to explain what she'd done, and why, and how. The *how* seemed particularly obscure, now.

"Just begin somewhere and tell it in any order," Niethe advised her, smiling. The queen must have allowed her ladies to breakfast earlier and then sent them away, because she was the only person present at breakfast aside from Mienthe and the captain of her royal guard, whose name, Mienthe knew, was Temnan. *He* was not smiling. He was a stodgy man in his fifties, not at all the sort of person who would agree to make a spontaneous raid across the river on the spur of the moment.

Mienthe was grateful that at least the queen's ladies weren't present. She knew she would become tongue-tied and clumsy in that graceful company. The ladies would exclaim in horror and assure Mienthe that she'd been foolish and she wouldn't know how to answer. Maybe the queen had guessed that and sent them away to allow Mienthe to speak freely—though it was hard to imagine Niethe understanding the shyness that afflicted Mienthe in that company.

"How did you come to lose that spy, and how did you get him back?" the queen asked in a kind tone. "You've taught Linularinum to be a little more respectful, perhaps. Iaor will be glad of that, at least! But how ever did they get, ah, Tan out of this house in the first place?"

That was as good a starting place as any, though Mienthe had to admit she had no idea. Captain Geroen entered the small breakfast room while she was saying so, but before she had to try to explain her strange but definite knowledge of Tan's position. This was good, because she didn't know how to explain that, either.

Geroen had cleaned up and no doubt snatched a bite to eat in the kitchens, but he looked tired. Though he didn't exactly droop where he stood, he somehow gave the impression he would have liked to. He gave a little dip of his head and said, "First off, Your Majesty, my lady— Iriene sends down word that our Tan will get back on his feet again soon enough, though he'll likely walk with a cane for a day or two. She says she thinks lately her own strength hasn't been just everything it should be, but the knee's not as bad as it could have been and she thinks he'll recover completely."

Mienthe only just kept from clapping her hands like a child. "Wonderful!"

Geroen's mouth crooked. He gave Mienthe the merest shiver of a wink. "Eh, and the esteemed Iriene said quite a bit more about the stupidity of putting a man with that kind of injury up on horseback, and it was a wonder he didn't fall off and break his other leg, or his neck, which she said would have saved her a lot of bother and we might keep that close in mind next time."

Mienthe hid a smile behind her hand. She hadn't realized Geroen knew Iriene, but even the acerbic healer would surely not say that to someone she didn't know at all.

Geroen had turned back to address the queen. "It was magecraft, Your Majesty. We know that right enough. Some Linularinan mage got their agents into the great house and stole the wits right out of my men's heads and wrapped Tan up in some kind of magecrafting so's he couldn't even yell out a warning and took him off. Only the lady, she knew all about it. I guess she's maybe going to develop mage-skill herself."

"Is she?" Niethe said, as astonished as if the captain had suggested Mienthe might change into a crow and fly away. She gazed at Mienthe with fascination, as though wondering whether she might suddenly turn the plates into crumbling loam or the polished glassware into budding flowers.

Mienthe blushed and said hastily, "I'm sure I'm not! We've never once had a mage in our family. Hardly any of my cousins are even gifted! I don't see how I *could* be a—a mage. I don't know anything about mages or mageworking or—or *anything*. I just knew...I knew what had happened, more or less, when I went back into Tan's room. I don't know. I just..."

"Well, Mienthe, ordinarily people *don't* just know such things," Niethe said reasonably.

"She told me she knew exactly where Tan was, direction and distance, and she made me believe it," Geroen said. "Nobody else did, or could, or I thought so, though I admit I maybe should have let that spy go before risking Lady Mienthe in Linularinum."

The royal captain snorted under his breath.

Geroen flushed slightly, but kept his eyes on the queen. "Well, but at first we thought maybe we could get him back without even crossing the river, and well, anyway, granting I never thought for a moment her lord cousin would approve, when that hope failed I thought we might risk a brief little excursion into Linularinum to get him out." Geroen paused again.

Captain Temnan drew breath to speak, but Mienthe leaped in before he could. "That was *my* doing, really." And then she went on, in her firmest tone, telling the rest of it so Geroen wouldn't try to take all the responsibility back on himself, as he clearly felt he ought to do. She explained how they'd crossed the river and found Tan. Geroen filled in some things she hadn't noticed about the barn and the people they'd surprised there, and the way Tan had been all chained up. Mienthe hadn't noticed the part about the slip-chain around his neck. She bit her lip and tried hard not to think about that, or about what might have happened if they'd been captured by the sort of people who would do things like that.

Temnan didn't look surprised by any of these details, but Niethe sat back in her chair, looking rather grim and ill. Mienthe thought the queen's imagination had taken much the same direction as hers on that topic.

To distract them both from any such ideas, she quickly picked up the story again. She explained about the strange things they'd found in the barn, the book and the other things. "I looked at the book; I've looked all through it, but every page is blank," she explained. "There are inks in six different colors, and nine kinds of quills, but they all look perfectly ordinary to me."

The queen nodded. "Well, *that* was well done, bringing all those things away with you." Her tone implied that it might be the only thing they'd done of which she wholeheartedly approved, though she didn't actually say so. "I'm very certain the mages in Tiearanan will be most interested in those items."

"But what do you suppose the Linularinan agents meant to do?"

Niethe lifted her hands in a pretty shrug and raised her eyebrows at Temnan.

The captain of the royal guard tilted his head. "One would hardly care to guess. Geroen, have one of your men fetch from her rooms the items Lady Mienthe described and bring them here."

Geroen's face, Mienthe thought, was really a good one for a guard captain: heavy-boned, rather coarse, and unusually hard to read. He was probably good at pian stones; nobody would be able to tell from his expression what stones he had in reserve. But she could see he didn't like to be commanded by Temnan, royal guard captain or not. She said hastily, "If you would be so good, Geroen."

Geroen nodded stiffly and stepped briefly out to give that order.

The queen said thoughtfully, "One ordinarily expects a legist to draw up contracts. I wonder what contract these men had in mind for Tan to write out? Well, and after that?" She listened intently and quietly, but once Mienthe had finished, she asked, "But *why* did they pursue Tan with such dedication?"

"For personal vengeance?" suggested Temnan.

Mienthe looked doubtfully at Geroen. "Would you say so?"

The captain hesitated, then shook his head. "Lady... no. As you ask me, I'd say no. I haven't questioned Tan, not seeing as he was in any condition to answer, but that was an interrogation, is what I'd say, not just some Linularinan fool indulging himself in a wild venture to get himself a chance at his personal enemy. Tan did say... Let me see. Something like, *That wasn't some petty street-thug; that was the Linularinan spymaster.* 'The' spymaster, he said, not just 'a' spymaster. He called him by name. He said it was Istierinan."

"I remember that name—" Mienthe began.

One of Geroen's guardsmen came in before she could finish her thought, bending to murmur to the captain.

"Tan?" asked Mienthe.

"He's unconscious and expected to remain so for some time," Geroen reported, dismissing the man with a curt nod. "I'll give orders for my men to stay on close guard, but I don't know how those Linularinan agents got through my men the first time."

"I'll give my men orders to stand alongside yours," said Temnan, and added, his tone a trifle supercilious, "if you'll permit me, Captain Geroen, and if Her Majesty approves. I've men from Tiearanan who might notice magework if anyone starts anything of that sort."

Geroen hesitated for a bare moment, then nodded abruptly.

"To be sure," agreed Niethe.

Mienthe said, "I'll go sit with Tan—" but surprised herself with a jaw-cracking yawn before she could finish her sentence. She put her hand over her mouth and blinked suddenly blurry eyes.

"You will not," the queen said firmly. "I'm sure our guardsmen can keep him safe. *You* will go to bed, Mienthe, and no matter it's just past breakfast time. Sleep till noon, if you like—or till supper." She stood up, came around the table, and touched Mienthe's shoulder. "Rest well, and never fret. Now we're all alert, I can hardly believe any Linularinan agents will try a second time. Just to be certain, I believe I'll send a formal courier across the river, inquiring whether Linularinum has deliberately attempted to provoke Feierabiand. *That* should make them pause."

Mienthe thought it certainly would. She hoped whoever had tried to kidnap Tan found himself in deep water. "Good," she said, and got stiffly to her feet.

CHAPTER 5

Tan was desperately bored. The servants were fine about fluffing pillows, but not very accommodating when it came to providing books or writing materials or anything else that would give him reason to sit upright. Iriene had plainly given orders, which the servants had proved tiresomely determined to follow, that he was supposed to be lying flat, keeping his leg elevated on pillows, and sleeping. Since he had been sleeping all day, this left Tan bored, nervous, and thoroughly irritated.

He looked up at the sudden murmur outside the chamber. He could distinguish the voices of his guards, of course, but also that of a woman. A servant bringing a book or two after all, he hoped, and moved uncomfortably, wishing he could sit up properly.

But it wasn't a servant who came in.

"Mienthe!" Tan exclaimed. Then he was immediately embarrassed that he'd been sufficiently startled as to forget his manners—in fact, he was embarrassed he'd been surprised at all. Surely it was not in the least remarkable that Mienthe would come find him and assure herself he was mending. He said more moderately, "Esteemed lady," and pushed ineffectually at the bed linens, determined to sit up after all, whether or not Iriene would approve.

Refreshingly, Mienthe did not command him to lie down flat. Evidently she hadn't been told he was supposed to stay down. She helped him sit instead, arranging the pillows so he could be more comfortable. Then she drew a chair near the bed and perched on its edge, like a bird ready to take flight. "Your knee?" she asked anxiously. "Did the esteemed Iriene mend it? It hadn't been too badly damaged?"

"I'm told it will heal well, so long as I restrain myself from overusing it now," Tan assured her. "I have no notion why everyone seems to feel compelled to emphasize that latter clause."

Mienthe laughed, but her voice was strained, and Tan realized—he should have perceived it at once—that the young woman was not anxious over his well-being, or not *only* anxious over his well-being. Something had frightened her. Something else. He tried to imagine what might have frightened or disturbed Mienthe more than the thought of enemy spies and mages sneaking about her home and kidnapping people. His imagination failed him. "Esteemed lady?" he said cautiously.

"Oh, Mienthe, please!" she told him.

She wasn't flirting. Tan had nearly reached the conclusion that, impossible as it seemed, Mienthe didn't know *how* to flirt. She simply preferred informality and, in her straightforward way, said so. Tan smiled. "I suppose the events of last night ought to constitute an introduction.

Not a proper introduction, perhaps, but thorough. So I suppose we might call one another by name, if you like, and then perhaps you might tell me what is troubling you?"

"Oh, well—" Mienthe eyed him cautiously. "Something else has happened. Shall I tell you, or do you need to rest?" She bit her lip. "You probably need to rest."

Not eager to be left again to lonely boredom, Tan declared, "I have been required to dedicate myself to nothing but rest all the long day. Be so kind as to tell me all." He lifted an expectant eyebrow at the young woman.

"Well…" Mienthe hesitated, though Tan thought she was merely trying to collect her thoughts rather than hesitating to tell him the news. He wondered what had possibly unnerved her. It was difficult to reconcile the collected young woman of the Linularinan raid with this diffidence. He tried to look encouraging.

"My cousin—" Mienthe began, but stopped. "I don't know…Do you know things?"

And how was a man to answer a question like that? Tan said, "Of course you shouldn't discuss with me anything your cousin told you in confidence," because it was important to establish a good, honest character if you wanted anyone to tell you their secrets, far less other people's secrets.

Mienthe nodded, but distractedly, as though she'd barely heard him. She declared, "You *expect* people to have lived their own lives before you ever met them!" Rising to her feet, she paced rapidly to one side of the little chamber and then back again.

"But sometimes it's a shock, to find out about those past lives," Tan suggested. He couldn't imagine what had happened. Something to do with her? With him? With someone else?

"Yes, exactly! I knew perfectly well my cousin did *something* to stop us fighting the griffins. And then something else when he was in Casmantium. But I don't know"—she flung her hands sharply upward for emphasis—"anything! Do *you* know about that? Especially about the Wall? The Wall in Casmantium, I mean, the one between the griffins and...and everybody else?"

"We had reports, of course." Tan watched her carefully, trying to think what might have prompted these questions. "Those events six years ago were the subject of some speculation in the Fox's court, I believe. I wasn't...I'd barely arrived in Teramondian that year. My attention was all for trying to win a place at court. I'd have assumed the people of the Delta would follow their own lord's actions a great deal more closely than even the most interested of the old Fox's advisers."

"I was only twelve," Mienthe said, not really to him.

"What happened?" Tan asked patiently

"Oh...this griffin came to see my cousin. Did anybody tell you that?"

Tan was rendered, for once, utterly speechless. Whatever he'd expected the young woman to say, *that* hadn't been it. He cleared his throat, but then only waved weakly for her to go on.

"No one did? Well, you were sleeping all day, you said, and then I suppose everyone thought you shouldn't be troubled." She gave him an anxious look.

"Don't stop there!" Tan said, and laughed. "*That* would trouble me!"

"Oh...yes, I suppose." Mienthe smiled, too. "Anyway,

yes. A griffin. A mage. A griffin mage, I mean. He wore the shape of a man, but…I didn't know griffins could do that. Not even their mages. Not that you'd have ever mistaken him for an ordinary man. Anasa—I don't remember his whole name. Something Kairaithin."

"A griffin mage." Only long practice allowed Tan to keep the disbelief out of his tone.

"Yes. Oh, yes. He was very—he was—you could tell. He helped my cousin six years ago, and he helped build the Casmantian Wall. I think," she added, somewhat more doubtfully, "I think he *is* my cousin's friend, but…"

"But he didn't just slip down from the griffins' desert to wish your cousin a pleasant evening," Tan prompted her when it became clear that the pause might lengthen.

"Well, I think he came to warn Bertaud that the Wall is going to break," Mienthe said, simply, as though she were in the habit of constantly providing amazing information in the most casual way.

"Ah." Tan hadn't seen *that* coming at all. He tried to think of everything he'd ever heard concerning the great Casmantian Wall. He knew that some Casmantian makers and mages had gotten together and built it in a day and a night and another day, or so the wonder of the making had been reported. He knew it was supposed to forever divide the country of fire from the country of earth…He gathered that "forever" had been a slight overestimation.

"He said the…the balance had been disturbed. Between earth and fire, he said. He said the Wall is—is cracked through. At both ends, I think he meant. When it breaks, something terrible will happen, and he said it will shatter in a few days or a few weeks—" Mienthe's voice was rising.

"But not tonight, I hope," Tan said, deliberately wry to offset any incipient hysteria. "So what did your lord cousin do about this?"

"Oh, he and the king went north, to look at the Wall, above Tihannad, you know…"

"Of course." *That* explained why her cousin had not stopped Mienthe from joining that little raid into Linularinum, which Tan supposed made the griffin's warning a good thing for him, if for no one else. He asked cautiously, "What disturbed the balance, did this griffin explain that? What terrible thing will happen if the Wall breaks?"

Mienthe shook her head, meaning she had no idea. "Only, I think, the griffins are very angry, and I think that if the Wall breaks, there will be a war…"

"Well, how many griffins can there be?" Tan asked reasonably. "It's hard to imagine there could be more than a very small war, after all."

Mienthe shook her head again. "I don't know…That wasn't what I thought he meant."

Had her cousin's visitor actually been a griffin? In human shape, Mienthe had said. But you would never mistake him for a man, she'd said. Why not? How could one tell? Especially if one had never encountered a griffin before at all, either in his true shape or disguised?

On the other hand, her cousin truly had, by all reports, been closely involved with the problems Feierabiand had had with griffins six years ago. He would certainly know a griffin when he saw one. And if anyone might find a griffin mage on his doorstep, it was likely Bertaud.

And if that much was true…He said at last, "Well, esteemed Mienthe, you've certainly given me a good deal to think over," which was true.

"But you don't know anything."

"Very little," Tan admitted. "Or very little about griffins. It's amazing how seldom the subject comes up in Linularinum—except as a consideration for determining what the King of Casmantium might do."

Mienthe drooped slightly with discouragement.

"Please don't rush out, however," Tan said quickly, afraid she might. "Perhaps you might try telling me everything *you* know about griffins. Lord Bertaud is your cousin. Perhaps you've learned a bit more than you think you have—"

"No, I don't think so. He never speaks of those things." Mienthe hesitated, and then added slowly, "He never has. Never. I think…" But she stopped, feeling perhaps that she had come too close to private things. She opened her hands in a shrug, then gazed down into her palms as though she might find the answer there.

Then she glanced up. "But…I'm so sorry. Here I am telling you all about the griffins and the Wall when there's nothing either of us can do about the trouble there. How are *you*? Do you do well enough?"

"Well," Tan said, trying not to laugh, "I'm here and not chained in some dismal barn on the other side of the river, so not only am I very well, I must also suppose no one's been able to get past your care of me. For all of which I am, I assure you, very grateful indeed. I shall hope we are not so distracted by this other problem that Istierinan is permitted a second opening."

"Oh, I'm sure Linularinum won't—"

Tan dismissed this assurance with a wave of his hand. "It obviously took a mage to get me out of this house. I am not confident what this mage might do next, if

Istierinan insists. Istierinan Hamoddian can be uncommonly single-minded."

Mienthe looked at him expectantly. "So why *did* your Istierinan kidnap you at all, if you'd already finished writing everything out for Bertaud? Or did he not know you'd already finished?"

"After three days in the great house? He can't have not known." Tan paused. He rather thought Mienthe was clever, and he knew she had found him by some sort of odd magecraft. And he owed her a debt. And, besides that, he could think of absolutely no reason to keep this particular secret. So he said slowly, "Istierinan wasn't after vengeance—or not *only* after vengeance. He asked me where 'it' was. Whether I still held 'it' myself or had given 'it' away. Not to the Lord of the Delta, he said. He said maybe I'd been able to give 'it' to one of Bertaud's people."

"*Able* to give it," Mienthe repeated blankly.

"That's what he said. Very odd, yes. He wanted me to return what I had taken. I never could get him to tell me what I was supposed to have stolen. Nor did I have enough time to guess its shape from the pattern of his questions. Fortunately, to be sure."

"But you must know what it might have been?" Mienthe asked, leaning forward in intense curiosity.

Tan flung up his hands. "Nothing but information! Nothing I could return, even if I wanted to return it—no more than I could return spoken words to the past that existed before they were spoken."

"Well," Mienthe said reasonably, "Istierinan thinks you stole something else, doesn't he?"

Tan opened his hands in a gesture of bafflement.

"Nothing occurs to me. Except that someone else took advantage of my, ah, of the confusion I caused, to steal something else. Something more tangible. And Istierinan thinks I stole it." Some lying dog-livered bastard was using Tan to conceal his own crime. Tan was offended, and then amused, since he hardly had any right to protest another man's dishonesty.

"Well, that's not good, if Istierinan is going to keep coming after you to try to get it back. And not good for anyone else, if he's willing to cross into the Delta and invade even our great house to get it," Mienthe observed, with some justice. "And with the king himself in residence! Or the queen, at least—I suppose Iaor was actually gone before they came after you. I suppose that might be why they thought they had a chance, right then; everything *was* confused, with everybody coming and going."

Tan thought about that, and about the scene in the barn, and about the agonizing but surprisingly uneventful flight back through the marshes and across the river. He said slowly, "Do you know, I wonder whether Istierinan is operating on his own in this. Mariddeier Kohorrian is a clever, ruthless man and a good king, and I don't think he would send agents to strike openly across the river into the Delta."

Mienthe made an interested sound.

Her eyes were quite pretty when she was so intent, Tan noticed—she was rather a pretty girl overall, but she didn't show herself off—indeed, she was so little given to flamboyance a man could simply look right past her.

She said, "Maybe he's the only one who knows something got stolen, and he's trying to keep it that way."

And, yes, she *was* clever. Tan cleared his throat. "Yes,"

he said. "That seems very possible." He began to smile. "And he thinks I have whatever was stolen, and so he let the real thief get away. Poor Istierinan! Going after the wrong man is no way to win back the regard of the old Fox!"

"It won't seem nearly so amusing if he keeps coming after you," Mienthe observed tartly.

"No, I imagine not." Tan tilted his head, letting his smile broaden. "One might as well enjoy these little moments of irony, esteemed Mienthe. Appreciating the humor life presents to us is what keeps us young. What a lot it is presenting us with at the moment, to be sure. Griffins and mages, legists and spymasters—"

The door opened.

Mienthe rose with a slightly guilty air, though by the time she turned she had done a creditable job of putting on an air of innocent inquiry.

Tan made himself smile as well as he waited for the door to swing back far enough to show him their visitor. Probably it was not Istierinan or his pet mage—ah. Almost as frightening: Their visitor was Iriene herself.

The healer was frowning. That much did not surprise Tan at all.

"You," Iriene said severely, with only the briefest nod for Mienthe, "should be lying flat. I left strict instructions. In fact, as I recall, I gave *you* strict instructions. And here you are sitting up."

Tan rapidly considered and discarded half a dozen possible replies, from the flippant to the meek, and replied with almost no hesitation, "Truly, esteemed Iriene, I'd rather try standing and walking. One never knows what necessity might arise. Sitting upright seemed a reasonable compromise, besides being more respectful to Lady Mienthe."

Iriene gave him a hard stare and a short nod, acknowledging both the impudence and the possibility of sudden necessity. "Just so you understand that if you undo all my fine work through impatience, I won't bother finding the time to do it over again. It's not easy doing work that detailed, you know, even when I'm at my best. Which I'm not, lately, so don't push your limits or you might find them before you want to, you hear me?"

"Yes, esteemed Iriene," Tan agreed meekly.

"Esteemed Iriene—" Mienthe said hesitantly.

The healer-mage turned her hard look on Mienthe. "And don't you be fussing my patient," she warned.

"No, I won't—I haven't," Mienthe said, just as meekly as Tan had. "I don't think I have. But, Iriene, I wondered…that is, people think…people say…I must have found Tan by magecraft. But I don't think I have any mage power. I don't feel as though I do."

Iriene's gaze became inquisitive. She looked Mienthe up and down. Then she shrugged. "You don't have the look of it to me," she said. "But I'm not the best one to ask, Lady Mienthe. I'm barely a mage myself—I heal. That's what I do. That's all I do." She paused, glanced at Tan, and shrugged again. "Him now. Events want to slip around *him*. Even I can see that."

"Events want to—?" Mienthe began.

"And what precisely does that mean?" Tan demanded at the same time, much more sharply.

Iriene said to Mienthe, "You don't see it?"

Mienthe looked closely at Tan, who found himself flushing under her regard. But then she only opened her hands in bafflement and said to Iriene, "No, esteemed healer, I don't think I see anything."

"Huh," said Iriene. "And that griffin who came to see your lord cousin. You were there when he was? You met him? That's right, is it?"

Mienthe nodded.

"And did you hate him, then?"

"*Hate* him," Mienthe repeated, clearly still baffled. "No, I don't think so. I thought he was frightening—and beautiful—and dangerous. But I didn't see any reason to hate him. I mean, he's my cousin's friend. Or something like a friend, I think," she added, with a finicky air of conscientious precision that made Tan want to laugh, though at the same time he appreciated it; so few people could manage to say anything at all with precision.

"Then I don't think you're rising into mage power," said Iriene. "I couldn't say what else might be coming along for you."

Mienthe gazed at her. "Do our mages detest, um, theirs?"

"Oh, yes. Passionately," Iriene assured her. "Overpoweringly. Not that I've ever seen a griffin mage, you know, but that's what I understand. Meriemne—that elderly mage in Tihannad, do you know her?—she wrote up a warning and sent it around after all that bother six years ago. She said the loathing earth mages feel for fire ruins their judgment when they encounter a griffin mage." The healer lifted a sardonic eyebrow as she added this last. "As though anything's likely to ruin *Meriemne's* judgment. Hah! I don't think so. Anyway, I don't suppose it's ever likely to matter, down here in these marshes, but I don't think you can be rising into mage power."

Mienthe nodded solemnly. Tan couldn't tell whether she was relieved or disappointed by this verdict. He said, "Esteemed Iriene, before you go, may I ask also about the odd book Mienthe—Lady Mienthe—brought back from Linularinum?"

"Oh, yes," Mienthe said, clearly much happier now that they weren't talking about her. "It had blank pages. All the pages were blank. Have you seen it? I think it's in my cousin's study—I could get it—"

Iriene held up a hand, shaking her head. "Books and such are matters for a legist, not a mage," she said firmly. "Healing's my business. Let me look at that knee of yours, esteemed Tan, and we'll see if you might be able to hobble down to a proper breakfast tomorrow morning, if not supper tonight. Though I warn you, you are not to attempt to walk without a cane, much less run, regardless of any unfortunate *necessities* that may arise."

"Queen Niethe's sending a formal protest across the river," put in Mienthe, before Tan could produce his own sharp response.

"Is she?" Tan was amused. "Yes, I imagine if the old Fox realizes that Her Majesty's taken official notice of Istierinan's indiscretions, he might very well haul Istierinan around on a close rein. And if he *hasn't* known, what a treat for him when he finds out."

Mienthe's mouth crooked. "I'm sure. So rest easy, if you please, and try not to press the esteemed Iriene's goodwill too hard, do you hear?"

Tan bowed his head, trying to present the very image of perfect docility.

Mienthe laughed and rose to her feet. "I'll leave you, then, but I hope I'll see you at breakfast tomorrow—if not supper tonight." She made a face. "Supper will be with the queen and all her ladies."

She did not actually say *And I'm going to hate every minute of it*, but Tan heard that in her tone, and no wonder. A girl with so little artifice, thrown in among all those court ladies? Even ladies of Feierabiand's court would not be short of artifice. Mienthe would be like a sparrow caged among canaries in that company. Though he was a little surprised he cared how the girl fared among the queen's ladies, Tan found himself wishing he could attend the supper himself. He could support Mienthe—he could be so subtle neither she nor anyone else would realize what he was doing, and yet make certain she did herself proper credit.

But he knew without asking that the healer wouldn't change her mind or her prescription for rest. Tan didn't protest Iriene's swift, ruthless examination—he wouldn't have dared, and anyway he, too, hoped to see Mienthe at breakfast. No doubt a passing urge for the young woman's company was quite well explained by boredom. And she was, after all, reasonably pretty.

Mienthe was sorry to leave Tan—he was so interesting, and he seemed clever, and she knew he must be terribly bored left on his own with nothing but orders to rest. But if she was the Lady of the Delta, it was her task to make sure her cousin's household was fit to entertain the queen without shaming the hospitality of the Delta, and she'd neglected that duty terribly.

Very soon thereafter she found she had developed a raging headache.

First Eris, the cook, had sent a kitchen girl running to

say that the mutton had gone a bit off, and the morning's catch out of the sea had been disappointing, and could they possibly serve Her Majesty fish out of the marshes? And if not, whatever should they do? Did Mienthe know of any dishes Her Majesty particularly favored? Or disfavored? That they could actually prepare, nothing made of air and rose petals such as they made at court, no, and would plain cream pastries suit Her Majesty at all, could Mienthe guess?

As a deluge is foreshadowed by a single drop of rain, this first problem was followed by others from every corner of the house. The master of the stables sent a boy to inform Mienthe that the queen's favorite mare wouldn't be fit to ride for a few days as the animal had been kicked by another horse when the beasts had been turned out into the house-pasture, and could Mienthe possibly tell the queen herself so the staff wouldn't have to risk displeasing her? And then the upstairs maids sent a girl to tell Mienthe that in all the flurry of the previous night no one had remembered to cut flowers for the vases, and would the queen insist on flowers on her supper table tonight or might they possibly wait to cut some for tomorrow? And then the laundry maids reported that a cat had had her kittens right in the midst of the finest bed linens and now there weren't enough for all the queen's ladies, as Her Majesty had brought twice as many as they had expected, and what could they possibly *do* when there wasn't time to wash the linens before bedtime and all the shops in town were closed at this hour?

If Tef had still had charge of the great house's cats, that last problem would never have arisen. It was thinking of Tef that gave Mienthe the headache, she was fairly certain. She longed to go sit on his gravestone and plait grass stems and flowers into a bracelet as he'd shown her, and forget all about the queen and her ladies.

Instead, she told the kitchens that fish of whatever origin would be delicious, and she suggested they round the menu out with duck and agreed that the queen would assuredly love cream pastries.

Then she sent the boy back to the stablemaster with the suggestion that the queen, if she wished to ride out in the next few days, might like to try the paces of that pretty gray mare her cousin had just purchased—the animal had nice manners, didn't she? The stablemaster might make sure the mare was kept clean and perhaps the boys might braid ribbons into her mane. Or early flowers. The queen liked flowers and would undoubtedly find the gesture charming. Although Mienthe was quite certain, she assured the upstairs maids, that no one would mind doing without flowers on the dining table just this one evening.

Then she patiently sent two of the younger maids, along with one of the guardsmen, to rouse out the proper shopkeepers and buy new bed linens, instructing them to pay extra for the favor even if the shopkeepers didn't request it.

After that, Mienthe had the headache.

She would have liked to beg off from supper, but of course she could not do anything of the kind. She wished Tan could have come down for it, or if he couldn't, she wished she might simply have a tray in her room. The little princesses, not even needing broken legs to excuse them, were not present, their nurses having taken them away to have their suppers privately.

That left Mienthe and the queen, and the dozen or so ladies Her Majesty had brought along on this progress—indeed, twice as many as she ever had before. No wonder the maids were fretting about the linens. Nearly all of the ladies were older than Mienthe, and all of them wore more elaborate and stylish gowns, and more ostentatious and expensive jewels. And they all chatted with one another in an oblique way that, Mienthe thought, might fit right in at the Linularinan court, because she didn't understand more than a phrase here or there.

Mienthe smiled and nodded when anyone spoke to her, and fervently wished Tan were at the table. He would probably be able effortlessly to translate all those little barbed comments, even though he was more closely acquainted with the Linularinan court than the one in Feierabiand.

The fish was good, though, and the duck superb.

"How quiet you are this evening, Mienthe!" the queen said at last, gazing down the table. She spoke with warm good humor; if she even noticed the edged tone of her ladies' chatter, it wasn't apparent. She said, plainly intending to avoid any difficult topic, "Tell us all the gossip of Tiefenauer and of the Delta, do. Such a large and complicated family you have here! There must be all sorts of interesting frivolities and nonsense we might hear of, to lighten the hour."

Mienthe's smile slipped.

However, even the most interminable evening must end at last, and to Mienthe's great relief the queen professed herself weary before the sweet wine was poured. That allowed Mienthe to declare her own exhaustion and retire, if not altogether in good order, at least not in an obvious rout.

Breakfast would be better. Not only would Tan be there—probably—but also the queen would rise early and breakfast while most of her ladies-in-waiting yet drowsed. Even if Iriene didn't permit Tan to come, Mienthe could ask the queen about her daughters. Niethe could chatter on endlessly about her daughters, so that would work well, and Mienthe would not be required to do anything more demanding than nod occasionally.

Also, perhaps by then this truly ferocious headache would have cleared away.

Mienthe was very tired. She missed Bertaud suddenly and fiercely; she wanted to be able to run up to his suite right now and find him there. Oddly, she also wanted to visit Tan once more. That was odd and a little embarrassing—what if he thought she was flinging herself at him?—but it was true. She wanted to go up and see that he was still safe and well. She found she had turned, without consciously deciding she would, toward his room.

The headache pounded. Mienthe lifted a hand to press against her eyes and walked blindly down the hall and around a corner, down a short flight of steps and around another corner, and at last out a side door into the garden, where a shortcut might take her to the house's east wing by a shorter path. But then she lingered. The breeze tonight had much less of a chill to it; though it was not exactly warm, one could feel the promise of the coming summer in the air. She could hear, out in the darkness where the lamps did not cast their glow, the urgent piping of the little green frogs. Somewhere a night heron

made its harsh croak and after a moment its distant mate
answered. The headache eased at last, and Mienthe sighed
and straightened her shoulders. She was very tired. But
she still wanted to see Tan—at least to glance in on him
and see that the maids hadn't forgotten him in the midst
of this royal visit.

The headache returned between one step and the next,
pressing ferociously down upon Mienthe as though it
came from something outside her, something in the air
or in the very darkness. Half blinded by it, Mienthe sat
down right where she was, on the raked gravel of the
path, and bent over, pressing both hands hard against her
temples. She had never had such a headache in her life.

Mienthe reached out with one hand and, with her fingers, scraped a spiral in the gravel of the path. Something
in the air or the darkness twisted about, echoing the shape
she'd drawn; she felt its movement as it followed the spiral
pattern. Her headache eased suddenly, then pounded with
renewed intensity. She found herself on her feet, walking
in a spiral, from the inside out. Something walked with her
and behind her like a shadow. That was how it felt. It was
her headache, or she thought it was. It wasn't part of her
at all, but followed her as closely as her own shadow. Her
actual shadow flickered out madly in all directions because
of the house lanterns and the moon high above, but the
thing that followed her stayed right at her heels. She drew
a spiral in the gravel and the earth and the air, a spiral that
opened out and out and out. The thing that followed her
followed the spiral, followed it farther than she had drawn
it or could draw it, ran in a spiral out into the night and
dissipated like mist.

In the house, someone shouted. Then someone else.

Someone was speaking. His voice echoed all through the house and the grounds, but Mienthe could not understand the words. No, not speaking, exactly, there was no actual voice. But someone was doing something *like* speaking, and the whole house seemed to bend around to listen to that person. Only that person's voice, or whatever, twisted around in a spiral that opened up and out, its power dissipating. The house seemed to shudder and settle firmly back upon its foundations.

There was more shouting. Someone ran out of the house, past Mienthe, too far away for her to see anything about him; his shadow trailed at his heel, strangely constant in its direction despite the multitude of lanterns. He vanished into the lamplit city below the hill, his shadow tucked up close behind him. Someone else followed the first man. Several more people, pelting through the garden in different directions. Mienthe stepped back out of the way, pressing close to the wall of the house. It stood solidly at her back, a warm, strangely solid presence—why *strangely* solid? How should a house be but solid? Mienthe rubbed her hands across her face, trying to think. Her mind felt sluggish as mud. Within the house was an uproar that reminded her of the wild tumult that had swept through the house one autumn when a hurricane had come off the sea and lifted the roof off half a wing.

But her headache was completely gone.

The Linularinan agents had tried again to come at Tan. Mienthe, her thoughts still confused and slow, got that clear only gradually. They'd tried to come and go unseen, as they had before—to steal Tan away without sound or breath or any sort of fuss. They nearly had. They'd slipped through the gaps between the Delta guardsmen and the royal guardsmen like mist in the night.

Mienthe felt horribly embarrassed. Bertaud had left her his authority, hadn't he? That made it her duty and responsibility to protect Tan, and she'd so nearly failed. She could imagine, far too easily, how disappointed Bertaud would have been in her if she'd let Linularinan agents kidnap a man *twice* from his house. She'd meant to check with Geroen about how all his men had sorted out with the queen's, but she'd forgotten, and then her forgetfulness had nearly cost Tan—everything, probably, Mienthe guessed.

"I'm sorry," Mienthe told Tan, once everything seemed to have been sorted out and peace had descended once more on the house.

Tan, seated on a couch in the queen's sitting room— well, in Bertaud's sitting room, made over for her royal presence—raised his eyebrows at her. There was an air about him of somewhat affected theatricality, as though the attitude was one he put on for his own amusement and that of his companions, not to be taken seriously by any of them. This dramatic air was aided by the cane someone had found for him, a handsome thing of carved cypress wood with a brass knob on the top, the sort aged gentlemen might carry. Mienthe's own father had carried one, and had always given the impression he might hit the servants with it, though he never had.

Tan folded his hands atop his cane and gazed over it at Mienthe, in exaggerated astonishment. "You're apologizing to me? For what? A second timely rescue?"

"You shouldn't have *needed* a second rescue!" Mienthe exclaimed.

"You're quite right! I certainly shouldn't have." Tan's tone was light, but then he hesitated and went on in a lower voice, "I'd picked up a quill. I was only going to write out some small thing, poetry for you, maybe—I don't know quite what I had in mind. I think now—in fact, it now seems abundantly obvious—that it's my legist gift Istierinan's mage is using. Somehow. I think he finds me when I touch a quill. I have no notion how, but then I'm not a mage. But if you hadn't provided a second rescue, I'd likely have needed nothing after my misjudgment but a timely funeral, and more likely have had nothing but a muddy hole in the swamp, at that."

The queen, seated in the room's most delicate and expensive cherrywood chair, leaned her chin on her palm and let them argue. She looked less frightened than Mienthe had expected, but thoroughly exasperated. Half a dozen of her ladies hovered around her, whispering behind their hands to one another, looking uncertain and worried and far less sophisticated and ornamental than they had a few hours earlier. The rest of the court ladies, to Mienthe's considerable relief, were not in evidence; they had been replaced for the moment by several grim-visaged royal guardsmen who did not speak at all. They looked exactly as embarrassed about the failure of their guard as she felt about her own lack of forethought.

The door across the room opened, and Geroen came in. Iriene came with him, which was a little bold of her, since that brought her into the queen's presence when she hadn't been sent for. Mienthe decided she didn't care.

Geroen gave the queen a low bow and turned, quite correctly, to Mienthe as the Lady of the Delta. "Lady," he said stiffly. "There's no sign of any of those dog-livered

Linularinan cowards anywhere in the city. Not that my men seem overdependable in setting eye or hand on them. But the esteemed Iriene agrees."

"Not that I might know," the mage said, wryly acknowledging her own lack of power.

"I think Istierinan's mage must be uncommonly skilled," Tan murmured. "How else would it be possible to come and go so silently in so crowded a house? Never mind so boldly," he added, with a nod to the queen.

"We'd all be glad to know how they could be so bold," Geroen growled.

Niethe was silent for a moment. Then she touched a graceful hand to her temple for a moment, dropped her hand, and asked, "How exactly did we send those...those dog-livered Linularinan cowards...on their way?"

"Lady Mienthe did it," Geroen growled. He gave Mienthe a quick look. "The esteemed Iriene says."

"I?" asked Mienthe uncertainly.

"You did," Iriene said crisply. She was looking at Mienthe with something like sympathy, but without doubt. "I don't understand it, but I'm sure."

"I don't..." Mienthe hesitated. She rubbed her forehead, searching for...something. The memory of pain? The echo of a shape she had drawn into herself, into the earth? "I don't...I don't truly know. I don't think...I don't think I *did* anything, exactly. There was something strange, something about shadows, and spirals..."

"You most certainly did do something. You did magecraft. I saw it." Iriene's voice had gone oddly gentle. "You sat down on the path and drew in the gravel, and the Linularinan working tangled up in the shape you drew and spun away and out."

Mienthe stared at the mage. Iriene had said she couldn't be a mage because she didn't hate her cousin's griffin friend. And she didn't *feel* at all like a mage. And yet...yet...she supposed she didn't really know how a mage was *supposed* to feel. And if she'd done magecraft, didn't that mean she *had* to be a mage? She said uncertainly, "No one in my grandfather's family has ever been a mage. Hardly any of us are even gifted..."

"Well, you will be the first, then," Iriene said practically. "Perhaps you have it from your mother."

Mienthe stared at the mage. She had never been able to recall the least detail about her mother. Tef had described her for Mienthe long ago, when she'd wondered with a child's curiosity about the mother she'd never known. A pale little mouse of a woman, he had said, always tiptoeing about in terror of drawing the attention of some stalking cat. A woman with colorless eyes and delicate bones and a pretty voice, though she seldom spoke. She had been afraid of Mienthe's father. Mienthe understood that perfectly, but she wished now that she could remember her mother.

"Fortunate for us, wherever you have it from!" declared the queen, speaking for the first time in several moments. She studied Mienthe with a lively curiosity that made Mienthe feel rather like a fancy caged songbird. "You must have a great deal of natural talent, surely, to notice this skillful Linularinan mage and know without training or study how you might expose and dismiss him. And you truly had no least inkling of your power?"

Mienthe truly had no least inkling of it now, except she couldn't deny that she seemed to have somehow used it. She began to answer the queen, found she had no idea what answer to give, and stopped.

"We all have an inkling of it now!" said Tan. "I would kiss your hands and feet, esteemed Mienthe, except I would have to rise, so I hope you will excuse me. How very splendid you are! An ornament to the Delta, to the city, and to your cousin's house!"

Somehow this excessively flowery speech settled Mienthe where the queen's warm approval had only worried her.

"I don't know about ornaments," Iriene said, with a lowering glance toward Tan, "but it seems to me that broad events are tending to pivot here, that this year the Delta has become a linchpin for the world. I suppose that's Mienthe, too, or else those Linularinan mages. I don't know. Everything looks strange."

"It's not me!" Mienthe said at once. She thought she might understand what the mage meant about pivot-points and linchpins, and this made her almost more uncomfortable than being accused of being a pivot-point herself, because she could see that no one else in the room understood at all.

"I don't know," Iriene said doubtfully. "It seems to me it *is* you, lady, but then everything looks strange in this house right now. I could almost think it was him"—she nodded toward Tan and finished—"except if anybody's at the heart and the hub of whatever's moving in the Delta, lady, it should be you and not some nice young Linularinan legist."

Tan tilted his head, looking curious and amused at this characterization.

Mienthe understood the amusement. So little of that description was actually true. How very strange and uncomfortable, to be aware that someone's appearance was deliberately cultivated and thoroughly false. She wondered whether Tan could possibly be at the heart and hub of all these recent events. That seemed much more likely than that she was. She said aloud, "It isn't *me* they're trying to kidnap."

"That's true," said Geroen, and glowered at Tan. "What was it you brought away with you from Linularinum, huh? What *did* you steal from the old Fox's house?"

Tan opened his mouth as though to say, as he had said all along, *Nothing*. But then he looked suddenly extremely thoughtful. He said instead, "Esteemed Captain...I'd have said I took nothing from Mariddeier Kohorrian save information. But it's clear Istierinan believes I took something more, ah, tangible. He must indeed hold this as an adamant conviction. I thought...I had concluded that someone else was using my, ah, my work to disguise his own theft. But before this, I would not have said the Fox's spymaster could so easily be led astray by mere clouds of obfuscation. Certainly not to acts of war."

"War!" exclaimed Queen Niethe, and then, as she realized this was obviously the case, looked sorry she had spoken.

Tan politely pretended not to notice the queen's embarrassment. "The Linularinan actions can hardly be seen in a less serious light. Only King Iaor's generosity will allow it to be cast otherwise—if he is generously inclined."

"To be sure—yet he will surely wish to be generous—no one can want a *war*," the queen said earnestly.

"Anyone would suspect, from the actions of his agents, that the Fox is in fact inclined toward war," Tan said, and looked around at them all. "But I have observed Mariddeier Kohorrian closely for better than six years, and I would swear he is never pointlessly aggressive. He might wish to reclaim the Delta, so often held by Linularinum and not by Feierabiand—"

Everyone nodded, fully aware of the Delta's complicated history.

"But he is not as, ah, forcefully acquisitive by nature, as, say, the Arobern of Casmantium. I still suspect Istierinan is acting alone and without Kohorrian's knowledge. But if the Fox himself is directing these activities, I believe it is with some restricted object, and not with any desire to provoke His Majesty to answer directly."

From Geroen's pessimistic glower, he was not confident of this assessment. Queen Niethe, on the other hand, seemed to have been rather too thoroughly reassured. Mienthe suspected that this might be because the queen simply did not want to believe that anything very dramatic was likely to happen. Niethe thrived in her well-ordered life and hated uproar and all disarray.

Mienthe herself thought that Tan would not have put his conclusion quite so firmly if he was not confident, but she also wondered just how infallible his judgment was. He'd thoroughly underrated the Linularinan spymaster's determination, evidently. And the Linularinan mage's ability to find him. Whom else might he have underrated? But she said only, "If either Kohorrian or Istierinan acts to gain a limited object, then that must be recovering the thing they believe you stole. I think it would be nice to know what that thing is supposed to be."

"It certainly would," Tan said fervently. "I would try to write it out, assuming it's a legist-magic of some sort, only after, well, everything, I confess I'm afraid of what Istierinan's mages might do if I pick up a quill."

"Nothing," the queen said firmly. "Not while we are all alert and watching—not while *I* am actually here in this room, surely, do you think?"

Mienthe did not find herself confident of this.

"I'll just write out the briefest line—I'll see what comes to me," Tan promised. He looked sidelong at Mienthe. "If you will permit me? It's your house—and you I've depended on, all unknowing, for rescue. Twice, now. Shall I risk a third time?"

"Perhaps not," murmured the queen, gazing at Mienthe with concern.

"Lady Mienthe?" Tan asked.

Mienthe wanted to refuse, but somehow, with Tan seeming to expect her to bravely agree, it was hard to say no. "Well," she said, not entirely willingly, "I want to know, too. All right. All right. Geroen, could you bring Tan a quill and a leaf of paper, from the desk over there?"

Captain Geroen handed Tan a long black feather, which he ran through his fingers. Nothing happened. Tan smiled reassuringly at Mienthe, dipped the quill in the bottle of ink Geroen wordlessly held for him, and, for lack of a proper table, set the paper on his knee.

Mienthe fell asleep before the ink touched the paper. She fell asleep sitting up, with her eyes open. That was how it seemed to her. She dreamed about a thin black spiral that glistened like ink. It was a different kind of spiral than the one she'd drawn earlier. This kind of spiral led inward and down to a concentrated point rather than rising and diffusing outward. She closed her eyes and followed the spiral down and down, and in, and farther in... She blinked, words writing themselves in spidery black script against the emptiness of her inner vision. Though the writing itself was black, colors bloomed behind the script: emerald and dark summer-green, primrose yellow, rich caramel gold and brown, the blues and slate colors of the sea. The fragrance of honey-suckle and spring rain filled the air, and behind those fra-grances, the heavier, more powerful scents of new-turned earth and sea brine.

She could not read even a single letter of the words she saw. Nor did she hear them. Though they seemed real and meaningful, they were not at all like spoken words. But she knew what they said. Or she knew, at least, that part of their purpose was to close tight and hold hard, and yet another part was to flex and move against pressure, only all those concepts were wrong—Mienthe didn't mean "hold" or "flex" or "pressure," or even "purpose." It was very strange to have concepts in her mind that she couldn't actually grasp.

Then Mienthe found herself blinking once again at the ordinary sitting room. Tan was sitting with his head bowed against his hand, his face hidden. He made no sound, but obviously he was in some distress, though she did not know exactly why. There were no marks of any kind on the paper that rested on his knee.

Iriene was staring at both of them. "Well," she said. "Well...that was no ordinary mageworking, was it? It wasn't anything I recognize. How strange. Was that legist-magic?"

"Yes," said Tan, not looking up. "Though it wasn't anything I recognize, either."

"Oh," said Mienthe. "Legist-magic? That explains the words, and why they're written out rather than spoken, and I suppose it also explains why I couldn't read them—because I'm not a legist."

"Words?" asked the queen, puzzled.

"Written?" said Iriene, at nearly the same time. "Did *you* see something, Lady Mienthe? What did you see?"

"*Purposeful* words?" asked Tan, looking up at last.

"But surely you saw them, too?" Mienthe asked him. "You're a legist—didn't you understand them?"

Tan touched his forehead gingerly with the tips of two fingers, as though not perfectly certain the top of his head was still attached. "I don't...nothing's very clear... I wonder *what* Istierinan had hidden in that study of his? Something that only a legist could take, and not even quite realize he'd taken it?"

"Oh!" Mienthe jumped to her feet and was through the door before she'd even realized that she'd forgotten to take proper leave of the queen. But the book was right there on the shelf where she had known she would find it. The fat little book with its expensive leather binding and its thick, heavy, blank pages, with no sign that anybody had ever written a single word in it.

Mienthe found she had no difficulty imagining thin, ornate writing filling the book, black and spidery across all its fine pages. She only wondered what the writing might have said.

CHAPTER 6

Tan recognized the book, of course—recognized it at last not merely as the blank-paged book Istierinan had brought to that memorable interview in the barn, but from before that as well—from that last rushed day and frantic night in Teramondian, when everything had suddenly fallen into order and he'd slipped past Istierinan's watchful eye and into his private study. Years of work used up in that one night, years of moving in all the right circles to gain knowledge of disaffected younger sons and yet with all the right steps to gain the trust of their weary fathers as well... Tan had not in the least minded acting as one of Istierinan's close-held Teramondian agents. He'd gradually established himself as one of Istierinan's most useful agents in the Fox's court, and that night he'd poured out every last drop of credit he'd ever gained. But he'd judged it worth the cast, and so it had been.

And now here this one small book was again, which he had hardly noticed at the time. Not that it was poorly made. It was, in fact, superior workmanship all through: top-quality paper that would take ink beautifully, a tooled leather binding. He was afraid to touch it himself in case that, too, might serve as a trigger for Istierinan's mage—and surprised again by the blaze of anger he felt at being forced to such timidity. But he asked Mienthe to page through the book for him. He watched in growing unease as the young woman turned one blank page after another. Finally he asked her to shut the book again.

Queen Niethe, curious, held out her hand, but one of her ladies took the book instead and held it for her so the queen would not touch it. That seemed a wise precaution to Tan, though he doubted it was necessary. Nevertheless, a weak-minded fear of the book ironically filled him now, when it was too late to evade whatever magic it had contained.

He had looked at this book and evidently taken the writing out of it, and he did not even remember what it had said. It was some trap Istierinan had left for a thief or a spy, and he had fallen into it. The writing in the book had got into his mind. Of course it had. Where else would it have gone? What had it done to him? What might it be doing still? No doubt it had rendered him vulnerable to Istierinan's mage—no doubt he was still vulnerable—and who knew what Istierinan might be able to do to him through it? Tan wanted to run in circles, screaming. Only years of hard-held discipline, a disinclination to look like a hysterical fool in public, and his injured knee allowed him to stay sitting calmly in his chair.

He said, trying for a calm tone, "I'm only surprised I did not recognize it at once. But I had other things to think about when Istierinan was, ah, making inquiries."

He hesitated. Then he admitted, "This book was in Ist-ierinan's study, on a shelf with a few others and a trinket or three and several jars of ink. I glanced through it... it wasn't set apart. I didn't think it special. I suppose I thought it might contain the key to a cipher or such, but..." He stopped.

"But it was blank?" Mienthe said.

"No..." Tan said absently. Why *had* he concluded that this little book held nothing of interest? Not because its pages were empty; at the time, it had held writing. But he had no memory now of *what* writing it had held. That... that was unexpected. Both the current state of the pages and the failure of memory. Tan could read a dozen books in quick succession and afterward give a very close approximation of what each had said; a fine memory for written language was part of the legist gift. He rubbed his palms on his sleeves as though he had touched something unclean and looked at Iriene.

The mage, frowning, held her hand out for the book. The queen's lady gave it to her.

The mage ran her fingers across the leather of the book's binding, opened it to touch the fine, thick, unmarked paper within, closed it again, held it briefly to her lips, shook her head, and declared, "I can't tell a thing about it, but I don't think it's ever held any kind of magecraft."

"Of course not," Tan said, just as Queen Niethe asked, "Oh, but surely it must have, esteemed Iriene?" and Mienthe said in a surprised tone, "But that can't be right," and Captain Geroen snapped, "Of course it has! Why else would Linularinan agents be so interested?"

Everyone stared at Tan.

Tan cleared his throat. But, since he was committed, he also said, "It's a legist's book. Or it was. It held law. Written law—law a master-legist set down stone-hard. Binding law. Until I read it. I wonder if any legist reading this book would have stripped the words out of it, or if it was something about me? My gift?"

From their expressions, Tan rather thought that neither the queen nor any of the guard officers in the room understood what he was saying. Geroen gave a wise, knowing nod, but that was only bluff, Tan could see. The queen looked honestly blank—well, likely she had little to do with any legists or legist-magic. Iriene at least knew that the legist gift was not the same as magecraft, but Tan took leave to doubt whether the healer knew much more than that.

Mienthe, now...Mienthe had taken the blank book back into her hands. She, too, had nodded, but in her case, and not really with surprise, Tan thought what he'd said might have actually made sense to her. She was stroking her fingertips across one of the book's empty pages, her expression abstracted.

What law was it, that Tan now held? He could feel nothing foreign or unfamiliar set into his mind...Would he feel it? Or had it simply restructured his mind and he had not even noticed? *There* was a pleasant thought!

But whatever the book had done to him, whatever he'd done to it, he knew with a profound certainty that he did not want to touch it again himself.

A guardsman came in, hesitated for a moment just inside the door, and finally came over to murmur to Captain Geroen. The captain's expression, from stern, became thunderous. He bowed his head awkwardly to the

queen, begged Mienthe's pardon with a vague word about
seeing to his duty, and went out. Queen Niethe seemed
to think little of his going, but Tan found himself meeting Mienthe's eyes, a common thought of Istierinan and
secretive Linularinan agents occurring, he was certain, to
both of them. Tan had, once again, this time knowing the
risk, set his hand to a quill. Who knew what Istierinan's
mage might have done in that moment?

"Not twice in the same night," murmured Mienthe,
aloud but more or less to herself. "Not once we are
alarmed and alert. Surely not."

"No," Tan agreed, but heard the doubt echo behind his
own words.

Queen Niethe glanced from one of them to the other,
but said nothing. They were all silent for a long moment
and then another, waiting for any alarm to ring through
the house. But there was nothing. The queen said at last,
"No, indeed. Of course not." She rose with practiced,
stately grace and said to Iriene, "So the mystery has
begun to be solved, has it not? We know about the strange
book and the legist's magic in it; we know why the sly
Linularinans have become so bold; we are alarmed and
alert. There is nothing more to do tonight?"

Iriene did not quite like to declare one way or another,
but thought they might send the book to Tiearanan,
where the best mages in Feierabiand studied and wrote
and crafted their work. Or maybe they should look for a
skilled legist who might know what a book like this one
had held?

Tan did not say, *You will hardly find a legist more pow-
erfully gifted than I am on this side of the river*, though he
might have, and rather tartly. It was true that he would not

mind another competent legist's opinion, but he doubted the competence of any Feierabianden legist that might be found. Linularinum for law; everyone knew that, and it was true.

But he did not object. He collected his cane and his balance, rose, bowed his head courteously to the queen, and retired so that she could, as she so clearly desired, speak privately to her own people: to Iriene if she saw any point to it, and to her own guardsmen and perhaps to whatever ladies and advisers she most trusted.

Mienthe must not have been one of those, for she took the queen's words as a dismissal as well and rose, tucking the book under her arm, to accompany Tan. Well, she was young, and Lady of the Delta rather than a constant companion in the Safiad court, undoubtedly loyal to her cousin more than to the queen. On reflection, Tan was not astonished that Queen Niethe did not keep the girl close now. At least she did not seem to take her dismissal as a slight.

Then Mienthe gave him an anxious, sidelong look, and Tan realized that in fact she had deliberately excused herself from the queen's presence in order to stay close to him—that she did not trust any protection Iriene could provide, that she did not trust the guardsmen, no matter how alarmed and alert they might be. She had rescued Tan from his enemies twice, and felt keenly the responsibility of both those rescues. He was surprised he had not understood at once. He felt a sudden, surprising warmth of feeling toward this young woman, so earnest and so astonishingly ready to assume deep obligations toward a chance-met stranger who was not even truly one of her own people.

Mienthe, unaware of the sudden shift in Tan's regard,

tapped the empty Linularinan book against her palm, glanced quickly up and down the hall, and said hesitantly, "I'm—that is, I have a comfortable couch in my sitting room." She had clearly forgotten her own authority in this house, for she did not make this suggestion into an order, but ducked her head apologetically as she offered it. "You might…I know you have your own room upstairs in the tower, and I'm sure that is probably perfectly safe for you, now. But I wonder if you might rather…a couch where no one at all knows to look for you…where I would be able to see you myself…I know it's not really a proper suggestion…"

The windowless tower room seemed now, in Tan's reflection, rather less like a refuge and more like a trap. A couch in a room where no one would expect to find him, a last-minute offer no one had overheard, from this young woman who'd shown such a gift for extracting him from the hands of his enemies…That seemed very practical. He was not too proud to say so. He said, which was even the truth, "I think it's a very proper and brave suggestion, from the Lady of the Delta to a guest who's under her protection. I'll accept, lady, and thank you for the consideration."

Mienthe looked relieved. She nodded her head to show him the way. "I was going to ask one of my maids to bring tea, but maybe it would be better not to let the kitchen know where you are, either. Though my maids are discreet. I think."

In Tan's experience, maids were never discreet. He didn't quite know how to say so. He could hardly suggest young Lady Mienthe invite him to stay unchaperoned in her own rooms.

"Karin can be discreet," Mienthe said, in the tone of one coming to a necessary conclusion. "She chatters, but that's all just show for the young men. She won't talk about anything important."

Tan said nothing.

"I swear I won't tell," the young maid Karin promised solemnly when Mienthe told her that Tan might be spending the night on a couch in her sitting room. She was a buxom girl with an outrageously flirtatious manner. "Not even my string of lovers," she added at Tan's doubtful glance, and winked. Oddly, Tan felt the girl might actually be telling the truth about her discretion, if not her string of lovers.

Mienthe made Tan take the best couch and settled in a cane chair, tucking her feet under her skirts like a child. "Well," she said, looking at Tan, and stopped, clearly not knowing what to say, and small blame for that.

The maid had settled, more or less out of earshot, across the room on the hearth of a fireplace. She busied herself with some sort of needlework, pretending, in the immemorial way of maids everywhere, not to listen.

"So," Tan said, low enough that the maid might not overhear, "and are you rising into mage power, Lady Mienthe?"

"No!" said Mienthe at once, but then hesitated. "I don't know. I don't think so. How can one tell?"

Tan, not being a mage himself, had no idea.

"And you?" Mienthe said. "Do you feel anything? Have you, since you found that book?"

Tan had to admit he could not tell. "It's all very… very…"

"Alarming? Well, but exciting, too, don't you think?

It could have been anything, couldn't it? Well, anything valuable," Mienthe amended. "Something that your Ist-ierinan would be desperate not to lose. Something to do with the magic of language and law. Maybe you'll be able to speak all languages now, do you think? Wouldn't that be wonderful? Erich tried to teach me Prechen, but I couldn't get more than a word or two to come off my tongue. Or maybe you'll be able to tell when someone is speaking the truth, or when they're writing a contract with intent to deceive. It stands to reason a legist would put only some wonderful, strong magic in a book, doesn't it? Only he didn't expect another legist with such a strong gift to get it out again, did he? Only then you did." Mien-the paused, staring at Tan in speculation.

Tan tried not to smile. He liked her optimism, and hoped she was right, and hesitated to say anything that might reveal his own terror of what his mind might now contain.

Somewhere, distantly, there was a shout. Indistinct with distance, but definitely a shout. Mienthe jumped up in alarm, and Tan reached for his cane.

There was a firm knock on the door before he could get to his feet. A guardsman opened it, leaned in, and said, "Lady Mienthe?" He looked a little embarrassed, but determined—the very picture of a man driven by orders to a forwardness that was not his by nature. It was Tenned son of Tenned, which amused Tan even under these circumstances. "You do find yourself on duty at the most fraught moments," he commented.

"Yes," said the young guardsman in a harassed tone. "Nothing like this ever happened before you came to Tiefenauer. I don't think I'll ever complain of boredom again."

"What *now*?" Mienthe asked.

"Esteemed lady—" Tenned began, but paused. Then he said, out in a rush, "Captain Geroen says he's getting reports from riverside, they say there's an awful lot of activity across the river, and Captain Geroen wants to undeck our half of the bridge, and send men to watch all the fordable parts of the river upstream and down, and muster the men. And the other captains, as were in command of the different divisions before Lord Bertaud appointed Geroen above them all, they don't want to do any of that, they say it's a fool who sees smoke from one campfire and declares the whole forest is burning. And the captain of the royal guard, Temnan, you know, he wants to send after the king to see what he should do—"

"*That's* a fool," Tan murmured. "Indecisiveness is the worst of faults in a captain—other than shyness, and that *send after the king* could be a sign of either. Or both. I don't know what influential family the king would be accommodating to have promoted a fool to a captaincy, but I wonder if this is why he left the man behind?"

"To guard his *queen*?" Mienthe objected. "And his daughters?"

"He can't have expected anything to happen…"

"I'm sure Temnan is perfectly competent," Mienthe declared, but her eyes hid worry.

"However that is, Captain Geroen, he sent me to find you, esteemed lady, and beg you come and tell him he can undeck the bridge—"

"That can't be necessary," said Mienthe, rather blankly.

The bridge between Tiefenauer in the Delta and Linularinan Desamion had never been a truly permanent sort of bridge of stone and iron; the history of the Delta was too complicated. It was a timber bridge, which meant that rotted timbers had to be replaced from time to time, but also meant that either side could undeck the bridge if times became suddenly uncertain.

"Lady—" Tenned began.

"Esteemed Mienthe—" Tan said at the same time.

Mienthe held up her hand to quiet them both. Possibly Tan's comment about indecisiveness was echoing in her ears, because she said to the guardsman, "Go tell Captain Geroen to give whatever orders he sees fit about the bridge, and about setting sentries around Tiefenauer. Mustering the men—isn't that something we sometimes drill? Don't I recall my cousin ordering a muster once just to see how fast the guard could respond?"

"Four years ago, yes, lady," said Tenned respectfully. "Just after I joined."

"We could do that now. Couldn't we? But in the middle of the night? Maybe we ought to wait for morning?"

"The captain—"

"I'll come speak to Captain Geroen," Mienthe decided. "But I think—wait a moment." She caught up the blank-paged book and darted with it into the other room. But in only a moment she was back again, breathless, the Linularinan book gone. "All right, let's go," she said to Tenned, and waved at Tan to accompany her.

"Kohorrian cannot possibly be planning to march troops across that bridge!" the captain of the royal guardsmen was—not quite shouting, Tan decided, but very nearly. "Earth and iron, man, you'll have Her Majesty in fits to suit your own silly humors! Are you a guard captain or a little girl, to be afraid of moving shadows in the night?"

Geroen simply stood with his head down and his eyes half shut, in much the same attitude he might have shown in a storm. He seemed otherwise unmoved by the other's vehemence. Next to Temnan's polished courtier's grace, Geroen looked decidedly lower-class, mulishly stubborn, and even rather brutish. But he also looked like the very last man to be moved by tight nerves and silly humors.

"I'm not entirely certain we can be perfectly confident of what the old Fox may and may not do," Tan put in smoothly, in a tone of polite deference. "And, after all, though the move must naturally prove unnecessary, I'm certain the city guard will profit from a little exercise."

"What is Her Majesty's opinion?" Mienthe asked.

"The queen has long since retired for the night," Temnan said stiffly, by which Tan understood that he was not so confident of his own position that he wanted to risk the queen's overriding him. Not that Tan was in the least interested in the queen's opinion, personally. He glanced sidelong at Mienthe, wondering how to convey a suggestion that, at least tonight, they might best take any warnings very seriously.

Mienthe did not seem to need to hear this advice from anyone. She kept her gaze on the royal captain's face, lifted her chin and said, "Well, though I should be glad of Her Majesty's opinion, in the Delta my cousin's opinion is foremost."

"I've sent after His Majesty and Lord Bertaud—"

Mienthe continued as though the captain had not spoken, "And since my cousin is not here, I will decide what we will do." Tan, standing close behind her, was aware that the young woman's hands were trembling. She had closed them into loose fists to hide the fact. From Temnan's stuffed expression, he did not realize Mienthe was nervous—but he did know that she was right about where authority rested in the Delta, and that he'd been in the wrong to try to overrule Tiefenauer's own captain.

Mienthe turned deliberately to Geroen and said, "Do as you see fit to guard the Delta and the city and this house. We will say it was a practice drill, if nothing comes of it. Do as you think best in all matters, Captain Geroen, and then come and explain to me what kind of activity it *is* that you think you've seen on the other side of the river and what you think it means."

The captain gave her a firm, satisfied nod. "Lady."

"Very well." Mienthe looked around once, uncertainly, as though hoping to see good advice carved into the walls or the ceiling. She said, "I wish—" but cut that thought off uncompleted. She looked at Tan instead. He gave her an encouraging nod and no suggestions at all, because she was already doing exactly as he'd have advised her. She looked faintly surprised, as though she'd expected argument or advice and was a little taken aback to receive only approving silence.

Mariddeier Kohorrian, the Fox of Linularinum, might or might not have desired soldiers bearing his badge and wearing his colors to march across the bridge, but someone—Istierinan Hamoddian, or someone he was advising—had indeed pulled together a surprisingly strong muster and pointed it toward the Delta. Geroen brought Mienthe that news almost before they'd gone— not back to Mienthe's rooms to wait, but to the solar, the one room in the entire great house that offered the best view of the city.

It should have been a quiet view, a peaceful night in the city. But there were lanterns everywhere, and torches and bonfires down by the river. Men moving in the streets, some with aimless confusion, but many quickly and with purpose.

Geroen brought descriptions of what he'd done with the city guardsmen, how he'd arranged them—along with a grim assurance that the eastern half of the bridge had been successfully undecked and bowmen placed on the rooftops to be sure the Linularinan troops could not easily redeck it from their side.

"But they want to," the captain told Mienthe, without any satisfaction at being proved right. "They've tried twice, under shields."

Mienthe said, voicing the common shock, "I can't believe it. I can't believe they're really trying this. How can they *dare*? Are you sure?" Then she waved this away, embarrassed. "Of course you are, of course—I can't believe it, but I believe *you*."

"None of us can believe it, but there it is." Geroen didn't sound panicky, or even excited. He sounded, Tan decided, rather more morose than anything else. There was a scrape across one cheek and his shoulders were slumped with weariness, but he met Mienthe's wide-eyed gaze with commendable straightness. He said, "Now, that lot trying to cross on the bridge—they'll have a hard time getting the job done, too hard a job if you take my meaning, and it's my opinion they're just meant to draw the eye."

"What?" Mienthe did not, in fact, quite seem to take captain's meaning.

"Ah, well," he said, more plainly. "I can't see as any sensible man would start up a war over some fool magic book, but it looks a great lot like maybe someone over there's maybe not sensible. If it was me and I meant to do a right job of it, then I'd be sliding around through the marshes and never mind the bridge until I could get control of both ends of it, do you see?"

Mienthe nodded. "Go on."

"Well, so I've got men watching, but not enough, my lady. I want to rouse out anybody as ever's been in the militia and send them out to watch, if you'll give me leave. And south, right down at the river mouth, because if it was me over there, I'd be thinking about loading up a few ships and tucking around that way—"

"You've sent a strong mage down to the sea to wake the wild magic, I suppose," Tan said quietly.

"I did that, for which I hope you'll give me leave, Lady Mienthe, because I ought by rights to have asked before I did any such thing, but—"

"You sent for Eniad of Saum," Mienthe guessed.

Geroen looked a little embarrassed, as well he might, having made the broad decision to involve other Delta cities in Tiefenauer's trouble. "You did say as I should do as I saw fit, my lady."

"No, you were right to send to Saum," Mienthe said quickly. "I'd have told you to, if I'd thought of it. Eniad of Saum is just who we'll want to send the sea wild and close our harbor—all the harbors, I suppose, just in case—well, in case. How long ago did you send your man?"

"Oh … right after you said I might, Lady Mienthe. And I sent over to Kames with word that maybe there could be some trouble, and up along the Sierhanan, thinking it would be best to have the whole Delta alert, just in case."

"Just what you should do," Tan said quietly, as Mienthe was starting to look doubtful about just how broad the captain's actions had been.

Mienthe glanced at him, then looked back at the captain and nodded. "All right. And what else?"

"Oh, well…that royal—" Geroen visibly edited what he'd first intended to say, continuing only after a perceptible pause, "The esteemed captain of Her Majesty's guard, he's sent men of his north as fast as they can ride, after His Majesty, and that's all very well, but he's not proved willing to let any man of his stand duty more than half a stone's throw from Her Majesty, which is all very well, but I'm not having him stand like a stone statue with his— anyway, begging your pardon, my lady, but I'm not having it. I want those men of his used for something better than house ornaments, and I thought maybe you might see your way to asking Her Majesty about that, my lady."

"Yes," said Mienthe, nodding. "I can do that." She was clearly relieved to be given a task that she understood, one within her proper bounds. "Very well. I'll speak to Temnan, but I'm not sure you'll get any of his men, because I'm going to wake the queen. I think Her Majesty should leave the Delta—tonight, at once." She hesitated. "That is, if you think…"

"Yes, my lady," Geroen said stolidly. "I think that's well advised."

Mienthe nodded quickly, relieved. "But maybe she'll spare at least a few of her guardsmen to help us here." She turned to Tan and went on, her tone a mix of justifiable incredulity and wonder, "All of this for you?"

"I don't see that it can be," Tan said hastily. "Truly, Mienthe—esteemed lady, I mean; forgive me. But whatever was in that book, it cannot possibly have been sufficiently important to justify, well, all this."

"It must be," Geroen disagreed. "If Linularinum's willing to start a war over you, then they obviously think you're important enough to justify it, eh, or they wouldn't, would they? And they have, and what else do you think could have brought them to it?"

"The griffins' Wall," Mienthe suggested, and lifted her hands in a little shrug when they looked at her. "Well, I mean, suppose Linularinum learned about the Wall cracking even before we did, maybe, and Mariddeier Kohorrian thought if Iaor and Bertaud were distracted enough in the north, maybe he could try to interfere down here in the Delta? And maybe he's just decided to use Tan as an excuse? Is that possible?"

Tan honestly did not think it could be. "Kohorrian is a little too clever to try anything quite so blatant, I think. Not when he must know how little the Delta would welcome any attempt to forcibly change its allegiance."

"I don't know," said Mienthe, and then to Geroen, "I wonder if you might be able to send a man of yours across to the Linularinan force? With a wand, I mean." She meant a white courier's wand, which in this context would show a request for parley. "He could ask what it is they want. He could try to find out whether the man behind this is that enemy of Tan's, Istierinan, I mean, or whether it's someone else, or whether Mariddeier Kohorrian himself is provoking us, and why. Or, at least, why he says he's doing it. I'll write a letter for a man to take across."

"Yes, good," Geroen agreed. He rubbed his face with a big hand, blinking wearily. "I should have thought of it myself. At the very least it may set those Linularinan bastards back a bit by their heels. Begging your pardon—"

"Good. Good. All right. Send me someone, then, and Tan, would you see if there's paper in that desk? Or, no, I don't suppose you'd better touch any legist's things—"

"No," agreed Tan, startled at the sharp anger he felt at that casual statement. *I don't suppose you'd better touch any legist's things.* He hid the anger, put it down: how stupid, how unreasoning a reaction. The sort of emotional reaction that could get a man killed, if he wasn't able to set it aside. He was indeed sensibly afraid to use his gift; Mienthe was quite right. It wasn't her fault anyway, but Istierinan's. He closed his eyes for an instant and took a breath, then clambered to his feet and came to lean over the young woman's shoulder. "Perhaps I will be able to suggest some phrasing you might use."

"Yes, please. Geroen, find someone to act as courier, please, and find a white wand for him. I'm sure my cousin has some in his study. And do send word at once if anything happens, will you? And send someone else to tell the queen's captain I want to see him."

The captain braced his shoulders back. "Yes, my lady."

But they never had a chance to send the letter, nor even to speak to the captain of the royal guardsmen. Mienthe's idea to write a letter had been a good one, and there ought by rights to have been time to write out a dozen fair copies if she'd been so inclined.

But Istierinan, or someone, had evidently sent men

upriver and across the Sierhanan by boat long before he'd begun making threatening gestures toward the bridge. Linularinan soldiers must have crossed into Feierabiand, along some quiet, dark stretch of river where no one was watching—maybe the Linularinan commanders had sent a small force across first to establish a bridgehead and stop any warning being sent south, because it was from the north and east that Linularinan soldiers first made their way into Tiefenauer.

"This night has been past imagining! How I wish Bertaud was here!" Mienthe said passionately when they had this last news. She stared in despair at Tan.

Tan shrugged helplessly, not pointing out that the night was far from over even yet. But he said, "Though it might be as well if your lord cousin was here, Lady Mienthe, you're doing well enough on your own."

Mienthe stared at him, but Geroen himself flung open the door and strode in before she could say anything, if she meant to.

Her Majesty, Geroen informed them, had agreed that she and her daughters should withdraw at once, north toward Sihannas. Niethe wanted Tan and Mienthe to come with her. Tan agreed that the queen's withdrawing was a fine idea, but he said at once, "But not with me in her party. No."

Mienthe met his eyes, and he knew she agreed with him: He must not accompany the queen's party, in case they were all wrong and the Linularinan force was in fact moving solely because of Tan.

Tan said, "You, however, should certainly go with the queen."

"Oh," said Mienthe, appearing very much surprised

by this idea. "No, I can't possibly. No, I'll stay here. It's only right—"

"It's only foolish," growled Geroen. He glowered at Mienthe.

Mienthe lifted her chin. "I can't possibly abandon Tiefenauer. I'm staying."

Geroen glared at her even more furiously. "Out of the question!"

"I won't—I'll—" began Mienthe.

"Anyway, Her Majesty's ordered you to make ready, so if she says you're going, you're going," Geroen said with clear satisfaction. "Better tell your maids. I'll tell them in the stables to get horses ready for you and your women."

Tan tapped his cane gently against the floor, waited a beat to collect both Geroen's and Mienthe's attention, and said gently, "Captain Geroen, you are captain of the Tiefenauer guard and therefore Lady Mienthe's servant. You are not her lord cousin, to bid her come and go."

Geroen flushed. He opened his mouth, but shut it again without speaking.

Mienthe, having recovered something of her ordinary poise, said firmly, "My maids may certainly go north, Captain, but Queen Niethe will assuredly reconsider her command to me." She was furious. Her eyes snapped with anger and determination. "I'm quite certain that Her Majesty will not be comfortable commanding the Lady of the Delta. I will not abandon the Delta or Tiefenauer or this house, Geroen; not for your urging or the queen's command. I'm certain my cousin would agree."

Geroen glared wordlessly at the young woman, then gave Tan a grim look. "Well, *you*, I guess, won't give me such trouble, so you think which way you want to ride out," he snapped, and strode out before either of them could argue.

Tan shook his head, trying not to laugh. "That's an uncommonly determined man, is my opinion. I've no astonishment he was slow of promotion and tended to be assigned hard duty—night captain of the prison guard, indeed! He's hardly a courtier, is he?"

Mienthe gave Tan a long look. Then she did laugh. "You like him, don't you? I'd think you'd prefer men who were, what, subtle and obscure and quoting poetry..."

Tan smiled back at her. "Ah, well...I like a man who knows his mind and his duty, and it's novel to meet one who doesn't give a thought to arranging his words prettily. One can understand his frustration."

The young woman shook her head and insisted, "Yes, but, Bertaud would perfectly well understand that I can't leave." But her tone was uncertain.

Tan wondered who had taught her to doubt herself. It seemed to him she needn't. Not at all to his astonishment, later in the stableyard, while everyone sorted out horses and baggage by the light of torches and lanterns, Mienthe continued her steady refusal of all invitations and exhortations and, eventually, commands to the contrary.

Queen Niethe thought Mienthe's stubbornness was perfectly exasperating and terribly dangerous and possibly illegal, but, as Mienthe was not shy of pointing out, Tiefenauer was not merely another Feierabianden town. Neither the queen nor the captain of her guard nor even Geroen quite dared put Mienthe on a horse by force, especially after she said flatly that they'd have to tie her hands to the pommel to make her stay in the saddle.

Tan was not actually surprised that the young woman could hold with such firm purpose to her refusal, though he saw that everyone else was, possibly excepting Captain Geroen. He gazed after the queen's retreating party with an obscure feeling of satisfaction, though when he caught Mienthe's gaze he shook his head in mock dismay. "So sad!" he exclaimed. "There they all go, and us left behind bereft."

Mienthe gave him a distracted glance—then looked again, more carefully. "Should you be standing on that leg?"

Perceptive girl. Tan had thought his grip on his cane was subtle. Evidently not. Rather than pretend he hadn't been leaning heavily on the cane, he smiled and said, "This leg does insist on joining me, even in locations bereft of chairs. The esteemed Iriene is not here to scold me, fortunately. I'm sure I'll soon be seated. On a horse, unfortunately, but we all have one or another burden to bear."

Mienthe stared at him, and then laughed—a little grudgingly, but she laughed.

"Ah, look," Tan said, tipping his head to indicate she should turn, "here are some of those earnest young men of Geroen's—Tenned, my friend, and how does this fine night find you?"

The young guardsman in question, in company with another of the same kind, ran an exasperated hand through his hair and then glared at Tan, perhaps mimicking Captain Geroen. "I'd thank you twice over, esteemed sir, to get into the house and out of our way." He looked at Mienthe and added in a far more conciliatory tone, "And you, my lady, if you would be so kind."

Tan threw an exaggerated glance around. "Anybody might be out here," he said in a low, urgent voice. And then, speaking in a normal tone, "Unfortunately, that's even true." He hesitated and then looked at Mienthe. "Esteemed lady—"

"Yes," Mienthe said, meeting his eyes. "You should leave, of course. Tenned and Keier can go with you." She gave the two young guardsmen a stern look. Neither of them objected.

"Not north," said Tan.

"No," Mienthe said distractedly, and might have gone on, but a distant ringing, clashing sound cut her off. For a long moment, everyone in the stableyard stood perfectly still, listening.

"There's fighting to the south," Tan said, which they all knew. "And the west, of course. I'll go east."

Mienthe hesitated an instant and then came unexpectedly to take Tan's hands and look seriously into his face. "Be careful, Tan. Be careful, don't take chances, be quick, be safe! Go to my father's house, it's just north of Kames. Use my name— Keier, they'll know you in Kames, won't they? Tan—" She pressed his hands in hers and then let go. "You'll be well. See to it that you are. You still need to write out some Linularinan court epics for me, eventually. I'll expect it, do you hear?"

"I'll look forward to it," Tan said, bemused and oddly pleased. "And you, don't take foolish risks, esteemed Mienthe. I need someone who will properly appreciate Linularinan court poetry."

Mienthe managed a smile and then turned to run inside. Tan would not have laid odds on what Mienthe might do. Too brave for her own good, and then a deep sense of personal responsibility…He discovered that he was personally concerned for her safety, a good deal more so than he'd have expected, and blinked in surprise.

But the young woman, and the great house, and the city entire, would likely be safer after Tan was safely away. He looked at Tenned and Keier.

"We'll get on the road at once, esteemed sir," said Tenned, indicating a waiting horse. "East should be safe enough, but if you'll pardon me, I think we should hurry—"

The distant sounds of battle underscored his words.

"I suspect you're right," Tan agreed, and limped rapidly toward the horse one of the grooms held. He even allowed Tenned to help him mount, when ordinarily he would not lightly have let anyone see such evidence of his weakness.

But as they rode out of the stableyard, he could not help but glance back over his shoulder at the great house, defiantly lit with lanterns beside each door and lamps in each window. He wondered at which window Mienthe was standing, watching everyone ride away. She would have guardsmen all around her, and perhaps one or another servant too loyal or elderly to flee the house. Tan knew that. But somehow he pictured her standing alone, with the lamplight catching in her eyes and glowing through her wheaten hair, and the dark violent night pressing against the glass before her.

CHAPTER 7

Two rivers ran out of Niambe Lake: the little Sef, which fed into the great Sierhanan, whose width divided Feierabiand from Linularinum; and the larger and more southerly Nejeied, which ran right down the middle of Feierabiand all the way to Terabiand on the coast.

Two rivers likewise fed the lake. One, the upper Nejeied, had its source in the high, distant mountains of the far north, beyond Tiearanan. But the other river, the one that came down to the eastern tip of the lake, had no name. That river came down out of the wicked teeth of the mountains where men seldom ventured. There was no reason to brave that place, for if a man did, with enormous difficulty, crest the difficult pass where the river ran, he would look down only into the savage desert where griffins flew on a fiery wind and no man could live.

There, at the top of the world, among the high, jagged peaks where the nameless river had its source, stood a cottage. It had been built below the sky and above the world, in a small, level place surrounded by tilting planes of stone and ice. It was solidly made of rough stone, chunks of pale granite mottled with dark hornblende and darker iron ore; the chinks and cracks between the stones were sealed with packed moss and ice. Within, the cottage was plain but surprisingly comfortable, not least because of a fire that burned continually, with neither fuel nor smoke, in a ring of stones in the middle of the floor. This had been a gift from the desert, a contained fragment of fire that would probably continue to burn even when time had long since reduced the cottage to a heap of tumbled and broken stones.

Above the cottage, the polished, ice-streaked granite faces of the mountains raked up into the sky, so that on bright days light was thrown back and forth above the thatched roof. On those days, with sunlight striking at every angle through the clear air, mist rose from the ice to wreathe around the cottage.

The true source of the river was invisible among the sharp peaks and the drifting mist and the clamor of cold, brilliant light, but a silver thread of moisture ran down the stone beside the cottage. This narrow stream fed a tiny alpine meadow surrounding the cottage, as it fed a string of similar meadows on its meandering route down toward the lake that was its eventual destination. The trickle of water sparkled with more than ordinary brilliance in the sun, and in fact it sparkled more than any water had a right to even when the clouds piled up thick around the tips of the mountains, for the nameless river carried something of the wild magic of the mountains down from the heights.

There was little snow this high in the mountains, for

the air was too dry. Even so, ice glittered in the shadow of the cottage. Yet the meadow seemed like a cup into which the brilliance and warmth of the sunlit afternoon had been poured, so the meadow was not, in fact, so terribly cold.

A dozen small, hardy brown hens and one white-feathered cock pecked around the cottage, taking advantage of the relative warmth. A long-legged goat with a tawny coat stood in the sun and gazed, with a meditative expression, into the empty vistas below the cottage. Above the cottage, clinging to a broken edge of stone and singing in a voice that rose through the still air like sparks from a bonfire, perched a bird.

The bird was about the size of a common jay, the gray-and-black jay that sometimes ventured up to these high meadows. But this bird was not a jay, nor anything like one. It was feathered in fire. Its head was orange, with black streaked like ash above its black eyes. Its breast was gold, its wings orange and crimson, the long trailing feathers of its tail crimson and gold. When it sang, its throat vibrated and sparks showered down across the ice that glittered on the stone below its perch. When it flew, which it did suddenly, darting high into the sky and then down again and away to the east and north, flames scattered through the air from the wind of its wings.

The bird did not come to the cottage every day. But sometimes, especially on afternoons such as this, when the air was brilliant and still as glass, it came to sing for him. Jos, who had few visitors, liked to think the bird scattered luck as well as fire from its wings. He regarded any day on which it appeared as a lucky day. And he thought, pausing with his hands full of grain to throw out for the hens, that luck would be a good thing, today.

Far down below the cottage, yet well within sight, stood one end of the Great Wall. Jos thought of it that way: the Great Wall. It was impossible not to set that kind of emphasis on it, if you looked down upon it on every clear day. The Wall dominated his world, even more than the jagged peaks of these wild mountains. It was made of massive granite blocks carved out of the heart of a mountain...more than one mountain, for this Wall wove its way from this place to the other end that anchored it, two hundred miles or more to the east. South of the Great Wall lay the wild wooded hills and great fertile plains and rich, crowded cities of Casmantium, where Jos had been born. To the north lay the desert.

The griffins' desert was nothing in size compared to Casmantium, but from Jos's vantage, looking down on both simultaneously, this was not perceptible. The desert ran down the far slopes of the mountains and then away farther than sight could discern: red sand and knife-edged red stone; molten light thick as honey and heavy as gold; winds that hissed with sand and flickered with fire. The northern face of the Wall, its desert side, burned with a hard, brilliant flame so bright it was painful to look directly at it. The other face...on the side of earth, the Wall was glazed with ice and veiled with mist. Above the Wall, all the way to the vault of the sky, the air shimmered, for the Wall was more than a physical barrier. It barred the passage of any winged creature of fire or earth as thoroughly as it barred those that were land-bound.

At two points, where the Wall had cracked through, massive clouds of white steam billowed up into the sky.

Judging by the amount of steam, the cracks had not gotten any worse today, Jos estimated. Or not much worse. Was that luck? Or had Kes found something better to do on this day than pry at the cracks, try to pull down the Great Wall, try to burn through to the country of earth? He peered carefully into the burning sky above the country of fire, but he could see no griffins riding their hot, dangerous winds. Perhaps they had all allowed those winds to carry them back into the heart of their own country. Perhaps Kes had gone with them. Perhaps Kes had called up that wind, a wind that would lead her adopted people away from the Wall that constrained them...

More likely the griffins had simply caught sight of a herd of fire-deer and allowed themselves to be distracted. Most likely they would come back soon. If not before sundown, then probably tomorrow.

And even without Kes or her companion mages pushing at the Wall, Jos thought the cracks would probably get worse. He was almost certain they had been worse this dawn than last night's dusk. Damage that worsened overnight was probably not due to the griffins' mages.

Jos only wished he knew what had caused the damage in the first place, what was still causing more damage every day. And, of course, he might wish as well that knowing what had caused the problem would let him see how it might be fixed. That was a separate issue.

There was a ripple in the air, a shift in the light, and Kairaithin was suddenly present, lying on the high winds, far above. His shadow swept across the meadow, brilliant and fiery-hot.

In his true form, Anasakuse Sipiike Kairaithin was a great-winged griffin, not the most beautiful griffin Jos knew, but one of the greatest and most terrible. He was a very dark griffin. Black feathers ran down from his savage eagle's head and ruffled out in a thick mane around his shoulders and chest. His black wings were edged and barred with narrow flickers of ember-red. They tilted to catch the wind, shedding droplets of fire into the chilly mountain air. His lion pelt was a shade darker than crimson, his talons and lion claws black as iron.

The chickens scattered beneath his fiery shadow, squawking in desperate terror, heads ducked low and wings fluttering. The goat, wiser than the chickens, bolted straight through the door into the cottage where it would, judging from past experience, crowd itself under the bed.

Jos tilted his head back to watch the griffin come down through the thin air—air imbued with the natural, wild magic of the mountains and the river. No griffins but this one could come to this place. That was why the Wall had been allowed to end down below: because it ran out into thin, cold air and wild magic inimical to griffin fire, and no griffin could simply pass around its end. Except this one. Anasakuse Sipiike Kairaithin seemed to have no difficulty going wherever he chose, whether in the country of fire or the country of earth or this wild country that belonged to neither.

Kairaithin landed neatly in the middle of the tiny meadow. Heat radiated from him. In his shadow, the delicate grasses withered. But in the rest of the meadow, flowers opened and tilted their sensitive faces toward the griffin's warmth as toward the sun.

Jos said mildly, "If you would come in your human form, I would not need to spend hours prying the goat out of my house and collecting terrified chickens."

Kairaithin tucked himself into a neat sitting posture

like a cat, tail curled around his eagle talons. He tilted
his head to one side, the mountain light glancing off his
savage-edged beak as off polished metal. He said, *Have
you other pressing amusements with which to occupy
your hours?*

A joke. At least, Jos thought that question had probably been intended as a joke. Sometimes griffin humor
seemed a little obscure to an ordinary man. He said after
a moment, "Well. Little enough, I suppose, except for
watching the Wall."

The griffin's eyes were black, pitiless as the desert sun
or the mountain cold or a fall from a bitter height. But
they could glint with a kind of hard humor. They did now.
The griffin said, *One hopes observing the wall is not an
activity that calls for your constant attention.*

Jos said straight-faced, "I suppose I might be able to
spare an hour from my scrutiny." Then he added, much
more tentatively, "The damage seems very little worse
today than it did yesterday. Do you think perhaps the
cracks through the Wall are becoming more stable?"

The griffin did not answer this, which might mean that
he was uncertain or might mean that he thought not, but
probably meant that he did not wish to dwell on a false
hope. He asked, *Kes?*

"She has not come today." To the endmost block, Jos
meant, the block that anchored this end of the Wall—the
block that was most seriously cracked. Once, he would
have meant, *She has not come here to speak to me.* He
did not have to say that, now. Now, she never came to
the cottage or to Jos. She ventured up into the mountains
only to cast fire against the Wall, to try to shatter the stone
or throw it down.

Opailikiita Sehanaka Kiistaike? Ashairiikiu Ruuanse Tekainiike?

Ruuanse Tekainiike was a young griffin mage, hardly more than a *kiinukaile*, a student. Griffins might be students for a long time or a short time, and became full mages and no one's subordinate, as Jos understood it, simply by waking up one morning and declaring themselves masters. Ruuanse Tekainiike was not a student because he admitted no master, but he was in no way Kairaithin's equal. He did not worry Jos at all. Or very little.

Opailikiita was different. Opailikiita was a young griffin as well; she, too, was nothing like as powerful as Kairaithin, though Jos had reason enough to respect her power. But, much more important, she was a particular friend to Kes. *Iskarianere* was the griffin term for it—like sisters. Jos knew the word, though he was aware he had only a dim idea of its true meaning.

But then, as Jos also knew, griffins had only the dimmest idea of human concepts like *friendship* and *love*. He said, "Not them either."

Kairaithin was silent for a time, gazing down from the little meadow toward the Wall. The sun had slid down past the tips of the highest mountains, so that great shadows lay in the valleys in the lee of the mountains. The temperature was already falling—or would be, if not for Kairaithin's presence in the meadow. Alpine bees made their determined way from flower to flower, taking advantage of the warmth the griffin had brought into their meadow. Jos wondered whether the griffin's presence was, on balance, useful or detrimental to the meadow. He might shed warmth and light all about, but those grasses and flowers his shadow had burned would be a long time recovering.

Of course, if the Wall shattered, a little patch of burned grasses in a high meadow would be very far from the worst problem they would all face.

Bertaud son of Boudan is coming here, said Kairaithin, still gazing downhill. *Your king is coming with him.*

"Here?" Jos was dismayed—then he asked himself, Why dismay? On his own account, or merely at the thought of his silent mountains being overrun by the king and his company? Either way, he smothered that first sharp reaction and asked instead, "Why? I mean, what do they expect to do?" Something useful? He could not imagine what.

The griffin's long lion-tail tapped once, twice, on the ground at his feet. Though he had been acquainted with Kairaithin for some years, and on tolerably good terms for several of those years, Jos could not guess whether that movement signified annoyance or satisfaction or nervousness or predatory intent or something else entirely. When Kairaithin spoke, he could recognize nothing in his voice but a strange kind of patient anger, and that had informed the griffin for as long as Jos could remember— since the Wall, indeed. Which Kairaithin had helped to build, after which he'd been cast out by his own people. Jos knew little more about it than that, for the griffin had never spoken of it. But he thought he understood Kairaithin's anger. What he did not understand was the patience.

I carried word to Bertaud son of Boudan, Kairaithin said. *I, as though I were a courier, bearing a white wand and the authority of your king.*

The idea of the griffin as an official Feierabianden courier made Jos smile. He turned his head to hide his expression. In Feierabiand, nearly all the royal couriers were girls of decent but not high birth; they tended to form a tight-knit alliance, married one another's brothers and cousins when they retired from active service, and brought up their daughters to be couriers as well. And they were all, that Jos had ever met, passionately proud of their calling. However Kairaithin viewed the service he had performed—and it seemed both a wise and a very small service, to this point—Jos thought he understood the griffin well enough to be certain he was not *proud* of it.

Jos wondered whether Kairaithin was, in fact, ashamed of his role in building the Wall, whether he was ashamed of once again defying the will of his people in carrying word of the damage to the Wall to human authorities. If he were a man rather than a griffin, that was a question that Jos—Jos in particular, all things considered—might even have found a way to ask him. But even when he wore the shape of a man, Kairaithin was nothing like a man. Jos could not imagine a way to pose such a question to the fierce, proud, incomprehensible griffin, whatever shape he wore. He said instead, "When will they get here?"

The griffin turned his narrow eagle's head to look at Jos.

He was angry, Jos realized. The griffin's black gaze was so powerful he half expected the granite of the mountain to crack and shatter under that stare. Jos stopped himself from taking a step backward by a plain act of will. It helped that he was sure—well, almost sure—that the griffin was not angry with *him*.

Soon, said Kairaithin. *Within the hour.*

"Oh." Jos hadn't realized that when the griffin said King Iaor and Lord Bertaud were coming, he meant *right now*. He glanced uncertainly around the meadow, down the slope where riders might come at any moment around the corner of the mountain. He did not know what Kairaithin had in mind, but he was almost completely certain that he did not want to meet the king or Bertaud or anyone in their party. "I could go…I could go somewhere, I suppose." Though he did not know where. He would need the shelter of the cottage at dusk…

You will stay here. You will speak for me, said the griffin.

Jos stared at him. "I will? What would I possibly say?"

What occurs to you to say. But Kairaithin paused then, and Jos realized he was not as arrogant as that command had made him seem; that he was, in some way, actually uncertain. He said, *Bertaud son of Boudan knows me… as well as any man. But you have gazed down at that Wall from almost the time it was made, and you know it well. And you know Kes.*

"Not anymore," said Jos grimly.

As well as any creature living. Better, I believe, than I. In some ways, better even than her iskarianere. *I wish you to explain what you know to the king of men and to his people. It is better for a man to speak to men.*

The belief that the King of Feierabiand would listen to *Jos*, of all men living, showed a certain wild optimism coupled with a complete lack of understanding of the way men made decisions. Or possibly, Jos realized bleakly, it showed an accurate assessment of how dangerous matters were, that Kairaithin considered that, regardless of all else, the King of Feierabiand would indeed feel himself compelled to listen respectfully to a Casmantian spy—an ex-Casmantian spy, a traitor to his own king, a man who had betrayed his own people for the sake of a Feierabian-den girl. And—to cap the tale—a man who had then not even managed to keep the girl.

Iaor Daveien Behanad Safiad was not an overtall man, nor overbroad, nor did he care to make an excessive display, except now and then and to produce a specific effect, at court—usually at his more formal summer court, in high northern Tiearanan. Or so Jos had heard, long ago, when he had heard everything from everyone. Then, poised at a small, neat inn at Minas Ford, on the road that led from Terabiand on the coast up the length of Feierabiand to graceful Tiearanan, he had been so placed as to hear and overhear both the most urgent tidings from the indiscreet servants of important lords and merchants and the most trivial gossip from farmers' wives and the servants of courtiers. Though Jos was generally quiet himself, other men tended to speak freely in his presence. This was a natural gift that had served him well…until the time came when he had been commanded to definitively act against Feierabiand, and chose not to. For Kes's sake.

He hardly remembered the state of mind and heart that had driven him at that time.

But he remembered Iaor Safiad, who, though he was not an exceptionally big man and though he made no great display, nevertheless drew the eye. And he remem-bered Lord Bertaud, the king's servant and friend, whom Jos had once gone out of his way to mislead regarding the number and disposition of the griffins that had come into Feierabiand... None of that had ended in any way as Jos or his master in the Casmantian spy network had expected. No. Events had unrolled down a different path. Because of Kes. Who now was still driving events, and still in no manner anyone could have foreseen.

Jos strongly suspected that neither King Iaor nor Lord Bertaud had forgotten him, or the role he had played— the role he had tried to play. No more than he'd forgotten them.

And Kairaithin thought he could speak to those men?

Jos stood in front of his cottage, his arms crossed uneasily across his chest, watching the riders come around the curve of the mountain. Kairaithin lounged near at hand, his great catlike body curved in a comfortable, relaxed pose against a shining granite cliff. Above him, sheets of ice became, under the griffin's influence, plumes of mist. Jos was grateful for his supportive presence, but he knew that Kairaithin's relaxed pose was an illusion—though it was a good pose and he was not quite certain how he could tell it was false. Nor did he understand the griffin's tension. Kings and lords, all the formal titles of men, what did they mean to a griffin? To one of the most powerful of all griffins; a griffin mage who, exile or no, undoubtedly still cast even his own former students thoroughly in the shade?

Nevertheless, Jos knew that Kairaithin was tense. The knowledge made him anxious in his turn. He had had a lot of practice, once, in masking his thoughts and emotions from the eyes of men. He hoped he had not lost the knack of it.

Iaor had brought only half a dozen men, besides Lord

Bertaud. Well, that was reasonable. They had come merely to look at the Great Wall, Jos presumed, and getting an army up into these rugged mountains would be a nightmare. If it could be done at all. This broken rock where the nameless river had its birth might be called a pass, but that was nearly a courtesy term rather than a strictly accurate description. One could get horses less than a third of the way, and to get all the way up to this high meadow, even mules needed considerable luck, shoes made specially by the best makers to provide better grip, and perfect weather. Jos tried to work out the logistics that would be required to bring an actual army through these mountains and gave up at once. Definitely a nightmare.

Probably King Iaor hoped that *looking* was all he and his people would be required to do. They would come up to this vantage, look down at the Wall, and worry over the cracks where the steam plumed out into the air. But then they would find that the cracks after all grew no worse. That the damage, whatever had caused it, had ceased. That the Wall would after all hold for a hundred years, or a thousand, and that no one now living would need to concern himself about the antipathy between fire and earth because the two would not, in this age, come actively into conflict. That was probably what they hoped. Jos had no conviction that they would discover any such happy outcome. He certainly could not give them any reassurance.

The riders slowed as they breasted the crest of the path—if one could call that rugged cut through the stone a path—crossed the silver thread of the stream, came single-file into the little meadow and up to the cottage, and reined in their mules. The mules were too tired and too glad of the meadow to object very strenuously to Kairaithin's presence, though the goat, wiser or not as weary, had not ventured from its hidden nook beneath the bed.

King Iaor had changed very little, was Jos's immediate judgment, but Lord Bertaud had changed a great deal.

The king had grown perhaps a touch more settled, a touch more solid—that was how Jos described the quality to himself. More solid in his authority and his confidence. Though by no means an old man, Iaor Safiad had been king now for some decades and had grown by this time comfortable with his kingship. He had married just before the...trouble, six years ago. Jos knew nothing of recent events at the Feierabianden court, or any court, but looking at the king now, he was willing to lay good odds that the Safiad's marriage had prospered. He had that air of satisfaction with himself and with life, though rather overlaid just now by weariness and unease.

King Iaor was a hard man to read, kings having as much need to conceal their thoughts and emotions as spies. But to Jos, as the king gazed down at the Wall and the plumes of steam rising from it, he looked tired and a little disgusted, as though he found the possible failure of the Wall a personal provocation. That, too, was the reaction of a man with a family as well as the reaction of a king who was concerned to protect his people.

Then Iaor pulled his gaze from the imposing, disturbing sight below to give Jos a little nod of recognition and acknowledgment.

Jos nodded back, not bowing because this was not his king. He said formally, "Your Majesty," which was the proper form of address in Feierabiand.

"Jos," said the king in a neutral tone. His gaze shifted to the griffin lounging near at hand. "Anasakuse Sipiike Kairaithin. What have we here?" He nodded down the pass toward the Wall.

Kairaithin did not answer, leaving Jos to speak—a man to speak to men, indeed. Jos said, "The plumes show where the Wall is cracked through. The cracks appeared some days ago." He was embarrassed to admit that he did not know precisely how many days. In these latter years, he had become unaccustomed to counting off each passing day according to the proper calendar and found the habit difficult to reacquire. He said instead, which was perhaps more to the point, "The fire mages on the desert side have been trying to split the Wall open along those cracks. Not Kairaithin. Two young griffin mages. And Kes." He glanced at the somber Kairaithin, whose student the girl had been, then turned his gaze back at the king, who had known her, briefly, when she had been human. Or mostly human.

King Iaor lifted an eyebrow, but it was Lord Bertaud who spoke. "She has become wholly a creature of fire, then." It was a statement rather than a question, and there was an odd note to the lord's voice, a note that Jos did not understand. He gave Lord Bertaud a close look.

Where the king had grown a bit more solid and comfortable over the past years, Jos thought that Lord Bertaud had grown darker of mood and more inward. There was a grimness underlying his manner and tone, not something born of the anxieties of the moment, Jos thought, but something that had been shaped out of a deeper trouble or grief. Some grief of love lost, or some private longing deferred? Or something less recognizable? Jos saw

the deliberation with which Bertaud avoided meeting
Kairaithin's eyes, and wondered at it. *I carried word
to Bertaud son of Boudan*, the griffin had said. Why to
Bertaud?

Jos knew very little about Lord Bertaud; nothing about
what the man had done with himself after those strange
and difficult events six years ago. He had not been curious about the world for years. He had, indeed, been
determinedly incurious, and it left him uncomfortably
ignorant now.

In the early years, when she had still remembered
dimly what she had been, Kes had come sometimes to tell
him about her life among the griffins. She had described
to Jos the beauty of fire and the empty desert, and sometimes she and Opailikiita had carried him high aloft
through the crystalline fire of the high desert night. It had
been beautiful, and Jos had longed for wings of his own,
that he might ride those high winds himself. But Kes had
never been very interested in the human world even when
she had been human, and after she became a creature of
fire she cared even less for the affairs of men.

In those years, and from time to time even now, it was
Sipiike Kairaithin who brought Jos the odd tidbit of news
from the human world. Certainly it had been Kairaithin
who had explained how and why the Great Wall had been
made, though never why he had bent his strength against
his own people to help build it. The griffin had mentioned
Bertaud now and again, however, and Jos understood,
or thought he had understood, that Kairaithin stood as
something of a friend to the man—as much as a griffin
could befriend a man. He had envisioned a relationship
something like the one he himself shared with the griffin:

ill-defined, perhaps, and awkward to explain, but a relationship nevertheless.

But what he saw in Bertaud, when the lord let his gaze cross the griffin's, was something he did not recognize at all.

She has become wholly a creature of fire, the lord had said. Jos looked at him for another moment and then answered slowly, "Well, lord, yes, I fear so. She has forgotten her past, or I expect she remembers it like a dream, maybe. She's a mage now. The most powerful fire mage in the desert, I imagine—excepting Sipiike Kairaithin." He gave Kairaithin a little nod.

"I see." Bertaud was looking at Jos now. His tone had become almost painfully neutral.

Jos tried not to wince. He kept his own tone matter-of-fact. "Tastairiane Apailika is her *iskarianere* now. She's listening to him, I guess, and she's trying to break the Wall from the far side. And she will, too, eventually, if she keeps prying at those cracks."

"Tastairiane," said King Iaor. "That white griffin. The savage one."

"Yes," said Jos, not adding that all griffins were savage. Anyway, the king was, in every way that mattered, right about Tastairiane.

"Little Kes has become that one's friend?"

"Friend" was not precisely correct, and though Kes was far from large, no one who met her now would say "little Kes" in anything like that tone. But Jos merely said, "Yes," again, because this, too, was enough like the truth to serve. He added, "She and Tastairiane Apailika are alike in their ambition to see the desert grow, I think, and alike in their scorn for all the country of earth. The Wall was well and wisely made"—and how he wished he'd been there himself to watch that spectacular making!—"but now it's started cracking, it won't hold long, not with fire magic striking through against the earth magic on the other side. Do we know what caused the cracks in the first place?"

King Iaor looked at Bertaud, who looked at Kairaithin. The griffin said nothing, only the feathers behind his head ruffled a little and then flattened again. Bertaud glanced uneasily away and said, "We've discussed this. We have an earth mage in our company, though under strict orders to keep hold of himself. But his first thought is to wonder whether the wild magic of these mountains, allied to ordinary earth magic but not of it, might possibly work against the magecraft set in that wall." He cleared his throat and added to Kairaithin, "You might discuss this with him, if both of you can bear to, well, speak to one another." He cleared his throat again, ducked his head a little, and finished, "We did send a message to Casmantium. To the Arobern, and his mages, and most particularly to Tehre Amnachudran Tanshan."

Lady Tehre was the Casmantian maker who, along with the last remaining cold mages of Casmantium, had been responsible for raising the Wall. Jos had got a brief sketch of those events from Kairaithin, but only a rough one. From the significant glance Bertaud gave the griffin mage, Kairaithin might have left out a good many details.

Of course you have, the griffin said, without any inflection in the smooth, dangerous voice that slid around the edges of their minds. *I will speak to the earth mage,*

*as he is here and perhaps may understand the southern
side of the Wall. But if this making does not stand*—he
meant the Great Wall, of course—*it is difficult to imagine
what more Casmantian strength can do.*

This was hard to argue, and for a long moment they all
stood in silence.

"Well," said King Iaor, glancing around at them all
and then looking away, down toward the Great Wall and
the rising billows of steam where the magic of earth met
inimical fire, "at least we are here, where all these events
are unrolling before us. We must be grateful for fair
warning and a chance to prepare, or else we would all be
standing in the south with no idea what might be coming down on us and no opportunity to influence events at
all." He looked at Kairaithin. "We are grateful for that.
And for any other assistance you might see your way to
offering."

The griffin said nothing.

After an awkward moment, the king added to Jos,
"If you would be so good, I think we would welcome
a chance to speak further—of Kes, and Tastairiane
Apailika"—he stumbled only a little over the name, awkward for a human tongue—"and of what you think might
happen if that Wall breaks."

"Yes," said Jos, without enthusiasm. He had no idea
what would happen if the Great Wall shattered, or what
they would be able to do about it in the event. But he said,
"I have little. But there is a fire, at least, and if Kairaithin
would be good enough to take the shape of a man, we
may all be able to fit under my roof." If they could get
the goat out from under the bed, they would also be more

comfortable, he did not add. And wondered whether he might be able to send a couple of the king's men to find the scattered hens.

But even that thought was not quite enough to make him smile.

CHAPTER 8

Mienthe had been glad to see the queen and her little daughters heading out of Tiefenauer. She was relieved to know they would soon be safe in Sihannas. But she'd never for an instant intended to leave the town herself. She didn't understand why anyone had supposed she would flee. Even if she wanted to—and she was willing to admit to herself that maybe she did—she couldn't. How could she? She was sorry Bertaud would worry when he heard she had refused to leave Tiefenauer, but he would understand. She thought he would. She was fairly certain.

Anyway, by the time her cousin heard about Linularinum's boldness, she hoped that Tan's enemies would have learned that he had escaped them. Then the Linularinan force would go away again and she could send her cousin *that* word, which would be much better than having him just hear that Tiefenauer was under attack.

Anyway, Bertaud must be in the mountains now, as

hard as he and the king had intended to ride. He might be looking down at the Wall right now. Then he would have other things to worry about than herself or even the Delta.

As few as five days for the Wall to break, that's what the griffin mage had said. Maybe as many as ten, but maybe as few as five. Four, now. Or even three, by the coming dawn. But maybe as many as seven, she reminded herself. And anyway, the Wall wasn't *her* concern. Bertaud would fix the Wall. He would get his griffin friend to help him and put things right.

And after he did, she wanted him to find a message waiting for him that assured him she was safe and the Delta was safe and the Linularinan force had once more withdrawn to its proper side of the river.

She hoped she would be able to send him that message. She thought she would. Anyway, she doubted she was personally in any danger. No matter how enraged Tan's enemies might be, they would undoubtedly think backward and forward before doing harm to the Lady of the Delta.

No. She was safe enough. *Tan* was the one who, Mienthe thought, might face pursuit and danger; Tan, who despite any other suggestions he might have made, was clearly the Linularinan objective. Or one objective, at least, for it did not seem reasonable that such an outrageous Linularinan action had *only* Tan in mind. Though, indeed, in recent days, Mienthe had lost confidence in caution or good sense or even clear sanity on the Linularinan side of the river.

Mienthe stood in the unlit solar, looking out across the gardens and the town but following Tan cross-country in her mind. The road to Kames was rougher and narrower than the river road, deeply rutted by traffic in the muddy spring, despite all that makers had done to build the road properly. And the countryside was cut through by numberless streams and sloughs and even a small river or two. A man couldn't ride fast on that road, never mind how skilled a rider he might be or how good the horse.

She wanted urgently to know Tan was safe—she even almost wished she'd gone to Kames with him. At least she wished she *could* have. She could have made sure he was welcomed by the staff at her father's house. Sighing, she turned away from the windows, went out into the lantern-lit hallway. There were three guardsmen there, assigned to stay with her while this strange night played itself out. She wanted to ask them what was going on out in the town, but of course they would know no more than she. Less, since they hadn't been gazing out the solar windows. Unless— "Has there been news?" she asked them.

They shook their heads. "We'd have sent any messages on to you anyway, my lady," one of them said. "But there's nothing. Only what we knew already. There's fighting. But so far as we know, for all they caught us by surprise, we're still holding them on the other side of the square."

Mienthe nodded.

"We'll send immediately if there's any other word," the guardsman promised her.

"Yes," murmured Mienthe, and went back into the solar. She opened one of the windows and let in the chill of the night air and the distant sound of shouting and battle. Closer at hand there was almost no sound at all: The few remaining servants were keeping close and quiet, as though if they were very still, danger might not find them. Though in fact there was another faint sound, like someone singing ... Well, no, that was ridiculous; the sound was nothing like singing, but then Mienthe did not know how better to describe it.

The sound was getting louder, too, though it was still very faint. It might not be at all like a melody, but it was also not the sort of patternless sound the wind might make whistling past thin leaves or knife-edged grasses. It wound up and around, up and around, up and around.

Mienthe found that she was trying to follow the sound, only it turned and turned back on itself, wound itself higher and higher ... She could not actually hear it; it had become too high and faint to be heard. Only she could *feel* it, turning and turning, and that was when she realized at last that she was somehow listening to some kind of mageworking. That she had been listening to it for some time, and that she'd somehow been wound up in it herself. She could no longer see the shine of lamplight against the glass of the windows, or the dim shapes of the town outside, or the stars above, or the sparks from the torches guardsmen carried out in the gardens. In fact, she could not see even her own hands, though she thought she lifted them and opened and closed them before her eyes. She might have been sitting in a chair, or standing, or lying in her own bed, dreaming. She could not tell. She could see nothing, hear nothing. There was only the dark, winding tight all about her, and the sound that was not exactly a sound and that she could no longer hear.

Young people who discovered the mage gift waking in them went to high Tiearanan to study, those who found in themselves the necessary dedication. That was not all of them, not nearly. Mienthe had known one boy, a servant's son. When the boy, whose name was Ges, had been about twelve or fourteen, his mother had shown Bertaud a kitchen spoon made of delicate, opalescent stone and nervously explained that it had been ordinary wood until her son had stirred soup with it, and now look! Bertaud had run his fingers over the spoon and asked the boy whether he had indeed changed it, and Ges had answered, even more nervously, that he didn't know but he was afraid to touch anything else. He'd said that he thought he'd started to hear the voices of the earth and the rain—the earth spoke in a deep, grinding mutter, he said, and the myriad voices of the rain flashed in and out, glittering.

Mienthe had been jealous of the boy, not because of the spoon or even because he could hear the voices hidden in the rain, but because he'd gone to Tiearanan. Her cousin had given Ges money, and more to his mother, and sent a man of his with them, and though the man and the mother had returned to the Delta before the turning of the year, the boy had not. Mienthe supposed he was a mage now—or maybe still studying to be a mage, because his mother had said they studied for a long time and she didn't know how any boy could have the patience for it, but that Ges had seemed to like it. But then, he'd always been a quiet, patient sort of boy, she'd added, with understandable pride.

Mages—young people who woke into magecraft and then actually decided to be mages—studied for years to learn how to use their power, and here Mienthe was, trapped in the dark, with a single high-pitched note winding up around her, and neither teachers nor time to study.

She did not panic. Or maybe she did panic. She had no way to run in circles, and no way to hear herself if she screamed, so how could she even tell? There was nothing in the dark with her except the inaudible whining note— other people heard the glittering voices of the rain, and here she was with nothing but this unpleasant mosquito-whine. That seemed almost funny, though not really.

Mienthe followed the sound she almost heard because it was the only thing she could follow and she could not think of anything else to do. She could not have said how she followed it, because she had no sense of actual movement. Nevertheless, she pursued it up and around, up and around, up and around. She found herself curving in a tight inward path. It wound infinitely tight, she knew. It would never, ever let her out…she might have panicked then. She wanted to panic, but she still had no way to scream or flail about or cry, so instead she fled back the way she had come, down and around, down and down further still.

The sound deepened and deepened. Mienthe found she could *see* it, running before her, a narrow, faint ribbon of glimmering light—well, it was not light and it did not glimmer, but it was like that, in a way. It widened, and widened again. Mienthe could not see her own body, she could not see anything but the ribbon of light, but she imagined herself running, her legs moving, her arms, the impact of her feet on the road, the wind of her own motion against her face.

The ribbon widened and widened, and opened; Mienthe skidded down it at a great rate so that she began to be afraid of falling, of the height from which she might fall, of where she might fall to, only she was more afraid of stopping, of being trapped motionless within the confines of the path. Though it was not very confining, anymore. It had widened so far it seemed to encompass the world. Its faint light surrounded her, pale as the glimmer of moonlight on pearl, and then she saw that a faint light *did* surround her, that it *was* moonlight, and with a tremendous sense of motionless, forceless impact, she found that she was standing once more in the night-dark solar, with the windows open before her and moonlight pouring through her hands and the breeze chilly against her face.

There was no whining spiral wrapping itself around her, no blind darkness. Only the ordinary night, and the sounds of men calling to one another and of distant battle. But in a way, she almost thought she could still see that rising ribbon of light twining through the darkness, and the deep hum the spiral had made still echoed somewhere—she could not tell whether she was only remembering the sound it had made or whether she was still truly hearing that sustained note that was not quite music. Or, if she was still hearing it, whether that was only in her mind or actually out in the world.

Blinking, she set her hands on the windowsill and shook her head. She tried to decide whether she'd ever truly heard—seen—experienced that strange magecrafted spiral at all. Whether she'd drawn it into the night air herself, or . . . No, she knew, even as the thought occurred to her, that *she* hadn't drawn this spiral.

A Linularinan mage had drawn it. Someone who had meant to trap her in his crafting? She was afraid that might be so. Tan's enemies might not have known she existed earlier...Could that have been only the previous night? Everything had been happening so fast, and nothing that happened made any sense. Except that maybe the Linularinan mages had discovered her, or had realized that she was their enemy, or had decided that they needed to clear her out of their way before they renewed their search for Tan. *That* made sense.

Mienthe took a breath that was half a sob and pushed herself away from the window.

The guardsmen who had previously been in the hall were gone, replaced by three others. Mienthe wondered whether the shift had been about to change when she'd stepped out earlier or whether she had been caught in that magecrafted spiral much longer than she'd thought. Though it couldn't have been *so* much longer, or she supposed it would not still be night. Unless it was some other night? No—it couldn't have been that long, or the guardsmen would surely look a great deal more disturbed. She felt relieved but also surprised, as though it would really have been easier to believe that days had passed. Or weeks. Or years.

"I'm going outside," she said abruptly.

"My lady—" the senior of the guardsmen protested, but Mienthe went past him without pausing and ran down the stairs, taking them two at a time like a child, and thrust open the door that led to the gardens and, past the gardens, to the stables and mews.

She stopped there, right outside the door. The clamor of battle seemed much closer—much too close—she could make out individual voices shouting within the clamor, hear the thudding of horses' hooves on cobbled streets, see the flash of swords through the shrubbery. A single arrow rose in a long, high arch, its wicked steel point shining like a chip of ice in the moonlight. The long smooth track of its flight caught Mienthe's eye and she watched it rise, seem to hesitate at the apex of its flight, and then fall. It sliced through the air with a high, singing sound and, by some singular chance of battle, buried itself in the garden earth directly before Mienthe's feet. She stared down at the humming feather-tipped shaft and thought how oddly like the hum of the spiral its whistling flight had sounded.

"Lady!" one of the guardsmen said urgently, catching hold of her arm. "Lady—"

"Yes," Mienthe said dazedly.

"You can't stand here in the garden!" the guardsman said. "It's not safe!"

This was abundantly clear, yet Mienthe resisted his pull. She did not even know why. She began to speak, but then did not know what to say. Somewhere near at hand, men were shouting. Somewhere even closer, someone screamed, a high, agonized, bewildered sound.

"It was a horse, that was only a horse!" said the guardsman when Mienthe flinched and gasped. "But it might be *you* next time, lady! You can't stay here!"

Mienthe stared at the man. If she'd meant to flee Tiefenauer, she should have gone with the queen. She'd thought the Linularinan commanders would send someone to the great house. She'd thought...It was hard to remember what she'd thought. But it certainly hadn't occurred to her that Linularinan mages might specifically attack *her*. And if they did—*if* they did—she turned suddenly and looked east, as though she could see right through the town and the surrounding marshes and past the rivers and upper woodlands, right to Kames at the very edge of the Delta. Where she had sent Tan. Where, she found herself convinced, his Linularinan enemies would pursue him. Even there.

And she would not be with him. She would not be there to counter any Linularinan mage who found him. Because the Linularinan mages had found her here, and if their first attack had failed, then they would only try again. Unless the ordinary swords the Linularinan soldiers carried killed her first.

Mienthe caught her breath, shook free of the guardsman's grip on her arm, and ran for the stables.

There were no horses there. "They took them all—the town guard needed them," said the senior guardsman, looking sick with dismay. "We didn't know—we didn't know you'd need them, my lady."

Mienthe stared at him. She said at last, "How could you have known? Where's Geroen?"

The guardsmen did not know.

"East," said Mienthe. "East. I'll go on foot." She took a step that way and found the three guardsmen falling in around her. She started to protest, but then did not know why she should object. And then she did: If the Linularinan mages found her again, she knew she would not be able to protect these men. But she could not send them away. She needed their help, and besides, they would not go.

There was fighting immediately to the south and west of the great house, and more than a few disturbing sounds to the north, but the east seemed relatively clear. The cobbled streets were narrow and dark, well suited to barricades, and there were plenty of barricades. The

Delta had always been pressed between Linularinum and Feierabiand; a large proportion of all the male townsfolk belonged to the militia, or had, and most of the rest were willing to fight. Even some of the women would fight: Plenty of upper windows held a woman with a bow, overlooking her husband or son in the streets below.

And the people recognized Mienthe, which surprised her—they would look at her guardsmen and then at her, and then they would haul back an overturned cart or some other part of a barricade to let her through. At first she thought they would be dismayed to see her fleeing the great house, but instead they nodded to her and smiled grimly and promised her that those Linularinan bastards, begging her pardon, would have a hard time getting through *these* streets.

Mienthe hoped they were right, but she couldn't believe how quickly the Linularinan soldiers, however careless their fathers might have been, had pressed through the town to come to the great house. She thought she could almost *feel* them, or someone, behind her: a dark, looming, seeking presence that pressed hard at her back, humming with power. She thought they knew where she was—she found herself terrified, certain that if she looked over her shoulder she would find someone there. When one of her guardsmen put a hand on her arm, she whirled, only the tightness of her throat keeping her from a scream.

"There's some Linularinan company up ahead there," whispered the man, not so much to Mienthe as to the other two men. "Hear that? That's not townsfolk up there."

Mienthe realized he was right. Up ahead, where the

town gave way to farms on the drier bits of land and marshes between the farms, there was a low sound of men moving. A lot of men, moving through the darkness, coming into the town from the east. Muttered curses as they moved without a light over rough ground and muddy roads...The east should have been clear, but some clever Linularinan officer had thought to send a force around this way, either to block Tan's escape or to flank Tiefenauer's defenders. Mienthe found she had no doubt that the Linularinan officers knew about Tan, or at least that someone in Tiefenauer might break for the east and that they should stop him. It occurred to her that they might even have caught him—no. She took a breath and let it out again, slowly. Tan was, she knew, well away, far to the east. If this Linularinan company had been sent around to the east to stop him, it had gotten to its position too late.

But not too late to block *her*.

The senior of the guardsmen touched her arm again and jerked his head to the right, *This way*. Mienthe followed him down a narrow lane until he stopped in a doorway. The door was locked and no one answered the guardsman's cautious rap, but the doorway was in deep shadow and offered at least a little shelter. "Likely they'll go on past," whispered the guardsman. "Likely they won't search too close—only enough to be sure there's not a great lot of militia or guardsmen ready to come after them and stick them in the back. But then, we're obviously guard, and that means you're obviously a lady, and I don't know what they'd do if they found us."

The guardsman was probably thinking the Linularinan soldiers might take Mienthe as a hostage, but what

Mienthe thought was someone in that company might recognize her as the one who had rescued Tan from their hands. She had a vivid, awful picture of coming face-to-face with Tan's particular enemy, Istierinan. He would... if he caught her, he would...She had no idea what he might do, and she didn't want to find out.

The guardsman must have read some of this in her face because his expression became, if possible, even more grim. He said, "You two, lead them off if they come this way. My lady, if you will please come with me." He led Mienthe farther down the lane. "There'll be a side street or alley," he muttered to her. "We'll get around them in the dark. Even if they do spot us, they'll not look too close. A man and a woman fleeing the town, that's nothing to draw attention. Here, lady, watch your step."

Mienthe was well past worrying about a little mud. The street was too narrow for the moonlight to provide any illumination; it was too dark to see even the cobbles of the street. It was so dark there was a constant risk of running headlong into an unexpected wall, but she could hear—she thought she could hear—the tramp of soldiers entering the town. The sounds echoed oddly in the narrow streets so that it was hard to tell their direction and distance, but she was sure it was soldiers. Boots, mostly, and the unidentifiable sounds of a lot of men moving in company, but occasionally also the ring of shod hooves. That was bold, but then maybe the Linularinan soldiers had a few people who could speak to horses in that company; the gift wasn't possessed *only* by the folk of Feierabiand, any more than straight light brown hair was possessed only by the people of Linularinum. But the sound of hooves made her check and turn her head, wishing *she* had an affinity for horses and could call one away from those soldiers.

"Lady!" whispered the guardsman, realizing Mienthe had paused. He, too, was all but invisible in the darkness.

Mienthe took a step forward.

Light bloomed beyond the guardsman, lamps carried high on poles so that their light shone out before the approaching soldiers—another company, or part of the same one, but either way wholly unexpected. The guardsman spun around, his hand going to his sword and then falling away because there were far too many soldiers to fight. But then he drew after all, setting himself in the middle of the narrow lane.

"No!" Mienthe cried, understanding that the guardsman meant to delay the Linularinan soldiers just that small time that might let her escape, and understanding as well that if he fought, he would die. "No!" she said again. "Don't fight them!" Then she whirled and fled back the way they had come, hoping that once she was clear, the guardsman would let himself surrender, knowing that if she stayed he would certainly fight, and anyway she did not dare be captured herself.

Behind her, swords rang. Before her, the darkness offered not safety—there was no safety anywhere—but at least some measure of concealment, at least until she ran into the other company of Linularinan soldiers. She looked for a way to get away from the lane, to slip away sideways. She tested one door and then another, but both were locked and no one came when she pounded her hand against the doors. She dreaded every moment that she might see the shine of lamplight off the painted wood

of the buildings and the damp cobbles, or hear the sounds
of approaching soldiers. Above, the moonlight slid across
the shingles of the roofs.

Ahead of her, Mienthe heard the flat sounds of boots
on the cobbles. Light shone dimly, not yet near, but coming nearer. Behind her, she was almost certain she could
hear more boots. She stopped, looked quickly about, and
then leaped for a handhold on the windowsill of a house.
The window was shuttered tight, but she got her foot up
on the doorknob of the house and hauled herself upward.
The windowsill provided her next foothold, and she tried
hard not to think about falling—she would break her
ankle on the cobbles and then she would certainly be
caught—the moonlight picked out the details of the upper
story of the building, but also mercilessly revealed Mienthe to anyone who glanced up from below. The upper
windows were also shuttered, but besides the balcony
there was a trellis with vines. The vines would never hold
her weight, but she thought the trellis might, and anyway
she could not find any other foothold.

Below her, the two companies of soldiers approached
from opposite directions. They would meet almost directly
below her, and then how long would it take someone to
look up? Mienthe gingerly committed her weight to the
trellis. The sweet scent of the flowers rose around her as
she crushed the vines. It seemed to her that the fragrance
alone would draw someone to gaze upward, and on this
clear night there was no hope of clouds to veil the moon.
Mienthe tried not to make a sound as she pulled herself
upward, got first a hand and then a knee onto the balcony railing—the railing had seemed sturdier before she
needed to balance on it. She laid one hand flat against the

rough wood, reached upward with her other hand, and felt along the edge of the roof.

Below her, someone suddenly called out.

Mienthe didn't glance down. She was obviously a woman. Would they shoot a woman when they didn't even know who she was? Or, if there was a mage with them, would *he* know who she was? Then they might shoot her—or just climb after her—probably a soldier would think nothing of this climb. Mienthe gripped the edge of the roof with both hands and scrambled to get her foot up to the top of the trellis. For a sickening moment she thought she would lose her hold and fall. Her arms trembled with the strain. Then she got a proper foothold at last, kicked hard, heaved, and managed to haul herself up to the roof.

The roof tiles proved more slippery underfoot than Mienthe had expected. She made her way up the slope of the roof as quickly as she dared and then over the peak and down the other side. Behind her she could hear soldiers scrambling up the wall after her, and then a loud ripping, tearing sound as—she guessed—the trellis pulled away from the wall under their greater weight. The crashing noises and curses that followed were gratifying, but how long would it take the rest of the soldiers to get out of the lane and around to the other side of the buildings? So long that Mienthe would be able to get down and run for some other hiding place? What hiding place, that they could not immediately find?

Reaching the edge of the roof, she indeed found a handful of soldiers there before her, along with a mounted officer. Two of the soldiers had bows, but it was the officer on the horse who frightened her. Without even thinking about it, Mienthe crouched, ripped up a heavy tile, and flung it down. Though she had not stopped to aim, the tile sketched a wide curving path through the air and hit the man in the face.

The Linularinan officer crumpled backward off his horse, but Mienthe, in flinging the tile, lost her precarious balance, staggered sideways, tried helplessly to catch herself on the empty air, and fell off the roof.

She did not have time to cry out, but also she did not exactly fall, although she did not know what other word she could use to describe what happened. It was as though she followed the same curving path along which she had thrown the tile; it was as though she rode a sense of balance she had not recognized until she fell along an invisible current in the wind or an unseen ribbon of moonlight. There was no time to be amazed. She fell, and then she was standing on the muddy ground next to the startled horse. The animal shied violently, only Mienthe caught his rein and flung herself into the saddle, wrenched his head around, and let him go.

Only one soldier tried to catch her, and he missed his grab for the horse's rein. The horse's shoulder struck him and flung him aside, and then Mienthe was past, weaving through the maze of the town's last scattered buildings and then pounding along a muddy moonlit road, heading out into the marshes and sloughs of the wide Delta.

She did not look back. If anyone followed her, she did not know it.

Mienthe did not stop again until near dawn, after putting miles of tangled, difficult country between herself and Tiefenauer. She had not kept to the road but headed straight for Kames. Or, at least, straight for Tan. She knew exactly where he was. Despite everything, she felt a great lightening of her spirits to know that he was far away to the east and that she was heading toward him. She found it difficult to imagine how she had let him ride east without her, almost impossible to picture herself heading, now, either north after the queen or back toward Tiefenauer.

The ordinary night sounds of the marshes surrounded her: the rippling splash of a stream, the rattle of the breeze through reeds, the rustle of leaves and the creak of leather as her tired horse shifted his weight. Above, the moon stood low over the dark shapes of the trees. To either side, water glinted like metal. Mienthe was cold, shivering; she could not feel her feet and her fingers were cramped on the reins. No one else was in sight, and though she held her breath and listened, she could not hear any voices calling.

Birds called, though, sharp trills and buzzes and one rippling little song that rose and rose until it seemed it must go beyond sound to silence, but after the song had climbed as high as it could go, it tumbled down again in a burst of notes. Mienthe knew the bird that made that song. It was a little speckled brown bird with a yellow throat. Though she could not see it in the undergrowth, she realized that she could see branches against the paling sky and that dawn had arrived.

There was a raw chill in the air. Though she worried a little about the smoke, Mienthe made a small fire. Steam rose from her clothing and boots. The boots, which had been good ones, ankle-high and embroidered around the tops, were undoubtedly ruined. She hoped they would be wearable for a little while yet; a day at least, until she reached her father's house in Kames. She did not know what she would find there. She did not actually expect a welcome, or, unexpectedly determined as Tan's enemies seemed to be, much safety. But she thought she might at least hope for dry boots.

Now, on her own and more or less safe, she had time to think—too much time and far too much solitude for her peace of mind.

She wondered where the queen and the royal party might be. Safe in Sihannas? She wondered about Tan. How far in front of her was he? Would he find her father's house—would he be safe there until she could come? Would *she* be safe until she got there?

If there was a Linularinan mage behind her, he was probably much better trained than Mienthe. Only stubbornness and luck had got her out of that strange magecrafted trap in Tiefenauer, and then more luck had kept her from falling right into Linularinan hands when she toppled off that roof. She hoped the guardsmen she had left behind were all right. She did not know enough to guess whether the two might have gotten away, or whether the Linularinan soldiers might have spared the one who had set himself in their way to guard her flight.

Where, she wondered, was the Linularinan mage now? As soon as the question occurred to her, Mienthe was certain he was somewhere close by, far too close—just out of sight—probably hidden at the edge of the tangled undergrowth on the far side of the stream, looking at her. Telling herself that this was unlikely to the very edge of impossibility did no good at all. Mienthe stood up, peering intently back across the stream, but she could see nothing. Birds called: long liquid trills and rattling buzzes and a sweet three-note song that sounded like someone calling *mock-e-lee*, *mock-e-lee*.

There was, Mienthe gradually realized, no one there. The birds would not be singing so freely if anyone was hidden there—and no one was, anyway. A Linularinan mage would hardly have crept after her by himself and hidden to watch her. How silly she had been, to feel one might have! The conviction was fading—it was gone, and Mienthe could not even really remember how it had felt to be so certain. A ridiculous certainty! No mage would be slipping about by *himself*, and she could hardly fail to notice a whole Linularinan company stomping through the marshes after her. And the Linularinan mage, whoever he might be, could not really be *very* powerful, or Mienthe would never have been able to wind herself backward out of his magecrafted trap.

There was nothing to fear. Any sensible person could see that there was nothing at all to fear in the marshes, however damp, or in this clear spring dawn, no matter how chilly or uncomfortable. She told herself this, firmly, and as she cast one final uneasy glance across to the west, the sun came up above the trees and the moon became pale and transparent against the brightening sky, and then it was full day. At last. The last of her nervousness lifted like mist, warmed away by the sun. She rose stiffly and, having nothing better, rubbed the horse's legs down with handfuls of coarse marsh grass. The animal deserved better of her than muddy grasses and a tired pat, but she had no grain to give him. At least he seemed to have no serious cuts or bruises.

She could see no sign of pursuit, no suggestion that any

Linularinan in the wide world had ever defied the proper bounds of his country to cross into Feierabiand. Indeed, now that her earlier fear had eased, Mienthe found it difficult to believe that any Linularinan soldiers had actually crossed the Sierhanan at all. She felt as though she had probably dreamed everything of the past night. She thought she might awaken at any moment to find herself in her own room, lilac-scented lanterns glowing in the predawn dimness and the gentle sounds of the stirring household around her. It was hard to believe that she was already awake, that she really was cold and muddy and in desperate need of hot water and soap and tea, and that the great house lay miles and miles behind her.

No maid called her name, and neither hot water and soap nor tea appeared, alas. Only the horse shifted restlessly across the damp hillocks of mud and grass, his hooves crunching through the winter's litter and leaving deep marks in the muddy ground. Mienthe sighed, climbed to her feet—her joints creaked—and went to investigate whether there might be a bit of hard bread in the saddlebags.

There was no bread, but there was a little cloth bag of dried apples and another of tough jerky. Mienthe ate the jerky and fed the apples to the horse, and after that felt rather more cheerful. The horse, a big sorrel animal that looked as though he had Delta blood in him, pointed his ears forward and seemed a little more satisfied with the morning as well, even when Mienthe put on her wet boots, kicked out the fire, and lifted herself—rather awkwardly, with neither mounting block nor helpful groom—back into the saddle.

The horse picked his way slowly among broad-boled

trees in woodlands that did not seem ever to have known an ax, lipping at leaves and the grasses that grew in sunny glades among the trees. While the horse might breakfast on leaves, Mienthe was not finding the jerky she'd eaten a wholly adequate breakfast with which to face the long day. And her feet slipped and chafed inside her clammy boots.

It was all rather disheartening.

Mienthe kept as far as possible to drier ridges, which provided brief, welcome respites from the mud of the lower-lying regions. Her boots had begun to dry at last, but water came chest-deep on her horse in some of the unavoidable marshy areas. Mienthe kicked her feet out of the stirrups, tucked her feet up, and stubbornly kept riding east, until at last she found herself emerging from the shadows of the marshes and riding down a final bank onto the broad, hard-beaten surface of a true road, and lying before her, in the brilliance of a clear afternoon, the wide brown width of the lower branch of the Sierhanan River.

She encouraged her horse to trot. He did not want to do that, laying his ears flat and jigging sideways when she tried to make him, and after the night and day they had had Mienthe could hardly blame him. But the horse was good-tempered enough to lengthen his stride into the fast, swinging walk that was almost as fast as a trot would have been, the walk that made Delta horses so desirable as plow animals. That was good enough. Mienthe did not really want to sit a jarring trot, anyway.

There were plenty of hoof marks and the tracks of wagons and carts in the packed earth of the road, and Mienthe practiced in her mind the sorts of things she might say to startled folk she might pass, to explain her solitude and muddy, bedraggled appearance: *I barely got out of Tiefenauer in front of Linularinan soldiers … I had to cross through the marshes.* Perfectly true. Yet she did not feel she had any ability to explain what had really happened, what still might be happening. She could visualize merchants or farmers rolling their eyes: *Chased out of Tiefenauer by Linularinan mages, were you?* Mienthe knew she simply did not have the ability to make anybody believe anything of the sort. Especially not while her horse and skirts and boots were caked with mud, and her hair straggling down her back—she could not look less like a granddaughter of old Berdoen and a cousin of the Lord of the Delta.

But there were few other travelers, and although they gave Mienthe curious, sidelong glances, none of them stopped to speak to her. She passed the occasional farm-track, and from time to time pasture fences ran along the road for some way. Sometimes big, flat-faced white cattle gazed at her incuriously from behind those fences. Tall shaggy farm dogs watched suspiciously as she passed, in case she should be a swamp cat or a cattle thief, but they did not come out to the road.

This branch of the Sierhanan, like the northern branch, was cleaner and wider and better for traffic than any of the smaller Delta rivers. Boats ran along with the current— flatboats, mostly, heading downstream; now and again a keelboat being heaved back upstream by a team of oxen. But the keel road was on the other side of the river and the drovers much too far away to call to or see clearly.

For the first time, it occurred to Mienthe that even when she found her father's house, the staff there might not know her. Certainly they would not be able to see in her the nine-year-old child she had been...Would any of them even have known her when she *was* nine? A sudden, vivid memory of Tef, in the cutting garden gathering flowers for the house, came into her mind. She could almost make herself believe he would be at her father's house, living still. Tears prickled behind her eyes.

She would have felt so much more that she was riding to her proper home if she had really expected to find Tef there waiting for her. She couldn't think of her father's house as her home at all. It occurred to Mienthe that she did not even know exactly where her father's house actually *was*. Well, she knew that it was set on the river a little north of Kames proper, so she must go right past it if she kept on south on this road, but would she recognize its drive when she came to it? She experienced a sudden conviction that this was impossible, that she would not, that she would have to ride all the way into Kames and ask there for directions, like a beggar hoping for generosity from some relative who had a place at the house as a maid or stablemaster...She flushed and checked her horse, looking indecisively left toward the river, and then right, up the low wooded hill that ran up away from the river...and there were the gates.

She somehow knew the carved wooden posts at once, and the wrought-iron bands that spiraled around them; she knew the graveled track that led between avenues of great oaks and how it would curve through neatly kept woodlands to the wide gardens surrounding the big house. Though she would have said she had no clear memory of any of this from her childhood, she knew it all. She checked her horse and sat for a long moment simply staring at the gates and the graveled drive. She did not feel excited or happy to have come back to this house; was she simply too tired? But she did not even feel very relieved to have arrived. She must be much more weary than she had thought.

Or more frightened of the reception she might meet.

As soon as she thought of this, Mienthe knew it was true. She knew the people in that house would not recognize her. She wondered if they would even admit her. They might think she was an impostor who was trying to mock them and steal things to which she had no claim. Or they might think she was a madwoman who claimed to be Berdoen's granddaughter and Beraod's daughter and Bertaud's cousin because…because…Mienthe could not quite imagine why anybody would claim to be Beraod's daughter. Probably that was because her memories of her father were a little too vivid…

But Tan would be there, and *he* could tell them who she was. Mienthe found she had no doubt that he was there. That was a heartening thought. She lifted the reins, clucked to the horse, and rode up the curving drive, between the oaks and through the woodlands, and out into the gardens in the last light of the day.

The gardens were not as well-kept as she remembered them, and the house was smaller, and down the hill the river blazed through the trees as though the slanting evening light had set the water afire. Someone called, and someone else answered, and there was a sudden confusion of movement and voices and faces. Suddenly nothing was familiar, and Mienthe tried to speak to an older man who had come out to hold her reins but could not think of anything to say. She wanted to dismount but was afraid to, although she did not know why she should

be afraid—she told herself she should not be—she knew
she was being foolish—

And then a familiar voice said, "Mienthe!" and Tan
was beside her horse, offering her a hand to dismount.
His was the only familiar face she saw. She took his hand
gratefully and slid down from her horse with a sense that
she had, after all, come at last to a place of safety, a place
she knew.

CHAPTER 9

The griffins' fire mages came again to test their strength against the Wall early in the afternoon on the second day following the arrival of the King of Feierabiand and his people.

King Iaor Safiad was not there to see them. After that first icy, brilliant night, the king had taken nearly all his people and gone away again, down the difficult mountain path. He would rouse his people and make them ready—his men, of course, but most especially his mages: the earth mages of Tihannad and all those in high Tiearanan. And he would set all the smiths of both cities to make arrowheads and spearheads infused with the most solid earthbound magecraft possible. So he had said, after looking down upon the cracked Wall and consulting the young earth mage he had brought, and Lord Bertaud, and Anasakuse Sipiike Kairaithin. He had not asked Jos for his opinion, but Jos had not disagreed.

"It might hold a hundred years like that, I suppose,"

the king had said, not with any great conviction. "But it might break tomorrow, and then where will we be?" Then he had added, a touch more hopefully, to Kairaithin, "You are certain your people intend to come down upon Feierabiand if they can break that Wall? *We* have never offended them—or I had thought not. I had thought we had become something like allies…"

Had you thought so? Kairaithin had asked him. *Well, something like, perhaps, for that brief moment caught out of time. But fire cannot truly ally with earth, king of men. That wall will not shatter along all its length; it will break here, at this end, where its balance has been disturbed and where it comes hard against the mountains. If the People of Fire and Air will come past its barrier, they will do so here, in this wild country, and thus they must strike into Feierabiand and not against Casmantium.*

"But—" the king had protested.

"Tastairiane Apailika makes no distinction among the countries of men," Lord Bertaud had put in, in a low voice. "He never has. And he likes killing and blood."

Tastairiane Apailika means eventually to burn all the country of earth, Kairaithin had said. *He is determined to leave nothing but fire in all the world, with the brilliant sky above and the world empty of everything but fierce wind singing past red stone.*

"We won't permit that," Lord Bertaud had said. His voice had still been low, but Jos had heard odd notes of grief and anger and warning mingled in it. He had understood the anger and he'd thought he understood the grief, but he did not understand the warning at all. King Iaor had given him a sidelong glance, and Jos had wondered what the king might have heard in his voice. Kairaithin had not looked at him at all. Jos thought the griffin probably did not know how to hear all the undertones of a human voice.

"Indeed, we will not," King Iaor had agreed, and at dawn the next day he had taken his very silent and subdued earth mage—struck dumb by the near edge of the desert or by the Great Wall or by the enormous, contained threat of Kairaithin himself, for Jos had not heard the young man utter a single word that day or all that night—the king had taken his earth mage and the rest of his retinue and gone down again from the mountain pass to Tihannad, to make what preparations seemed possible and practical.

Lord Bertaud alone had stayed to watch the Wall. He, with his mule and another, and Jos, and the goat, and the frightened chickens, rather crowded the cottage. The rear part of the building, built out in a simple lean-to, had provided ample room for one goat but was hard put to accommodate two mules as well. Their ears brushed the rough stones when they lifted their heads and they seemed rather inclined to eat the thatch. Fortunately, the goat and the mules were willing to be amicable even in their crowded quarters. Perhaps the memory of the griffin lingered even once Kairaithin had gone, so that the presence of any other creature seemed more welcome to all three animals.

In the griffin's absence, the white cock and all but one of the hens had crept back at last to their roost, attached as it was to the cottage and providing the only reliable warmth in all the mountains. Jos was sorry about his missing hen, though. She had not been one of the most reliable layers of the flock, but he did not like to think of her lost in the cold. He gave the remaining birds an extra handful of grain to help them forget their fright, watching carefully to make certain the larger hens did not keep the smaller from the grain. Such small concerns occupied him when he did not want to go back into the main part of the cottage.

Once the king and his people had gone and the immediate subject of the Wall and its possible shattering had been exhausted, Jos did not know what to say to Lord Bertaud. Once, Jos had had the gift of speaking easily, of drawing out anyone to whom he spoke, of putting anyone he met at ease. Somewhere during the past six years, he had lost all those skills. Now he did not know how to speak to anyone but the echoing mountains and one griffin mage exiled from his own people.

Nor did the Feierabianden lord seem to know how to speak to Jos. He had too much natural tact, it appeared, to ask anything like, *So, how have you lived? How has it been for you here in these mountains, belonging neither to fire nor to earth?* Far less would he ask any such question as, *How long was it before Kes forsook your company for that of Tastairiane?* And if Lord Bertaud—thankfully—possessed too much delicacy to ask any of those questions, Jos certainly did not intend to volunteer answers.

Or it might have been that Lord Bertaud simply despised Jos too much to speak to him, aside from the commonplaces necessary in such close accommodations. Though Jos would have liked to ask about the world below the mountains, he did not care to invite any rebuff by asking questions. He did not speak. Nor did Lord Bertaud. So it was a silent day that stretched out after King Iaor had departed. There was only the clucking of the hens to break the quiet, and the song of a hardy finch or two that had come bravely up from the lower meadows, and the muted hum of the bees, and the ceaseless winds above that always sang with more or less violence through the heights.

And after the long day, it was a silent evening, and later still a deathly quiet night. The dawn that followed was cold, of course, as every dawn was cold in these mountains. But the stream did not freeze. It seldom froze even in the depths of the most savage winter; its own inherent wild magic kept it running freely across the clean stone when any sensible water would have turned to shimmering ice and frozen mist.

Jos filled his single pot and made tea from his small store. He was glad to see Lord Bertaud's saddlebags still held some good bread and hard cheese, and some dried beef, and a handful of last fall's wrinkled apples. As it happened, Jos did have two mugs, for occasionally Kairaithin took the form of a man to visit him and then the griffin mage liked tea—or perhaps was simply amused to go through the motions of human hospitality; Jos was never confident he understood the griffin's motivations in even so simple a matter. But there were two mugs. He added sugar and a pat of goat's-milk butter to the tea in each mug and handed one, steaming, to his... guest, he supposed. For a sufficiently flexible understanding of the word.

Bertaud set out the bread and other things, and took the offered mug with a nod that seemed civil enough. He took the chair nearest the fire, less inured than Jos to the chill that seemed to creep through the stone walls of the cottage. There was actually an abundance of chairs—four, recalling the days when Kes and Opailikiita and Kairaithin had all occasionally come to visit Jos. Opailikiita had never, so far as Jos knew, taken human shape, but in those days he had thought it best to be prepared in case one day she might.

Instead, Kes had gradually lost her own human form, in every sense but the least important, and had ceased to visit the cottage. Jos had more than once thought of flinging two of the chairs down from the heights, letting them shatter on the stone below. He did not know whether it was hope or apathy or sheer blind obstinacy that had held him back from doing it.

"Is it all Tastairiane Apailika?" Lord Bertaud asked at last. He was not looking at Jos. He was staring into the fire. If he had noticed that the fire burned ceaselessly without wood or coal, he had not commented. Perhaps he had not noticed. A lord would not be accustomed to building up or maintaining his own fires. And he seemed much absorbed in his own thoughts. He asked again, "Is this Tastairiane, all this determination to defeat the Wall? Without him, would the People of Fire and Air so passionately desire to burn their way across the world?"

He, too, spoke of the Wall with the slight pause and distinct emphasis that Jos felt the Great Wall deserved. And, Jos noticed, the lord called the griffins by the name they called themselves without hesitation, without even appearing to think about it. He thought once more of how Kairaithin had said, *I carried word to Bertaud son of Boudan*, and again he wondered what the relationship between the two comprised.

But he did not know the answer to the lord's question, and only shook his head.

Lord Bertaud looked Jos in the face for a moment and then suddenly got to his feet and turned away, the sharp motion of a man who could not bear to sit still. He said harshly, "I cannot—they cannot be permitted to do as they wish to do." Going to the cottage's single tight-shuttered window, he put back the shutters with quick, forceful motions and let in the cold, brilliant morning light. Then he stood perfectly still for some time, gazing out. From the direction of his gaze, he was staring down toward the Wall.

The pale dazzling light that poured in through the open window was welcome, the harsh cold much less so. Jos opened his mouth to say, *Close the shutters, man, are you mad?* but then, watching the Feierabianden lord, he did not speak. The constraint he felt was, he realized, due far less to his fear that Lord Bertaud would take offense than to his surety that the lord would not even hear him. Jos thought the other man was so deeply absorbed in his own thoughts and fears that he would not have heard the crash and roar of an avalanche coming down from the frozen heights. For the first time, it occurred to Jos that the lord's enduring silence might be due to his own distraction and worries and not to any distaste or scorn he felt for his company.

After a moment, Jos went to stand behind Lord Bertaud and look over his shoulder. The Wall glowed in the morning light, but the light that struck it from either side was entirely distinct. On the desert side, the molten sunlight poured down from a savage white sky that seemed oddly metallic. The light on that side of the barrier seemed to pool against the barrier of the Wall, thick as honey, pressing against the huge granite blocks as though it possessed actual body and weight. On the other side, ice flashed and glittered in a pale, thin brilliance that came down from the high, blue vault of the heavens, carrying no warmth at all.

From both sides, light seemed to gather and pool in the cracks in the Wall. Light ran down from the cracks like liquid; steam billowed up from them, glowing in the sunlit air, gradually dispersing as it rose into the sky.

And the griffin mages flicked abruptly into view high against the white-hot brilliant desert sky and plunged downward like striking falcons, crying in their high, fierce voices.

Ashairiikiu Ruuanse Tekainiike, youngest and most arrogant of the fire mages, burned in fiery metallic colors, bronze and gold with flickers of blazing copper. Opailikiita Sehanaka Kiistaike, a smaller and more graceful griffin of gold-flecked brown, carried Kes on her back. Even at this distance, the girl was visible as a streak of white and gold against the darker, scorching colors of the griffins.

They blazed downward without pause, straight toward the burning sands of the red desert, far too fast. But at the last moment before they would have struck the sand, they blurred into wind and light and reshaped themselves, at rest and laughing beside the towering Wall. At least Jos imagined they were laughing—at least Kes would be laughing, and the griffins blazing with their fierce silent humor, so like and yet unlike the humor of men.

Kes stepped forward and laid her hands on the Wall. Fire blazed up at her touch, licking in rich, blazing sheets up the side of the wall. Fire found the longest, deepest crack and poured into it, filled it, pried at it. Great white clouds of steam plumed upward. Jos could hear, in his mind if not in truth, the hiss of fire meeting ice. He fancied he heard the stone shift and crack under the assault of the flames; he imagined he could even hear the powerful magic of making and building that had been woven into the Wall groan with the strain as it tried to maintain the cohesion of a Wall that suddenly wanted to explode into a chaotic storm of shattered, knife-edged shards of granite and crystal.

Beside Jos, Lord Bertaud uttered a low oath. He had stepped back in shock at the deadly plunge of the griffins, and now, recovering himself, he gripped the cold stone of the windowsill and stared downward. His expression was odd. Jos had seen creatures of fire many times, but was still struck anew each time by their ferocity and beauty. He was not surprised by Bertaud's shock. What he did not understand was the intensity of grief and longing hidden behind the man's hard-held calm.

Bertaud spoke at last, his tone flat with the effort it took to contain his emotions. "Tastairiane Apailika is not there."

"If the Wall breaks, I'm sure he'll come," Jos said. He kept his voice light, dry, inexpressive.

Nevertheless, something in his tone must have caught Bertaud's attention, for the lord turned his head, his glance sharp and, at last, attentive. But what he said was, "I'm sure he will. When he does..." But his voice trailed off, and he did not complete this thought. He turned instead, caught up his fur-lined coat, and stepped across to the door. He fumbled for a moment with the cold iron of the latch and the stiff leather of the hinges, then thrust the door open and stepped out into the chilly light of the morning.

Jos followed, though his coat was nothing like as good.

He found Lord Bertaud standing out in the middle of the meadow, scowling down through the brilliant freezing air toward the distant Wall. His arms were crossed over his chest. Despite his forbidding expression and solid stance, something about his attitude struck Jos not as aggressive but as defensive, even hesitant. But when he spoke, he did not sound hesitant at all. He sounded sharp and commanding, every bit the court lord.

He did not speak to Jos, however. Instead, he called out into the crystalline silence of the heights, "Kairaithin!"

At once, as though the griffin had been waiting for that call, fire blurred out upon the meadow. Anasakuse Sipiike Kairaithin drew himself out of fire and air and the piercing stillness of the mountains. For that first moment, he wore his true form: fierce black eagle head and feather-maned neck and chest, black-clawed red lion rear, his eyes blazing with fiery darkness. Then his wings beat once, scattering fire through the air, and closed around him like a cloak as he reared up and dwindled to the shape of a man. But the black eyes he turned toward them were unchanged, strange and unsettling in the face of a man, and his massive winged shadow stretched out behind him with the same fiery black eyes.

He said, his tone unreadable, "I am here."

Lord Bertaud gave an uneasy little nod, but now that the griffin mage had come, he did not seem to know what to say.

Jos came forward, with a deferential glance for Lord Bertaud and a welcoming nod for the griffin. "Kairaithin," he said, and gestured down the slanting, jagged pass toward the Wall. "What shall we do? Shall we go down and speak to them?"

"They will not hear you," the griffin mage answered, his tone strangely bleak. He glanced at Bertaud, half lifting a hand. But when he spoke, it was to Jos. "I will take you down to them, if you wish. But a day of blood and fire is coming, and I see no way to prevent it. Only to turn it in one direction or the other. But whether it turns right or left, still there will be blood and fire."

Jos waited a moment, but still Lord Bertaud did not speak. So he asked, "If your king and the fire mages you trained and all your people call for a wind to carry them to that day of fire, why should you want to turn it?"

He thought at first that Kairaithin would not answer. The griffin mage did not look at him, but glanced once more at Bertaud and then down toward the wall. But Kairaithin said at last, "If the People of Fire and Air try to ride that wind, they will find an unexpected storm which carries all before it. They believe the earth alone will burn, but fire and earth alike will be torn asunder."

Bertaud still said nothing, but somehow Jos found that his very silence commanded attention. He looked from man to griffin and, with a spy's trick to encourage others to speak, refused to say anything himself that would disguise or slip over the palpable tension that sang between them.

"You should go down to the Wall," Kairaithin said abruptly. His black gaze was on Bertaud's face, but he was speaking to Jos. He said, "You should go speak to Keskainiane Raikaisipiike. Kes. Perhaps she will hear you. Neither Opailikiita Sehanaka Kiistaike nor Ruuanse Tekainiike are important. Kes calls their common wind and sets its direction. If Kes is turned toward a different wind, all the mages of fire will turn, and the Wall may yet stand."

"I have spoken to her," Jos protested. "You know she will not listen to me." Then he paused, because Kairaithin did know that. Jos belatedly understood that Kairaithin wished to speak to Lord Bertaud and did not want Jos to overhear what they would say to each other. He looked from one of them to the other, seeing that Lord Bertaud, too, understood Kairaithin's intention.

Bertaud did not seem surprised by this, however. He stood looking aside, down toward the Wall, his shoulder turned toward both Jos and Kairaithin. His expression was closed and forbidding. Jos thought the man was not angry, or upset, or even frightened—he would have understood any of those emotions. He did not understand what he saw in that set, rigid face. He did not understand the strange relationship between the Feierabianden lord and the griffin mage, but he was abruptly certain that it was somehow important.

Jos wanted to argue, insist upon staying here by the cottage. He wanted badly to know what the other two had to say to each other that they did not want him to overhear. But no argument of his would matter if Kairaithin did not choose to hear him. Kairaithin could simply take the Feierabianden lord elsewhere if he wished to speak to him privately. Or if the griffin mage commanded Jos to leave, Jos had no power to defy him.

But Lord Bertaud said unexpectedly, "We might all go down to the Wall, perhaps. We might all speak to Kes. I'm curious to see her." He glanced at Jos. "If you say she has forgotten us, forgotten the country of earth, then of course I believe you. But even so, I would like to speak to her."

Jos found he wanted to know what the Feierabianden

lord might find to say to Kes—and what answer Kes might give him. He nodded wordlessly.

Bertaud turned back to Kairaithin. "Those young griffins, they were your students, were they not? Have you so little influence with them now? Or have they sufficient strength to challenge you? I admit, that would astonish me."

Kairaithin did not answer at once. He regarded Lord Bertaud with close attention, as though wondering, as Jos was, what might lie behind these comments. But he said at last, "Neither Ruuanse Tekainiike nor Opailikiita Sehanaka Kiistaike could challenge me. You might well be astonished at such a suggestion. But your Kes has become in all truth Keskainiane Raikaisipiike—her intimates may perhaps still call her Kereskiita, the little fire-kitten, but she is no more a kitten."

The griffin mage looked for a moment down along the broken stone of the pass, at the white fire that blazed around Kes and poured away from her to tear at the crack in the Wall. But at last he added in a low voice, "Well, I thought that one day she might challenge me. That day has long since come. I should never have made that human child into a creature of fire. Though that was not the greatest of errors I made six years ago." He glanced back at Bertaud and away again.

Bertaud said quietly, even gently, "We can none of us turn time to run back, nor say what would have happened if we had acted other than we did. We all do as best we can. Who is to say that we would not have come to this in the end, your people and mine, whatever we did?"

After an almost imperceptible pause, the griffin mage answered. "Not to this. Not without the wind I called up.

Not without Kes." He paused again, very briefly, and corrected himself. "Keskainiane Raikaisipiike."

Bertaud looked down toward the pass. "Even now, I can't think of her by any name but Kes."

Jos wanted to say, *Speak with her for five minutes together, and you will learn to.* But he kept silent, not wishing to stop either of the others from speaking further if he wished.

Besides, even Jos, who had spoken to her not so long ago, still thought of her by the human name she had long since ceased to use.

"We will go down," Kairaithin said, and on that word shifted them all out of the bright airy heights and straight down into the powerful desert.

For the first moment, the heat was welcome, even pleasant. Jos found his numbed fingertips and his ears thawing instantly. He had almost forgotten what it was like to be really warm. This heat spread through him, unknotting muscles in his back and neck, so that he relaxed and stretched and stood straight.

After that one moment, the desert heat rapidly became excessive, and then overwhelming. The red sands were alive with delicate flames that flickered upward with every motion and then subsided, ebbing like water. The air sparkled not only with red dust but also with sparks of fire that settled downward as flecks of gold. The wind was hot and gritty and bone-dry. The very sunlight was entirely different here than it ever was in the country of earth: It hammered down upon them, brazen and heavy.

Kes turned. The young griffin mages turned with her: Opailikiita Sehanaka Kiistaike, as dependably good-humored as any griffin ever could be, the rich brown of her feathers flecked and stippled with gold, slim and beautiful. A pace to the rear, Ashairiikiu Ruuanse Teka-iniike, dark bronze and gold, his eyes brilliant gold and his temper far less certain.

Kes herself looked less human even than Kairaithin, for where the griffin mage had deliberately put on human form as a mask and a convenience, Kes was not making any pretense of being human. Only her shape was human. She seemed to have been formed out of white gold and alabaster and porcelain; she glowed from within as though white fire flowed in her veins. Maybe it did. Fire filled her hands and poured down her arms, pale fire scattered from her hair when she turned to look at them. Fire glowed in her eyes, pale and brilliant and terrible. Her shadow, flung across the red sand, was as molten as her eyes.

She was smiling, an expression that expressed nothing human. She looked happy, even joyful, but hers was a dangerous joy that held nothing of ordinary affection or gentleness. She said, "Jos!" and came to take his hands.

Jos was absurdly flattered that she would speak to him first, that she would come to greet him before she even acknowledged Kairaithin, much less Bertaud. Though he knew she spoke to him first partly as a deliberate slight against Kairaithin, though he knew she had her griffin *iskarianere* now and never thought of him, he could not help but find the pleasure in her voice flattering. But he stepped backward as she came toward him. He could not help but step back, for the fire that filled Kes, unleashed as it was now, would burn him to the bone and she had plainly forgotten this.

She realized this an instant after he did, and stopped.

The white fire that burned so bright in her did not exactly
fade, but it ebbed lower and lower, until standing near
her was not quite so much like standing near an oven.
She reached out to him again, and this time Jos let her
take his hands. Her fingers did not seem exactly human
in his; they were slender and graceful, exactly as he
remembered, but holding her hands was like holding the
hands of an alabaster lamp shaped like a woman. She said
again, not gently or cheerfully, but with a kind of pleased
possessiveness, "Jos."

He knew perfectly well that she spoke to him and
ignored Kairaithin in this pointed way in order to deliver
a subtle affront. He knew this. But it did not stop his
heart from coming into his throat in the most foolish and
childish way. He said, "Kes," and found he could not say
anything else.

"Why do you wish to break the Wall?" Lord Bertaud
asked her, very simply and directly, when Kairaithin did
not speak.

Kes released Jos's hands, turning to gaze at the Feierabianden lord. Her smile had grown somehow both more
brilliant and sharper-edged. She was wilder than a griffin,
less fierce but more capricious, less high-tempered and
passionate but more whimsical. Or so she seemed to Jos,
who had known her when she was a human girl and then
while she had been made from a creature of earth to one
of fire and then afterward, when the fire had taken her
completely. She said, "Why should any such constraint
be allowed to stand? It is an offense against all the country of fire. Besides, Taipiikiu Tastairiane Apailika wishes
the Wall to be broken, and why should I not please him if
I can, now it has been cracked through?"

"Tastairiane?" said Bertaud, as though even saying the name hurt him.

"You recall Tastairiane Apailika? He is my *iskarianere* now," said Kes. She spoke with pleased amusement, but the edge to her humor was sharp enough to cut to the bone.

"Yes," said Bertaud in a low tone. "I had heard so."

"Had you? Well, one would never predict what word might be carried on some errant wind," Kes said, and laughed.

It was a cruel laugh, like no sound she would ever have made when she was human. Jos winced from it. He knew, none better, how pitiless the griffins were by nature, but pitilessness was not the same as cruelty, and it hurt him to hear that note in her voice.

Bertaud said, not as though he expected Kes to understand or believe him but as though he felt driven to speak despite this, "If griffins turn once-for-all against men, if it should come to true battle, Kes, I promise you, no one will win. Least of all the People of Fire and Air." He hesitated and then added, "Even you, swift as you are to heal the injured, even you cannot bring a griffin back to life after he has been killed."

Kes only laughed, shaking her head in dismissal of this warning. "Oh, no. You're mistaken. You're entirely mistaken. If I'm swift enough, no injury need be mortal."

"You cannot be so swift, not when thousands upon thousands of men draw together to face a mere few hundreds of griffins—"

"I can be as swift and attentive as I must be," Kes answered with perfect confidence. She reached out to lay her hand on the Wall. Fire ran up along the great blocks, playing over her wrist and hand. The flames were ruddy where they rose from the red sands, but white where they crossed her hand. She smiled.

"Kes," said Kairaithin. "Keskainiane Raikaisipiike."

"*Siipikaile*," said Kes, turning to face him directly for the first time. *Teacher*, that was. But she pronounced the word with a mocking edge, and met his powerful black gaze without the slightest flinch. Her eyes were filled with fire, black and gold and paler gold, set in a face that might have been carved of porcelain. Jos remembered when Kes had had eyes of a pale grayed blue, like water. He tried to remember when they had turned to fire. Not at once, he thought. Not in those early years, when they had built his cottage and kindled the fire that burned within it. There had still been a touch of humanity about her in those days. But the last of it had burned away a long time ago.

Neither of the young griffin mages flanking her acknowledged Kairaithin at all. They would not, Jos knew. No griffin would speak to Kairaithin, from what he had said about flying alone. Brawny, powerful-shouldered Ruuanse Tekainiike crouched down a little; the feathers of his neck and chest, feathers that might have been beaten out of bronze and inlaid with gold by some master metal-smith, ruffled up with a stiff rattling sound. He looked brutal and dangerous, but he did not meet Kairaithin's eyes. He was not a match for his former teacher and no one, least of all Tekainiike himself, mistook it.

Opailikiita was a question. Opailikiita Sehanaka Kiistaike . . . she had been Kairaithin's student long before he had stolen Kes from the country of earth and made her into a creature of fire. Slender and small, her beauty was subtle rather than flashy. She was more powerful than she seemed to any first glance. Jos had once known her rather well. When Opailikiita turned her head to avoid looking at Kairaithin, Jos suspected it was not acknowledgment of his superior strength that made her look aside. He thought it was regret for what her old teacher had lost. Or at least some griffin emotion similar to regret; some emotion hotter and more violent than mere regret. A sort of angry grief, perhaps.

Kairaithin would not be goaded, neither by the scorn in Kes's voice nor by the overt indifference of his former students. Perhaps he truly did not care. He said, "You understand less than you believe," but when he took a step forward and lifted a hand, it was not to remonstrate with Kes, as Jos at first thought. Instead, he struck at her with a wholly unexpected blaze of power that burned right through her and hurled the rest of them violently aside.

Kes shredded into fire and air under that blow. She did not even have time to cry out. Opailikiita did, the harsh scraping shriek of an enraged griffin. She flung herself fearlessly at Kairaithin, who merely called up a hard wind that threw her aside, tumbling her over. Young Tekainiike, also shrieking, reared back in shock and then leaped into the air, his wings thundering as he strove for height—fleeing, to Jos's shock, who would not have expected any griffin to fly from such a battle.

Jos had also shouted aloud in shock and grief. He had been flung to his hands and knees, for even the glancing edge of Kairaithin's power was like the blow of a smith's hammer. Half blinded by flying wind and whirling sand, conscious of the furious griffins above and about, he

could not even crawl out of the way. He was aware of
Kairaithin rearing up, of his human shape exploding to
match his immense shadow, of black feathers raking the
air above him; he was aware of fire cracking across the
sky and of the flaming wind roaring down from the high,
hard sky—

Then Bertaud seized Jos by the arm. He had been the
first of them all to regain his balance, and the only one
among them to make no sound. Jos had a fleeting realization that the other man might actually have guessed that
Kairaithin might strike at Kes, for he had evidently been
ready for it. Now he dragged at Jos, who with the other
man's help managed to regain his feet; they both ducked
away from the violence of wind and fire, their arms over
their faces to guard against the rushing sand.

"You knew—" Jos began, shouting over the fury
of wind and griffins, but then coughed and could not
continue.

He did not know what answer the Feierabianden
lord might have made, for the other griffins came then,
rushing down out of the storm; the harsh desert sunlight struck off their wings and flanks as off bronze and
copper and gold. The ferocious light flamed on their
knife-edged beaks and talons and glowed in their eyes.
Behind them, the sky turned crimson with driving sand,
and below them fire fell like rain from the wind of their
wings.

In those first moments, Jos thought that all the griffins
in the world had come to avenge Kes. Then he realized
both that only a double-handful of griffins were actually
plunging down that fiery wind toward them—though
that seemed enough and to spare—and that Kes did not

need to be avenged. Kairaithin had not succeeded in his
aim.

At least not yet. A streak of white and gold fire poured
itself through the wind, shaping itself back into the form
of a human woman. Kairaithin, beautiful and terrible,
rearing huge against the sky, the wind of his power roaring through his black wings, struck at her again. Again
she shredded away into fire and wind. She could not
answer him, or would not, or at least she did not. She
fled. But Kairaithin used his strength to block her flight,
pinning her against the Wall and dragging her ruthlessly
back into shape. He meant to kill her—to destroy her—
she could not match him. Jos made a wordless sound
but did not know he had tried to leap forward until he
found Bertaud blocking his way, the other man's grip on
his arm so fierce even Jos could not break it. He wanted
to hit him. He stopped instead, leaning forward, his fists
clenched.

Kiibaile Esterire Airaikeliu, the Lord of Fire and Air,
the king of all the griffins, swept down out of the sky. His
immense power came before him like a motionless hurricane—Jos did not know how else to express it. All other
power flattened out before him, crushed to stillness. The
wind itself died; the air cleared of its red haze of dust; the
flames that had blazed up from the desert sands died.

On all sides, the struggle quieted. Kairaithin settled
back slowly to the ground, folding his great wings. Kes,
looking tiny and helpless and frightened, drew herself
slowly away from the Wall and turned to face them,
one hand still braced against the fire-washed stone for
support. The Lord of Fire and Air landed near her, his
gold-and-crimson mate on his other side and the savage

white Tastairiane Apailika beyond her. Ruuanse Tekainiike, looking much younger and smaller in such company,
came down warily near them. The young griffin mage
had not fled after all, Jos realized belatedly, but had gone
to bring the king and his company to this place.

And now that the king was here, Kairaithin had lost.
There was no more mockery in the look Kes gave him,
but rather wary respect. But even the greatest griffin
mage could not threaten her again, not—

Kairaithin, who had turned to face the Lord of Fire and
Air, flung a slender blaze of power like a knife at Kes. He
did not even look at her; his blow took everyone by surprise, most of all Kes. It was a thrust of such power and
strength that it passed right through the forceful stillness
the king of griffins had imposed, and unable to block or
answer it, she leaped away. But anyone, even Jos, could
see that she was nothing like fast enough.

Everyone moved in a blaze of speed and fury:
Opailikiita with a blaze of magecraft of her own to
block Kairaithin's blow, the Lord of Fire and Air casting
himself forward to protect Kes, the king's mate lunging after him, Tastairiane and a half dozen other griffins
flinging themselves simultaneously against Kairaithin.
And Kairaithin *was* overset by their combined force, but
only momentarily, for he was a very powerful mage and
neither Tastairiane nor any of his own former students
could match him.

But though the griffin mage was forced back, and back
again, until he was pinned against the Wall himself, his
blow had found its mark. There could be no mistake on
that account, for even Jos and Bertaud, out of place as
they were, felt the reverberation of power and loss and

destruction echo and reecho through the desert. It happened very swiftly, but there was a whirl of blinding sand and fire and an explosion of red dust, and then a single hard, savage cry of fury and anguish, and then, suddenly, stillness.

But it was not the same stillness that the king had imposed.

At first, even after the griffins drew back, Jos thought Kairaithin had after all managed to achieve his aim. He thought that Kes had been destroyed. Even though the woman he had known had ceased to exist years ago, grief rose up into his throat and choked him. He started to step forward, blindly, wanting at least to look down at her body, or at least at the ebbing fire and white sand and flecks of gold that she might have left if she had been too little human to leave a body.

As he had before, Bertaud stopped him. Jos started to knock the other man's hand away, and then stopped, for he saw with astonishment that again, though he could not imagine how, Kairaithin had missed his mark. Kes was still alive. She was standing beside Opailikiita, her hand buried in the soft feathers of the slender griffin's neck, staring at Kairaithin. Her expression was very odd.

It took Jos much longer than it should have to realize that the Lord of Fire and Air had taken Kairaithin's blow in her place, and that in her place he had been destroyed. He understood this only when the red-and-gold griffin who had been the king's mate, crouching low to the desert sand, gave another loud cry, of such despair and grief and fury that Jos was frozen speechless and motionless by it, as a mouse might be frozen among its tangled grasses by the scream of a stooping falcon.

Everyone seemed equally frozen, griffin and human alike. Kes was holding one hand out to where the king had been. Red dust sifted through her slender fingers. She looked stricken. Beside her, almost as close as Opailikiita, Tastairiane Apailika stood so still he might have been hammered out of white gold. His fiery blue eyes blazed and his immense wings were half spread, the feathers like the flame at the white-hot heart of a fire.

The red-and-gold griffin who had been the king's mate— her name was Nehaistiane Esterikiu Anahaikuuanse— flung herself abruptly into the brilliant air and exploded violently into flaming wind and red sand, and was gone.

For a long, long moment, no one else moved.

At last, Tastairiane Apailika turned his savage, beautiful, white-feathered head and looked deliberately at Kairaithin.

All the lesser griffins fell back and away, as though at a signal. Kairaithin came a pace away from the looming Wall and stood, outwardly impassive but, to Jos's practiced eye, looking weary and heartsick and very much alone. The black feathers of his neck and shoulders ruffled up and then smoothed down again. His great wings were nearly furled. He turned his head to look at Kes—no. At the place where the Lord of Fire and Air had died, where now nothing remained but drifting red dust and flickers of fire. He did not look at Kes herself. Nor did he look at the white griffin who stood near her.

But Tastairiane Apailika looked at him. The white griffin said in a smooth, deadly voice that sliced across their minds like a knife, *Kiibaile Esterire Airaikeliu is gone. Nehaistiane Esterikiu Anahaikuuanse is gone. Who will challenge me?*

From the depth of silence that followed, it appeared no one would.

The shining white griffin continued to regard Kairaithin. He was poised with supreme grace and confidence, wings angled aggressively forward. The hot sunlight blazed off his terrible beak as though striking edged metal. He lifted one eagle's foot clear of the sand, his talons glinting like silver knives.

In contrast, Kairaithin clearly did not want to fight. He still looked dangerous—nothing could stop his looking dangerous. Jos did not think he was exactly afraid, for fear was not something griffins understood. But he looked as though, if he were to challenge Tastairiane Apailika now, he would lose. And he looked as though he knew it.

The Lord of Fire and Air has gone into the fire and the air, the white griffin said. His tone was not exactly triumphant, but it held pride and strength and something more, an awareness of his own strength, and a willingness to command. He said, *I am become the Lord of Fire and Air. Will any challenge me?*

All the other griffins shifted, not exactly rushing to put themselves at Tastairiane Apailika's back, but reorienting themselves around him. They accepted him as their lord, Jos saw, and he saw that even Kairaithin felt the new power and confidence in the white griffin, that he could not help but respond to it, for all he was unalterably opposed to the other.

Kes said, in her smooth, light voice that was so nearly the voice Jos remembered, "Lord of Fire and Air! What wind will you call us all to ride?"

Tastairiane Apailika turned to her and said, *Break the Wall.*

"I will break it," said Kes. She looked at Kairaithin. She was not laughing now. She reached out with great deliberation to set her palm against the burning stone, in a gesture that was very clearly a challenge, and a challenge that she very clearly knew her former teacher could not take up.

Come, said the new Lord of Fire and Air, to Kairaithin. There was a new depth and power to his voice. Tastairiane Apailika had come fully into his strength. Something about declaring himself had done that for him, or else something in the recognition of the other griffins. He commanded Kairaithin again, *Come here.*

Kairaithin seemed to shrink back and down—not very much, not even with any perceptible motion. But Jos saw very clearly that the griffin mage had nothing left with which to defy the new king of the griffins: neither strength nor pride nor even the certainty that recently had sustained him.

Then Bertaud, with a courage and presence of mind that astonished Jos, walked across to Kairaithin's side. He turned there, setting one hand on the black-fathered neck, and regarded Tastairiane Apailika with an expression Jos could not read at all.

Well, man? the white griffin asked him impatiently.

Bertaud began to answer him.

What answer the Feierabianden lord might have made, Jos could not guess, but he did not have a chance to speak. Before Bertaud could utter even a single word, Kairaithin, with more decisive speed than Jos had imagined he could yet command, swept him up, and Jos with him, and took them with him, away from the Wall and out of the desert entirely.

The world tilted and turned, and raked away behind and beyond them, and they were standing abruptly on solid stone. They stood now in the mountains, in a high, clear morning above Tihannad, with Niambe Lake shining beside the city.

The city lay below them, quiet and peaceful, with no sign of any impending peril. Here and there bright-coated skaters raced along the lake's edge where the ice was still firm enough to be trusted, but little wavelets rippled across the middle of the lake. Mist rose from the lake into the cold air. Out in the town, threads of darker smoke made their way gently up into the sky.

It was almost impossible, in this place, to really believe in the desert, or in griffins, or in the Wall that had so briefly held fire from the country of earth and that was now so near failure.

Kairaithin had taken on human form again, perhaps because he had brought them to a place of men. He stood now with his head bowed and his eyes closed, as though he had used up the last of his strength in bringing them here. Perhaps he had, for when he took a step, he swayed. Catching his arm to steady him, Jos looked at Bertaud in alarm.

The Feierabianden lord was not looking at him, nor even at Kairaithin. He was staring down at Niambe Lake and at the city, his expression closed and forbidding, his mouth set hard. He said abruptly, "We will go down to the king's house."

Jos only nodded.

"Unless you have another suggestion to offer? Or to force upon us?" Bertaud said to Kairaithin, with a coldness that astonished Jos.

But the griffin mage did not respond in kind. He did not seem offended, or even surprised. He only nodded in weary acquiescence and gestured for Bertaud to lead the way down from the shoulder of the mountain to Niambe Lake, and thence to the king's house in Tihannad.

CHAPTER 10

The road through the mountains from Minas Ford in Feierabiand to the town of Ehre in Casmantium was the greatest road in the world. Mienthe had not seen every road in the world, but she was certain none could rival the one through the pass above Minas Ford. The very best Casmantian makers and builders and engineers—Mienthe was not quite certain of the proper bounds of any of those terms, in Casmantian usage—had been years in the building of this road, which even now was not quite completed.

In some places, Casmantian builders had cut the road back into the sides of the mountains; in others, they had swung it right out over wild precipices, supporting the great stones with ironwork and vaunting buttresses, rather as though they were building a massive palace. Sometimes bridges seemed to have been flung across from one high place to another just out of the builders' exuberance. The longest gaps had been spanned by tremendous iron arches from which were suspended the most amazing bridges, hung on iron chains. All her life, Mienthe had heard of the splendid skill of Casmantian makers and builders. Now she decided that she had never heard even half the truth.

With this new road, it was possible to ride straight through the pass without ever picking one's way far down a mountainside into a steep valley and then laboriously climbing back up the other side, as the old road had required. It was even possible for a long train of heavy wagons to cross straight through the pass, with never a perilous turn around the narrow shoulder of some mountain where a cross-footed mule might drag an entire unfortunate team off some terrible cliff. It was not, unfortunately, always possible for a few travelers mounted on swift horses to swing wide around such a heavy train of wagons.

Mienthe stood up in her stirrups, trying to peer ahead over the long train of wagons making their slow, cautious descent around a long curving angle of a mountain. She was quite certain her horse could have taken that same descent at three times the speed and been up around this mountain and up the next rise as well, and across the bridge dimly visible far ahead, all before these wagons would reach the lowest turn of the road and begin the next ascent.

"There will be room at the bottom to get around them," Tan said, his expressive mouth crooking with amusement.

Mienthe thought his unfailing good humor about the minor discomforts and irritations of their journey might eventually become unbearably provoking. There was some irony in that, since Tan was the one who had argued against making this particular journey at all. After alert guardsmen had reported possible Linularinan agents in Kames, asking questions about the house and grounds, Tan had wanted to go straight north as fast as he could ride, drawing the most persistent and dangerous Linularinan agents away with him. But Mienthe had worried that his enemies might also have already got ahead of him, waiting for him to run north and right into their hands.

With a quite terrifying quirk of humor, Tan had been very much inclined to oblige them. "The day I can't outwit and outrun an ordinary shaved-penny spy or two, Linularinan or otherwise, I'll retire from the game and take up turnip farming," he had said, with altogether too much complacency for his own good, in Mienthe's opinion.

Mienthe had wondered aloud just how many of those shaved-penny spies might actually be Linularinan mages. That had blunted the edge of Tan's amusement. Then she had asked him how many times he meant to put her to the trouble of rescuing him, and that had done for the rest.

"You should be glad to see me go north," he had said. "I can get past anyone Istierinan has in my way, Mie, and then let him try the skill of his mages against the mages of Tihannad. I know you're longing to get back to Tiefenauer. You should let me go."

Mienthe hadn't been convinced that any such flight would succeed. But she was afraid for Tan to stay in her father's house in Kames, doubly afraid now that they were both certain Istierinan knew where he was. At the same time, she knew exactly which unexpected direction they could take that would lead them straight to safe shelter.

"The Arobern is on good terms with my cousin," she had pointed out. "And however bold your Istierinan is here, he won't lightly try his hand in Casmantium, do you think? You can take shelter with the Arobern, I'm sure he'll have no objection, and then once you're out of Linularinum's reach, surely Istierinan will pull his people back. Kohorrian will probably even apologize to Iaor for any *misunderstandings*."

Tan had stared at her. "There are times, Mie," he had said at last, "when your utterances blossom out with a most peculiar complexity, as the flowers of some wondrous country. Some might consider a confidential agent who delivers himself over to a foreign king not merely foolish, but actually treasonous, you know."

"The Arobern won't do anything like that!" Mienthe had protested, shocked.

"Anyway, isn't the information you carry nearly all about Linularinum? What does it matter if Casmantium has it, too?"

Tan had had to admit that this was a point.

Mienthe had argued, "We don't know I can protect you from Linularinan mages, but we know I *have*. I'm afraid to ask you to stay here and afraid to see you go north alone. But I think if we can get through the pass into Casmantium, we'll both be safe."

"We?" said Tan, sounding both startled and for once quite serious. "Out of the question, Mie—"

"I'm not leaving you for Istierinan!" Mienthe had insisted, thoroughly exasperated. "Nor staying here to wait for him myself. You could even be right about being in danger from a foreign king! But I'm Bertaud's cousin and the Arobern's friend, and that changes everything. I'm going."

"Well," Tan had said after a moment, "I know how stubborn you are, and—" He had paused and then added, his manner suddenly almost serious, "I admit, Mie, I would find your company a welcome reassurance, under the circumstances. But your cousin is probably going to kill me for putting you in such danger."

The thought occurred to Mienthe that, though plenty of people might find her company welcome, no one, not even her cousin, had ever said he found her company *reassuring*. She did not know what to say to that. But in the end, she and Tan, and a handful of guardsmen, and the maid from Kames whom her steward had demanded she take with her for propriety's sake, had all headed east and not north.

Mienthe had not even known she'd had a steward, though she supposed she'd have guessed if she'd ever thought about it. She had never wanted to hear about anything to do with her father's house or her inheritance. But, after all, someone had to look after her father's house and see that it remained in good repair, and keep an eye on the land to prevent too much clandestine wood-cutting or poaching or grazing. She supposed Bertaud had approved the man; at least he seemed competent and reliable. A little too forceful, perhaps, when insisting that Mienthe have a female companion.

Not that the maid was with her now, which Mienthe actually did regret. But they had lost two of the guards-men finding out just how swiftly the Linularinan agents had moved to surround Kames. After that, Tan had given up any idea of heading north, and Mienthe had insisted that the maid be left in a little village along their way, with the other guardsman to keep the woman safe and eventually see her back to the house at Kames. Propriety and appearances were all very well, but the maid had been rather too old for a fast journey, and frightened by the close pursuit they'd encountered.

After that, by common accord, Mienthe and Tan had skirted any larger village or small town they'd passed and slipped right by the rebuilt Minas Ford in the fading light of evening, camping in one of the recently deserted engineer's camps right in the pass itself. And now they were here, entirely out of Feierabiand, in these mountains that belonged to no country at all. And they did not even have any clear certainty about whether they were truly riding toward shelter in Casmantium, far less whether they were riding toward allies.

But, though Mienthe did not know how likely they were to find friends in Ehre, she knew that if they turned back, they would find enemies behind them. And she was certain that the King of Casmantium, once he knew she was Bertaud's cousin and Erich's friend, would be very polite. She was certain he would offer the hospitality of his court and that he would not harass Tan at all, even if he learned that Tan had been one of King Iaor's important confidential agents, which she supposed they would have to tell him. At least, they would have to explain their presence somehow.

No, she was confident of the Arobern's courtesy and hopeful of his goodwill. She even wondered whether he might lend her a few men…say, a company…to see them safe back through the pass and north to Tihannad. Even this did not seem unlikely.

But how far was it, from the mouth of the pass at Ehre to the Casmantian capital city?

Tan did not know the answer to this when she asked him. "I can tell you every distance in Linularinum, from Dessam in the far north right down to Desamion," he said, and shrugged. "But I never expected to visit Casmantium. I don't even speak Prechen. I don't suppose . . . ?"

Mienthe didn't, either, aside from a few laborious words. She could say *Please* and *Thank you*, and she thought she could manage *My cousin is Bertaud son of Boudan, Lord of the Delta*, which might be very much to the point. But she did not know how to say anything as complicated as *Linularinum has invaded the Delta and their agents are trailing us, or at least Tan, because he accidentally stole some powerful legist-magic out of a special book, so we need to see the Arobern right away.*

She wondered whether Linularinan agents had actually dared come after them into the pass. She glanced uneasily over her shoulder. But the road behind them was clear all the way up the long sweeping curve of the mountain they had just descended, and beyond that she could not see.

"We're well ahead, I'm quite certain, even if Istierinan has the nerve and resolve to send a man of his right to the very doorstep of Brechen Arobern himself," Tan said.

He meant this to be comforting. It would have been more so, except he'd said something very like it before. That had been just prior to the loss of the two guardsmen. But Mienthe did not comment. She merely nodded and wondered whether, once they got past the wagons, they might possibly be able to beg or bribe the men driving the mule teams to slow to an even more deliberate pace and block anyone coming behind them.

As it happened, once they reached the wide gap at the bottom of the slope, the muleteers drew politely to one side to allow swifter travelers past. When Mienthe—very tentatively—put her request to the drivers, they seemed oddly eager to assure her they would be very slow on any upward stretch, and assuredly did not care to have any overbold travelers startle their mules by coming up alongside when there clearly wasn't room.

It dawned on Mienthe, rather too slowly, that the muleteers thought she was with Tan in a very specific sense. They thought that she must have slipped away from her father, or maybe from her proper husband. Mienthe, horrified and offended, wanted to correct them. Before she could, Tan caught her eye and her hand and proceeded to encourage the muleteers' assumption by putting on an understated air of nervous, half-embarrassed smugness that would have got the idea across to men far less romantically inclined. The muleteers grew even more amused and accommodating. Mienthe smiled until her face hurt.

She was too angry to speak to Tan when they at last left the wagons behind and rode up the next neatly angled slope of the road.

"It's very convenient for them to assume—" Tan began once they were well away.

"I know," Mienthe said through her teeth.

"It's only practical—"

"I know!" said Mienthe, and put her hood up to make it clear she did not want to be mollified.

They did not speak again until they reached the middle of the pass, with its welcoming public house and stables and twelve lamps glowing along the road on either side to lead weary travelers in out of the cold.

The public house was set up on a low place where mountains climbed away in serried ranks in all directions. The mountains, glittering with ice, were rose-pink and gold where the late sunlight slanted down across them; the shadows between and behind them were violet, and the road running away toward the east seemed picked out in gold where it twisted up across the face of the nearest. Where the road flung itself across a chasm, high above, the iron bridge looked like a stark black thread.

The public house had a stable behind and two long wings, one angling in from the east and the other from the west. These met in the middle in a handsome square-cornered three-story building of dressed stone with carved wooden doors and real glass in the windows, blazing gold in the light. The whole was substantially larger than her father's house, much more elegant than the great house in Tiefenauer, and a great deal more elaborate than anything Mienthe had expected to find in the middle of what was still, despite the fine new road, a rugged mountain pass.

Mienthe, wordless, gazed down and up and around in amazement.

Tan said in a low voice, "Would we might rise on eagle's wings, mount above the heights where the rising sun strikes music from the stone, and fall again through the silence that is song."

"Oh," said Mienthe softly. And after a moment, "If there's a poem that catches an echo of this"—Mienthe opened her hands to the surrounding mountains—"then someday you really must teach it to me."

Tan nodded. But he also said, "We might be wiser not to stay at that inn."

Still stunned by beauty, Mienthe hardly understood

him for a moment. Then she did, and, unreasonably, resented it. She said grimly, "Of course," and nudged her horse forward again. She wondered if Tan thought they could get all the way through to Ehre without stopping. She knew she couldn't.

"There must be good places along the road for a cold camp," Tan said, not quite looking at her. "I'm sure travelers used to have to camp three or four nights from one side to the other, or many more than that for slow wagons such as those we passed. I should think the builders will have let their road encompass some of those old campsites."

"Yes," said Mienthe.

"I'm sorry—"

Mienthe snapped, "For what? Of course we can't stop there. You're perfectly right."

"For being right," Tan said gently. "It hasn't happened often of late, Mienthe; do grant me my one moment of reasonable competence in these days of striking idiocy. I do think we oughtn't stay there, but I hope we may stop for supper."

"Oh," said Mienthe, in a much smaller voice. She felt she ought to apologize as well, but wasn't sure for what, or how. She said merely, "All right."

The public house offered hot spiced wine and roasted kid, soft flatbreads, a compote of dried apples and raisins, and little cakes dripping with honey, "Which my wife makes them special," said the host, a big man from Feierabiand, with a generous belly and a booming laugh. "With honey from her sister's bees, down near Talend. The bees there, they make a special honey from the trees that flower at midsummer, dark as molasses. Good to keep off illness, they say it is, and good especially to sweeten a dark heart, not that that matters to *you*, esteemed lady, eh?"

He winked down at Mienthe, clearly assuming, just as the muleteers had, that she was with Tan. At least Tan did not suggest to him that they were running away together. Not where Mienthe could hear him, anyway. She tried not to wonder what he told the host to explain why they were not staying the night at the house.

But at least the host also told them of a cold campsite a little more than an hour's ride up the east side of the pass.

Even so, Mienthe was certain for some little while that the lowering dusk would catch them still abroad on the road. Certainly the host's estimate seemed a little over-optimistic, or else he'd been thinking of riders with fresh horses, or at least riders coming down from heights rather than trudging upward.

They had lanterns. The road was, after all, good. She tried not to be frightened by the mere idea of riding up the twisting length of any mountain road, no matter how fine the road or how bright the lanterns.

But at last they came up a rise that had been, by the worn and rugged look of it, part of the old road, simply incorporated into the new. Then they crossed one of those improbable iron bridges and came onto a section of the road where the stones were so new and fresh they looked all but polished, and beyond that the new road ran again into a section of the old. "Yes," Tan said, gesturing away down the rugged slope that fell away from the road, "you can see where the old road plunged way down into that valley and then crawled slowly back up to this height."

Mienthe nodded obediently, although she was far too

cold and tired to appreciate how much effort the new road had saved them, just so long as it had. But then they turned along a long switchback and came out at last, with the last of the slanting light, onto a broad flat place that had plainly been used as a campsite for many years. A cliff reared out a tight little nook, just right to keep off the weather, and circles of firestones were laid ready before the cliff. There was even a neat stack of firewood against the cliff, which someone must have gathered with considerable labor, because even the small twisted trees of the heights were rare so high.

Mienthe arranged wood with numb fingers and struck a fire while Tan unsaddled the horses. He did not hobble the beasts, which were as tired and cold as their riders and very willing to be led into the nook. He was limping, Mienthe saw; he had been only very slightly lame in Kames, but he'd used himself hard on their flight and the limp was much worse now. She was immediately worried, and then resented the necessity of worry, which she knew very well was unfair. But there was nothing she could do if the half-healed knee had been reinjured—nothing either of them could do, this side of Ehre. So she worried. "Your leg?" she asked Tan.

"It will do," he said, and stopped limping, which made Mienthe feel guilty and more resentful still. Even worse, Tan did not seem to notice her bad temper.

She got up and went herself to pour out handfuls of grain for the horses and check their feet. At least there were few other camp tasks, as simply as they were traveling. Tan settled by the fire and stretched his leg out carefully, with a saddle under his knee.

Mienthe wrapped herself up in a blanket and tucked

herself, not too close to Tan, between the cliff wall and the fire where the reflected warmth would, she hoped, eventually thaw her fingers and toes. She was acutely aware of his presence. And of the absence of the maid. And of the silence and solitude that surrounded them. She did not know what to say, but found herself suddenly unable to look at him.

"Tomorrow should see us out of the pass and down at least to Ehre," he said, throwing another branch on the fire. His tone was utterly prosaic.

Mienthe nodded, staring fixedly into the fire.

"I could bring you something to eat—"

She shook her head and leaned her head back against the cliff. Then she lay down right where she was, closed her eyes, and opened them what seemed mere moments later to a spectacular dawn.

Clouds had piled up in the east, rose-pink and deep carmine and gold. The sun, rising behind the clouds and among the teeth of the mountains, flooded the valleys between the peaks with a streaming pale light that seemed almost solid enough to touch. To either side of the road, the luminous faces of the mountains glowed gold and pink with reflected light; ice streaked the high jagged tips of the mountains with crystalline fire. Violet and indigo shadows stretched out below the mountains, and the iron bridge, a surprising distance below their campsite, gleamed like polished jet.

"Good morning," Tan said, smiling rather tentatively at Mienthe from beside the fire. He was heating pieces of last night's roasted meat on sticks over the coals and folding them into flatbreads, and it was the savory smell of the dripping fat that had woken her.

Mienthe found herself suddenly and unexpectedly happy. It might have been the clarity of the air and the brilliance of the light, or the deep warmth that had built up around her through the night from the fire, or the feeling of safety. She had not realized how frightened she had felt, or for how long, until she woke secure in this stony nook high above the world, with no company but Tan and the horses. Somehow, in the bright light of the morning, it no longer seemed nearly so strange or worrisome to be alone in the mountains with only Tan for a companion.

She sat up, then got to her feet, shook out her traveling skirt and rubbed her face with her hands—Tan had put out a bowl of water and even a surprising bit of soap, so she could wash her face like a civilized person. Then she knelt down by the fire while Tan saddled the horses and rolled up the blankets. She didn't even feel guilty about letting him do all the work. He looked wide awake and energetic, like he'd been up for hours, and he was hardly limping at all. Besides, there wasn't a great deal of work involved in cleaning up their camp. So she peacefully ate the hot meat and exactly half of the honey cakes out of the packet. The honey *was* very good, spicier and somehow wilder than the honey from Delta wildflowers.

"We'll be out of the pass and in Casmantium by noon," Tan said, leading her horse up to her and offering her the reins. "Shall we lay odds on it?"

Mienthe couldn't help but laugh. She laid Tan odds of three to one that they wouldn't reach the far end of the great road before midafternoon, because that way she couldn't lose—at least, she would rather lose than win.

"Your knee is better?" she remembered to ask.

"A night's rest was all it required. It'll be well enough as long as I leave the stirrups long," he assured her.

He sounded so very sincere that Mienthe wondered if he was actually concealing a good deal of pain, but so far as she could see he looked calm and relaxed, without any of the visible tension of pain. So in the end she simply nodded and guided her horse out of the sheltered nook and up the long curve of the road that led east.

There was room to ride abreast, and for a while they did. But neither of them spoke, and after a little while, Tan fell back behind Mienthe. She did not mind. She liked the illusion that she was riding alone between stone and sky, the morning light pouring through the cold air around her, the granite glittering in the sun and the clean wind against her face. She could imagine she was the only living creature within a hundred miles—and her horse, of course. The horse also seemed cheerful this bright morning, moving willingly along with a long stride, its head up and its ears pricked forward.

This road truly was wonderful, Mienthe decided. She enjoyed its long spiral climb around the curve of a mountain and the artful way it doglegged up a narrow pass between two broken crags, with the sky an amazingly dark blue above and the mountains luminous with reflected light. She enjoyed the sharp thrill of crossing a graceful bridge spanning a gulf between two narrow spires. The chasm must have been at least four hundred feet long—she counted her horse's strides to make that estimate and, turning at the end to look back at the bridge's graceful, narrow length, wondered whether it was the longest bridge in the world and what magic of making kept it from collapsing down into the gulf.

The road climbed and climbed, and then they came up and around a particularly steep and awkward turn around a dramatic cliff that raked against the sky. Mienthe immediately understood exactly why the engineers had designed the curve as they had, despite its awkwardness. As they came around the last sharp turn, they found the whole world spread out unexpectedly before them in one long eastward sweep of stone and sky, down and down and dizzyingly down, until they could see the green of trees far below, and the town of Ehre, its high wall and wide streets and granite houses faintly blurred by a haze of smoke and distance.

Mienthe had checked her horse without noticing, and now she turned to Tan and smiled.

He gazed back at her, not smiling himself. Indeed, he looked rather pale and serious. Mienthe had not realized until that moment how nervous Tan was about entering Casmantium, about delivering himself into the Arobern's hands. But he only said after a moment, lightly, "Casmantium before noon, as I said. No doubt it shall tremble at our coming. What were those odds?"

As it would not be kind to notice his anxiety, Mienthe laughed and said, "It's farther than it looks, I believe, and noon's not so far away. I think I'll win our wager yet—which is good, as you know perfectly well it was three to one!"

She patted her horse on the neck and nudged it forward, in no particular hurry—not that she would mind losing the wager, but because she found herself oddly reluctant to arrive at Ehre, and thus in Casmantium, with the freedom and peace of the mountains behind them.

*   *   *

They came down out of the mountain pass and rode through the great iron gates, the gates that marked the border of Casmantium, exactly at noon, when the sun stood precisely overhead and all shadows were as small and unobtrusive as they ever could be. On the mountain side of the gates, the paving stones of the mountain road ran broad and smooth up into the pass behind them. Before them, on the other side of the iron gates, the road was narrower and made simply of pounded earth, with plain timbers to keep it from washing too badly when streams fed by melting snow came down from the mountains in the spring. Ehre, westernmost town of Casmantium, stood with its imposing square stone towers rising up behind its high stone walls, less than half a mile farther on down this ordinary road.

They had actually come to the iron gates a scant few minutes before noon, but Tan caught Mienthe's reins and held her back until they could tell by the shadows of the gates that the sun stood precisely at noon. Then he led her horse through the gates onto Casmantian soil and solemnly offered Mienthe three coins. It was absurd, of course, but she nevertheless gave him one back. Then they traded again, so that both of them were back where they'd begun. She tried not to laugh, but it was impossible not to smile. It was hard to remember the fear that had dogged their steps for those last days. Mienthe did not know what they would find in Ehre, but she was at least confident it would not be Linularinan agents.

After they passed through the iron gates, she turned once more to look wistfully back up the long sweep of the road behind them. The achingly brilliant blue of the sky stretched infinitely far, above gray and silver mountains that shaded away to violet as they rose to meet the sky. Mienthe could make out the narrow thread of the road, snaking its way up and up until the narrow thread of it tipped at last over a curve high above. She sighed and began to turn away for the final time, toward Ehre and the last long stretch of their journey. But then she paused, her attention caught by the movement of tiny black figures high above, coming slowly over that last high curve. They were so far away and so tiny that she probably would not have seen these other travelers at all except they paused, gazing down from the crest of the road as she and Tan had done, and as they paused there they were clearly silhouetted against the brilliant sky.

Though she knew other travelers must use the great road, though she knew there was no reason to suspect those barely visible flecks were anything sinister or anything to do with them at all, she nevertheless found her pleasure in the day instantly quenched, as swiftly as a smothered candle flame. "Tan," she said.

He turned, following her gaze up to the high curve of the road, and stilled. He said at last, deliberately calm, "The road is open to anyone, after all."

"Yes," said Mienthe, and heard her own voice come out small and tight.

"There's no reason to think they're anything to do with us."

"No," Mienthe agreed.

Tan gave her a level glance and added, still in that calm tone, "But we might ride on, even so. We might ride straight through Ehre and be well out in the countryside by dusk, do you think?"

"Yes," said Mienthe. She had hoped to rest in some pleasant public house in Ehre. She didn't say so, but only pressed her horse into a swinging trot toward the walls of the town, so near at hand.

But she could not believe, now, that those walls would offer anything but an illusion of safety.

Mienthe had thought Ehre a small mountain town, larger than Minas Ford, no doubt, for all the building that had been done at Minas Ford and Minas Spring in the past years, but still far smaller than Tiefenauer. Certainly Ehre had not seemed very large from above, but it was intensely busy; busier and far more crowded than she had expected. She thought it was probably a market day, for farmers with empty carts were passing in and out of the stone gates that pierced Ehre's walls. Well, mostly out, for they'd clearly disposed of their produce earlier in the day. But plenty of other people were going in or coming out. Not merely ordinary folk, either, but an astonishing number of fancy carriages and riders dressed not for the practical necessities of travel, but in finely dyed linen with lace at their wrists and delicate embroidery, and fancy rings for the men or bangles for the ladies. Mienthe thought she wouldn't have been able to wear so fine an outfit for an hour on the road without snagging a thread or ripping the lace.

"Do you suppose there's a spring fair?" Mienthe asked Tan. "Or perhaps the lord here is celebrating the birth of an heir?"

Tan had a thoughtful, wary look on his face, but it fell away almost before Mienthe had noticed it, and he smiled and shrugged with every evidence of good humor.

"Perhaps a fair," he agreed. "It's useful. I much doubt anyone will look twice at strangers passing through." He touched his reins to direct his horse toward the gates that led into the town.

At first Tan's prediction seemed accurate. There were guardsmen at those stone gates, but they seemed unconcerned about travelers and simply waved everyone through after a brief exchange of words. Mienthe knew that they would do the same for herself and Tan, but she could not help feeling as though the hunted, anxious days just past must show somehow. She felt very strongly that the guards would stop them and demand knowingly, *And just what brings you to Ehre, eh, esteemed lady? Bringing trouble at your heel, are you? Linularinan agents, is it?* And while she wanted to explain about all of that to the Arobern, she certainly did not want to be taken for a hysteric or a madwoman by provincial guards here in Ehre.

She wished that Bertaud was here with her—visiting Casmantium wouldn't be frightening at all if her cousin were with her—even if he'd come bearing news of trouble and disorder in Feierabiand, everyone here would respect him and believe everything he said. She had been desperately eager to arrive in Ehre, but now she looked anxiously sideways at Tan, riding beside her on the road. He did not look in the least concerned about the guardsmen. Mienthe did not for a moment believe his confident pose. She wished she did.

But they could hardly go back through the pass.

The guardsmen asked, without much interest, what business had brought them to Ehre. Tan, with a discretion Mienthe thoroughly approved, did not go into any details.

He gave his name as Teras son of Toharas and did not give hers at all; he merely said that they were on their way to Breidechboden—he pronounced the name quite creditably—with an important message from Lord Bertaud of the Delta to King Brechen Glansent Arobern.

They had agreed he would say so much, because Tan said that complicated lies were difficult to put over properly and Mienthe had suggested that she might well pass for a courier; that, indeed, after their recent hasty days of travel across country with never a decent chance to pause at any civilized house or inn, she would be hard put to look like a respectable lady. She had flatly refused, this time, to allow Tan to imply they were fleeing together from an outraged husband.

But after that nothing in the encounter followed any outline either of them had envisioned.

"You plan to go to Breidechboden?" one of the men said, in accented but quite accomplished Terheien. His gaze, from bored, had become intent. "You wish to speak to the Arobern for the Lord of the Delta?" He did not sound, as Mienthe would have expected, doubtful. He simply gave Tan a long look and Mienthe a polite nod and said, "I am glad to save you many miles. The Arobern is not in Breidechboden. He is here."

"Here? In Ehre?" Mienthe said blankly, before she could stop herself. She had meant to leave all the speaking to Tan, but in her startlement she had forgotten.

"In Ehre. Yes," said the guardsman. "This is good news, yes? Because you bring an important message. You do not have a wand?"

He meant the white wand Feierabianden couriers carried. Mienthe shook her head mutely, mindful of what

Tan had said about complicated lies. She said, trying
to sound confident but finding her voice coming out
small and nervous, "But I do carry an urgent message,
esteemed sir."

The guardsman gave a little nod. "I will escort you
to the king myself, honored courier, and bring him word
you have come. From the Delta, as you say you are sent
by the honored Lord of the Delta." He was watching them
closely, Mienthe realized, in case they had lied and the
news he gave them was actually very bad news indeed.

But when she met the man's eyes, he smiled deferentially and ducked his head, and she saw he did not think
they had lied at all. He thought she was probably a true
courier, that she did bring word of some kind to his king,
and that Tan was her proper escort. Though Mienthe *did*
carry an important warning and *did* urgently want an
audience with the King of Casmantium, she felt oddly
like an impostor under the regard of the guardsman. She
tried not to let this show.

"It's good news indeed, esteemed sir," Tan said with
smooth sincerity. He drew his horse aside with hardly a
hesitation, nodding to Mienthe to precede him. He, too,
had understood the conclusion the guardsman had drawn
and now played precisely to that conclusion. Mienthe
thought probably Tan would be best pleased to step out
of view, play the role of servant and protector. He would
tuck himself in her shadow so that everyone would see
and remember only her. She understood why he wanted
to do that, so even though she found the attention of the
guardsmen uncomfortable, she nodded and rode ahead of
both men into the town.

It occurred to her before they had gone very far that

they were going to see the King of Casmantium and that, much worse, he was actually going to see *them*. She wondered what her hair looked like—she had not managed to wash it since Kames—and might there be visible dirt on her face? Though the mountains had been clean stone and ice, mostly. But her traveling skirt was terribly crumpled, and once she discarded her coat, she was almost certain she would find a grease mark on her blouse from the previous night's dinner. She wondered whether they might really need to go *straight* to the Arobern. Might the guardsmen let them stop at some inn or public house, first? One with decent bathing facilities and a laundry?

But a sidelong glance at their escort told her how little hope there was of such a stop. They were accompanied by several guardsmen, not merely the one who had said he would escort them, though that one was clearly in charge. He looked very serious and determined. If Mienthe and Tan had wanted to break away and lose themselves in Ehre, this would have been inconvenient. As it was, except that her sudden burst of self-consciousness made her wish for a little less efficiency, the presence of the guardsmen was very convenient indeed. The streets were terribly crowded and Mienthe had no idea in the world where she was going. But the guardsmen cleared a way for them, guiding them around in a confusingly circular path that seemed to lead them strangely out of the way if they meant to go, as Mienthe had assumed, toward the center of the town.

Just as she started to wonder very seriously where exactly the guardsmen were taking them, the streets suddenly opened up and there before them was a very large stone fortress, a building not without a certain grace, but obviously intended far more for defense than for beauty. There was no evident garden, only a small courtyard of raked granite grit, with stables to one side and one massive tree on the other.

"The governor's palace," said their guide. "The Arobern is there now. I will show you where to wait and then I will take word to the king's...ah, the word is...the king's chamberlain, yes? Forgive me; I am clumsy with your language."

"But you speak Terheien very well," Mienthe said.

The man ducked his head again. "The honored courier flatters my poor skill," he said politely, and swung down from his own horse to hold hers.

Mienthe dismounted. So did Tan, though no one held his horse for him. He kept a grip on his horse's saddle, Mienthe saw, and his mouth tightened with pain as his weight came down on his bad leg. She gave him a worried glance, to which he returned only a short nod. He let go of the saddle and took two deliberate steps away from his horse, hardly limping at all, though Mienthe did not like to guess what that effort cost him.

The door to which the guardsman brought them was a plain one, set out of the way, well around the palace from the main doors. It opened onto a narrow hall, but the rugs on the stone floor were good ones, and the walls paneled in carved wood. At the end of the hall was a surprisingly pretty receiving chamber, furnished with clear attention to elegance and style. The floor was stone, with rugs of violet and blue to muffle the cold and noise. The furnishings were all wood save for the small tables, which were each topped with a sheet of polished granite. A bronze statue of a leaping stag stood in one corner, and a pewter tree with silver leaves and little birds of copper and black iron in another. There were no windows, but lamps of copper and glass hung from the paneled ceiling, and porcelain lamps stood on the tables.

"I will leave you here," said the guardsman, speaking to Mienthe. "I will tell the chamberlain. I will be very clear. I think the Arobern will send for you quickly, but I will tell them to send tea. You will wait? This is acceptable?"

"Yes," said Mienthe, wondering what he would say or do if she said *No*. She said helplessly, "But my hair—" and stopped, blushing in embarrassed confusion.

The corners of the guardsman's mouth twitched uncontrollably upward before he tamped his lips out straight again. He said very firmly, "The King of Casmantium is accustomed to receive urgent news from couriers and agents. Honored lady."

"Yes," Mienthe said, though not with nearly the firmness the man had managed. She told herself it was perfectly true. The guardsman bowed, rather more deeply than she had expected, and went out. None of the guardsmen stayed in the room with them, though she was not at all surprised to see two of them stop outside the door— there was only one door—with a patient attitude that suggested they might be there for some time.

"Your hair looks perfectly charming," Tan told her, without the hint of a smile, after the door had closed. "There's a tiny bit of ash on your chin, just—" He brushed his thumb across his own chin.

Mienthe scrubbed her face vigorously with her sleeve, sighed, and looked around. At least there were chairs, nice ones with thick cushions. She thought hot tea sounded wonderful, especially if it came with cakes or sweet rolls, and she thought even more strongly that Tan should sit down. She sank into the nearest chair herself, by way of example, and said, "I suppose the Arobern really is here."

"Yes," agreed Tan. "For a brief time, I was afraid our friends there might be taking us somewhere other than to the king, but now I rather suspect they are royal guardsmen and not merely local men who prefer soldiering to farming." He lowered himself slowly into a chair, not grimacing at all, and carefully stretched his leg out before him.

Mienthe did not ask about his knee, since the way he moved told her everything she needed to know. Anyway, she had some hope he would be able to rest it properly now. She asked instead, "You do intend to tell the king who you are, don't you? If he will see us, I mean? Because I don't know how to explain everything without explaining that." She considered for a moment and added, "I don't know how to explain *anything* without explaining that."

"If the Arobern actually sends for us, I suppose he must have the entire wretched story from top to toe," Tan said, not as if the prospect pleased him. He tilted his head against the back of his chair, closed his eyes, and let his breath out, slowly.

"I hadn't known—" Mienthe began worriedly, and stopped.

"I had no difficulty until I tried walking on it," Tan said, not opening his eyes. "I'm sure it will soon be better. You will do me the favor of not mentioning the problem to anyone."

"No, of course I won't," Mienthe promised, though she couldn't decide whether this request—or command—was based on any practical consideration or merely on Tan's habitual unwillingness to let anybody know the truth about anything.

There was a sound at the door, and she turned, thinking of the promised tea. But the sound did not presage a tray-bearing servant, but rather an elegant man in lavender and gray who bowed his head briefly to Mienthe and said, in smooth, perfect Terheien, "The Lord King Brechen Glansent Arobern is pleased to grant you audience, esteemed lady, and you, sir, if you will please accompany me."

The King of Casmantium looked very much as Mienthe had expected.

Bertaud had never spoken to her—not even to her—of the summer of the griffins, nor of his months in Casmantium that had followed. Mienthe had clearly understood, as so few people seemed to, that whether he had achieved some sort of triumph or not, whether or not he was honored for whatever he had done, her cousin had suffered somehow in that year and did not like to think of that time.

She had once believed, with a child's natural romanticism, that he had probably fallen in love with a Casmantian woman and she had broken his heart. Later, it had occurred to her that this was, perhaps, a simplistic explanation. Also, she had come to understand that her cousin's grief, whatever its source, was in some way deeper—no, not deeper, that wasn't fair. But then perhaps somehow *broader* than the grief that afflicted men who were merely unlucky with a woman. Though this assessment was based largely on the lovesick and forlorn men who trailed behind her maid Karin like a line of goslings piping piteously behind a swan—well, that was a silly image, but anyway, perhaps comparing Bertaud to her maid's hopeless collection of would-be lovers wasn't quite fair.

Whatever the source of his distaste for the subject, she had never asked her cousin any questions about that time. Even as a child, she had very well understood how someone might wish to forget the past. Or, if the past could not be forgotten, at least to keep from dragging through unpleasant memories. She had been wordlessly determined that, with her, Bertaud might speak or keep silent, exactly as he wished.

But that had not stopped her deep curiosity to know everything about her cousin and what he had done. After he had brought her to live with him in the great house, she had admired him enormously and had longed to know all the details about every admirable thing he had ever done. She had asked his guardsmen, and the servants, and she had once found the nerve to ask King Iaor, and although no one knew everything, she had learned by heart the bits they all knew and had made up stories to tell herself that explained the parts they did not know.

But she would have known the King of Casmantium anyway, because he looked so much like his son, Erich. When she saw Brechen Glansent Arobern, she almost felt as though she recognized him. It was odd to think that he could have no idea who she was.

The Arobern was a big man, burly as well as tall, who looked more like a professional soldier than a king, except for the sapphire and amethyst buttons on his shirt and the heavy gold chain around his throat. He wore unornamented black and had a black-hilted sword slung at his side, and as his close-cropped hair and heavy beard were also black, he made rather a grim, aggressive impression, which Mienthe supposed was purposeful. Certainly it was effective. His jaw was heavy, but his deep-set eyes, glinting with wit as well as forceful energy, prevented him from looking dull or brutish. She would have been afraid of him, except she saw him through Erich's memory as well as her own eyes, so she saw kindness and generosity in his face, as well as aggressive energy.

The king sat in a plain chair of polished granite, in a room that was not large and yet managed, with its violet-draped walls and thick indigo rugs and the sapphire-blue glass of its lanterns, to seem ostentatious. Though there were other chairs in the room—plain wood—everyone else in the room was standing.

There were several guardsmen and servants, but there were also some few people who were clearly more important than these attendants. Close by the king's side, leaning casually against the back of the stone chair, stood a slight, fine-boned man with perfectly white hair. Mienthe immediately recognized this man. Bertaud might not like to speak of Casmantium, but both King Iaor and Erich had described him to her. Though King Iaor had disliked him, Erich had told her that while he was impossible to deceive, he was also wise and kind. *He's the only man in Casmantium who isn't a little afraid of my father*, Erich had said. *When he's kind to you, it isn't because you're a prince.*

This was Beguchren Teshrichten, who, Erich said,

had been a mage but who, so King Iaor had said, had
somehow lost his magecraft—used it up or burned it out,
or the griffins had burned it out when they defeated him.
Something had happened to him, but King Iaor had not
been clear about exactly what that was.

But Lord Beguchren *looked* like a mage. Despite his
white hair, at first she did not think he was very old.
Then she looked again and was not sure, because his
opaque pewter-gray eyes somehow seemed ancient. He
was a very small man, no taller than Mienthe herself—if
anything, he was a little shorter than she was. Despite his
small size, the impenetrable calm in his pewter-dark eyes
made Lord Beguchren rather intimidating, especially
because he was also thoroughly elegant. There was delicate white embroidery on his white shirt, which had buttons of pearl and just a little lace at the wrists—Mienthe,
who was not ordinarily much interested in fine clothing,
instantly longed for a gown made by his tailor—and there
were very fine sapphires set in the silver rings on three
fingers of his left hand.

Behind this man and a little to the side stood a man who
was so much taller that he made Beguchren Teshrichten
look as small as a child. He had broad shoulders and big
hands and a strong, bony face that was not exactly handsome. Yet he owned, Mienthe could not help noticing, a
lanky, raw-boned masculinity that was, in its way, more
striking than ordinary handsomeness.

The tall man was also particularly perceptive: For all
Tan was working to stay quietly in the background, the
greater part of his attention was definitely fixed on Tan
and not on Mienthe. She wondered how Tan had caught
his interest so quickly and definitively. The tall man did

not seem to wish to stare, but he looked again and again
at Tan with quick, covert glances, each time looking
away at once. Mienthe frowned at him. He noticed it
after a moment, took a deep breath, closed his eyes for a
moment, and then gave Mienthe a carefully attentive look
and a smile. She did not find his gaze aggressive like the
Arobern's nor unfathomable like Beguchren's, but curious and even friendly. If not for his strange reaction to
Tan, she would have thought it the look of a warmhearted
man who wished to believe the best of every stranger.
But there *was* that reaction, so she did not know what to
think.

Beside the tall man stood a small, delicate woman with
lovely molasses-dark hair and great natural poise. By the
way she rested her hand possessively on his arm, she was
clearly his wife. There was no sign of warmth or friendli-
ness from her, but there was no hostility, either. Her gaze
was, Mienthe decided, professionally intent and curious.
She did not seem to share her husband's fascination with
Tan, but gazed steadily and analytically at Mienthe. It
was the sort of look Mienthe expected from a mage.
Probably she *was* a mage, whether Lord Beguchren was
or not. For all her cool dispassion, Mienthe was absurdly
glad to see another woman in the room.

Mienthe wanted to look at Tan, but he was a step behind
her. So after a moment, since there was plainly nothing
else to do, she walked forward, offered the Arobern a
very small bow—he was not her king, so although she
longed to be able to ask someone, she thought it must be
wrong for her to do more. Then, straightening, she waited
for the king to address her.

The Arobern nodded back, very grave and regal. He

said without preamble, in strongly accented but understandable Terheien, "You did not send me a wand, but I
think you are a courier. From the Delta, I am informed.
Also from the Safiad, yes?"

Mienthe stared at him for a moment. She remembered
Tan saying, *I suppose he must have the entire wretched
story from top to toe.* But she did not know how to
begin.

Then Tan breathed in her ear, "Whose cousin are you?
Well?"

Mienthe blinked. She took a deep breath and said, her
voice only wavering a little, "Lord King"—she thought
that was the correct Casmantian form of address—"Lord
King, I am not precisely a courier. But it is true I carry a
warning from the Delta. From my cousin. I'm—my name
is Mienthe daughter of Beraod. Bertaud son of Boudan is
my cousin. He—I—I know you are an honorable man and
a strong king. So I came to you, because there is trouble
in the Delta and I did not know where else to go."

There was a pause, during which the King of Casmantium looked hard at Mienthe. He did not smile or
nod, and for a moment she was afraid he did not believe
her. Then he stood up and inclined his head to her, and
she saw that though she had taken him by surprise, he
did not doubt her. She supposed few people dared lie to
him. Certainly not with the rather alarming Beguchren
Teshrichten by his side.

"A chair for Lady Mienthe," the Arobern commanded,
and waited for one to be brought over before he dropped
back into his own chair. He made a broad gesture that
dismissed most of the guardsmen and nearly all of the
servants. Then, once the room was more nearly private,

he said, "I have had word from the Safiad. That is why I came to Ehre, so that couriers from Feierabiand could come to me more swiftly. Now you say you are come directly from the Delta, not from the Safiad but on your own account? Tell me your warning."

It seemed an unbelievable tale when Mienthe laid it out, which she tried to do in order, from Tan's appearance in Tiefenauer carrying secrets he'd stolen from the Linularinan spymaster, straight on through his kidnapping right out of a guarded house by that same spymaster and then the immediate invasion of the Delta by Linularinan soldiers. It sounded unbelievable even to her. She stumbled embarrassedly through an explanation of how she'd found Tan, of how she might be waking into the mage gift, though she didn't feel like she was becoming a mage, but really she did not know what becoming a mage felt like—here, though no one interrupted, Beguchren Teshrichten and the tall man exchanged a significant look, and Mienthe stopped.

"Go on," said the Arobern, with an impatient frown for his own people.

Mienthe hesitated for a moment, but when no one else said anything, she went on to describe the book, the one with the empty pages, that the Linularinan spymaster had brought with him from Teramondian. She looked again at Tan in case he should want to explain about the book. He only nodded at her again, so she explained how they thought Tan must have taken some powerful legist-working or law out of the book and how the Linularinan spymaster, or someone, seemed amazingly determined to get it back.

Mienthe looked from one to another of her audience,

unable to gauge what anybody thought of any of this. She said uncertainly, "And then when we thought we might go north, Tan and I, we were afraid we might find Linularinan agents before us. They won't *stop*. I don't know if King Iaor knows all this yet, though some word must surely have got north by this time. But I don't know whether he's free to respond to Linularinum's provocation, because of the griffins. You do know about that? That's what was in the message you were sent, isn't that right? A mage of theirs, named Kairaithin, I think, brought word that the Wall, the Great Wall my cousin helped build, that it was cracked through. But was there anything about Linularinum in that message?"

"No," said the Arobern, looking at her.

"Well, then I bring you that word," Mienthe said simply. "We don't know why they are so horribly determined, but we think—that is, I think—"

"We," said Tan quietly, the first time he had spoken.

Mienthe nodded, grateful for his support. "Maybe it's not so, but we think it's something to do with the book and the magic of law it held, and we think there were Linularinan agents still behind us in the pass. Maybe three hours behind? Just at the crest of the mountain when we had reached the iron gates. Though it might not have been—that is, honest travelers might also have come behind us by chance."

The Arobern looked at Mienthe for a moment. Then he studied Tan for a much longer moment. At last he said to Beguchren Teshrichten, "What do *you* say, hah?"

The small man gave his king an impenetrable look and then glanced up at the tall man with the quirk of one frost-white eyebrow. He asked, "Gereint?"

The tall man looked carefully at Mienthe and then glanced at Tan, though he looked away again at once with a slight wince. He took a deep breath, shrugged, and said to Beguchren, his voice exactly as deep and gravelly as Mienthe had expected, but somehow not harsh, "I don't know whether the honored lady is a mage. I'm looking right at her and still I can't tell. I told you how oddly magecraft has been behaving of late. That may be inter-fering with my perception. I look at the honored lady and sometimes I think she's a mage and sometimes I think she's nothing like a mage." He glanced at Tan once more and away.

"But the man?" Beguchren Teshrichten said patiently.

"Oh, well…the man. I don't think *he's* a mage; that's not what I'm seeing. But forces are not simply bending around him as they bend around a mage." Gereint pointed one powerful finger at Tan, who flinched just perceptibly. "Forces—events—every chance in the whole world is twisting, distorting, and folding right *there*. I've never seen anything like it. I've never heard of anything like it. I can't think of a single passage in Warichteier's *Principia* or any other book that refers to anything remotely like it. I certainly can't do the phenomenon justice, not being a poet, but if you'll forgive a poor attempt, I'd say it's as though this man here is the hinge around which the whole age is trying to turn."

This time Beguchren lifted both eyebrows. Then, while everyone else, including Tan, stared at his tall friend who had come out with such astonishing statements, he gave the Arobern a significant look.

The Arobern said to Mienthe, "Three hours behind you, hah?" Then he turned to one of the guardsmen, the one who had escorted Mienthe and Tan through Ehre, and commanded, "Set a guard on the iron gates. At once, do you hear? I wish to see anyone who comes through those gates. I wish to see these travelers personally, you understand, whoever they might be. And set a stronger guard on all the gates into Ehre—be quick to do that. Anyone who seems perhaps a little out of the ordinary, you understand? Men who are neither merchants nor farmers nor of any trade you can name. Look at these people for me, and send me word if you have any doubt what you have caught in your net."

The guardsman bowed without a word and went out quickly.

The Arobern got to his feet. Mienthe jumped up immediately, not to stay seated while the king stood, and looked anxiously at Tan. Practiced as he was at showing only what he wished to show, he looked faintly stunned. Mienthe thought his expression was sincere. She certainly thought he had every reason to look stunned.

To Mienthe, the king said, "Honored lady, I will ask Lady Tehre Amnachudran Tanshan to grant you the hospitality of her household, if this is agreeable to you and if Lady Tehre will permit me the liberty."

The tiny woman had been staring, with everyone else, at Tan. Now she transferred her interested gaze from Tan to Mienthe and said, in nearly accentless Terheien, "Yes, I am pleased to make such an offer. That will do very well." She smiled, a sharp expression but not unkind, and added, directly to Mienthe, "I'm sure you wish to wash and shift your clothing. If I haven't anything to suit you, I've got some cloth we can easily run up into a nice gown—I've been considering cloth lately. Working with cloth is more complicated and interesting than you'd think. Of course everything is fine if you apply any tension straight along the threads, and cloth distorts symmetrically if you apply tension at forty-five degrees to the angle of the warp and weft threads, but what I can't make out is the equations that allow you to predict the degree and kind of deformation if the tension is applied at some intermediate angle—"

Gereint broke into this discourse without the least surprise or fuss, "Tehre, if you please, I imagine Lady Mienthe would like to have something to eat at a civilized table while you find appropriate clothing for her." He added to Mienthe, "I think I am able to assure you, Lady Mienthe, that no Linularinan agent, mage or otherwise, will trouble your rest in *my* household."

Mienthe nodded, trying not to laugh. *Tehre's Wall*, the griffin had said to her cousin. So Lady Tehre had made that Wall. Mienthe found she was not at all surprised. She wondered what sort of protections might surround a household that included Lady Tehre and her husband. Very secure ones, probably.

Then she realized the king had not said he would send *Tan* with Lady Tehre, and hesitated, wondering whether she should say something, or ask, or protest.

Before she could speak, the Arobern said to Tan, "You, I wish to give into the hands of my friend Beguchren Teshrichten and my mage Gereint Enseichen. Will you permit this?"

For once, Tan did not seem to have any smooth response to hand.

CHAPTER 11

The king's house in Tihannad, where he held his winter court, was tucked close by the shore of Niambe Lake. It was a comfortable, rambling house built out of the native granite, with shingles of mountain cedar, nestled in the center of a comfortable, rambling town also built out of stone and cedar. A low wall ran about the king's house, as a greater wall encircled the town, but neither wall had been called upon to defend against enemies for hundreds of years and the gates of both generally stood wide and welcoming, with neither guard nor even a clerk to count who came and went.

But the gates of Tihannad were guarded now, and all but hidden by the crowd of folk waiting to be admitted. Jos saw at once that very few folk were leaving, or at least not heading south; all efforts were bent toward getting in.

Lord Bertaud paused when he saw the crowded roads and the press at the gates, his eyebrows rising. He might

have been wondering, as Jos certainly was, whether the
folk pressing into Tihannad expected walls of stone and
timber to defend against griffins who rode upon the wind.
Though perhaps it was not the walls themselves but the
lake so near those walls that was expected to ward away
fire. Perhaps it even would.

"I would have thought Tiearanan would be the retreat
of choice," Bertaud commented, gazing down toward the
press at the gates. "Though perhaps it is, for those who
are able to climb that steep road at speed. These may be
local folk who fear they may not come swiftly enough to
any more-distant shelter."

Jos only nodded distractedly, and Kairaithin did not
even seem to hear these comments. After a moment, Bertaud shrugged and led the way down across the slope of
the mountain toward the town.

For a few minutes, they walked in silence. Jos thought
about the wall, and a little about Kes, but that was too
painful and he tried to think about other things—anything
else—only then he thought, *So here we are, walking
down toward Tihannad*, and that was such a strange,
uncomfortable thought that he hardly knew what to do
with it. Six years alone in the high mountains had surely
unfit him for human company, and what would he possibly do now in a clamorous town? A *Feierabianden* town
crowded with fearful farmers who hoped their walls or
their lake would protect them.

Lord Bertaud would hardly have brought Jos trailing at
his heel to any purpose. Only the exigency of the moment
had compelled Kairaithin to shift them all, and he had
brought them here. But though that was well enough for
Lord Bertaud, Tihannad was no place for Jos.

His steps slowed, and then stopped. He looked uncertainly up into the broken country of stone and ice, east and north, back toward the high pass and his abandoned cottage. His fire would burn without ceasing, but would his goat and all the foolish chickens know how to make their way from meadow to meadow along the silver length of the nameless river, down to warmer country and better pastures? The goat, perhaps, he thought, but probably not the hens or the vain white cock.

But he could hardly make his way back up through that rugged pass on foot and alone and without anything at all in the way of supplies. Even if he could, when the Great Wall finally shattered and the griffins came through the pass, he doubted whether they would spare anything they found in their way, man or goat or bird. Probably they would tear every stone apart from every other stone merely with the fiery wind of their passage.

Kairaithin, too, had halted. He had followed Jos's gaze, up and east and north, but there was nothing a man could understand in his eyes. Jos wondered what the griffin mage was seeing. Not these mountains, nor a small abandoned stone cottage. Fire, and the Wall, and the red dust where the king of the griffins had lunged forward just that little bit too fast...

Jos regarded the griffin mage with worry. Kairaithin did not seem to have recovered his emotional balance, whatever that properly comprised, from the brief, shocking battle by the Wall. He seemed stunned, perhaps by his failed attempt to destroy Kes; or by his awareness that the Great Wall must surely break; or, most likely of all, from the awareness that the king of the griffins was dead and that Kairaithin himself had killed him.

Jos had expected Kairaithin to leave them here above Tihannad once he had brought them here, to let them make their own way down to the lake and into the town. He had expected the griffin mage to take himself away alone to some deserted bit of desert where he might think or curse or worry or consider the new span of his options, or whatever it was that a griffin might do at such a moment of personal loss. He had little idea what that might be, but he did believe that Kairaithin felt the king's death as a personal loss, and far more bitterly for how it had happened.

Instead, the griffin mage had followed the men down along the side of the mountain toward the lake, as though, Jos thought, he simply could not imagine where else he might go. Now, standing with his face raised to the high mountains, his expression closed and still, he looked, for the first time, not only drawn and weary but also old.

Then Lord Bertaud looked over his shoulder and impatiently snapped at both of them, "Come!"

Jos flinched, more in startlement than in alarm. But, after all, where else could he go? He took a step after the Feierabianden lord.

But, to his surprise, Kairaithin also flinched and lowered his head and came, like a servant or a dog. Jos had not precisely expected a flash of anger or offended pride; he had not thought about that command or its tone enough to expect anything. But he was deeply shocked by the weary compliance he saw in the griffin mage's bowed head.

It seemed to shock Bertaud as well, for he turned quickly and came back toward them—toward Kairaithin, because he was not looking at Jos. He began to reach out a hand as though he would touch the griffin mage, grip his arm or his shoulder. But then he stopped and his hand fell back to his side. But the intensity of his gaze seemed to compel a response from Kairaithin, who lifted his head and met Bertaud's eyes.

They stood on the cold windswept stone of the mountain, the two of them, Feierabianden lord and griffin mage, as though for that moment they were the only two living creatures in the world. Jos could not understand what he saw between them. He thought it was neither friendship nor enmity, but perhaps some strange kind of understanding that owed something to both.

Bertaud said quietly, "I beg your pardon."

"You need not," Kairaithin answered. He bowed his head again, and this time Jos saw that he did this with a kind of deliberate effort, yet not precisely unwillingly. He said, "Everything I have done has led to this moment. All the important choices fell to me, and I was wrong, and wrong again, and all that has come or will come now is due to my lack of foresight."

"No," said Bertaud at once, forcefully. "Six years ago, if you had not made Kes into a creature of fire, everything that you feared for your people would have happened exactly as you foresaw it. Your diminished people could never have faced both Feierabiand and Casmantium, and it would have come to that eventually. Those Casmantian cold mages were determined to destroy you all, and they would have done it. I believe they would, if not right at that moment, then very soon—"

"I should have foreseen what a weapon I made, when I made Kes—"

"You did! Of course you did! Why should you mind

giving your people a potent weapon? It was me you didn't foresee, and how could you have? How could anyone have?"

"You call *griffins*?" Jos exclaimed, utterly shocked by this sudden realization—Feierabiand for calling, yes, very well, but calling *griffins*?

Then, as both Bertaud and Kairaithin turned toward him, he understood just how foolish he had been to cry this realization aloud to the listening mountains. Six years alone had been too many—he would never have exclaimed aloud when he'd been practicing proper spy-craft, no matter how shocked he'd been—he took a step back.

Kairaithin, his mouth tight, the expression in his black eyes unreadable, began to lift his hand.

Jos took another step back, knowing there was no point to it, no flight possible, nothing to say. He had in one flashing moment—too late—understood what it would do to the griffins to know that they could be commanded like dogs, and understood as well that no one in the world knew they could be, except those standing here on this mountain above Niambe Lake. It was impossible that any oath of silence could possibly satisfy Kairaithin. He took a hard breath, straightened his shoulders, and looked the griffin mage full in the face. He saw no mercy there. He did not expect to, for he knew that mercy was not some-thing griffins understood. He found himself thinking of Kes, beautiful and inhuman and just as merciless as a griffin. He tried to think of her, instead, as she had been years ago, when she had been merely human. He could remember, though with some effort, the shy, graceful girl who had shunned company—though not his—and liked to run barefoot in the hills. He shut his eyes to better hold her image before his mind's eye.

"No!" snapped Bertaud.

Jos opened his eyes.

The griffin mage had stopped, his hand only half raised. He was looking at Bertaud.

"He won't speak of it." Bertaud did not look at Jos, only at Kairaithin. "It's not his fault he realized. We were careless—I was careless. But he's accomplished at keeping secrets, and he'll tell no one. Whom would he tell, and to what purpose?"

"He will cry it from the rooftops of your human town; to everyone and in every direction of the wind he will call it out. He will do it to compel you to act."

"*Events* will compel me to act! Unless we find another choice! Another wind to ride, not one that rises from anything that has yet happened!"

"Great secrets are always safest if no one knows them—as anyone accustomed to secrets is well aware!"

Jos couldn't quite keep from flinching. For a long moment they all stood in silence. Jos did not move. He tried not even to breathe. But Lord Bertaud and the griffin mage were glaring at each other; for the moment they both seemed to have forgotten him.

He found himself turning over this new and shocking revelation in his mind—Lord Bertaud could call griffins, so he could command them to cease their attack, only he did not want to command them. Because—and if Jos had not been so closely acquainted with griffins over the past year, he would never have understood this—because they could never accept being commanded. The knowledge that they could be called to heel by a man would *destroy* them—in fact, if they knew that it was possible for a man to command them, they would probably become even more determined to kill everyone and tear down all the country of earth.

Several odd comments he had not quite understood, from both Bertaud and Kairaithin, suddenly fell into place.

He said suddenly, without truly knowing beforehand that he was going to speak at all, "What if you get Tastairiane by himself? What if you demonstrate to *him* what power you hold? No, better, not merely a demonstration and a warning; what if you simply command him to turn away from this wind, to bid Kes leave be the Wall, to keep his people in their desert?"

Both Lord Bertaud and Kairaithin turned to stare at him. Jos tried not to flinch—he had not exactly meant to make himself the renewed focus of their common attention, only the idea had occurred to him—likely he had not understood properly—there was probably some very good reason that wouldn't work—

Bertaud said at last, "Kairaithin?"

"A dangerous wind," the griffin mage said, not looking at him. He was looking at Jos, but now with something like his accustomed fierce power in his fiery black gaze. "As goes the Lord of Fire and Air, so go the People of Fire and Air. If Tastairiane Apailika is filled with fury and despair, then fury and despair will burn through the country of fire. But…"

Bertaud said nothing. Jos thought he was probably trying not to exclaim, *Well, that's all right, then!* Though perhaps not. Jos had lived in Feierabiand for many years, more than long enough to know how violently a man who could call an animal hated to do anything to harm that animal. How much more intense would that revulsion of feeling be if you could command not animals, but a fierce and beautiful people? A people who would surely die if they knew they were constrained, either in violent resistance or simply in outraged bursts of fire and sand?

"But no king is eternal," said Kairaithin, continuing his earlier thought. "At some time in the future, Tastairiane Apailika will no longer be the Lord of Fire and Air, and at that time, so long as the People of Fire and Air remain, another king might set a new and better direction." His eyes were on Bertaud's. He said, "I do not know how I may come at Tastairiane Apailika, or how I may bring him alone to you. But I will try. If you give me leave."

Lord Bertaud said flatly, "Go."

Kairaithin blurred away into the air and the cold sunlight, and was gone.

Bertaud stood rigid for a moment, looking at nothing; at the slant of the cold light across the lake, perhaps. Then he shuddered and rubbed his hands across his face, and looked up at last at Jos.

Jos did not speak. He did not know what to say.

"Your suggestion might prove a good one," Bertaud said at last. "I thank you. I certainly bear you no ill will. But I don't know whether I should have stopped him. You understand the price of forbearance? You must *never* even imply that there is a shadow of a chance that you might ever tell *anyone*—you must swear to me you will *never*—"

"I understand," Jos assured him fervently. "I promise you, lord." He hesitated. Then he said, "You know I don't hate them? I'm afraid of them, but I don't hate them and

I don't want them destroyed, and I don't know how many other men could swear to that, but I can. I do. I'll tell no one, lord. I do swear it. I'm sorry I ever guessed, except as it may let Kairaithin take down that bastard Tastairiane. I wouldn't be sorry if *he* were destroyed."

"Earth and stone." Bertaud rubbed his face again, then looked up and nodded. "Very well. I accept your word and your promise. *Keep* it, man. You may. In the end, if I must, I'll reveal it myself."

Of course he would. So long as… "Kairaithin cannot find a way to slip sideways around this… affinity of yours and kill you himself?" Jos tried not to sound too diffident. "To him, that must surely seem an acceptable solution, lord?"

Bertaud laughed, without much humor. "I'm confident he wishes he had when he had the chance. No. It's too late now for him to reach after *that* wind. He can't approach me without my awareness, and I'm alert to the possibility, I assure you." He gazed down toward Tihannad for some time in silence.

Jos supposed the Feierabianden lord knew the measure and limits of his own gift. Nevertheless, he resolved to stay near him if he could, so he might at least cry a warning if Lord Bertaud was mistaken.

Bertaud nodded to Jos at last and led the way that last little distance down to the lake and then along the lakeshore road to the gates of Tihannad and, with some difficulty, through the crowd that pressed forward. But once at the gate, the men there recognized him, of course.

"Begging your pardon, but it's the king's orders, my lord, because of the trouble in the south," an officer of the guardsmen told Bertaud. "Everyone to be let in, but we're

to direct them as best we may. Everyone's taking in one
or two families, and the king's ordered temporary shelter
set up for the rest—"

"Trouble in the *south*," Bertaud said. He and Jos
exchanged a baffled look.

"So they say, my lord," said the officer. "Couriers have
been riding in and out all today and yesterday, until one
would expect them to wear out their wands as well as
their horses. His Majesty is in his house, so far as we've
had word here, and I'm sure he'll be glad to see you, my
lord, if you'll go up. I'm sure we can find horses for you
and your companion—"

"Thank you," said Lord Bertaud, with a shake of his
head that suggested, not that he was rejecting the offer,
but that he had no more idea than Jos what might have
happened in the south. "Yes, we would be glad if you
could find an extra beast or two. *Where* in the south, do
you know?"

The officer gave Bertaud a close look and lowered his
voice. "Ah, my lord, I'm sorry if I'm the first to tell you
so, but what we hear is those sly Linularinan bastards
have crossed the river into the Delta, taking advantage
of what they hope will be trouble here. I don't know as
whether that's true, my lord. You should ask at the king's
house—"

"Yes," Bertaud said, in a blank tone.

King Iaor received them without formality, in a large,
plain room with five tables, where at the moment maps
were spread out on all but one of the tables and pinned
up on three of the walls. The king was attended by two
of his generals and by the captain of his personal guard,

and by another man for whom Bertaud spared a sharp look.

"Yes, my queen is returned, and my daughters, thankfully all safe," said the king, evidently in explanation of that man's presence. He opened one hand in a curt gesture, signaling that they need not bow or stand otherwise on ceremony. "They are come weary and bedraggled, but safe. Earth and iron, if I had known we rode on *campaign*, I would hardly have invited them to accompany me! Tell me that they will be safe here." He cocked his head at Bertaud, who wordlessly shook his head.

"No?" said the king, and gestured for two of his attendants to unroll another map on the only clear table. He said, "One may possibly expect Tihannad itself to be protected by the intrinsic magic of the lake...we do expect so. Nevertheless, I think I will send the queen and my little girls north to Tiearanan. If there is trouble from any direction, it will surely come there last."

"And from what direction do we expect trouble? From what other direction," Bertaud amended. "From the south, is it? What is this I hear about Linularinum coming across the river into the Delta?"

The king nodded sharply. "Would I was able to deny that word! But I fear it is true enough. Niethe herself tells me she fled only just in time. Bertaud, I regret that I must inform you that your cousin Mienthe insisted on remaining in Tiefenauer."

Lord Bertaud stood very still, as though he had received a blow and was waiting to feel the extent of the damage.

"Likely she is perfectly safe. Kohorrian will surely not allow his men to pillage, least of all your own house in your own town. He will not wish to offend the Delta so seriously—"

"He has offended me," Bertaud said. His voice had gone quiet and hard, with an undertone of ferocity nearly as dangerous as a griffin's.

"Well, he has assuredly offended me!" snapped the king, and slammed a fist down without warning onto the nearest table. "My Niethe, *my little girls*, riding night and day through dangerous sloughs and along animal trails, because Kohorrian thinks if we are sufficiently distracted in the north, then he may make as free as he likes with the south! We shall find a way to sort out this trouble with the griffins, I trust we shall, and then we shall assuredly ride south and explain clearly to Kohorrian the depths of our offense."

"May we find it so," said Bertaud grimly.

Iaor nodded. "There is word that Linularinan forces are active west of the Delta as well, over toward Minas Ford and Minas Spring. Nevertheless, we believe that the greatest part of his ambition, whatever ill-conceived notion informs it, concerns the Delta itself. I should send you south—"

Bertaud opened his mouth, but then closed it again without speaking. Clearly he longed to take a fast horse and as many men as the king would give him and ride south as fast as he could go. But, thought Jos, even more clearly he knew that if the Wall above Niambe Lake shattered, he would need to be right here, right *here*, where the griffins must come through the narrow pass and pass by the lake. He could not possibly ride south, not on any account, not even if his pride were scored beyond bearing at this extraordinary Linularinan insult, not even if he had a wife and a dozen children in Tiefenauer and far less if his greatest hostage to the exigencies of war were a mere cousin, with which in any case the Lord of the Delta was reputedly well-endowed.

"So I am to gather you have no good word to bring me?" Iaor asked, regarding Bertaud narrowly. "Advise me, my old friend, and we shall consider what we may best do."

Lord Bertaud took a slow breath. Another.

Jos wanted to say, *You cannot possibly go south*, only Bertaud would not likely welcome advice he knew already, nor Jos's temerity in offering it. He said nothing.

"As you permit me," Bertaud said at last. "Yes, send Niethe and the girls to Tiearanan. Then, my king, take what force you have gathered and ride south yourself. See to the Delta. Reprimand Kohorrian. Leave me a small force here. If the Wall breaks and the griffins come through the pass—and I think it likely will, and so they may well—in this exigency, my king, trust me to turn them, with such allies as I am able to persuade. Or if I cannot turn them, then nothing can, and as that is so, your armies will be better occupied elsewhere."

From the king's blank expression, this was not the advice he had anticipated. He met Bertaud's eyes in silence. There was something between them, Jos guessed; something difficult of which this moment reminded them both. But neither man spoke of it. The king only asked at last, "Shall I trust your judgment in this? Do you trust your own judgment in this?"

"Yes," said Bertaud, his tone flat. "As I beg you will, my king."

"Ah." The king glanced around at his maps, down at the nearest. Up again. He glanced questioningly at Jos.

"He does well enough with me," Bertaud said. He offered no explanation, as he had offered none in all this tangled implication and half-truth.

However, the king asked for none. He only nodded and glanced again down at the map. Then he looked up again. "My generals"—he nodded right and left at the sober, quiet men who attended him—"have been gathering men this past day. They will be able to ride the day after tomorrow, or possibly the day after that. Perhaps with me, perhaps with you, perhaps with neither of us. I will wish to hear in more detail of what you have discovered regarding the Wall and the griffins; we will both wait for further news from the south. Then we will decide, in all good order, what we shall do."

"My king, I can desire nothing but what you desire," Lord Bertaud said formally, and bowed.

Jos was already certain that, whatever the king wanted and whatever he thought was important, the final decision would place Bertaud firmly in the path of any incursion of griffins through the northern pass. It was absolutely essential that the decision fall out that way, and so Lord Bertaud would say whatever he must, do whatever he must, to be certain it did.

But he was also certain that unless Kairaithin said and did whatever *he* had to, in order to ensure a private meeting between Lord Bertaud and Tastairiane, and quickly, quickly—before the Wall shattered—no good outcome was even vaguely possible, whatever men and the kings of men might arrange among themselves.

CHAPTER 12

In his life as a confidential agent, and even before that, Tan had lived through his share of terrifying moments. Yet, oddly, he could not recall ever being so frightened in his life as he was when the door shut behind him and closed him into a small, private, comfortable room with the small, elegant Casmantian lord Beguchren Teshrichten and the tall mage Gereint Enseichen.

It was perfectly reasonable for the confidential agent of one country to be afraid if he fell into the power of a different country. Certain obvious events were likely to unfold from that point. But an awareness of that fact did not explain Tan's fear, and he knew it did not.

Mienthe had insisted on staying close by him, which Tan considered very nearly heroism as it meant she must postpone her bath. He had considered prompting her to go with the Casmantian lady, as the Arobern clearly wished. Compliance with the Arobern's wishes might well have been tactically the wiser course. But, though he was ashamed of the depth of his own need for her support, he was too grateful for her presence to make any effort to send her away.

Because he was ashamed and angry as well as frightened, Tan said sharply, "Well, Lord Beguchren, as there is no great need to dissemble, shall we be plain? You mean to pry open my mind and heart and discover what is written there. Is that not true?"

Mienthe, shocked and distressed, took half a step forward, but Lord Beguchren only gave Tan a slight, imperturbable smile, tipped his head toward a chair drawn up near a wide fireplace, and said mildly, in smooth, unaccented Terheien, "If you will sit, we will make an effort to discover whether or not that will be necessary."

Tan did not move.

"He is frightened," said the tall man. Gereint Enseichen. His tone was matter-of-fact, utterly lacking in censure. He added wryly, "You have this effect on ordinary men, my lord. I well remember our own first meeting." As he spoke, he rearranged the chairs in the room so that four of them formed a neat rectangle in front of the fire, a porcelain lamp hanging behind each. Then he settled in one of the chairs, folding up his long limbs with every sign of satisfaction. "Honored lady, if you will?" he said to Mienthe, indicating one of the remaining chairs, and, "My lord? Honored sir?" he added, nodding toward the others.

The white-haired Casmantian lord was not quite smiling, but nevertheless he looked amused. He said mildly, "Well, but I was constrained by a royal command to terrify you, Gereint," but he also moved to take the indicated chair.

"You terrified me for a great long time after that," the

mage said. "You still do." He did not sound in the least terrified, but rather warmly affectionate.

Tan saw very clearly that the two men, however different they might seem, were close friends. For some inexplicable reason, he found this reassuring. And he did not want to frighten Mienthe by letting her see his own fear.

She laid a tentative hand on his arm. "You probably should sit, do you think?"

Tan's knee *was* making itself a trifle obvious: A long, slow ache had spread from the knee all the way up and down his leg. He gazed for a moment at Mienthe's anxious, earnest face and then found himself able to walk forward, almost without limping, and take his place in the appointed chair. The stiffness of his movements owed nothing to his bad knee. He did not understand why he could not mime relaxation, amiability, dense stupidity… He had drawn one mask or another across his own manner for so long that he would have thought the exercise had become effortless. But all masks seemed far out of reach today. He said sharply, to the mage, "What is it you see in me? What do you mean by saying that, what, events turn around me?"

"A very good question," agreed the Casmantian mage amiably. He regarded Tan with great curiosity for a moment, then looked away, wincing slightly. He told the fire, "One certainly understands why mages have no difficulty tracking you. It's quite a remarkable effect, when you try to examine it closely."

"I wish I—" Lord Beguchren began, but cut that thought short.

"As do we all," said Gereint Enseichen, in a tone both wry and deliberately brisk.

Mienthe gazed at him for a moment, then at the elegant Lord Beguchren. She started to speak, then visibly changed her mind about what she meant to say and said instead, "Whatever Tan is, *I* can't be a mage. Isn't that right? I don't see anything strange when I look at him. And my cousin said I couldn't be a mage because I didn't hate his friend. Kairaithin, I mean. The griffin mage."

Lord Beguchren regarded her thoughtfully. "If I remember your story correctly, after you were forced to flee Tiefenauer, you went directly to your father's house at Kames, to which you had directed the honored Tan. Why did you go there, rather than north to find your lord cousin?"

"Well, I…I don't…" Mienthe frowned. She opened her hands in a gesture of bafflement. "I don't…I don't really know why. Only…" She shook her head and looked back at Tan, her brows drawing together in puzzlement.

"You were drawn to find the honored Tan in Linularinum, after Istierinan Hamoddian had taken him; you found him without difficulty; and then again you were drawn after him to Kames. Gereint? You do not believe the lady is a mage?"

The tall man sat forward, turning so he could study Mienthe without looking also at Tan. He tilted his head in polite curiosity. "Perhaps you may have a very weak mage power, Lady Mienthe. That might explain why you have found yourself drawn toward the honored Tan without being exactly aware of what draws you, and also why you were able to endure the presence of a griffin mage without distress."

Mienthe nodded uncertainly.

Tan said sharply, not uncertain at all on this point,

"Whatever gift or power the lady holds, I can assure you, it is hardly *weak*."

"Thus the world insists on defying our expectations," Lord Beguchren murmured. He steepled his hands, regarding both Mienthe and Tan over the tips of his fingers. "The lady holds a powerful gift, but nothing a mage can recognize. Though your presence, honored Tan, distorts the world, we are told that you are not yourself a mage." He paused, his expression becoming even more bland and unreadable. "Mages do not ordinarily devote great attention to the work of ordinary gifts. Possibly this has constituted an oversight."

"So, now?" Tan challenged him.

"I, too, have directed only scant attention to the gift of law," the elegant lord said softly. "A regrettable neglect." He paused, but then went on, speaking directly to Tan, "While the lady's gift is interesting, it is yours that appears to require urgent attention. Your current condition has clearly come about not because of the working of any actual magecraft, but because of the great influence of the legistwork you have taken into yourself. The conclusion to which we are guided by events is that very influential factions within Linularinum are so distressed by the fact that they have lost this work that they are willing to provoke Iaor Safiad to war to regain it." He paused.

Tan said quietly—he could manage a quiet, civil tone if he concentrated—"I suspect Istierinan—or, yes, I know, possibly some faceless, nameless Linularinan faction—knew that your Great Wall had cracked through. So they wagered that King Iaor would be compelled to commit his strength in the north, giving them a relatively free hand to act in the south."

"And yet," murmured Lord Beguchren, "if I were a clever Linularinan spymaster, I should have assumed that the goodwill established six years past between Feierabiand and the griffins might possibly hold. That Wall was not built because the griffins intended to strike against *Feierabiand*. Why would any Linularinan faction, no matter how prescient, have guessed that the breaking of the Wall would draw peril down across Feierabiand rather than Casmantium?"

Tan had no answer to this.

"I think," Lord Beguchren said quietly, "that we have perhaps gone as far as ignorance can carry us. I think perhaps it is time to seek a clearer understanding of this book and the work it contained. I think it will after all be necessary to, as you so neatly put it, open your mind and heart and discover what is written there."

Mienthe said uncertainly, "If you'll permit it, Tan?"

And if he would not, Tan had no doubt that Lord Beguchren would compel him. That would horrify Mienthe. And to what point, when the Casmantian lord was so clearly correct? But he still could not make himself speak.

Lord Beguchren, though undoubtedly aware of Tan's sharp terror, said mildly to Mienthe, "He is aware there is no other reasonable course open to any of us. He was aware of it from the first."

Mienthe was, Tan regretted to see, indeed beginning to look horrified. He reached out toward her and managed to say with a quite creditable imitation of calm, "That's true. That's true, Mie."

Mienthe, unmollified, jumped to her feet and came over to stand behind him. Placing her hands on his shoulders, she glared at the Casmantian lord, looking young, small, unkempt with hard travel and, Tan thought, also quite courageous and resolute. He was distantly amused at his own appreciation of the young woman, grown more and more acute through the recent days. How foolish to allow himself to feel any attraction whatsoever toward Lord Bertaud's cousin under these circumstances! Or, to be sure, under any circumstances.

"Of course you must stay with him, Lady Mienthe," conceded Lord Beguchren, so gracefully that one was hardly aware he was making a concession. He gave Gereint Enseichen a glance that combined inquiry and command.

The tall mage unfolded himself from his chair with a slightly apologetic air, as though he knew he tended to loom and wished not to alarm anyone. Nevertheless, he alarmed Tan, who gripped the arms of his chair.

"Only if you're certain," Mienthe declared, color high in her face, glaring both at the mage and at the inscrutable Lord Beguchren beyond him.

Tan would in fact have been glad to refuse if refusal had been possible. But he was well aware that the Casmantian lord would not in fact allow defiance, and even more clearly aware that the disorder resulting from any attempt to stop this could not serve anyone. Least of all Mienthe. He reached up to lay his own hand over one of hers and concentrated on producing an expression of mild acceptance.

The mage took the one step necessary, reached out with one big hand, and touched Tan's cheek with the tips of two fingers.

Tan had thought he'd prepared himself for the mage's

intrusion, but he found he had not begun to imagine what
that intrusion would be like. No kind of preparation could
have been sufficient. Gereint Enseichen sent his mind
slicing through every mask Tan could put in his way,
striking ruthlessly past every illusion of calm acceptance
and through the shock and fury and terror beneath, laying
open the privacy of mind that Tan cherished more than
affection or honor or any other quality that he might have
claimed to value more highly.

Tan would after all have fought this incursion, if he
had been in any way able to fight it. He could not. Memories shifted rapidly before his mind's eye, a confused blur
of images and emotions, with anger and fear underlying
them all, so that even memories of his childhood, of the
house by the river, of his mother's face became colored
by dark flashes of rage. He cried out...would have cried
out, but he had no voice. His first sight of Teramondian
whirled by him, of the Fox's court, of Istierinan...He had
liked Istierinan on that first encounter, as nearly everyone
liked him on first acquaintance, even those who did not
approve of the dissolute face he showed the court; not
many ever saw his other face...

He saw Istierinan's study, all his traps and locks and
codes defeated. The wild, reckless pleasure of that morning swept through him again...He had got past all the
Linularinan spymaster's defenses and now everything
was open to him, defenseless, save for the trifling exercise of getting away again. The thought of Istierinan's
white-hot rage when he discovered Tan's depredations
made him laugh. He turned, took a small, thick book off
a shelf.

He had not planned to take it. It had not caught his

eye. He did not know why he had reached for it. He only found it in his hand as though it had come there by some odd chance of the day. He hardly paid it any mind even as he flipped it open, glanced down at a random page—

He was standing somewhere warm and close and not in any way Istierinan's study. His throat felt raw; his eyes burned as though he had been working all night by the poor light of inadequate candles, writing out some complicated, tight-binding contract with a thousand codicils and appendices; his leg ached ferociously from hip to foot. He was violently angry.

Mienthe was clinging to his arm with both hands. Tan nearly struck her—he might have hit her, except the Casmantian mage grabbed his arm.

Turning in the mage's grip, Tan hit him instead, hard, a twisting blow up under the ribs. It was the sort of blow a spy learned for those scuffles that might happen in the shadows, where no one involved had the least interest in the civilized rules of proper encounters.

Big the Casmantian mage might be, but he was not a brawler: He collapsed to one knee with a choking sound, his arms pressed against his stomach and side. Tan stared down at him. He felt strange: half satisfied and half appalled and entirely uncertain about what had just happened. The only thing he remembered with perfect clarity was hitting the mage. A powerful Casmantian court mage, it gradually occurred to him. In front of his friend, the even more powerful Lord Beguchren. And in front of Mienthe. Whom he'd possibly come near striking as well.

"Appalled" began to win out over "satisfied" as his anger ebbed at last. Tan looked up cautiously.

Mienthe was standing several paces away, her hands over her mouth, staring at him. Lord Beguchren had one hand on her arm, having drawn her back out of Tan's way. His expression was unreadable.

At Tan's feet, the Casmantian mage began, with a pained noise and some difficulty, to climb back to his feet. Tan cautiously offered him a hand, more than half expecting a stinging rebuff. He knew he should offer an apology as well—he searched for suitably abject phrases, but his normal gift for facile speech seemed to have deserted him.

But the mage accepted his hand, levered himself upright, touched his side tenderly where Tan had hit him, and cast a distinctly amused glance toward Lord Beguchren. He said to Tan, "How very gratifying that must have been. All men so provoked should have such recourse. Though I'm grateful you did not have a knife to hand."

Tan did not know what to say.

Gereint glanced once again at Lord Beguchren, turned back to Tan, and added, in a far more formal tone that nevertheless still held that unexpected note of humor, "Though my actions were unpardonable, may I ask you nevertheless to pardon them?"

Tan managed a stiff, reluctant nod.

The tall mage inclined his head in formal gratitude. Then he sighed, limped back to the grouping of chairs, lowered himself into one with a grunt, and stared into the fire for a long moment without speaking, presumably ordering his thoughts. Or the images and impressions he'd taken from Tan's heart and mind.

Tan closed his eyes for a moment against a powerful

urge to hit him again, possibly after finding a knife. It was the urge of a fool. A hot-hearted, intemperate fool. He tried to put it aside, dismiss the anger, assert a more reasoned calm. In the event, unable to force calmness on his heart or nerves, he settled for what he hoped was a composed expression. But he did manage to give Mienthe a brief smile that he hoped was reassuringly natural, and walk with an assumption of calm across to take his place in one of the other chairs. Mienthe followed, though hesitantly, and Lord Beguchren came to lean on the back of the fourth chair, regarding them all with bland patience.

Gereint Enseichen looked up at last. He turned first to Tan. "I give you my promise," the mage said formally, "that I shall not speak to any man, nor for any urging, of anything I glimpsed in your heart. Can you trust me for that?"

As a rule, Tan did not trust anyone for anything. But if he'd had to wager on the big mage's essential honesty, he would have felt reasonably confident of collecting his winnings. This helped a little. He produced a second nod, not with great goodwill, but a trifle less stiffly, and looked at the fire so that he would not have to look at anyone else.

"Possibly an overbroad promise, under the circumstances," Lord Beguchren observed. His tone was unruffled, but with an almost imperceptible bite behind the calm.

"No. The little that I glimpsed of the book is not, ah, does not—" He lifted a hand in frustration at the limits of language.

"Lacks emotional context," Tan said tonelessly. He did not look around, but kept his gaze fixed on the fire. There was a pleasant smell in the room from the mountain cedar in the fire. He tried to fix his mind on that.

"Yes, well put. Exactly." The mage paused.

"You only glimpsed a little?" That was Mienthe. She sounded disappointed and decidedly offended. "You did that, that—you did whatever that was to Tan, and you didn't even see anything?"

"Even a fleeting glimpse may reveal a great truth," Lord Beguchren said quietly.

"There was a book," the big mage said slowly, and in a tone that suggested he was not certain even of this. "There *was* a book...or a working that *looked* like a book. Tan...the honored Tan..."

Tan said curtly, not lifting his gaze from the fire, "Now we are so well acquainted, I think we need not be overly concerned with formality."

This produced an uncomfortable pause. Then Gereint Enseichen said, "Tan, then. Tan had, I think, something like an affinity for that book. I wonder whether any of the rest of us would have had that book fall into our hands, if we'd been in that room? I think not; I do think it unlikely."

"I believe it is Andreikan Warichteier who discusses the various meanings of 'affinity' in magework and among the various natural gifts," Lord Beguchren commented.

"Warichteier has one discussion of the subject," Gereint agreed. "And I believe Entechsan Terichsekiun developed a theory of affinity and similarity, though not in exactly this context. I don't know of any philosopher who described a marked affinity between a piece of legistwork and a legist—but I'm not as familiar with Linularinan philosophers as I should be."

Tan shook his head. He asked after a moment, managing a more natural tone than he had expected, "We knew there was a book; that's no great revelation. Did you manage to glimpse anything at all *in* the book?" He hesitated, almost believing he might remember—but no. There was nothing. He rubbed his forehead, frowning.

"A word. A line perhaps." The Casmantian mage frowned as well. "I couldn't read it."

Tan dropped his hand and gave the mage a cold stare. "Of course you cannot read Terheien as well as you speak it. We might have considered that earlier."

"Ah," said the mage, with a quick gesture of apology. "No, in fact that should not signify in such an exercise—not so long as *you* understood what you read."

"You are not a legist," Lord Beguchren murmured.

Everyone looked at him.

"*Gereint* is not a legist," the small, elegant Casmantian lord repeated. "That was legistwork and nothing, perhaps, meant for other eyes. What does the legist gift encompass?" He paused, looking expectantly at Tan.

"Law," Tan said, since it was clearly expected of him, though everyone knew this. "Especially written law. Contract law. You do have legists in Casmantium."

"Yes," agreed Lord Beguchren. "Not as Linularinum has, however. You look very Linularinan yourself, you know. You are Feierabianden by conviction, perhaps, rather than by birth?"

"Does it signify?" Tan snapped.

Mienthe said quickly, "There's thorough mixing of blood along the river, you know, Lord Beguchren. Especially in the Delta."

"Yes," the Casmantian lord repeated. His expression

was unreadable, but a subtle intensity had come into his voice. He tapped the arm of his chair very gently. "You are a very strongly gifted legist," he said to Tan. It wasn't a question. "The legist gift has to do, as you say, with written law, contract law. They say one should count one's fingers after signing a Linularinan contract—"

"And the fingers of your children and grandchildren in the next generations. So they do." Tan was not pleased to have that old censorious line recalled. He said, "In Linularinum, tight contracts are admired; in Feierabiand, and Casmantium as well, no doubt, signatories frequently have more concern with how contracts can be broken than with how they may most advantageously be kept."

"Even the most ambitious Casmantian merchant would probably say, 'How they might be most *honorably* kept,'" Lord Beguchren said. "But then, Casmantium is not a nation of legists." Perhaps fortunately, he held up a hand to forestall Tan's first, intemperate response. He said patiently, "What I am trying to say, perhaps with less grace than I might, is that a mage, most especially a Casmantian mage, is not likely to immediately grasp the more complicated elements of legist-magic. What was in that book was law—written law—contract law, and well set about with the strongest possible legist-magic. I doubt whether Mariddeier Kohorrian would provoke Iaor Safiad over any specific contract, however important. I greatly doubt whether Istierinan Hamoddian would so vehemently pursue a confidential agent who stole from him long after the stolen information had been passed on, if the only other item stolen were a specific piece of legal work, no matter how elegant."

"Well?" Mienthe asked. "So it was some sort of

important magic Tan took. We knew that already! But meant to do what? We still don't know! We haven't gotten anywhere!"

A terrible binding, Tan thought. An immensely strong legal binding, something the kings of Linularinum needed to bind their courts or their country to order. Or something else, something worse. Something that would undoubtedly do terrible things to any careless legist strong enough, and unfortunate enough, to accidentally lay his hand on it. Particularly a legist who had deliberately deceived and betrayed the Linularinan king and court.

"Indeed, this remains an excellent question," said Lord Beguchren at last, still very softly. "To discover what Linularinum has lost and we might have gained...Gereint. Do you suppose you might find, somewhere in this house, a decent quill and a book of blank paper?"

Gereint shook his head. "My lord, forgive me; I have evidently not been clear. I believe that very book, as well as the writing it contained, is an integral part of the work." He looked at Tan. "I feel certain—please tell me plainly if I am mistaken—but I feel certain that you cannot possibly write out any part of that work save you have the book itself to write it in."

Tan turned this idea over in his mind. He saw...he thought he saw...at least he thought it was *possible* that he saw a faint glimmer of how to do that sort of work. One would make a book that was not precisely a book, or not *only* a book; one would write in it with quills that were not ordinary quills, cut with special care to pick up precisely the right kind of ink...One would take this book and write in it using words that were not ordinary words, language that was not everyday language, the sort of language that could not be spoken, for it was meant only for the eye and hand and mind of another legist...

"But it's true I'm not a legist. Perhaps my understanding is not correct," said Gereint.

"No," Tan said absently, and then glanced up. "No," he repeated with more decision. "No, I think your understanding is without fault. I think only a legist could make a book like that, and only if he knew precisely what work he wished that book to encompass. And I suspect Istierinan made this thing, or at least I think he believes he can make it over, if once he reclaims both that book and me."

"But," Mienthe said, looking from the mage to Lord Beguchren in some distress, her hands clasped urgently in her lap, "but the book, we don't have it with us. It's in Tiefenauer!"

"Then Istierinan Hamoddian has undoubtedly reclaimed it, and lacks only our friend, here"—Lord Beguchren nodded toward Tan—"to reclaim the work entire."

"Oh," said Mienthe quickly. "No, I don't think he does have it, unless he could find it by—by magic, you know. I hid the book in my room. I don't think Istierinan will find it. Not even my maid has ever found my hiding place, and you know how maids find *everything*." Then the young woman ruined this confident assertion by adding, with sudden doubt, "I think."

The corners of Lord Beguchren's eyes crinkled with humor, and Gereint Enseichen tilted back his head and laughed out loud.

But Tan had never felt less like laughing.

There was a quiet rap on the door, and a servant—no, a guardsman—entered. The man ducked his head in apology and said to Lord Beguchren, "Begging your pardon, my lord, but the Arobern bids me inform you that a Linularinan agent has been captured. He requests you will come." The man's eyes went to Mienthe. "He asks whether his honored guests will be pleased to come as well."

Mienthe was not surprised to find that there had indeed been several Linularinan agents behind herself and Tan in the pass, but even though she was not surprised, she was still horrified. They had been so close behind—she could not help but think, *What if we had not been able to get around the mule wagons? What if we had decided to stay the night in the guest house? What if we hadn't woken early this morning?*

The Arobern's guardsmen thought there had been three agents altogether. Two, it seemed, had been killed. But the third man had been properly and thoroughly apprehended. Once his advisers and guests were ready, the Arobern signaled his guardsmen and they brought their prisoner forward and flung him down before the Arobern, on his knees on the cold stone floor.

The man caught his balance, his bound hands flat against the floor, and then straightened his back and lifted his head. He was very obviously Linularinan: He had not only the sharp face, with narrow eyes and angular cheekbones and a long nose; the straight light brown hair, and the graceful hands with rings on his long fingers; but also, despite his current position, the indefinable air of superiority.

He did not fight the guardsmen, but flung back his head, glaring up and to both sides and then focusing on the king—no, not on the *king*, but beyond him, on Tan. Tan returned only a bland look, but the Arobern scowled.

The man abruptly transferred his glare to the king and snapped, "You have no idea what you have there! You can have no idea, or you'd immediately repudiate him and give him into my hands!"

The Arobern said, his deep voice as mild as he could make it, "Maybe. Maybe that's right. So tell me what he is, and maybe I will give him to you, yes?"

Tan raised one eyebrow and smiled, very slightly. It was the most extraordinarily insulting smile. Mienthe wondered how he *did* that, and whether she might be able to learn how.

The captive swelled with outrage, but he did not fling himself forward or rant wildly. He glowered, at Tan and at the Arobern, and then, craning his head around, at Gereint Enseichen. "*You* should know I speak the truth!" he said to the tall mage.

Gereint Enseichen gave a mild shrug. "I know events are in sweeping motion. I know that chance and opportunity turn around this man." He nodded at Tan, but without taking his eyes off the prisoner. "I know Linularinum is responsible."

"Linularinum! Responsible!" cried the man, and stopped, breathing hard. Collecting himself, he said in a more moderate tone, "Is it the proper owner of a jewel, or the thief who steals it, who is responsible for the man who covets and kills for it once it is out in the world?"

"Neither," said Lord Beguchren. His light, cool voice

drew all their attention; his gray eyes effortlessly held those of the prisoner. He moved a step forward, out of the Arobern's shadow. "It is the man who does murder who is responsible, and neither the jewel's owner nor the thief. Or would eminent scholars and philosophers argue otherwise, in Linularinum?" He paused for a heartbeat and then went on, even more quietly, "And who is responsible for what some strange and powerful legistwork might do? Or might fail to do? The legist who created the work with quill and ink and his mastery of language? The mage who hid it out of the view of ordinary men? The king who guarded it from one age to the next?"

"It's too perilous to have out in the world!" shouted the Linularinan prisoner. He tried to get to his feet, but the soldiers hastily caught his shoulders and held him from rising.

"Of course it is," murmured Beguchren, catching and holding his gaze. "What is it, man? What is this thing that is so perilous for anyone but a Linularinan to hold?"

The prisoner stared at the small, elegant Casmantian lord in very much the way a bird was said to stare at a serpent. He said in a quick, sharp tone, "Do you not understand? Not even yet? This was a working against— for—it was a working of natural law. Do you not perceive the terrible distortion of the world around this thief, as the world seeks the proper bindings of law? Do you not understand what desperate peril we are in, now the strands of natural law are breaking?"

"The *proper* bindings of law," murmured Lord Beguchren.

The prisoner sat back on his heels and stared at Beguchren, furious, his bound hands raised in urgent supplication. "You must understand. A thousand years ago, we founded the age by binding into place the laws of earth and fire, and pressing aside the unbounded wild magic of mountains and forest. And then that fool"—he glared furiously at Tan, who looked merely blandly attentive—"that *fool*," the Linularinan prisoner repeated, "undid half our bindings in a day. The rest will break in time. And you *shelter* him? From *us*? Give him to me—for all of us. Let us recast our bindings, if any legist of our age has such power—will you leave the law of the world unsettled and wild?"

"The law of the world," Lord Beguchren repeated. He still spoke quietly, but his tone had become biting, cold as the gray heights of the mountains, and his storm-gray eyes were dark with fury. He took a step forward and said, "The laws of earth and fire, do you say? Gereint has described to me a certain strange quality he has recently found echoing behind the magecraft he has tried to work. We had assumed this strangeness was due to the cracking of Tehre's Wall. Now I wonder whether both the breaking of the Wall and this disturbance to mage power might be due instead to a common cause." He paused and then added, his voice dropping even further, "I wonder why Linularinum seems so untroubled by the threat the griffins pose to all our countries? Certainly Mariddeier Kohorrian seems perfectly ready to distract and weaken Iaor Safiad, and this at a time when one would expect him to see the necessity of supporting Feierabiand against griffin-fire."

The Linularinan agent did not answer.

"Indeed..." said Lord Beguchren. "Indeed, one might almost wonder why it is that *Casmantium* has endured the continual threat of fire, why it is that Feierabiand's border with the desert has now and again been breached and is now threatened again, and yet *Linularinum* has never seen so much as a grain of red sand blowing in the wind. Fire stays well clear of Linularinum. It always has. I wonder why that is? Just how have the legists of Linularinum written their binding law, this law that their clever kings have owned from the beginning of the age, and have hidden from the rest of us?"

"Only *we*—" said the prisoner, and stopped.

The Arobern, whose grip on the arms of his granite throne had tightened until his knuckles whitened, stood up at last. He seemed to loom massive as the mountains. The expression in his deep-set eyes went well beyond rage.

The Linularinan prisoner flinched back from the king, for which Mienthe did not blame him at all. She would have backed away herself except she could not move. But then the prisoner abruptly reached down with both his bound hands, sketching a swift line of writing on the stone floor with a fingertip. The letters that followed his tracing finger were sharp, angular, jagged things, nothing like ordinary letters. They were black, but not the shining black of fresh ink. They were a strange, bodiless, empty black, as though the man were carving narrow but bottomless cracks right into the stone, so that the blackness at the heart of the earth showed through.

To Mienthe, it seemed that the whole world abruptly tilted sideways. She did not lose her balance; it was not that sort of tilt. But everything seemed to stutter and pause, and the cracks ran swiftly out across the stone and yawned wide—she thought someone was shouting

and someone else was cursing and someone else was
screaming, or maybe that was all the same person. She
seemed caught in a timeless moment that did not contain
alarm or movement, around which urgent sound pressed
but into which it did not intrude. She seemed to watch
the empty black letters slashed into the stone lengthen;
they sliced out like knife cuts toward Tan. But Mienthe
felt neither frightened nor rushed. She seemed to have all
the time in the world to move; indeed, she seemed to be
the only person in the world who was moving, or who
could move. She stepped dreamily through the slanted
world to intercept the black writing before it could reach
Tan, and stooped, and drew a spiral on the floor to catch
the sharp letters. Then she straightened and stood quietly,
watching.

The black letters reached her spiral, and rushed into
it, and the deep-cut writing swept down and around and
around and down and disappeared into the depths of the
earth, and the polished stone closed over the place where
they had been, and suddenly time, too, rushed forward,
and the world slammed back toward its ordinary level
with a tremendous silent crash. Mienthe staggered.

Before she could fall, Tan caught her elbow with one
strong hand, steadying her until she could recover her
balance. He was not looking at her, however, but at the
Linularinan agent—a mage, Mienthe realized belatedly.
Or, no, with that strange writing, a legist, of course. Then
she followed Tan's gaze, and found it did not matter, not
for any immediate practical purpose. In startlement or
terror or outrage, one of the prisoner's guards had cut
his throat. A great wash of crimson blood ran across
the stone, filling the deep-carved letters the agent had

drawn into the stone and trickling across the floor of the hall.

There was no sign, now, that the carved letters had ever sliced out toward Tan. But there was a crystalline spiral set directly into the stone a step away from where he stood with Mienthe. It was no wider than a man's hand at its widest diameter: A perfect spiral of smoky quartz set right into the polished granite, turning and turning inward until the fine pattern in its center became too fine to see. Tan glanced down at this spiral, his brows drawing together in bemusement. Then he looked at Mienthe. There was no surprise in his face. He only gave her a little, acknowledging tip of his head: *Did it again, didn't you?* As though he'd have expected nothing less. Mienthe blushed.

The Arobern, too, stared at the spiral for a moment. Then he turned his head to look at the dead man and the blood, and at last at the guardsman who had killed him.

The man ducked his head in uncertain apology and came forward to offer the hilt of his bloody knife to the king. "If I was wrong—" he began and stopped, swallowing. Then he drew a quick breath and met the Arobern's eyes. "Lord King, if I was wrong, then I beg your pardon."

The Arobern shook his head. He reached out to touch the knife's hilt, but he did not take it; instead, he folded the guardsman's fingers back around the hilt. "He meant his blow for my guest, a man under my protection. I would not like to have my protection fail. Your blow guarded my honor, and I thank you for it."

The guardsman, looking much happier, bowed his head and backed away. Other men came deferentially forward to take away the body and clean up the blood. There was a surprising amount of blood. Mienthe tried not to look. She stared down at the crystalline spiral she'd drawn instead, though it pulled at her eyes and made her dizzy. It was still better than looking at the blood.

"It was *your* blow that protected me," Tan said to Mienthe in a low voice. "So I'll thank *you* for that."

Mienthe shook her head. She rubbed her foot cautiously over the spiral. It gleamed dully, a spiral of ordinary smoky quartz that might have been there since the stone was carved and carried into this house and laid down to be part of the room's floor. Tears prickled unexpectedly in her eyes, and she blinked hard. "I do things," she whispered. "I feel things, and I don't know why or how. There's something in me that makes me do things, but it isn't me and I don't know what it is."

Tan shook his head and, to Mienthe's surprise, took her hand in both of his. "It's you," he said. "It's all you. You simply have a gift you haven't yet recognized. But it's guiding you well, Mie, don't you think? You've done all the right things so far, and which of the rest of us can claim as much? Until you learn to recognize and understand your gift, you might simply try trusting it—and yourself—a little."

Mienthe stared at him. Then she tried to smile.

"Quite so," said Lord Beguchren, approaching unexpectedly. "One does wonder what sort of gift you hold, Lady Mienthe, but it seems one might do far worse than trust it." He knelt to trace the quartz spiral with one fingertip. Then, rising, he lifted a frost-white eyebrow at her.

He was still very angry, Mienthe knew that. Although

she knew he was not angry with her or with Tan, she did not know what to say to him. She did not know what she thought about anything. She was shaking and found she couldn't stop. Tan put his arm around her shoulders, and she leaned against his solid weight gratefully.

The Arobern had been glowering down at the bloody granite and the crystalline spiral. Now he turned abruptly and said to Gereint Enseichen, "Assist my guardsmen, if you please. If there is another Linularinan agent in Ehre, I think this may be a matter of some urgency. Also see to the safety of your own household. I will assuredly ask you and your lady wife to extend hospitality to my guests."

"Yes," agreed the tall mage, inclining his head. He smiled reassuringly at Mienthe and went out.

The king said, to Mienthe and Tan and Lord Beguchren, "Come."

Mienthe thought drearily that the Casmantian king was going to want to go over everything again, and she knew she didn't want to. This day had been unpleasant enough living through it just once. Tears pressed again at her eyes. Tan tightened his arm around her shoulders, and she thought of his voice asking tartly, *Whose cousin are you?* She straightened her shoulders, blinked hard, lifted her head, and followed the Arobern.

The king guided them no farther than down a short hall, to a much smaller and less formal chamber with thick rugs on the floor and cushions on the chairs. He waved to the chairs without ceremony and said shortly to Lord Beguchren, as soon as they were all seated, "Well?"

The small lord hesitated. Then he opened his fine

hands and said, "From what that…person…described, I surmise it is possible to reorder the natural law of the world to a degree I would have previously believed impossible. I surmise that the honored Tan may be able to effect such a change."

Tan said sharply, "It would be pleasant to think so, no doubt." He was rubbing his knee, an absent, unmindful gesture that was utterly out of character. Mienthe guessed by that how very disturbed he was by everything that had happened. She rose from the chair she'd just taken and went to lean on the back of his chair, resting her hand on his shoulder. The muscles were rock-hard under her touch. But he looked up at her and managed a small nod.

Lord Beguchren only said smoothly, "If Tehre's Wall shatters, then an effort to alter and bind natural law might seem suddenly very wise indeed, no matter with what doubt any of us may now regard the prospect. It does not seem wholly beyond the bounds of possibility that the honored Tan might be able to, if I may be forgiven the term, 'rewrite' a certain element of the natural law of the world. A small element, a trivial item that would not disorder the world to any great extent…I wonder, for example, whether he might be able to use this book and the work he holds himself to more thoroughly subordinate fire to earth."

There was a pause. Tan did not look at the Casmantian lord, or at the Arobern. He looked at Mienthe. She thought he needed something from her, but she had no idea what he wanted her to say and could only gaze back at him.

There was a subdued cough at the door, and a guardsman said apologetically, "Lord King, forgive me. We have had another messenger through the pass. A courier—a royal courier, from Feierabiand."

The Arobern scowled but laughed at the same time. He waved an impatient hand. "Of course I will see the courier. At once." He threw a harried glance around the room, ran a broad hand through his short hair, and said to Mienthe, to the rest of them, "Of course you must stay. You must all stay."

The courier was a young woman, no older than Mienthe, who looked just as tired as Mienthe felt and twice as travel-ragged. She glanced at the rest of them, but was clearly too weary to be curious and turned at once to the Arobern, bowed, and held out her white courier's wand.

"Yes," said the Arobern. "I will assuredly hear you. What message does Iaor Safiad send to me?"

"Lord King," said the courier in a faint voice, then took a breath and continued more strongly, "His Majesty Iaor Safiad sends me to say to you: He believes the Wall will not hold, that it is impossible it should hold, and that as it is the fifth day since the warning was given, we are even now within the period of greatest peril. He bids me say: The griffins have a new king who is furious and intemperate. This king of theirs scorns men and detests all the country of earth. His Majesty says that the king of the griffins will not likely stop in Feierabiand. He warns you to look east as well as north and guard the passes through the mountains." The woman stopped, swallowed, and added in a faint voice, "That's all. Will there be a response?"

The Arobern said, "Honored courier, I must consider. If there is a response, I will tell it to you in the morning. Go. Rest. My household will see to your comfort."

The courier bowed once more—she staggered a little as she straightened—and allowed herself to be led away.

Mienthe stared at the Arobern, stricken and wordless.

"My friend," the Arobern said to Beguchren Teshrichten, "what is in your mind?"

The elegant lord inclined his head. He said, "Here in this extremity, where fire threatens to burn across all the world, an unlooked-for weapon has flung itself into our hands." He met Tan's eyes and went on, quietly, "You are pursued. You have enemies. Well, so do we all. It seems to me we may well consider how we may confound all our enemies at once, and if we also forever shift the balance between earth and fire to favor earth, is that not also very well?" He turned to the Arobern. "Shall we not send agents to recover this book? Shall we not bring it here and see what the honored Tan might make of it?"

"What say you?" the king said to Tan.

Before Tan could answer, Mienthe said quickly, "But—" She stopped as everyone looked at her, but then remembered Tan saying, *You might try trusting yourself a little*, and went on, "But, Lord King, if you will pardon me, is it wise to send a small number of men through the pass, when we have no idea what they might find? Even if Linularinum doesn't have its own agents in the way, which I'm sure it does, wouldn't it take a terribly long time for men to go all the way to Tiefenauer and then come all the way back here? From the—the word about the Wall and the griffins, can we take so much time?"

The Arobern tapped his fingers on the arm of his chair. "Very well! What do you wish me to do?"

"I want you to send an army into Feierabiand!" Mienthe declared. "You have one; of course you do, with all the, the warnings flying back and forth across the mountains! So you have an army ready, haven't you, and here it is, right at the mouth of the pass, just where we need it to be! I want you to send an *army* through the pass and press back the Linularinan forces and confound their mages and make a safe road for Tan to go *himself* back to Tiefenauer—and me, of course—and then we can get the book and see how useful it might be."

Tan was staring at her, looking appalled by this idea. "A wise man does not leave be the hart at bay to pursue a glimmering fantasy by moonlight, nor forsake his house of stone to build a palace of sunbeams," he said, with some force. "I admire your boldness, but you cannot possibly set all your hopes on—"

"I'm not!" exclaimed Mienthe. "If the Arobern sends an army to the Delta, then at least Linularinum will be out of the Delta, which is one thing we want." She turned back to the Arobern himself. "And if you do that, then you'll have an army in place to help block the griffins before they can come into Casmantium, which has to be something you want, and if Lord Beguchren is right about that book and about Tan, then we can stop the griffins entirely, and we all want that, don't we? So why not do everything at once?"

There was a slightly stunned pause.

The Arobern himself broke it, rising to pace several strides away and then turn and come back. He moved with sharp energy, glowering at Mienthe with uncommon ferocity. "I thought of exactly what you say, yes?" he growled. "But you have forgotten: I cannot take men through that pass and march them through Feierabiand, because Iaor Safiad has my son in his court and within his reach! Do you think he will stop to ask me what I do, when he sees the spears of my soldiers flashing in the sun?"

The Arobern flung himself back down in his chair and scowled around at them all. "I could send that girl back to Iaor Safiad, yes, and ask him politely if he would permit me to bring a few thousand men marching through southern Feierabiand. Except there is no time! Who knows whether the griffins have already come through the high pass and down against Tihannad? Nor will Safiad trust me or what I might do! Later, when he sees I kept faith with him, that will be too late!"

"You have another son now," Lord Beguchren said very quietly.

"A babe in arms does not replace my first son!"

Mienthe stared at both men, utterly horrified. She exclaimed, "But King Iaor would never harm Erich! I don't care if—if Erich is supposed to be a hostage against you, it doesn't matter what you do, he would never touch him!"

"He is a king!" shouted the Arobern, lunging back to his feet. "He will do what he must!"

Mienthe jumped to her feet to face the King of Casmantium and shouted back, "He won't!" She found she was glaring as fiercely as the Arobern. "Who knows King Iaor better, you or I? He's spent a month out of every year in the Delta, in my cousin's house, and every year he's brought your son with him. He treats him like his own son! When little Anlin fell off her pony last spring and broke her wrist, it was Erich who carried her back to the house and sat up with her all night and told her stories so she wouldn't cry! He told her about the time he broke his arm falling off the roof of your palace in Breidechboden, and she made him promise that someday when she visited Casmantium he'd show her just where. He made her promise she wouldn't climb out and fall from the same place!" Mienthe stopped. Then she finished with dignity, "It doesn't matter what you think. King Iaor is honorable and kind and he might have taken your son as his hostage, but when it comes to the moment, he won't touch him."

The Arobern was gazing at her now with a very strange expression. "My son has stayed in your house for a month out of every year?"

Mienthe nodded uncertainly.

"You must know him now better than I do."

Mienthe opened her mouth and shut it again. She said at last, "He's a great deal like you, I think. Only not so hot-hearted. He loves you and Casmantium, but..."

"But he has learned to love Feierabiand and the Safiad as well," the Arobern said heavily. "Yes. That is what the Safiad meant to teach him, and better that than..." His voice trailed off. "It is true that I have gathered a small army here. It is also true that I have thought of taking this army of mine through the pass. I would be glad to keep any war on the west side of the mountains, away from my own country. But..."

"You are a king," Lord Beguchren said quietly. "You will do what you must."

CHAPTER 13

An hour before dusk, the Arobern and all his people came out of the western mouth of the pass and found themselves slowly descending the lower slopes of the foothills and approaching the soft new green of the spring pastures spread out below.

Beguchren found the long rolling view of Feierabiand's gentle countryside...troubling. He knew those foothills and pastures, for this was the identical view that had greeted that other Casmantian army six years ago, when the Arobern had come for the first time into Feierabiand. Then, his ambition had been conquest. He had intended to use the griffins as unwilling, ignorant weapons against Feierabiand. The cold mages of Casmantium...Beguchren and all his brethren...had hardly cared whether the king's plan succeeded. *They* had intended the ultimate destruction of all the griffins.

If the Arobern had not been so ambitious...if the cold mages of Casmantium had not encouraged him in his ambition...then, very likely, the griffins would have kept, within reason, to their desert isolation. The slow battle between fire and earth would have continued as it had from the beginning of the age: inconclusive and wearying, but never ruinous.

Casmantium would still have its cold mages. Beguchren would not have been required to consign each of his long companions to the cold earth. The Great Wall would have been neither built nor broken.

Beguchren himself would still have his mage-sense and his power.

This was not a new thought. Only the regret and grief had become suddenly more piercing in the face of the green Feierabianden spring, with its soft breeze and gentle warmth.

Beguchren looked for signs of the stark desert the griffins had made here among the gentle hills and farms of Feierabiand. Looking down from this height, those signs were not obvious even to his experienced eye. But below and over to the south, the grasses were different: longer and harsher and strangely wiry. And there was a faint reddish cast to the land underlying those grasses. There were no trees in that area, except someone had apparently planted some young oaks and elms; the saplings stood in rows much too neat for trees that had sprouted naturally. Farther away, almost at the edges of visibility, stood a twisted, jagged tower of stone. The sunlight caught on it oddly, with a bloodred glimmer that turned its sharp edges almost translucent. Beguchren bowed his head, fixing his gaze instead on the mane of his horse, on his own fingers gripping the reins.

"My friend," said the Arobern, and Beguchren drew a hard breath and looked up again.

The king had drawn up his horse, so that Beguchren had come up beside him. Their eyes met in a perfect understanding of shared guilt and regret. But neither of them would speak of the past, the Arobern because he was determinedly focused on the present and Beguchren because he was far too intensely private a man.

Leaning on his pommel, the Arobern gestured down the slope, west and a little south. "The ford is there, with its good bridge. The bridge is still there, I think. It was repaired when the rebuilding of the town began."

Beguchren nodded. Of course the king would know for certain about the bridge—he would have had reports from his agents about every bridge and ford that would allow men to cross all the rivers in Feierabiand.

"So," the Arobern said gravely. Lady Mienthe, her legist companion at her heel, had come up on the king's other side and was looking at him questioningly; he turned toward her and went on, "We will assume the Wall yet holds. Perhaps it does." It had been seven days since the griffin mage had brought his warning to Lord Bertaud. Perhaps the Wall held, and if it did not, still there was little they could do other than ride for the Delta and try an unexpected sideways blow against the griffins.

"We will cross the Nejeied," continued the Arobern. "We will go across the country, straight toward Tiefenauer, at least until we are closer." He had been practicing, as he managed the difficult Feierabianden names with only a little clumsiness.

"Yes?" Lady Mienthe said uncertainly.

The Arobern glanced sidelong at Beguchren and said, "If the Wall is broken, then Iaor Safiad will stay in the north. But if it still holds, then he may come south. If he comes, what will be his road? Will he ride down along the Sierhanan, straight for the Delta but always risking that he may find Linularinan soldiers have crossed the river and gotten in front of him? Or that he may find an attack coming from any direction, if Linularinum has crossed in force and laid a trap for him?"

"No," said Beguchren, as the Arobern clearly wished to have all these tactical considerations laid out for the lady. "If the Safiad moves south, he will come down along the Nejeied this far. His options are wide, once he is here. He could cross west toward the Delta if he finds the Linularinan assault his greatest concern, as I imagine he hopes; or continue down the Nejeied toward Terabiand if for some reason he thought that wise; or if his hopes fail him and he suddenly discovers Linularinum to be the least of his concerns, he might go south along the Sepes River to Talend and have the forest at his back when he faces the griffins. He might even, in extremity, retreat with his men into the pass. I imagine that the griffins would care for that even less than they would like the forest."

"That is also what I think," said the Arobern, and paused. From the king's grim expression, and from the way his gaze rested for a long moment on Lady Mienthe's face, he was probably trying to imagine what he might say to King Iaor, if they happened to find him on the road down there, on the other side of the bridge.

"We will go down to the bridge," the Arobern decided. "Lady Mienthe—" He frowned at her, though not unkindly. "You must speak to the people there and bid them to be calm."

"They will know they cannot fight us," Lord Beguchren said, watching her face. The lady was clearly thinking of how frightened her folk would be when they saw thousands of Casmantian spears flashing through the dust raised by thousands of Casmantian boots. He said, "They may scatter up- and downriver, however, with the most disturbing tales of Casmantian invasion. You might persuade them to send a second lot of messengers after the first, in the hope that we may not encounter too much difficulty as we move farther into Feierabiand."

"We will move too swiftly to encounter difficulty," the Arobern declared. "If Iaor Safiad comes upon us, we will hope he will listen to us with both his ears. I will send that little courier north today, this very hour, explaining what we are about and asking his pardon for our boldness. Lord Beguchren, I will ask you to stay here, athwart the likely road, so that if the honored courier does not reach the Safiad, you may meet him here."

Lord Beguchren, unsurprised, inclined his head in acceptance of this command. "I am honored by your trust," he said quietly, and to Lady Mienthe, who was looking openly surprised, "It is a mage you will need with you in the west."

"And it's a smooth tongue the lord king will need here in the east," said Tan, unexpectedly, for he had rarely spoken to any of them on this ride, and had assiduously avoided both Beguchren and Gereint. His tone now was stiff. But he went on, glancing from one of them to the next and ending with an earnest nod toward the Arobern, "King Iaor may even believe that you deliberately act

together with Mariddeier Kohorrian, and that you have
some plan for dealing with the griffins after you've finished partitioning Feierabiand between you."

Beguchren gave the legist a considering nod and
agreed, "Indeed. I shall hope that in such exigency, I will
be able to clarify matters."

The Arobern grimaced and then looked keenly at
Mienthe. "The Safiad knows you well, hah? Your cousin
is his friend as well as his adviser and a lord of his court.
Maybe I should leave you here also. Then you would be
safe and also you could speak for me to your king. Maybe
that would be clever, yes?"

"No—no, it wouldn't!" said Mienthe, plainly horrified. "I have to go west! I need to be in Tiefenauer! Or,"
she amended, "at least, I need to be with Tan." She said
this as she might have said *The sky is blue* or *Water runs
downhill.* As though it were a flat statement of such obvious truth that no one could possibly dispute it.

Tan said, a snap of temper in his voice, "I should hate
to go west without Mienthe. It isn't your mage who's so
far turned away three Linularinan attacks against me."

Lady Mienthe looked at Tan with surprise and pleasure, as though she hadn't expected his support. But,
when the Arobern began stubbornly to speak again of
her safety, it was to Beguchren she turned for help.
Though Beguchren had to acknowledge, without mod-
esty, that if the young woman was not confident of her
ability to carry her own point, she could not have chosen
better in looking for one who both could and would argue
for her.

He said, "Your feelings have been remarkable of late,
have they not, Lady Mienthe? Both in their strength and

then in their direction. We are assured that you are not a mage. However, even so, I think it very likely that you perceive the turn and tilt of the world." He paused.

Mienthe stared at him blankly. She clearly had no idea what it would be like to perceive forces, balances and events pivoting, and just as clearly doubted that she felt any such thing.

But Beguchren was confident of it.

He turned gravely toward the Arobern. "Lord King," he said formally, "I must advise against your suggestion, reasonable and wise as it seems. I believe the honored Lady Mienthe should return to Tiefenauer with the honored Tan, with all reasonable alacrity."

"Huh. I thought only to keep you safe—" the Arobern said to Mienthe. He glanced at Beguchren and shrugged. "But very well! You will assuredly go west, honored lady."

Beguchren said to his king, "I will speak for you to Iaor Safiad. I swear to you, I will not permit any harm to come to your son."

"I depend upon it," the Arobern growled. "I cannot give you many men, nor can I give you Gereint Ensei-chen. I will leave you—hah!—I will leave you Lady Tehre. *She* will make the Safiad listen to your voice. You must make him understand he must not press carelessly forward, that I have not set myself against him, that he must not interfere with me." The king paused.

"I understand you very well," Lord Beguchren said gently.

"Of course you do," agreed the Arobern, and swung around, waving for his officers to come hear his commands.

*   *   *

Iaor Safiad, if he left Lord Bertaud in Tihannad to find
such accommodation with the griffins as he might—and
Beguchren wished the Feierabianden lord joy of the
effort—would very likely race south to meet the Linularinan offense. Beguchren remained convinced that
the Safiad would come down the Nejeied. From Minas
Ford, he could angle west toward Kames and from there
strike directly toward Tiefenauer, exactly the route the
Arobern had taken. True, there were poor roads and
farmer's tracks all the way. But going that way, whatever
Linularinan troops one might meet would lack support
from across the river. This was what Beguchren thought
the Safiad would do, thus driving straight against the rear
of the Casmantian army, quite possibly leading to a very
unfortunate outcome. Thus the urgent necessity of pre-
venting him from pursuing any such course.

But if Iaor Safiad chose to ride south along the Nejeied
at all, he would certainly have in mind the broad, open
countryside west of Minas Spring, where the little Sepes
divided from the larger Nejeied. This was the ideal place
to rest his men and the fine Feierabianden horses.

Thus, this was where Beguchren set his own men, just
past dawn on the day following their arrival in Feierabiand. He arranged them right across the middle of the
open land, where the last of the precipitous hills leveled
out to gentle pasturelands before reaching the river. It was
a stupid position if he had meant to offer serious battle,
especially with so few men. If he had actually intended
to fight the Safiad, he would have wanted to arrange his
men a fraction more northerly, where the narrow road
lay between woodlands on the east and the river on the

west. He would have set archers in the woods, so that Iaor Safiad would have been forced to bring his men through withering fire in order to come at his lines of spearmen. So his officers—two captains, each with a half-strength company—earnestly told him, unnecessarily. They and Lady Tehre had joined Beguchren under the awning of his tent, to look over the lines once more and review the plan.

"The point is not to fight," Beguchren said gently, "but to hold Iaor Safiad from pursuing the Arobern in error. Or committing other acts in error." Lady Tehre looked blank, which probably indicated that she was considering something entirely unrelated to what Beguchren had just said. But both the captains nodded, even more earnestly than they had explained how their men should be arranged. They were not stupid men. They knew very well the possible error to which Beguchren referred.

"But how are we to hold the Safiad if we cannot fight him?" the senior captain asked. "And should we not *prepare* to fight wholeheartedly, in case all else fails? Or, if all else fails, are we to prepare to yield this ground and our men and allow the Safiad through?" He plainly did not much care for this idea.

"We would much prefer not to yield," Beguchren conceded. "One fears that events in the Delta may become altogether too delicate to allow even the best-intentioned interference from without. Possibly Iaor Safiad will give me his word to allow our king a free hand, but I think that unlikely."

Both captains nodded; one of them laughed grimly.

Beguchren barely smiled. "Just so. So we shall prefer to delay Iaor Safiad past the likelihood of any great interference. We should prefer to hold him entirely. But we will first show him a face that may make him pause to reflect, rather than merely gather his forces for an assault. We shall assuredly not draw the first bow." He glanced from one man to the other and added without emphasis, "Indeed, you may warn your men that I will personally see to it that any man who shoots without the command is bound under the *geas*."

Lady Tehre looked up at that, suddenly attentive, frowning. Both captains paled. "No one will draw without leave," the senior said earnestly. "We assure you, my lord."

"Indeed, I am certain of it," murmured Beguchren. "Now, if we should be *compelled* to fight, we shall hope Lady Tehre may compensate for our poor disposition of forces."

The captains glanced at each other and then, with the greatest respect, at Lady Tehre. They were northern men; that was one reason the Arobern had left them with Beguchren. They had seen the Great Wall.

"Well, but," said Lady Tehre, worried, "there is no stone here to break; the mountains are a great distance away. I think too far."

The lady was perched on a camp chair, her hands folded demurely in her lap, a few strands of her dark hair curling down beside her face. She looked fragile and feminine and markedly more beautiful than she had six years ago. Marriage to Gereint had suited her very well.

She said now, "I can tear up the road under their horses, to be sure, my lord, but that wouldn't be enough to stop them, do you think, if they are determined? This soft black soil is very deep here along the river. I don't know what I could do with it." A tiny crease appeared between her fine eyebrows as she slipped into a maker's reverie. "Soft earth might actually *flow*, in a sense, rather like very thick molasses," she murmured. "I wonder..."

Beguchren left the lady to consider how deep soil might flow like a liquid and said to the captains, without the slightest fear he would distract her, "I expect the Safiad to make his appearance, in considerable force, quite soon. Today, tomorrow, most likely not so late as the day after. Suppose he approaches this very afternoon. If we cannot halt him entirely, I think we must delay him at least three days." After that, if the Wall had held so long, it would probably break. At that point Iaor Safiad would have to forget about the Delta and set his men against the griffins. If that happened, Beguchren intended to support the Feierabianden king with his own men. Provided he had any left, which he would not if he had been forced to use them in battle. He did not intend to have events come to that.

He said merely, "We do not wish our king to find himself pressed from the rear when he has urgent matters to which he must attend elsewhere. We most particularly do not wish him forced to engage Iaor Safiad personally. Given the possibility of unfortunate errors attending that sort of engagement, even if they had been previously avoided."

Again, both captains nodded. One of them murmured, "No, indeed, my lord," in a fervent tone that made Beguchren suspect the man had young sons of his own, and sufficient imagination to flinch from the picture this statement called to mind.

"We shall hope, however, to persuade the Safiad to

hold using nothing more forceful than moral suasion," Beguchren said firmly, and dismissed the captains. As they drew away, he overheard one of them murmur to the other, "Well, my lord is the man for moral suasion, if anyone is," and the other answer, "He might bid the river flow backward and have it comply, but an offended king is likely to prove harder to turn than a river."

This summed the situation up tolerably well. Beguchren, too, would have much preferred not to be forced to depend wholly on his own personal persuasiveness. Lady Tehre was a weapon, but it was not weapons that would win this particular argument—not if it could be won at all.

He could not help but recall, as sometimes he did rather too vividly, that once his usefulness to his king had not been limited to the fluency of his tongue and the persuasiveness of his arguments. Sighing, he rose—stiffly, for he was no longer a young man—and, leaving Lady Tehre to contemplate the possibilities inherent in this gentle pastureland, went to once more look over the arrangements he had made.

The King of Feierabiand rode south along the river road and out into the broad pastureland just after noon. Scouts had warned Beguchren, so he had his men properly drawn up. The formality of their disposal made the thinness of their lines all the more apparent, which was not accidental. Nevertheless, they made a fine, aggressive display, with all their neat uniforms and their helms polished and their spears neatly parallel. The spear-and-falcon banner of the Casmantian king flew over their heads, sapphire and purple.

Only the officers were on horseback, and they would dismount if the Feierabianden troops rode forward, for there were certain to be horse-callers among the Feierabianden ranks. No Casmantian, whether soldier or officer, could possibly trust himself to even the best-trained horse. The long Casmantian spears, made by the best weaponsmiths in the world, were meant to compensate for this Feierabianden advantage. Ordinarily they might do so, though today, with so few men, and those arranged in long lines rather than a powerful defensive block, they would never compensate sufficiently if it came to battle.

Iaor Safiad had clearly had scouts of his own out ahead of his main force, for he did not seem surprised by what he found in the open country along the river. His men filed off the road and formed up in their own lines, broader and far thicker than the Casmantian lines, for this was the Safiad's main force, all that could be gathered hastily. Feierabiand was accustomed to having an uneasy neighbor on either side, and so that was a large proportion of all the male population, townsmen and farmers alike. The Feierabianden army might possess relatively few professional soldiers, but its militia was large, experienced, and swiftly available. And mounted. Feierabiand was proud of its horses and knew very well what a powerful advantage they possessed in their mounted companies. They rode to battle with other creatures as well: Hawks and even eagles perched on more than one shoulder, and the birds were greatly outnumbered by mastiffs with powerful shoulders and even more powerful jaws.

To be sure, though Beguchren might lack horses and dogs, he did have Lady Tehre by his side, and she was a weapon more to be valued than any number of spears.

He asked her, "How much are we outnumbered, do you think?"

"Hmm?" The lady was mounted on a pretty bay mare. She wore a practical traveling dress with split skirts, a set of copper bangles around one wrist, and an abstracted expression. "Not much above four to one," she said, glancing casually across the field. "Four and a fraction, I believe. About four and a tenth. You know, I don't believe there's much to do with all this deep soil after all."

"Oh?" said Beguchren.

"No, I think the thing to do is snap all their bows. Or perhaps their arrows. The bows themselves are quite resilient to breaking, you know, especially at these cool temperatures, but they will very likely break if the arrows are broken just as their strings are released."

"Ah," said Beguchren.

"Although the timing in that case would certainly need to be very precise, even if they shoot in volley," Lady Tehre added reflectively. "Perhaps it would be better to think about—"

"Please do nothing at all until it is quite clear that the Feierabianden force is actually attacking," said Beguchren. "And I would greatly prefer it if, in that case, you do as little as seems consistent with a reasonable possibility of success."

The lady's gaze sharpened. After a moment, she smiled. "I understand," she said.

Beguchren returned a small smile of his own, confident that for all her apparent absentmindedness, she did.

He rode out alone across the field toward the Feierabianden lines—rode, because it showed both confidence and peaceable intent to ride a horse within distance of the

Feierabianden horse-callers, and because the Casmantian commander could hardly walk on foot across the mud and grasses, and most of all because he needed the horse's height and beauty to make a proper show. The horse was a particularly fine white mare, not large, but pretty and elegant, with blue ribbons braided into her mane and tail for the occasion. Beguchren wore white to match her, embroidered with blue and set about with pearls. Together they would make a brilliant show, which was one skill Beguchren still owned, for all he had lost.

Iaor Safiad sat his own horse, a plain bay with good shoulders and powerful quarters and not a single ribbon, in the center of the Feierabianden lines. He did not ride out to meet Beguchren. Nor, which might have been more likely, did he send any man of his to ride out. He brought his horse forward only a few paces and then waited, compelling Beguchren to come all the way to him.

The King of Feierabiand was not as big a man as the Arobern, but he owned a kingliness all his own, and he had grown into his power as he had aged. His lion-tawny hair was just becoming grizzled, but he was one of those men, Beguchren thought, whose personal force would only deepen with time.

At the moment, the Safiad's expression was stern and his mouth tight with anger. A difficult audience, Beguchren judged. But he had not expected otherwise.

The Feierabianden officers were spread out, each to his own company, and so far as Beguchren could judge, the king had not brought any court advisers with him. But beside the king and a little behind sat a young man on a fine black horse, a thickset young man with black hair and dark eyes and the unmistakable look of his father. He carried neither bow nor spear, but he had a sword at his side; a good, plain weapon and no courtier's toy. He met Beguchren's eyes with a serious, uneasy intensity.

Beguchren was already well within arrow-shot. He came within an easy spear cast and then rode closer still, until he was very close; close enough to be easily heard without shouting. Then he drew up his mare and simply sat for a moment, meeting the furious stare of the King of Feierabianden.

"Beguchren Teshrichten," the king said at last, bare acknowledgment with no courtesy to it. But he had reason to be angry.

"Iaor Daveien Behanad Safiad," Beguchren answered, inclining his head in grave respect.

Iaor glared at him and lifted a hand, gesturing from left to right across all the field and the men arranged in their lines there. "What is this? Well? Brechen Glansent Arobern gave me his word he would be amicable, and now I find *this* in my way? What will he have of me?" He glared at Beguchren and then jerked a hand sideways to indicate Prince Erichstaben. He said, even more furiously, "I am aware he has a new young son; has he forgotten the one he gave to me? Does he believe my patience is without limit?"

Beguchren bowed his head in the face of the king's anger. He said softly, "The Arobern indeed has hope of your patience, Iaor Safiad, but he does not believe it to be limitless. He asks, if you please—"

The Safiad slammed a fist down on his own thigh, reining his horse back sharply when it flung up its head and jolted forward a surprised step.

Prince Erichstaben, breaking into the moment with a

sense of dramatic timing that might have been his father's, moved suddenly. He had not appeared shocked or frightened at the Safiad's threat, but had given Beguchren an involuntary glance that repeated the king's question, only with real anxiety to it: *Has my father forgotten me?* But he did not ask that question aloud. He did not speak at all.

Instead, the prince stripped off his sword belt with quick movements, slung his sword over the pommel of his saddle, swung one leg over his horse's shoulder, and slid down to the ground. Then, having collected all eyes, he walked forward to stand by the Safiad's horse. He took the king's reins and himself steadied the horse, absently patted its shoulder, and at last lifted his head to look up at the king. He did not speak, but his open, honest look spoke for him quite clearly and very well matched the courage and dignity of his gesture. Then he glanced at Beguchren and bowed his head, waiting.

The prince's gesture could not have been better suited to Beguchren's purposes if he had directed the boy through every instant. It changed everything about how Beguchren meant to proceed, for he had expected that he would need to slip every word he spoke past the Safiad's outrage. But Prince Erichstaben had created a silence in which any word spoken would carry several times its normal weight, and in which any gesture, too, would carry more than usual weight and force.

Beguchren carried no sword of his own to give up, not even a knife, so he could not quite match the prince's gesture. But he twisted his reins about the pommel of his saddle and swung down to the ground, came forward a measured few steps, and sank down to one knee. He said clearly and steadily, "Lord King, Brechen Glansent

Arobern remembers every oath he swore to you and repudiates nothing. He sends me to beg you hold your hand and your temper and your men." He deliberately touched his fingertips to the muddy ground and then to his lips in the gesture of eating dirt, met the king's eyes, and said, "I do not know how to beg more abjectly." He was satisfied to see that Iaor Safiad, taken aback, appeared at a loss for any answer.

Turning to the young prince, Beguchren added, with all the forceful sincerity at his command, "Your father has not forgotten you. However events fall, whatever these perilous days bring, he begs you believe that you have been always in his thoughts. He declares, with great passion, that no new babe can replace his firstborn son."

Prince Erichstaben's expression lightened. Though he still did not speak, he bent his head in an admirably dignified nod of acceptance and gratitude.

Beguchren shifted his gaze back to the Safiad. He said, "My king acknowledges that you hold the life of his son in your hand, but entreats you to hold." And then, once more directing his words to the prince, "I beg you will believe that only the hard necessity of a king could have driven him to risk you."

Iaor Safiad found himself constrained by Beguchren's meek humility on the one hand and by Prince Erichstaben's honest bravery on the other. He opened his mouth to speak or perhaps curse, but then only drew a hard breath. He said at last, still harshly but without the bright-lit fury of those early moments, "Get up, then—up, I say!—and tell me why the Arobern has committed this offense against my borders—for the second time!—and why I should hold."

Beguchren rose as quietly and smoothly as he could. He did not remount his horse, deliberately using his own slight size to further constrain the Safiad to a civilized restraint. He said, "The cousin of your lord Bertaud came to my lord king. Lady Mienthe daughter of Beraod. Through the pass she came, to Ehre, with a companion who gave his name first as Teras son of Toharas to the royal guardsmen and to my king only as Tan."

He had captured the Safiad's attention. Though the king did not speak, his curt gesture indicated that Beguchren should continue. So he outlined the alarming news the lady had brought them: Linularinum on the one side and griffins on the other and confusion throughout; the strange determination of Linularinan agents to reclaim the legist together with whatever mysterious working he had stolen. He drew, without allowing himself to flinch, on his understanding of mages and mageworking to describe the way events were bending wildly around Tan, and his own guess about the legist gift and what Tan had stolen, and what that theft might mean for them all.

He did not mention Lady Mienthe's odd gift or power, for fear the king's very familiarity with the young woman might lead him to discount her. But he gave an honest and almost complete account of the reasoning that had led the Arobern to come west, and their fear that the Safiad, though rightfully outraged, might perhaps err in his anger and prevent the recovery of the legist book. "If the Wall does not hold and griffins ride their burning winds across Feierabiand," he said quietly, "then we may all wish most fervently we had bent our efforts toward this work of legist-magic that might subordinate them."

The king lifted a skeptical eyebrow. "You think this is possible."

Beguchren met his eyes. "I think it likely," he said gently. "And who would know better than I?"

He had used that phrase many times in his long life, generally to good effect. Even here in this foreign country he saw the words go home and belief settle in the king's eyes.

The Feierabianden king said in a low tone far removed from his earlier anger, "I have heard a good deal of you, to be sure," and then paused.

Not for any reason would Beguchren have broken into that considering pause. He stood with his back straight and his hands open at his sides, his eyes steady on the king's face, waiting.

Prince Erichstaben waited also, his hand still resting on the neck of the king's horse. He did not look again up at the king, however, for pride forbade any faintest suggestion that he might ask for mercy, either for his father's sake or on his own account. There was tension in the set of his broad shoulders; nothing to wonder at with the recent vivid demonstration of a king forced to a hard necessity he would never have chosen freely. From that tension, Beguchren saw that the prince thought it was possible that the Safiad might still reject everything Beguchren had said and every plea he had made. But he also saw trust and even affection in the placement of the prince's hand on the neck of Iaor Safiad's horse.

The Safiad glanced down at the Casmantian prince. His expression was closed and cold, but only a man with a heart of stone could have been unmoved by the young man's quiet courage. Beguchren was not at all surprised when the king said, in the low tones of a man making an admission, "We should neither one of us forgive the other for such an act, nor for compelling it."

Beguchren bowed his head in acknowledgment.

The Safiad eyed him without enthusiasm. "Your king has presumed on my good nature, Lord Beguchren. He has greatly presumed. I am not in the least amused by his presumption, nor by your own effrontery. Nor is my patience endless. Get your men out of my way."

His head still bowed, Beguchren dropped again to one knee.

"Well you may beg," the Safiad said sharply. "It is indeed effrontery! You do not have men enough there to hold me. Well?"

"Lord King," Beguchren said, with a perfect humility that would surely have made the Arobern laugh out loud, "I am commanded in the strictest terms to see that the Arobern remains free to act, on your behalf and for us all. I beg you will forgive my effrontery and be so gracious as to permit me to obey my king. Only your generosity can redeem my honor. If you command me again, I shall have no choice but to comply, for, as you say, I have few men. I would never wish to compel a lady onto a field of battle, nor would the lady Tehre Amnachudran Tanshan wish to be so compelled. She would much prefer to ride north with all speed and see to her Wall; she was greatly distressed to hear of the damage that has come upon it."

The Safiad looked momentarily taken aback by this combined threat and offer. Then he actually laughed—a grim laugh, but with something like real amusement. "Get up," he said. "Get up, Lord Beguchren, and draw back your men. Set them in some less provocative order, and we shall discuss the matter. That is your pavilion down by the river? We shall retire to it and consider what we may do."

"Lord King, I shall do everything exactly as you command," Beguchren said smoothly, and rose.

CHAPTER **14**

What does one do to prepare for the swift and terrible arrival of fire? Where does one go to hide from the fiery storm? Where does one go if the storm will come everywhere?

Casmantian for making, as the saying went, and to be sure, Feierabianden makers were neither so common nor so skilled as those of Casmantium. But it was humbling to see with what dedicated hearts the makers of Tihannad bent to their tasks. Especially when everyone in the city, and they themselves, must suspect their efforts would in the end prove inadequate.

One would not look to Feierabiand for the best of makers, but still, it is makers one needs before battle. Certainly horses and hounds would be by no means so useful against griffins as they might be against men. So what makers Tihannad possessed were wearing the skin off their fingers shaping arrow shafts and putting decent edges on spear points. Feierabianden mages did not know how to tip arrows with points of ice, but even in Feierabiand a weaponsmith could make spears that would resist breaking and arrows that would turn in the air to seek blood.

"Not blood," Jos told the harassed weapon-makers, having sought out the weapons-hall, which was crowded and clamoring. "Have your arrows seek fire. And see if you can get them to resist burning."

"It's not so easy to make *wood* resist *burning*," the head of the king's weapon-makers snapped impatiently, but he had fires kindled through the weapons-hall so the makers could keep their enemy more clearly in mind. Before Jos left the hall, he saw the man run a long grayfletched shaft through his hands and then cast it into a fire, and when he lifted the arrow out again it was only smoking and not charred.

"That was well done," Lord Bertaud said to Jos when he heard of it. "I would dearly wish to have a hundred Casmantian makers here, and a dozen cold mages, but even advice may help. Have you any other suggestions for our makers?"

Jos wished he could say, *Oh, yes, only do this and avoid that and victory will be ours!* But he could only shake his head.

Bertaud nodded, unsurprised, and shifted a lamp over toward his maps. It was not yet dusk, but the room had only an east window and the light failed early this time of year.

He had been considering the lay of the land above the lake and before the precipitous hills, where they expected the griffins to come out of the broken country of the pass. "They will not care for those wild heights," he said

absently, not really to Jos. "Nor for the magic carried by
the gathering river and held by Niambe Lake."

This was true. Griffin-fire had little in common with
that cold, wild magic. Their hot winds would blow only
weakly through those mountains and near the lake. That
could not possibly compensate for the advantage Kes
would provide the griffins, however, not to any real
degree. Jos did not say so. He did not have to. They both
knew it.

"We will arrange our men here and here, I think," said
Bertaud, tracking figures on a map. "Archers here and
over along here. The griffins must come this way and
that will force them to pass through this killing ground,
here."

Griffin mages could burn arrows in the air, and Kes
would heal any injured griffins before they could fall. Jos
made no comment.

Lord Bertaud gave him a look. "Yes," he said. "But
my officers will expect us to arrange ourselves as though
we may do something useful. If the main body of men is
here, then it will not seem strange if I set myself with a
small, picked force"—he traced a line forward, right into
the mouth of the pass—"here."

Jos nodded. "You don't think you can hold them all?"
he ventured.

The Feierabianden lord did not look at him. "The pass
will force them down and keep them tight-packed. I think
I will be able to hold them all. But if I am wrong, I think
it would be as well if we have our men arranged so as to
be some use."

Jos nodded again.

"Tastairiane will be in the forefront of the attack, I

imagine, and if I can stop him, that will at least cast the rest into confusion."

"Kes will stay far out of arrow reach. And out of your reach?"

"I can't—she isn't—" Bertaud stopped.

"She'll be riding Opailikiita, I guess."

"And if I can't compel Kes, I should be able to compel Opailikiita. Yes. She has always been very careful to keep Kes far out of reach of any stray arrow, but the mountains may force her to fly lower, closer to the ground. And closer to me. I may be able to force Opailikiita to turn against Kes. That will allow our arrows to do useful work against the rest of the griffins." The lord did not look happy about this. There was a strained note in his voice, rather as though he were discussing his potential ability to impale children.

Jos nodded again, silent.

"I know," Bertaud said, looking up suddenly to meet his eyes. "I know it must be done, and better the griffins are destroyed than Tihannad, and after us all the country of earth. But—"

"I—"

Bertaud slammed his hand down on the maps he had been studying. He did not shout, but said almost in a whisper, "*Don't* . . . tell me you understand."

Jos caught himself, barely, before he could take a step backward. "No, lord. I beg your pardon."

The Feierabianden lord stared at him for another moment, his eyes narrow and his color high. Then his gaze fell, and he flung himself into a chair and rubbed his hands tiredly across his face. "Forgive me."

"There's nothing to forgive, lord," Jos said earnestly. He hesitated. "Kairaithin?"

"If he could bring me Tastairiane, or bring me *to* Tastairiane, he surely would have done it by this time, don't you think?" This began as a cry of despair, but ended as a question that pleaded for reassurance. "Do you think so? *Could* there still be time for Kairaithin to succeed? If he will try, in the end, and not merely delay and delay and hope I am overwhelmed in the end—"

"Until the last seconds run through the glass, there's still time."

Lord Bertaud laughed bitterly. "Ah. Thank you."

"It's an aphorism because it's true," Jos said gently, and heard the gentleness in his own tone, and was surprised by it. He had not realized until that moment that he thought the other man fragile.

"Well," said Bertaud, and hesitated, glanced around with an air of uncertainty that suddenly firmed into decision, and called into the air, "Kairaithin! Sipiike Kairaithin!"

The griffin mage came to that call, whispering out of the air like swirling ash. He drew darkness around himself as he came, rising to his feet out of black feathers and the sullen glow of a quenched fire. His shadow smoldered, brighter than either the lantern light or the pale daylight lingering outside the windows; the wooden floor under his feet smoked and charred.

Jos had never known the griffin mage to command his own power so ill. He wanted to exclaim, to remind Kairaithin to rule himself. Then the griffin turned his human face toward them, and they both saw the livid mark that ran across his cheek, and the way he held one arm tucked close to his body. Jos forgot what he had meant to say, and Lord Bertaud came to his feet, asking sharply, "Was that Tastairiane? Are you all right?"

"I am not defeated!" Kairaithin said fiercely. "Do *not* call me, man! Do you not understand I am doing all I can? Let me go!"

Bertaud lifted his hands in a helpless gesture of distress and grief, and the griffin shredded at once into the thin light, black feathers crossing the light like shadows, gone once more.

For a long moment, neither man moved or spoke. Then Bertaud laughed with no humor at all and pressed a hand across his eyes.

Jos said, "If he cannot get to Tastairiane Apailika..." He stopped.

"Do you know..." Bertaud began, and paused. But then he went on, speaking in a low voice. "He said once he would tell her. Kes. About me. About what she did, when she used fire to heal me, about how she'd woken this...gift...with her fire. He said the truth would do more than any lie to keep her from healing other men with fire; that she would understand she must never risk another man coming into this cursed affinity."

This explained a good deal. Jos only nodded, allowing the other man to talk, as he clearly needed to. It might be the only useful service he could actually provide, listening to secrets Lord Bertaud could not tell anyone else.

"He can't have done, of course. Or she would never support Tastairiane in this. And now it is too late. He'll never be able to come at her now, no more than he can come at Tastairiane himself."

Jos said quietly, "I suppose he saw, as the years turned on, how little she came to care for men. So he thought it was unnecessary to warn her not to heal men with fire. He thought, *Great secrets are always safest if no one knows them.* And he thought she would never care to heal a man so again. Even—" *Me*, he had meant to say, but that would sound hopelessly bitter. He did not finish the thought aloud.

"You're Casmantian. Not much chance you'd find yourself waking with any affinity, I imagine, no matter how much fire Kes poured into you. Though—" Lord Bertaud hesitated, and then finished a little grimly, "I suspect Kairaithin would have killed you if she'd ever happened to heal you with fire, just to be certain of it."

Jos winced a little. He had come to consider Sipiike Kairaithin as something almost like a friend. But he thought the lord was right. "I sprained my ankle once," he recalled. "That was during my first winter in the mountains. Kairaithin brought me splints…Kes did not come, not for several weeks. I wonder whether Kairaithin prevented her. He did not want to tell her this secret, but he would not risk her healing me…How does a fire mage heal a creature of earth?"

Bertaud only shrugged. "Go," he said. "Rest, if you can. This is, what, the ninth day since Kairaithin brought his warning? And Kes is still using her strength against the Wall, I'm sure. I imagine the last grains of sand are running through the glass. If Kairaithin cannot come against Tastairiane tonight or tomorrow, I think we will discover what will happen when unquenchable fire runs against unyielding stone."

Clearly the Feierabianden lord wished to be alone. Jos bowed and withdrew, leaving Lord Bertaud to pore once more over his maps. He could not imagine there was much chance of rest for either of them.

Jos walked slowly toward his room, an antechamber in

Lord Bertaud's own apartment, through the dim light of the hallway. He was thinking of Kes. She had been in the back of his mind without ceasing all through these weary days, and was only more so now.

For all her fierce power, she knew so little. She knew nothing at all of what her adopted people would meet on this side of the pass…He thought of Bertaud saying, *He can't have told her.* What a pity! And how ironic for a man who had once been a spy to think a secret too close-kept. But if she knew…if she knew…This one particular secret would do best if one more person knew it, if Kes knew it. Kairaithin could not come close to her, no. Her *iskarianere* Tastairiane Apailika, Lord of Fire and Air, would see that no enemy could come close to her.

But even the Lord of Fire and Air could not hold a fire mage from going where she would; no, not even if it occurred to the powerful white griffin to constrain her. Likely it would not occur to him, for griffins did not lightly accept or impose any constraint on one another. Kairaithin might not be able to reach Kes. But, though Kes might be wary of Kairaithin, she would not fear *Jos.* If she wished, she could come to him. And then he could tell her this dangerous secret. He had sworn silence—but Lord Bertaud, from what he'd said a moment earlier, would plainly release him to tell *Kes*, if he could.

Probably she would not come. But if she did, he could tell her what awaited her adopted people on this side of the pass. Then she would at last understand why the People of Fire and Air must not strike into Feierabiand—no, nor against any part of the country of earth. Then she would refuse Tastairiane's command to break the Wall, and all the coming storm might yet be averted.

Jos turned on his heel and headed, not toward his room, but toward the stairs. Up and up again, from the busy areas of the house to the upper hallways where no one went but servants, and up again, the remaining flight to the slanted door that led out to the roof. Not a very high roof, for the kings of Feierabiand did not care for tremendous ornate palaces such as those the kings of Casmantium built. But nevertheless above the town and out in the free air, where a creature such as Kes might come.

It was just dusk, a propitious moment because fire mages moved most easily through wind and light at dusk. Even Kairaithin preferred to come and go at dusk, especially if he moved out into the foreign country of earth. Jos was not certain that Kes *could* shift herself from the country of fire and right across the wild mountains into the country of earth. Especially with the Wall in her way. Nor was he sure that she *would* come, even if she heard him, and he was not confident even of that.

But he called her. He called her by the name she had owned when she was human, and then by the beautiful, complicated name she owned now: Kereskiita Keskainiane Raikaisipiike. He gazed up at the earliest stars, glittering cold and distant in the luminous sky, and dropped the long graceful words off his tongue as though he were reciting poetry.

And Kes came. Like a white star falling to the earth, like lightning called out of the sky, like a stroke of fire through the dark; the breeze shifted from the north to the east, and strengthened, suddenly carrying a scent of hot sand and molten air, and Kes shaped herself out of the wind and walked forward across the shingled roof. She moved as though she barely touched the roof, as though she might walk straight up into the sky if she ceased to pay attention to where she placed her feet. Her shadow, dim in the dusk, glowed like the last of the sunset. Her eyes, turned toward him, were filled with fire.

Jos stood still, watching her come. His heart had twisted the moment he'd realized she had actually come to his call, and it felt tight and painful still. He could feel the beat of his pulse in his throat. She walked toward him, smiling her fierce, beautiful smile, her eyes blazing with life and fire, and he forgot for that first moment why he had called her and what he had intended to say.

"Jos," she said. Her voice was light and quick and joyful, but behind the joy was something else, a strange wistfulness that was more nearly something he could recognize. There was no cruelty to her voice now—nor any kindness, but that he could endure, so long as the cruelty had gone out of her. She held her hands out to him.

She had settled her fire, contained it; he could touch her without danger. So he took her hands in his and looked down into her lovely, inhuman face. He said, "Kes."

"You called me," said Kes. "I came…I wished to see you one more time." Her ethereal white brows drew together slightly in puzzlement. "I heard your voice, and I wished to come," she repeated, speaking slowly, as though she found this curious.

"Kes," Jos said again. And then, with dawning fear, "One more time?" He had closed his hands too tightly on hers. She did not flinch from his grip, but he realized the strength of his grip and flinched on her behalf, opening his hands.

She did not draw back. She did not seem even to realize he had let her go. "I broke the Wall," she said simply.

"This past noon, when the sun struck down with all its power. Only a very little is destroyed, but that part was the anchor that locked the Wall tight against the wild mountains. The pass is open to fire now. At dawn we will call up the fiery wind. Tomorrow will be a day for blood and fire."

She did not speak, as Jos might have expected, with joyful delight. Instead her voice held an odd kind of wistfulness. She tilted her head to look at him, a quick, almost birdlike motion. She said, "I might take you away. Not into the pass. Somewhere the People of Fire and Air will not come…"

"They will come everywhere, eventually. Or they would. Kes—" Jos wanted to touch her face, run his thumb along the angle of her jaw. He did not let himself reach out, but said urgently, "Kes, I'm so glad you came. You don't know what will happen. A day of fire and blood, you say, but it's a day that will quench all fire. Bertaud—Lord Bertaud, whom you know—do you not realize he holds an affinity for griffins?"

For a long moment, Kes did not seem to understand what he had said. Then she did not believe him. "A creature of earth?" she cried. "An affinity for the *People of Fire and Air*? You speak fables and sunbeams, your words are as the ash that crumbles when the wind touches it! That cannot be true. It is not true. How could it be true?" She took a step back from him. Another. Cried even more sharply, her tone more plainly human than he had heard it for years, "How can you tell such lies?"

"You woke the gift in him yourself, when you used fire to heal him," Jos told her urgently. "No one knows but Sipiike Kairaithin. Think of Kairaithin and tell me it's all sunlight and ash! Think of what Kairaithin has done over these past years and what he has refused to do and tell me it's a lie!"

The fire within Kes brightened, and brightened again, so fiercely that Jos had to take a step away himself. But Kes did not disappear into the wind. She had become a burning figure of white gold and porcelain, but she did not go.

"Kes!" he said, and made himself step forward again. "If the griffins come riding their wind of fire out of that pass tomorrow, they will *all* find out. Do you understand? Do you understand what that will do to them?"

"Yes," said Kes.

"You must stop them. It's Tastairiane Apailika driving this wind, isn't it? You can go to him tonight—tell him—"

"I can't *tell* him!" cried Kes.

"—tell him you've changed your mind, you won't support this attack against Feierabiand; you can tell him something—tell him you remember your sister. *Do* you remember your sister, Kes? I'm sure she hasn't forgotten you. It's just the same this time as six years ago! All the power is in *your* hands. Tell Tastairiane you won't support him and that we're prepared, that if griffins come through that pass tomorrow, they'll face ten thousand arrows and a thousand spears, and you won't be there to make his griffins whole when they're struck down—"

Kes shook her head. "He will never stop now. Not now that the Wall is broken. He will never stop, and even if I tell him, he won't believe it can be true, he'll think you lied to me. Or if he believes it, he'll be so angry—it's Bertaud, you say? Lord Bertaud son of Boudan who has this affinity to fire?"

"Yes—" Jos said, and realized as he spoke—too late!—that he should never have given her Bertaud's name. She shredded into a blazing white wind, and Jos stared, appalled, for far too long a moment before he flung himself for the stairs.

Bertaud was still in the map room when Jos hurled himself through the door, and still alive, which Jos had not expected; it must have taken Kes a moment to find him—well, she did not know the Feierabianden lord well and *he* had not been fool enough to call her name out across the winds.

But she was there before Jos, even so. She was walking forward when Jos slammed open the door and ran in, panting in great heaving breaths. She had her hand out in almost a friendly manner, and Bertaud was not alarmed—or not alarmed enough. He was just standing there, not even backing away, far less running for the door—not that running would help; the air prickled with living fire. In a moment the house itself would blaze up, the maps and furnishings and the underlying structure itself, and Lord Bertaud would burn like a tallow candle at the center of that conflagration.

Jos could not get enough breath to shout a warning, but Bertaud took in his precipitous arrival and then seemed to see for the first time the white fire prickling across Kes's outstretched hand. He caught the edge of the map table and flung it over to block her way; worse than useless, for the papers caught fire as they spilled across the floor. Kes put her foot on the fallen table and stepped across it, so lightly it did not even wobble, but flames licked out across the wood—white flames, pale gold at the edges, burning with an intense heat that seemed likely to set the air itself on fire. Bertaud tried to shout, but the burning air drove him back, choking, his arms across his face.

Here at the edge of the room where Jos stood it was not so unendurably hot, and so Jos took a quick hard breath and shouted, "Kairaithin! Anasakuse Sipiike Kairaithin!" His voice, rough and half-strangled with heat and terror, fell flat and dead against the brilliant air. He lunged forward over the burning table and caught Kes's uplifted hand in his, dragging her back and swinging her around. He looked into her face, and he could not recognize anything he saw in those golden eyes. The fire that filled her burned his hand and arm, but to his astonishment she caught her fire back away from him after that first instant, containing it, so he did not instantly die for his temerity.

Then Kairaithin came. The eastern wall went up in a fierce blaze, and Kairaithin strode out of that sheeting flame as though he were coming through a door and took in all that was happening in one swift, summing look.

For one horrifying instant, Jos thought the griffin mage might simply lend Kes his own terrible power and rip fire out of the air through the whole house. Then his furious black gaze locked on Bertaud's, and although the man was coughing and could not speak, all the flames flattened sharply toward the floor, flickering madly, and went out, exactly like candle flames blown out from above.

"Kairaithin—" said Kes. Her tone was urgent, remonstrating. She stretched her free hand out toward her old teacher.

"Kairaithin!" Bertaud said in a much different tone, though just as urgently, and tried to catch his breath through the coughing.

"No!" cried Jos. He knew the Feierabianden lord

meant to command the griffin mage to kill Kes—he knew he should even agree, he knew very well he should agree, but he couldn't, not even now. He had not let go of Kes, not even yet, and now he jerked her back to put himself between her and Kairaithin. He shouted furiously to the griffin mage, "Get her *out* of here, get her as far away as you can, and *keep* her away! Don't you see, that will do, that will be enough, if she isn't there even that bastard Tastairiane won't press through the pass without her—" He ran out of breath, coughing helplessly; his chest burned and agony radiated from his hand all the way to his shoulders and he knew, he *knew* he hadn't said enough, hadn't said it *right*, he'd never been a man with a gift for words—

Then Kairaithin, with no expression Jos could read, called up a hard-driving wind right through the walls of the house, a wind shot through with wild darkness and rushing sand and flames, and that wind whirled all around them and swept them up, and the world tilted out from underneath them, and Lord Bertaud was left behind in the map room and the king's house as the griffin flung himself and Kes and Jos away into the wind.

CHAPTER 15

Mienthe came back to Tiefenauer only weeks after she had left it. It seemed like years. It had been raining from the moment they had entered the Delta, but the rain ceased at last as they pressed through the last of the countryside toward the town. Mienthe put back her hood and straightened her back, looking up as the first sunlight of the day struggled through the heavy overcast.

They were coming into Tiefenauer not from the east, but more from the south. The Arobern had taken them around that way so they could come up the coast road. "We turn only a little out of our way, and this road is better for marching, especially in the rain," he had said, with no explanation of how he came to know the quality of the roads in Feierabiand and the Delta. "And we do not wish to come without warning upon the Linularinan troops in the town."

Mienthe had been surprised.

"We do not wish to astonish and overwhelm them," the

Arobern had explained. "We wish them to see us coming so that they may back out of our way. If they do not back away, *then* we will overwhelm them."

But he had seemed to expect the Linularinan forces to retreat. Mienthe was surprised by this, too. After all, Linularinum had shown itself amazingly determined. The Arobern certainly could not look for any additional support from Casmantium, whereas the Linularinan forces on this side of the river must have everything they needed.

"That is all true," agreed the Arobern. "And Gereint Enseichen thinks as you do, that we may find Linularinum reluctant to give way. But, militarily, they must. This is all hostile country for them. Half the men all through this country are militia, or have been. We will have the favor of the countryside and the Linularinan forces only sullenness and flung stones."

It was true that the Casmantian king had asked Mienthe to go ahead and speak to militia officers at Kames, so they had acquired three good-sized militia companies. The militia rode under the command of the Arobern's professional military officers. Their combined force now flew not only the spear-and-falcon banner of Casmantium, but also the oak banner of the Delta and the golden barley and blue river of Feierabiand. Until the Arobern explained, Mienthe had not realized that he had purposefully set all those banners up where they could be seen.

And at first he seemed to be right: They met no stiff resistance, only from time to time they glimpsed Linularinan scouts or agents, and then as they pressed forward they would often find obvious signs of a larger force that had been encamped and had now withdrawn. A formal alliance approaching and a thoroughly hostile Delta population to press them: The Linularinan officers did not want to face that. They withdrew, and withdrew again. So there had been no fighting.

"It may be different when we come to Tiefenauer," the Arobern warned Mienthe.

"It will be, if they haven't found that book of theirs," agreed Gereint Enseichen. He gave Mienthe a nod, but really he was speaking to the Arobern. "They might not wish to fight, but I think they will, rather than give up the town where they know it hides."

"They won't have found it," Mienthe had answered with confidence, but the Casmantian mage only shrugged, and as they at last approached Tiefenauer, she gradually became much less certain. She brushed damp strands of hair out of her face, peering ahead for the first glimpse of the city. The sun fought its way through towering clouds, and the woods along the road looked heavy, thick with green shadows. The shadows were ornamented by flashes of yellow and crimson where a flowering vine tumbled down a great oak or a bird darted past. Mosquitoes whined in the heavy shade, and sapphire-winged flycatchers dipped and wheeled in the complicated sky overhead. The horses' hooves thudded dully on the packed wet earth of the road, and everywhere there was the sound of rushing water—it ran down the ditches on either side of the road and against the banks where the road had been built up through a slough; it dripped from leaves overhead and trickled through the wet leaves that carpeted the ground under the trees. The reins were stiff and cold in Mienthe's fingers.

"It always seems to be raining when I come back to Tiefenauer after any time away," Mienthe said aloud.

"If it were in the mountains, it would be snow," Tan answered with the ghost of a smile. He was riding at Mienthe's shoulder, his customary place through all these long wet days. He seldom spoke now. His attention seemed to be directed inward. But he had perhaps seen Mienthe's anxiety and so spoke lightly, to take her mind from her mood.

Mienthe was not willing to be cheered. "At least that would be pretty," she said. It seldom snowed in the Delta; usually there was only a cold gray drizzle for days on end. Mienthe liked snow. She thought wistfully of pretty, wintertime Tihannad. Up in the shadow of the mountains, there might even be snow this late in the spring. Bertaud was there now. As soon as she thought of him, she found she missed him terribly. Had he met his griffin friend again; had they discovered why the Casmantian Wall was breaking and how to stop it breaking right through? He must have heard now about the trouble in the Delta…

It occurred to Mienthe, for the first time, that her cousin might possibly be riding for the Delta right now; that he might have come before them, he might even be there at this moment. She had assumed that he would stay close by the king, and that Iaor Safiad would avoid the Sierhanan road, and that they would meet Lord Beguchren at Minas Ford and Beguchren would stop them, exactly as the Arobern had planned. But what if—? And then what would he do, when he saw what Mienthe had brought home with her? If he had even made it to Tiefenauer on that dangerous road…if Linularinan soldiers hadn't stopped him, hadn't…

"It's a pity your lord cousin is stuck away up in Tihannad and won't be waiting to scold us for our adventures and send for healers and hot soup and warm blankets," Tan said, having evidently guessed the trend of Mienthe's thoughts.

"You don't suppose...you don't think..."

"Never in life, Mie. Even if he's settled whatever difficulty it is with the griffins, he'd never be so lost to sense as to take the Sierhanan road."

Somehow this reassurance seemed more decisive and solid when Tan said it aloud than when Mienthe only whispered it to herself. She nodded, feeling happier, and then at last they came around the curve of the road and the woodlands fell away to wet pasturelands and unplowed muddy fields and scattered farmhouses. Farther on, the farms gave way to the outermost sprawl of the town, and beyond that they could just make out the city proper, all washed slate and painted cypress and gleaming cobbles. It took a surprising effort for Mienthe to suppress the strong urge she felt to lift her horse into a canter and race down the center of the road, straight for the great house.

That wild ride might almost have been safe. There was no sign of any Linularinan force. It occurred to Mienthe only after some moments that of course the Arobern had known the road was clear; he had scouts of his own way out, after all. She said tentatively to Tan, "Do you suppose the Linularinan soldiers have all gone back across the bridge?"

Tan flashed her a smile that was only a little strained. "We shall hope so."

He almost hoped they hadn't, Mienthe understood.

Of them all, Tan was the least eager to arrive, while no one but she seemed to feel this driving need for haste. But... *Trust your gift and yourself*, Tan had said to her, and though Mienthe thought she was probably foolishly impatient, she looked for the Arobern so she could ask whether they might press their pace to something a little less deliberate.

"We'll make haste, yes, but slowly," the Arobern told her. His tone was absent, but kind. He looked past her as he spoke, watching the road, watching the empty farmlands, studying the town they were approaching. "I thought they might get out and away across the river, but now I think they are there in the town, those Linularinan enemies of ours, you see? This country"—he made a broad gesture that encompassed the woods behind them and the cleared land near Tiefenauer and the town itself—"it is too empty. This is not peace we ride into, but a silence of waiting—ah. Do you see? Now we will find out what is there."

A small group of men had come warily up to the edge of the road to meet them. Farmers, Mienthe thought, and maybe a tradesman or two from the town. They stared at the banners, especially the Delta oak. And they looked at her, as the Arobern drew his horse up and waved a broad hand, signaling Mienthe to put herself in the forefront of the company. She was a little surprised, but only momentarily, for the militia companies were clearly pleased by his gesture and the waiting men as clearly reassured by it. The militia dipped their banners to her. Mienthe hoped she did not blush.

The men stepped up on the road to meet her, nodding respectfully and glancing warily past her at the Arobern,

waiting beneath the blue-and-purple Casmantian banner. Mienthe thought they would not recognize her, that
they might not trust her, but instead one of the townsmen
came forward another half step and said, "Lady Mienthe,
you won't remember me, I suppose. I'm Jeseth son of
Tamanes. A glazier. I did the windows of the solar up
at the great house for your cousin. That was some years
ago—"

"I do remember!" Mienthe exclaimed. She did. She
recognized the man's broad, weathered face and kindly
eyes and short grizzled beard; seeing him here was like
a promise of homecoming. She said, "You fixed my window, too, when I broke it." She had been fourteen, and
bent on rescuing a fledgling green jay that had got its foot
tangled in the flowering vines outside her room. The poor
creature had dangled helplessly upside down, cheeping
piteously, but Mienthe had freed it easily. She hadn't
slipped and broken the window until its frantic parents
had startled her, diving to protect their young one.

"I did," said the glazier, smiling at her. "You showed
me the little bird, which the esteemed Iriene had just fixed
its leg. You had a scratch on your cheek where its mama
had pecked you, and lucky she hadn't got your eye."

Mienthe blushed.

"It's good to see you safe," said the glazier. His gaze
went past her, to the Casmantian banner. "You *are* safe,
are you, lady?"

Mienthe blushed again, but nodded firmly.

"Well, and it's a strong ally you've brought trailing
home at your heel. Which that is an ally, is it?"

Mienthe nodded again and found her voice. "He is,
and he will be—I was afraid to come back, afraid I would

find Linularinan soldiers in Tiefenauer and Linularinan officers in the great house—"

"So you will, and so we came up to warn you, seeing as you might want recent word of the town and the river," said the glazier. He'd brought his gaze back to her face. "We've not known what to do, what with your lord cousin gone to Tihannad. Earth and stone, even if Lord Bertaud's trying to get back here right this minute, who knows what he might have run into? We've no word from him and none from the king, and every one of your uncles pulling in a different direction. Arguing like a pack of fighting dogs with one bone, they are, and not one as will give way to the rest. And now here *you* are, lady, cutting straight past that whole lot and bringing a *Casmantian* lord home with you! That'll make those Linularinan bastards sit up on their hind legs and take notice, and at the same time save a great lot of arguing among our Delta lords." He gave Mienthe an approving nod.

"That's Brechen Glansent Arobern himself," Mienthe said. She raised her voice and said to all the silent little group of listening men, "This is the Arobern himself, come as a friend to our king and to my cousin and to the Delta. He'll push all those Linularinan troops back across the river, whether they've got the bridge decked or have to swim, and too bad for them if all this rain's got the river up!"

The men cheered and laughed, nodding approvingly. One farmer called out, "The bridge isn't decked even yet, and let the lot of them be swept right out to sea on the salt tide!" and they cheered again.

Mienthe nodded and smiled, but she also said, "Well, all the Delta will have to help. Neither the Arobern nor

his men know the marshes or our town, and assuredly we
want to clear out the Linularinan troops as quick as we
may, so we can polish up Tiefenauer and present it properly to my lord cousin when he comes back!"

"That's right!" said one man, and another, "Hear the
lady!"

"So tell our ally your news, and we'll see what we
have to do," Mienthe concluded, and waved up the
Arobern, who gave her an approving nod, swung down
from his horse, and strode up on foot to speak to the men.
He was bareheaded and informal, speaking quickly in his
rough, accented Terheien, making farmers and townsmen
alike forget he was a king and nodding now and then,
respectfully, toward Mienthe.

All along the column there was a general easing, men
passing along flasks of watered wine and pieces of hard
cracker. "We can do better than that by you," one of the
Delta farmers broke off to say, and spoke to one of the
Arobern's officers, after which a half dozen Casmantian
soldiers and a good many Delta men went off down the
farm lane.

Soon after that there were loaves of good bread, and
cold roasted mutton, and baskets of fried chicken and hot
buttered muffins, brought by the farmers' wives and by
boys too young for the militia but eager to touch the
vicious heads of real Casmantian spears. "Which we had
word of your banners long since," said one woman cheerfully. "And then my Tamed brought word of yourself,
lady, and glad we were to hear *that* word! *You'll* teach
those Linularinan bastards they can't take us so light,
begging your pardon, lady."

Mienthe smiled and nodded and murmured whatever

seemed appropriate and cast longing glances down the
road. "Can't we get *on*?" she begged the Arobern at last.
The sun stood nearly directly overhead, and she found
herself fretting like a caged bird with all the bright sky
above calling out to her to *fly*.

"We don't want to rush the Arobern past what he
thinks is wise," murmured Tan, which sentiment collected approving nods from the Casmantian officers.

"We might wish to heed the lady's sense of urgency,"
said Gereint Enseichen, winning a grateful smile from
Mienthe.

"I think we can," said the Arobern. He looked sternly at
Tan and then transferred that heavy frown to Mienthe. "We
shall expect some resistance; we shall expect some fighting. You will both assure me that you will stay close by the
honored mage, do you hear? You will not ride ahead, no
matter this *sense of urgency*. You will not fall behind no
matter that you feel you have cause for alarm. Yes?"

"Yes!" declared Mienthe, trying to press the king and
the whole company into motion with sheer willpower.
Her grip tightened on her reins; her horse jigged sideways
and spun in an impatient circle when she checked him.
She longed to let the animal go, kick him into a gallop,
fling him straight ahead at the town that lay so quietly
before them.

"Yes," muttered Tan, his eyes on the damp road,
steaming now in the sun. He swung reluctantly into the
saddle. When Gereint took a step toward him, he flinched
and backed his horse several steps.

The mage paused and looked at Tan for a moment
without speaking. Then he went, still in silence, to mount
his own tall horse.

*   *   *

Tiefenauer was not a great city, with tall mansions of fine dressed stone and wide avenues paved with tight-fitted blocks of stone. Its streets were narrow and cobbled, its buildings tight-packed and mostly of painted cypress and oak. Cheap gray paint was favored in the poorer areas of the town because it was cheap, with dark red or tawny yellow for those who were more daring; white where families could afford to have their houses painted every year. The white buildings had shutters and doors of scarlet or bright green or sunny yellow, and vines with purple or crimson or orange flowers tumbling from their balconies.

In most of the town, homes were small and mostly set above equally small shops: tailors and cobblers and dressmakers all along one long, narrow street; furniture-makers and harness-makers and metalsmiths near the horse-market; butchers and sausage-makers in the south of town and fishmongers along the river; bakers and confectioners and apothecaries and all sorts of small crafts on the north side. In the middle of town was a wonderful fountain, three levels of falling water leaping from top to bottom with hundreds of green copper fish. Beside the fountain stood a huge oak, in the wide square where twice a week the market was raised, and beyond the square the low hill with the sprawling great house atop it.

It was in the square that the bulk of the Linularinan forces were set, and in the gardens around the great house. But there were Linularinan soldiers all through the town, occupying the apartments above the shops and making free of the shops themselves.

"But not too free," the townsmen had said, with the

grudging air of men bound despite their wishes to be fair. The glazier had added, "They'll let anyone out of Tiefenauer who wishes to go, which is a good many. There hasn't been much looting and less wanton pillage and no firing the buildings. While I was still there—I have a business to look after, but I sent my wife to her cousin down near Saum—but while I was still in Tiefenauer myself, I saw the Linularinan officers flog one of their men for theft and," he said with a grim nod of satisfaction, "they hanged a man for raping a girl, as well they might."

"A gentle occupation. They don't want your folk to hate them for generations," the Arobern had said, which was obvious.

"They only want that book—and Tan," Gereint Enseichen had added. "They must know the book is there. And Lady Mienthe is right: They haven't found it. But I can't imagine what's prevented them. If it's a twentieth-part as obvious as Tan himself, a blind mage should be able to walk right to it."

"So perhaps it isn't a twentieth-part as obvious," Tan had said, an edge to his tone. "Shall we stand here discussing it from one noon to the next, or shall we get on?"

They had gone on. Mienthe had no idea what the Arobern planned to do about the Linularinan soldiers in the houses or the ones in the square; she hadn't been able to make herself pay attention. She knew that Tan was near her, but she was barely aware even of Gereint Enseichen, though the mage rode close on her other side. All her attention was focused on the great house, on the book, on the pressing need to get to it and do—something. She could picture the book clearly in her mind's eye, but she could not picture what either she or Tan or Gereint might *do* with it. But she could not think about anything else. Images of the book occupied nearly the whole of her mind. She could have drawn every curve and line of its decorated cover; she could have told out how many pages it contained. She felt the textures of leather and fine thick paper against her fingers. She thought if *she* had been looking for it, she would inevitably have gone straight to it, with the same certainty with which the river knew which way to go to reach the sea. And, of course, she *was* looking for it, and when she was at last permitted to go freely forward, she headed for it with exactly that certainty.

So Mienthe did not know what disposition the Arobern made with his men, or with the militia companies; she did not know what arrangements he came to with the townsmen and surrounding farmers or even whether there was fighting in the streets of the town once they arrived. She noticed vaguely that she had gone largely blind. Or not really *blind*. It was not a malady of the eyes, but of the attention. She would blink and find quite a large block of time lost. She knew they were outside the town and then that they were in it, between gray-painted buildings, in a narrow alley that smelled of warm rain and steaming cobbles and horse dung and baking bread, with the angle and quality of the light quite different. Then she blinked again and only the cobbles were the same, for the buildings were painted white and the smells did not include bread but did include the fragrance of tumbling trumpet flowers, and the shadows were long and the air much cooler. Yet she had no sense of passing time: All her sense of time seemed to have narrowed to a single pressing urgent *now*.

She lost track of Gereint Enseichen, only noticing occasionally that he had seized her wrist to hold her back. Once when this happened, she stepped sideways and around in a neat circle that took her out of his hold and let her walk forward again, only then she found that Tan had not come with her, so she had to turn back to find him.

She neither noticed nor remembered to wonder whether any of the Arobern's men or townspeople had come with her. Tan was the only person she really noticed, and then only in his absence. She needed him to come with her, and when the world bent around her and behind her then she knew he had paused. If he would not come with her, then she, too, was constrained to pause. In those moments she tried to find him, take his hand, pull him forward after her. But he resisted her tug.

There was shouting, she noticed vaguely. And then she thought so again; she did not know if time had passed or if she was still caught in the same moment, but the shouting seemed to have become more violent and nearer at hand. Tan was refusing to follow her. Mienthe blinked, confused by the sweep of motion and color all around them; nothing would resolve to sensible form. She turned her head, but nothing she saw made sense. But Tan had a hard grip on her hand, and the book was now very close, it was right over *there*. She closed her own hand on Tan's and pulled him hard, around and into a circle that led around the violent motion and through brilliantly colored shadows, and there was the book— She pulled back the rug and shifted the wardrobe out half a step, leaned into the gap, tapped firmly against the upper edge of one panel of the wood that decorated the wall, and the panel swung open just a crack, and she pried it open just that little bit farther and reached into the dark gap behind the panel and the book fell neatly into her hand.

And the moment crashed into time, or time expanded to engulf the moment, and Mienthe found herself standing in her own apartment, her own bedchamber, with the last of the afternoon sunlight slanting in through her window, and the smell of smoke and dust hanging heavy in the air, and, not so far away, a clamor of shouting and screaming and the clash of weapons. Startlement made her gasp, and then rising fear might have made her cry out in earnest, only when she whirled about she found Tan standing in the middle of her room with a finger held to his lips and an expression of stifled hilarity in his eyes.

For a long, stretched moment, Tan was absolutely certain that Mienthe, having brought them by some strange mageworking right past who knew how many Linularinan soldiers and straight into the great house and her own room, would at this inopportune moment recover her senses and cry out some word of triumph or even, given her dazed expression, astonishment. As he could quite clearly hear the loud, authoritative voices of Linularinan soldiers directly without the room, this would hardly serve.

He had, however, for the first time in days—for the first time since Ehre, indeed—a wild desire to laugh. He felt very alert, and tremendously alive, and terribly frightened. He tried hard not to laugh. He bit his lips instead, and held out his hand.

Somewhere near at hand, a soldier called out and another answered: a formal sign and countersign, by the sound, as was the Linularinan practice in uncertain territory. Mienthe's eyes widened at the sound. She glanced over her shoulder, hesitated one more instant, and then darted across the room to Tan. She clasped the book—the book for which they had spent so much effort—in both her hands. For a moment Tan thought she might fall back into that trance of movement and magic that had so recently held her. But then she blinked, life and awareness returning to her eyes, and instead offered the book to Tan.

He did not touch it, but took her by the elbow and nodded aside, at the farthest doorway that led out of this room, and raised his eyebrows.

"Yes," Mienthe whispered, and ran that way.

The doorway proved to lead straightaway into a tiny, windowless corner room that was probably meant to be a maid's room, but fitted out not with its own narrow bed and tiny dresser but with a neat little writing desk and shelves of expensive books and little keepsakes. An illustrated herbal lay open on the desk, undisturbed, as it had no doubt lain since they had all fled so precipitously from this house.

The tiny room was surely as far from enemy soldiers as they might well find themselves. Mienthe closed the herbal and set it aside, then placed the blank Linulari-nan book down on the desk. She ran a fingertip over the curves and loops of its tooled leather cover and then looked rather blankly at Tan.

"You know what to do," Tan murmured to her.

Mienthe only shook her head. "I thought I would," she whispered back—she did not know that a whisper carried better than merely a low voice, but it should not matter, back in this corner as they were. She looked frightened and uncertain, and that was much worse. She whispered, "I thought I would know what to do, but all I see now is a book! All the rest is like, like a dream—misty, fading— We're here, we *have* this book, and now I don't know *anything*—"

"Shh," murmured Tan, touching her shoulder to quiet her. "All will be well. Everything will be well. Shh. Let me just see this odd creation now. The key to our hope and all our enemies' desire, and yet it is so very small."

Mienthe did not recognize the quote, of course. She only nodded, looking uncertain.

Tan did not try to explain. He only began to reach out—then caught himself and nodded to the young woman instead. "Open it for me, will you, please, for all kindness."

Mienthe managed a nervous little smile and a nod, and flipped the book open herself. She flipped past several of the heavy, ivory-colored sheets, each as empty as a cloudless sky. She said, "Maybe if you were to write in it—if you were to have nothing in your mind, but only touch a quill to its pages—do you think you might write out what you . . . what you have? What you hold in your mind?"

"What passes for my mind," Tan murmured absently. "Perhaps."

"But I don't have any quills—"

Without a word, Tan extracted a packet of quills from an inner pocket, held it up with a minor flourish, and set it down by the book.

Mienthe turned another blank page, and another. She shook her head. "There's nothing. It's so strange. It's almost as though there was never anything here at all."

Tan made a wordless comforting sound, not really

attending. He took a quill, a small but neatly made crow's feather, out of the packet and tested it on his thumb. The ink was black, a good, flowing ink without grittiness or stutters, contained within a well-made quill, exactly what one would expect from the Casmantian king's own mage. Or ex-mage. From Lord Beguchren Teshrichten, in either case, from whom Tan had acquired the packet of quills. He looked at the book, considering. But when he moved to touch it, to write in it, he could bring himself to do neither. He had a reasonless but intense dread of the book, especially of setting ink to its empty pages. He knew he could not possibly bring himself to write anything at all in it.

"Well?" Mienthe asked anxiously, forgetting to whisper.

Tan shook his head. He laughed, though quietly. "So far out and as far back, and what have we to show for all our weary steps? We are come not even to our beginning, but beyond that. We are looking over ground we shall have to recover to come back to the place where we began—"

"Write something!" said Mienthe sharply.

Tan shook his head again. "I can't. I daren't. I don't know how. This isn't a book, Mie, it's something else that's just in the *shape* of a book. If it's legistwork, it's nothing I recognize, not even now."

Mienthe's lips pressed together, and her jaw set in that determined expression with which she faced down mountains and kings. She said, "We'll take it back to Gereint Enseichen. All the way back to Beguchren Teshrichten, if we have to. *He'll* know what to do with it."

She did not suggest how they might get out of this

house and back across town; well, more than likely she did not remember anything of the twisting, difficult route they'd followed to get in. Or how they'd still be trapped outside this house now, save for that strange spiraling path she'd drawn across light and shadow to bring them the last little way, at the end...She flipped the book shut with a sharp, decisive movement.

Tan said suddenly, the pattern leaping out at him for the first time, "There's a spiral on the cover."

Mienthe blinked, and looked.

Tan traced the pattern for her in the air, the tip of his finger hovering above the leather. There *was* a spiral, when one looked for it—or not just one, indeed, but several: interlocking spirals set into the patterned leather among the circumscribed arcs of circles and ellipses. Some of the spirals were raised and turned right, but at least one was concave and turned left.

Mienthe traced the first spiral herself, with no need to be cautious about touching the book. She said, "Earth."

Tan looked at her, wanting to ask what she meant, fearing to interrupt whatever inspiration she might have discovered.

"Earth," Mienthe insisted, and traced the next spiral, a smaller one that interlocked with the first and then twisted away in its own direction. And the next, small and twining about the second. "Fire," she said. "And wind." She found another, this one pressed deep into the rich leather. When she touched it, her fine eyebrows drew together in something like pain. "Oh. The wild heights."

"Mie—"

"Yes," the young woman murmured. She stood up, took the crow-feather quill out of Tan's hand, walked back into the apartment's main sitting room, swung chairs aside every which way, kicked aside a rug, and bent to draw a spiral right on the naked boards of the floor.

Tan wouldn't have interrupted for the world. He hauled a couch out of her way; then, after a moment's consideration, stood it on end and leaned it into the little writing room. Then he stood in the doorway, watching with tense fascination as Mienthe completed the first big outer circle and began to bring the spiral inward.

There was a faintly audible alarmed shout. Tan jerked his head up, listening. The shout was repeated, nearer, he was almost certain. Mienthe did not seem to notice, but Tan was afraid the alarm might very soon press itself on her attention. He wished he knew what drawing spirals on the floor was going to do, or, which might be a more urgent question, how long it might take to do it. He had no weapons, and no particular skill with them even if he found a sword tucked away among the gowns in Mienthe's wardrobe. Chairs propped under the doorknobs of the outermost apartment door and then the sitting room door were all very well, but would hold professional soldiers for no more than moments—Mie might have found inspiration somewhere, but nothing useful occurred to Tan, and the shouting was now distinctly closer—

"Tan!" Mienthe called urgently from the sitting room, having either forgotten the need for quiet or justifiably concluded the precaution was now no use. "Tan! Oh—there you are, good. Get in the center. No, *with* the book!" She pressed it into his hands and pushed him toward the middle of the spiral that now nearly covered the floor: A dozen long, perfectly smooth turns ran away from the wall toward the center of the room. The black lines glistened as though with fresh ink, but not the best-made quill in the world could ever have held so much or drawn out such a broad, heavy stroke. And then in the next moment the black lines did not look like ink at all, but like shadows, like deep cracks that cut straight through into the heart of the world. He tried to follow the spiral inward with his eyes but found the center hard to see, as though it was very far away. The illusion that the overall spiral led downward as it turned inward was very powerful, even though when he looked across it rather than along its curving length, he could see perfectly well that the floor was level.

"Don't cut across the line!" she added.

"Don't cut the line?" Tan muttered. He cast a glance toward the door, which someone had just struck a rever-berating blow. "Mie—"

"What?" She did not seem to notice, not even when the door shook in its frame under another blow. She stared instead at the widely spaced curving lines of the spiral. Her expression was intent, not blank as it had been out in the town. But was the difference good or bad?

The door shook again, and the wood cracked.

"Tan!" said Mienthe, but not about the door, and how nice for her to be so caught up in her strange magic that she did not need to suffer fear. She pointed toward the center of the spiral.

With an effort, Tan turned his back on the door and, stepping firmly into the spiral, began to walk around the curving pathway it provided toward its center. He was careful not to touch the glistening black line with his foot, though he wondered, if he did, would the ink smear, or would he simply find his foot plunging through an open chasm toward the center of the earth?

Mienthe exclaimed, "Oh, *where* did I leave off the end?" but she sounded frustrated rather than frightened. Then she said, "Oh," sounding much happier. How nice one of them could be happy.

Despite her warning to Tan, she walked suddenly forward right along the line, placing one foot carefully in front of the next. The ink did not smear, nor did she fall. Despite the narrowness of the line and all her care, she walked quickly, so that she threatened to reach the center long before Tan. He did not know whether this mattered, but found himself hurrying to keep up, so that they walked shoulder to shoulder, Mienthe on the outside line and himself on the inside, keeping to the space between the lines.

The crashing at the door now seemed to linger oddly on the air; the sounds reverberated against the air as though from a great distance...Black sparks were falling away from Mienthe's feet. She seemed to be walking on a layer of translucent glass that lay across deep cracks... To Tan, she did not seem to have created those cracks, but rather to have *collected* them somehow, pulling them out of the very fabric of the world and arranging them in this orderly shape, but he could not have explained what he meant by this idea or why he thought so. He also thought the cracks were going down, down and in, even though when he remembered to glance up he could see that they were still in the room, that the world outside the spiral seemed unchanged...perfectly unchanged, as though frozen in glass, as a glassblower might lock a delicate flower or leaf into a glass weight, only it was as though the glass had turned inside out, so that everything outside it was locked into stillness and only within the spiral did motion and life remain possible.

But this was an illusion, for even as the strange idea occurred to Tan, the door flew soundlessly to pieces— well, not soundlessly; it was only that the crashing, splintering sounds did not seem important.

Linularinan soldiers surged into the room but then flung themselves aside rather than forward. Tan wondered what they saw; indeed, he wondered what *he* saw. Mienthe had come to the end of her line, and Tan to the open center of the spiral, but, though he stopped, she kept on, placing one foot neatly before the last. Though she had no quill or ink, the line drew itself out under her feet, or she drew it after her by the act of walking forward. Tan wondered whether he should follow after her, but he could not see how there was room for him to go forward—nor could he see how *Mienthe* found room to walk forward, only she made her own space as she made her own line. But Tan did not know how to do that.

Istierinan Hamoddian came through the door after the soldiers, who pressed back to give him room. Tan turned to gaze at Istierinan, across what seemed simultaneously an immense distance and the span of an ordinary, rather small room. The Linularinan spymaster looked old, much older than he had bare weeks ago. Old and ill. The bones of his face had become prominent, his eyes dark and hollowed, his hands skeletally thin. He was holding something—a quill, Tan saw, made of a white falcon's feather, its tip glistening with ink so dark a red it might almost have been blood. Then Tan blinked again and saw that it *was* blood.

Istierinan spoke—he was shouting: The tendons stood out on his throat. In a way, Tan could not hear him, or only dimly, as from a long way away. Yet if he thought about the sounds, he realized they were actually loud. "You don't know what you're doing!" he cried. "You don't know what you *can* do!" He started toward the entrance to the spiral, his white quill held out before him like a weapon.

At the same time, Mienthe faltered, but not because of Istierinan. "It's not enough," she said, her tone dismayed. "I can't finish it—the turns are too tight—it doesn't go deep enough—it's not right, I'm not doing it right, it's all wrong—"

"Ignorant child!" Istierinan was beside himself with fury and a terror so great it was almost exaltation. "Of course you're not! How could you? *Get out of it*, turn it around— *You!*" he shouted at Tan. "Give what you stole back to me now and I may *even yet* be able to set this right!" He strode forward, set himself at the entrance of the spiral, but then hesitated there, his breath coming hard, his hands shaking, gathering himself for that first step.

"You'll *never* set it right," Mienthe cried. "You can't, you won't, you don't even want to! Get out, get away!"

"Mie—" said Tan. "If you can't do this, if you can't do whatever needs to be done, then maybe—"

Mienthe turned to him. She was weeping with frustration and fear, and her voice was shaking, but even so she spoke with passionate conviction. "He can't! He set it up all wrong before; it was him, if it wasn't him then it was someone *like* him. I'm sure it was! And he didn't do it right! It's never been right, not from the first time it was ever set down!"

"Mie, *what* was set up wrong?"

"Everything!" Mienthe cried. "The law of the world! He's a mage as well as a legist! He hates fire, and if *he* writes the law down in that book, he'll write it all wrong!"

Istierinan stepped into the spiral, between the black lines.

Tan turned so as to meet him when he came around the last turn, but for all Istierinan's age and evident illness, he moved toward Tan like a superior swordsman might stalk toward a rank novice who's had the temerity to issue a challenge. Tan had thought he understood legist-magic. Now he knew he didn't understand anything, and the only thing he knew with perfect certainty was that he was afraid of the older man.

"I see the way it should go—if I could only *finish* it," cried Mienthe, but though she turned and tried to draw her spiral forward and inward and down, it was as though she leaned against something solid, tried to press herself forward through air that had become as sheer and hard and unyielding as glass, and not nearly so easily broken.

Without warning, fire blazed out of the air and into the outer reaches of the spiral, slapped against Mienthe's empty black line as against a physical barrier, and rose, towering to the ceiling.

Tan, staggering, dropped to his knees and tucked himself forward over the book he still held, as though it contained all his hope of life and sanity. But the fire did not rush into the center of the spiral at all; rather, it whipped outward around the curving lines of the spiral and roared out into the room. It sheeted past and over Istierinan, who staggered but did not burn.

Outside the spiral, the fire was much worse. Flames roared up the walls; the discarded chairs caught; flames licked across the boards of the floor. The soldiers fled.

Mienthe was screaming, Tan realized at last. He came up to one knee, twisting about to look for her, but she was untouched. She was crouched down upon the black line of the spiral, her hands pressed against her lips, shaking and white with terror, but never stepping away from the line she had drawn.

Someone else groaned, a deep, raw sound of agony, and the flames suddenly flattened low and flickered out. The walls and floor were charred, everything was charred except within the spiral, but there was no longer living fire anywhere.

A man stood near the entrance to the spiral. His posture was rigid, ungiving. His austere face was set in an expression of bitter resignation and anger. When he turned his head, taking in the room and Mienthe's spiral, his black eyes burned with power. Istierinan, straightening, stared at him with horror and loathing.

A little distance from him stood a big man and, tiny next to him, tucked half out of sight behind him, a pale, fragile girl. The man was gripping her delicate hand in his big one, gripping hard, by the clenched muscles of his forearm. But it was not the girl who had cried out with pain, but the man, and now he let her go, cupping one terribly burned hand in the other.

The girl looked dismayed. She came back toward the man, her steps quick and light.

"No," snapped the dark man. "Fool! Do you not understand yet what may wake when you use fire to heal a man?"

"He's right. He's right. You mustn't," said the big man, backing away from the girl, his face twisting with pain and with some strong, dangerous emotion.

"It's my fault, then!" cried the girl, and whirled away from them all, gathering herself as though she might spring away into the air.

"No," said the dark man again.

The girl whirled to face him. "Let me go!" she cried. "Kairaithin, let me go! If this is my fault, let me set it right! He cannot constrain *me*!" Her voice was high and light, furious and desperate and somehow not at all a human voice. And she *glowed*, Tan realized, as though she burned with her own internal fire. Flames flickered within the tangled gold-white hair that fell down her back; her eyes were swimming with golden fire.

"Get out!" roared Istierinan, his voice thick with fury. "Get out!"

"Impossible," said the dark man, Kairaithin, but to the girl. He took no more notice of the Linularinan spymaster than an eagle might have paid a furious songbird. Less. He said, still to the girl, "And untrue. Nothing that has happened is your doing. Though you may still pay the cost of it. As may we all." His taut posture had not eased; he tilted his head as though listening to the great wind that had brought them; as though listening to the roar of fire, or of some powerful music none of the rest of them could hear. His voice was strong, harsh, dangerous.

Like the girl, he was a creature of fire, Tan realized, though the fire that burned in him was darker and more powerful and far more tightly controlled. His shadow rose behind him, huge and wild and burning. It was not the shadow of a man, and at last Tan realized what he was, what he must be, for all he wore the shape of a man. *This* was the griffin who had come to Mienthe's cousin? *This* had brought the warning that had taken Bertaud and the king away to the north and left the Delta vulnerable to Linularinan machinations? Tan was amazed by the composure Mienthe had shown after meeting this creature.

The griffin mage turned suddenly, focusing all that dark, burning power toward Mienthe. She didn't quite manage composure this time, but flinched noticeably from the scorching heat of his stare. "It was *your* wind," he said harshly. "When I looked for a new wind to ride, it was *your* wind that swept across mine. And what direction do you mean for this storm you are calling?"

Mienthe flinched from the powerful Kairaithin, but in fact nearly all of her attention was on the pale-burning girl. She took a step toward her along her black spiral, holding out her hand. "It was *you* I needed all along!" she said. "Fire to balance earth! No wonder, no wonder— Was there a wind? Well, no wonder it brought you here!"

"No!" cried Istierinan. "Fool!" He did not leave the protection of the spiral, however, but turned and began to walk once more along the narrow passage between its black lines, toward Tan.

The pale girl said furiously to Kairaithin, paying no attention to either Istierinan or Mienthe, "It wasn't *my* wind! I know what wind *I* would call up!"

"Kes," said the human man. He spoke with difficulty, his voice ragged with pain, but his voice checked her where the others had only fed her fury. He said again, "Kes. You were a creature of earth, once. Try to remember. I know you remember a little, or you wouldn't have held your fire back for me—you wouldn't have thought of healing me—and you did think of it. You did. You had a sister whom you loved, do you remember? I know she hasn't forgotten you. Would you really call up a wind for Tastairiane Apailika, a fire to burn across your sister and her horses? Across everything you ever loved?"

Kes stood still, her golden eyes on the man's strained face. Her eyes held nothing human; her expression was unreadable. But she stood still, listening.

"Kereskiita," said the dark man, "the storm Tastairiane Apailika wishes to ride will carry the People of Fire and Air to destruction." He lifted a hand, pointed straight at Mienthe's black spiral. "Here is a different storm, when I had all but given up hope that any countervailing wind might arise. It is perilous and terrible, but surely set in a direction none of us had anticipated. It is too late to turn Tastairiane Apailika's wind. Call this wind, then, and let it burn!"

"Kes," said the man. He cradled his burned hand against his body and stared at the girl, his eyes purely human. He said again, "Kes."

"Jos," said the girl very softly. "I do remember." And, turning toward the spiral, she took a single step that suddenly whirled her around it and left her standing beside Mienthe.

Far too close, in Tan's opinion, but though he flinched violently, Mienthe reached out and laid her hand against the hand of the girl of fire, palm to palm. Nor did she jerk back as away from fire, but only looked into her face for a moment, her expression very serious.

"No!" shouted Istierinan again, his voice cracking in furious despair.

Mienthe lifted her hand from the other girl's, turned,

and began to draw out her spiral: around and in, around and in. Kes turned in the opposite direction and began to draw a spiral of her own, this one a narrow line of white fire that turned outward, rising. Though they both sketched their parallel spirals on the same level floor, somehow the black spiral seemed to turn down and down, while the burning white spiral rose as it turned.

Tan saw at once what Mienthe had meant by fire balancing earth, for now Mienthe moved much more easily, with no sign that she had ever or would ever come against a limit to how tight she might make her spiral, how deep she might send it. And Kes moved as easily, every step as light as though she were actually rising as she went, walking away into the air.

Istierinan cried out, an articulate sound. He dropped to one knee and drove the tip of his white quill straight across the line of white fire. The quill caught fire and blazed up with a flame as white as its feather, and the red ink ran out of it, hissing as it came against Kes's fiery spiral, quenching the flame and leaving only the black chasm of the spiral Mienthe had drawn.

Mienthe cried out, sounding furious as well as terrified. Then Kes cried out as well, her voice as piercing and inhuman as the shriek of a falcon. Their two voices blurred together until it was impossible to tell one from the other.

Tan began to stride forward, out of the center of the spiral, toward Istierinan.

"No!" said Kairaithin urgently. "No, man!"

"Yes, come to me!" called Istierinan grimly.

Tan stopped, looking helplessly from the griffin mage to the Linularinan legist, and Istierinan stood up and ran

the white feather of his quill through his fingers. The fire
that had caught in its feather went out, and he laughed.

Kairaithin, with no expression at all, took one step
forward and exploded violently into fiery wind and driving red sand. The power of that wind slashed across
the double spiral with incredible precision, slicing past
Mienthe and Kes, scouring away the bloody ink and
whipping up the white fire, hardly disturbing Tan's hair
as it whipped past him but driving against Istierinan with
terrible force, tearing at his face and eyes, flinging him
to his knees, ripping the white quill from his hands. But,
though the quill blazed up once more, it did not crumble
to ash but flew across the spiral like a burning arrow. It
fell point-down at Tan's feet, its tip deep in the wood of
the floor, its feather burning on and on with white fire,
like a slim taper that would not gutter out.

The power in that same great wind, unleashed, allowed
Kes, even as she screamed in grief, to raise her fragile
white hands and send her spiral racing infinitely wide and
high, until it cracked the edges of the world and broke
against the dome of the sky. Mienthe cried out, and her
spiral leaped forward in equal measure as though dragged
along by the fiery spiral, only hers broke open the day
and the dark and twisted in and down until it shattered
the center of the earth.

"Write down the law!" Mienthe cried.

As in a dream, Tan opened the book. He bent and took
up the burning white quill.

"Write down fire and joy!" said Kes. She seemed to
have forgotten grief. She lifted hands filled with blazing
light and shook fire out of her hair, laughing.

"Write down earth *and* fire," said Jos, leaning against

a wall that was, amazingly, still standing. "Write down sorrow as well as joy."

"You must subordinate fire to earth!" croaked Istieri-nan through burned lips and broken teeth, trying blindly to get to his feet.

Mienthe only watched Tan, her expression grave and trusting.

There was no ink left in the quill, so Tan tore its sharp point across his own wrist. He wrote in his own blood, across a page that would take no other ink, a single word. The word he wrote was

AMITY

He wrote it plainly, with neither flourish nor ornament. The word sank into the page and all through the book. From the center of the earth to the dome of the sky, from one edge of the world to the other, the writing remade the law of the world.

CHAPTER 16

It was nothing a mage would have thought of. Everyone agreed about that one thing, later. Everyone, at least, who was a mage, or had ever been a mage. Certainly Beguchren Teshrichten said so, so Mienthe was sure it was true.

"It required someone with a remarkable, anomalous gift," he said wryly to Mienthe. "Casmantium for making, Feierabiand for calling, and Linularinum for law, but I've never heard of anyone waking into a gift such as yours."

"Istierinan Hamoddian was anomalous, too," Mienthe pointed out.

"But not at all in the same way. Have some of these berries. What a splendid climate you have here in the Delta, to be sure. Fresh berries so early! No, we quite well understand Istierinan, anomalous as he undeniably was. One doesn't think of a mage being able to sustain any natural gift; indeed, we are taught that bringing out

the mage power smothers the inborn gift. Yet clearly there
are and have been exceptions." Beguchren tilted his head
consideringly. "Perhaps the legist gift is more amenable
to magework than making or calling. One does rather
hope that such persons are rare, generally not quite so
powerful, and now inclined toward a certain humility."

They might very well be so inclined, Mienthe thought,
considering what had happened to Istierinan. She had
thought they ought to leave him for King Iaor to judge,
or even send him back to his own king, but Kes had not
been patient or forgiving with the man who was, or so
she had seemed to feel, in some part responsible for her
old teacher's death. When she had destroyed him, she
had not left even ash. Nor, when it came to the moment,
had Mienthe tried very hard to stop her. She had not
confessed to anyone her deep relief at the death of Tan's
enemy. But she was relieved. All she said aloud was, "I
hope they are *very* rare."

They were in the Arobern's camp, set neatly to the east
of Tiefenauer, separate and self-contained. The Arobern
had thought it politic to keep all his people outside the
town, lest anyone should have any impression he'd ever
meant to conquer or hold it himself. Iaor Safiad himself
had firmly and pointedly occupied the great house as
soon as he'd arrived, two days after Tan had written his
new law to govern fire and earth. Bertaud had not yet
returned. Mienthe was almost certain her cousin was
well—the king assured Mienthe he was well—but she
longed to see him and be certain of it herself.

Iaor Safiad had not yet granted the Arobern an audience. He had sent only curt word refusing the Casmantian king leave to withdraw east toward the pass. He

had, however, sent almost every available Feierabianden healer to the Casmantian camp, thus demonstrating that while he might be furious with the Casmantian king, he was at least willing to admit that the Casmantian soldiers had suffered on Feierabiand's behalf. Everyone assumed that Iaor was much angrier with the King of Linularinum than with the Arobern—everyone assumed he would, in due course, forgive the Arobern's presumption. The Casmantian soldiers, nodding wisely, muttered about royal pride; three or four young men had already wistfully asked Mienthe about the Safiad's temper. She had not known how to answer their questions.

Beguchren Teshrichten had not asked Mienthe about either king. He said instead, "One does wonder whether your gift would ever have stirred if Tan hadn't happened to break the law Linularinan legists long ago imposed on the world." Then he paused and asked, very gently, "How does Tan do, today? May I hope that there has been some improvement?"

Mienthe began to answer, but tears suddenly closed her throat and she found she could not speak. Blinking hard, she opened her hands in a gesture of wretched uncertainty.

"I believe he will come to himself in good time, child. Recovery from such events does take time. He overused his gift, I suspect." The mage paused and then said plainly but not unkindly, "He might have lost it. Used it up. Such things can happen, in great extremity."

As Lord Beguchren knew better than anyone. Mienthe nodded. She swallowed, rubbed her hand across her mouth, and managed to ask, "Is there anything you might suggest?"

Beguchren lifted his shoulders in a minimal shrug. "I'm certain you are already doing everything I might suggest. Warmth, rest...the company of a friend..."

"King Iaor made me leave." Mienthe blushed slightly, remembering the king's blunt impatience. *You're too thin, Mienthe. How will it help him if you wear yourself to bone and nerve? Go for a walk, go for a ride, see the sky, have something to eat, have a nap, don't come back here until dusk. Trust Iriene to watch over him. That's an actual royal command, Mie. Now go away.* Though she suspected that Iaor had not actually meant for her to ride down to the Casmantian camp and visit Lord Beguchren.

"Undoubtedly wise. It serves nothing for you to fall ill yourself. Once you are both entirely recovered, I wonder whether you might care to visit Casmantium." Beguchren picked up another cluster of berries between his finger and thumb and gazed at it. "How very like a string of garnets! You might like to wait until your berrying season is past, perhaps. But I would be pleased if you—and Tan, of course—would visit me in Breidechboden. I would like very much to investigate the precise nature of your gift. I believe it is certainly a gift rather than any form of magecraft. But certainly an exceedingly odd gift. I wonder what other odd gifts we may find emerging now that the world is no longer subject to the constraints placed on natural law by Linularinan mages."

Mienthe thought she would be perfectly ecstatic if her gift, whatever it encompassed, never woke again. Drawing that last double spiral had left her with a persistent and not altogether comfortable sense of increased depth in the world. Well, that was an odd and entirely inaccurate way to describe it. It was more as though everything in the world was now attended by a faint reverberating echo—well, not precisely an *echo*. Mienthe frowned and ate a berry. The sharp sweet-tart taste seemed just a little bolder or darker or more distinct than it should have. She put the berries down and sighed.

Beguchren said gently, "Is it so very unpleasant?"

"Oh…it's not *unpleasant*, exactly." In fact, Beguchren's curiosity almost made her curious herself. "What other anomalous gifts?" she asked. "You really think other people might—might—" She waved a vague hand.

"Have gifts similar to yours? Or perhaps unique to themselves? Certainly. Why not? You demonstrate the possibility, and I do not believe the new law will constrain such gifts." Beguchren regarded her with a calm, detached interest that, oddly, made Mienthe feel more comfortable with her strange gift rather than less. He murmured, "I would like to see what you might do in the high mountains. I suspect your gift may be as closely related to wild magic as to the ordinary magic of the earth—an odd notion, and yet I do suspect so. I am curious to see what you might do with the winds. And perhaps with the sea. One might well understand both the winds and the sea to contain"—he made a circular motion in the air—"circles and spirals. Yet we have ordinarily envisioned the sea as allied to earth and the winds as allied to fire."

"Have we?" Mienthe, distracted by an odd thought, had barely heard him. She said instead, "I wonder whether, if a mage's power smothers the inborn gift and if you're no longer a mage—" She stopped. Looked up, with some trepidation. She had not meant to wake old sorrows.

But Beguchren was smiling slightly. "It doesn't matter," he said. "But, yes. I wonder that as well."

"If you—" Mienthe began hesitantly.

A Casmantian soldier, ducking his head in apology as well as to clear the low tent roof, came in, and she broke off, trying to decide whether she was glad or sorry for the interruption.

"Lady," the young man said to Mienthe, and to Beguchren, "my lord, the Arobern asks you to attend him. Immediately, he says, if you will forgive me."

Mienthe jumped to her feet. "I should go—"

"Not at all," murmured Beguchren, rising more slowly. "We may well value your advice, Lady Mienthe. Please accompany me."

"The Safiad has sent for me," the Arobern told them both. He paced nervously from one end of his much larger tent to the other, then spun to glare at Mienthe. "What will he say? What will he do? I am certain Erich is safe—" *Nearly* certain, suggested the stiffness of the Casmantian king's shoulders. "But what will he demand? An apology? An indemnity?" His deep voice dropped further, into a rumbling growl. "A longer term for my son to be held as a hostage at his court?"

Mienthe had to confess that she could not guess. "He *ought* to thank you," she added, but cautiously, because no one but she seemed to think this at all likely.

The Arobern grunted, jerked his head *No*. "I offended his pride. Twice. No. Three times. Once in coming through the pass without leave—twice in leaving Beguchren to delay him on his road—a third time, worst of all, because he knows he must be *grateful* to me." The

Casmantian king jerked his head again. "No. He will be *furious.*" He prevented Mienthe from exclaiming how unfair this was by adding, in a low growl, "I would be."

"He will be more furious still if you do not come as he bids you," murmured Beguchren. The elegant Casmantian lord looked faintly amused, so far as Mienthe could read his expression at all.

"Yes. True." The Arobern ran a big hand through his short-cropped hair, looking harassed. "Come," he said to Mienthe abruptly. "*You,* come. An apology is well enough, if that will satisfy the Safiad's temper, but if your king demands a second term for my son in his court, *you* tell him he should be grateful to me!"

Mienthe could hardly refuse.

Iaor Safiad was in the solar, in a big, heavy chair with ornate carving on its legs and back. Normally that chair occupied Bertaud's personal apartment, but Mienthe was not surprised to see that the king had claimed it, for it *was* very like a throne. Especially the way Iaor sat in it: not stiff, but upright, with his hands resting on the polished brass finials that finished its arms. There were other chairs near his, but none were much like a throne, and no one was sitting in any of them. There were guardsmen at the door, but they only stared straight ahead, with the most formally rigid posture possible, and did not even seem to notice the Arobern. Or Mienthe, standing nervously in his shadow. She did not know why *she* should be nervous, except that the Arobern's nervousness had communicated itself to her during the ride up to the great house.

Only one other person was with the king: Erich. Prince Erichstaben Taben Arobern, who was standing, his back

straight, his chin raised, and his face blank, at the king's
left hand. The Arobern stopped when he saw Erich. His
gaze went first to his son's face, shifted to take in the
young man's height and breadth of shoulder with silent
amazement, and rose again to his face with an unspoken
but unmistakable hunger.

Erich lifted his chin half an inch higher and met his
father's eyes for a brief, taut moment, then turned his
face aside as though the effort of sustaining that intense
contact had abruptly grown too great. He glanced instead
at Mienthe and tried to smile, but it was not a very con-
vincing effort and he gave it up at once.

The echo behind the tension in the room was so
powerful that Mienthe found it difficult to endure. She
stopped just inside the door and simply tried to breathe
evenly, hoping she would not be called upon to explain
anything to anybody.

Mienthe was not surprised the king had Erich with
him. What surprised her was how very much the prince
resembled his father. Erich lacked some of his father's
bulk, but none of his height. And their expressions were
alike, also. They even stood with the same upright pride.
She had not realized how very alike they were until she
saw them like this: together in good light.

At last the Arobern moved his gaze, as with an effort,
to Iaor Safiad. He walked forward with a heavy stride
and stopped a few steps away from King Iaor's chair,
his hands hooked in his belt. Mienthe could not read his
expression now. There was nothing simple or friendly in
the way the two kings looked at each other. She almost
fancied she could hear the ringing clash of swords when
their eyes met.

The Arobern said, his grim voice touched with irony, "Well, Iaor Daveien Behanad Safiad. I find the second time much like the first. Perhaps someday I will come before you as something other than a supplicant."

Iaor Safiad answered, with a flash of temper, "Perhaps someday you will come into Feierabiand *without* an army at your back."

So everybody else had been right, Mienthe saw, and she had been wrong. Her heart sank.

But the Arobern only lowered his eyes, like a man laying down a sword. He said, "Yes. I did not wish to offend you. But I expected you would be offended. You have been patient. And generous beyond measure."

"You left me little choice but generosity."

"You had every choice. You took that one. I am grateful." The Arobern looked deliberately at his son, then turned his gaze back to King Iaor. He sighed heavily, came one step closer to the throne, and began to kneel.

"No," said Iaor, stopping him. He turned one hand, indicating one of the other chairs. "Sit, if you wish."

There was a little pause.

The Arobern, moving slowly, seated himself in the chair. He set his broad hands on his knees and looked at Iaor Safiad without speaking.

"Your son," said King Iaor, with deliberate emphasis, "has grown into a fine man. He should make any father proud. No doubt Lord Beguchren told you."

"Yes," said the Arobern.

There was another pause. Iaor broke it. "You took every chance," he said, with the same slow, deliberate emphasis. "I am grateful."

The Arobern bent his head just enough to show he had

heard, then met the other king's eyes again with somber intensity.

"Shall we agree we are mutually indebted? And that we are not likely to find ourselves at odds during the lifetimes of our children? Feierabiand is glad to count Casmantium as an ally."

"Casmantium, the same."

Iaor nodded. He said grimly, "Then, as we are allies, I will tell you that I intend to send a courier to Linularinum. To Kohorrian's court. I will bid Mariddeier Kohorrian attend me here in Tiefenauer. Do you think he will obey my summons?"

"Ah." The Arobern leaned back in his chair. After a moment, he smiled. It was not a kind expression. "I will send a man also, is this what you intend? Perhaps a soldier, to stand behind your girl courier? And Lord Bertaud will send a man of his, am I to think so? Yes. Then, yes, Kohorrian will come. You wish me to leave a man of mine here also, to stand at your back when you scold Mariddeier Kohorrian?"

Iaor did not precisely smile in return, but there was a glint of hard humor in his eyes. "I thought you might be persuaded to leave me Lord Beguchren Teshrichten for the purpose."

"Ah." The Arobern tapped his heavy fingers on the arm of his chair.

"I should be pleased to see Lord Beguchren turn his tongue against Mariddeier Kohorrian rather than against me. And, in truth, I should value his counsel. I consider that he owes me at least so much. What surety would you require?"

The Arobern's eyebrows rose. "From you? I would be

ashamed to ask for any surety from you, Iaor Safiad. I will bid Lord Beguchren act as my agent in this matter. I think he may even be pleased by the task."

King Iaor briefly inclined his head.

The Arobern nodded in return, paused, and then asked, "And I? What will you have of me, Iaor Safiad?"

"I will expect you to withdraw from my country quietly and in good order. As, of course, you entered it."

The Arobern, regarding Iaor warily, made a gesture of acquiescence. "As soon as you give me leave to go."

"I give you leave." Iaor gripped the arms of his chair and rose. Then he paused, looking down at the other king, and added, "As a hostage one will not touch has no practical use, I will release your son. When you return to Casmantium, Prince Erichstaben may go with you." He added to Erich, in a much different tone, "I'll miss you, boy, especially when my daughters pester me to teach them dangerous tricks with their ponies."

The young man flushed, grinned, and answered, "Well, Your Majesty, and I'll miss the little girls! May I thank you, and beg you to make my apologies to them for leaving without bidding them farewell?"

"Perhaps I'll send them to Casmantium for a visit," Iaor said to him. "In two years. If your father approves." He gave the Arobern a hard stare.

The Arobern got to his feet and bowed, very slightly. "Of course, Casmantium would be honored to welcome the little Safiad princesses," he said formally.

Erich smiled, a swift, affectionate smile. He glanced at Mienthe and the smile became wry. But then he looked back at his father and the smile slipped altogether.

King Iaor crooked a finger at Mienthe and walked out.

Mienthe followed, all her nerves on edge. She hadn't said a single word, even to say good-bye to Erich. She wondered how soon the Casmantian force would leave—soon, probably, at dawn, perhaps— She wondered whether King Iaor would mind if she went out to the camp again, to bid Erich and his father farewell? Because the king was indeed very angry, she knew, for all he showed it so little. She might not have realized it, except that to her new perception, the echo of his anger filled the space around him like a dark mist.

The door closed behind them, and the king stood still for a moment in the hallway, breathing deeply. Then he turned to Mienthe—she tried not to flinch—and took her by the shoulders. "Mie," he said, smiling with forced good humor that did not touch his eyes. He let her go, but indicated with a nod that she should walk with him. "What I am considering—tell me, Mienthe, would you perhaps consent to escort my daughters to Casmantium in a few years' time? I believe I might not object to a possible connection between my house and the Arobern's, and my daughters are not so much younger than Erich. I do not like to ask Bertaud to go, but you seem on good terms—excellent terms—with the Arobern and his people."

"I'm sorry," Mienthe said, answering the most important part of this. "I mean, of course I will gladly do anything you ask me to do, but—Your Majesty, everything happened so fast, and I didn't know what else to do, but go through the pass. I'm sorry—"

The king shook his head, his taut anger easing at last. "No. No indeed, Mie. It was well done. You have done nothing which requires forgiveness. Nor has Brechen

Glansent Arobern. You need not tell me so. I am perfectly aware of it."

Mienthe nodded, relieved. She asked tentatively, "What will you say to Mariddeier Kohorrian?"

"Ah." This time, when the king smiled, the humor did reach his eyes. "I have no idea. I will think of something. Beguchren Teshrichten may advise me." He glanced up and smiled suddenly, a much kinder expression. "And perhaps your cousin may have some ideas of his own."

"Regarding Mariddeier Kohorrian? I could indeed make several suggestions," said Bertaud.

Mienthe whirled around. Her cousin was walking quickly toward them down the hall. His voice, light and ironic, did nothing to hide the shadows of grief and loss in his eyes, but he was alive, and not obviously injured, and he was *here*.

Forgetting the king, forgetting every reason for grief and fear, Mienthe ran forward to embrace him.

Bertaud caught her up as though she were still a child, in a hug that threatened her ribs, then set her down and held her at arm's length, looking searchingly into her face. "Cousin! You are well?"

"Yes, I am, but you? Are *you* well? Are you—" Mienthe hesitated. "You heard...Kes told you about your friend? I'm so sorry, Bertaud." She was dimly aware that the king had quietly withdrawn to leave them together, and even more vaguely glad of it, but she had no real attention to spare for anyone but her cousin. He looked, she thought, desperately weary and grieved.

Bertaud bent his head. "She told me, of course. He unmade himself to give you the power you needed to remake the law of the world. Or so I gather. I gather you discovered a gift in yourself which is not quite like anything else in the world." He touched her cheek gently, smiling. "My little cousin!"

Mienthe was embarrassed. "I...it wasn't exactly me. I just did things that came to me to do. Tan was much braver. Jos was *very* brave. And..." She stopped.

"I'm very certain Kairaithin was glad to know that the wind his death called up was so strong as to overwhelm any other gathering storm. He always—he always was determined to get his own way in everything. And he nearly always succeeded. Most importantly—most importantly at the end."

Mienthe nodded. She asked tentatively, "Do the griffins...Was there a ceremony?"

"Not as we understand such things." Bertaud paused, then touched her arm, inviting her to walk with him. "Kes told me that the red dust had blown all through my house and across my gardens and lands, and she kindled a fire for me. A fire for memory, that will never go out...If you don't mind, Mie, I thought I might set it to burn next to Tef's stone."

A lump came into her throat. She had to try twice before she could say, "I think that would be the perfect place for it."

They walked out to the gardens side by side. Standing among the stones of generations, Bertaud solemnly tipped a single glowing ember out of a small earthenware pot beside Tef's low, polished grave marker. The ember flickered twice, and for just an instant Mienthe feared it might go out, but then flames crept up from it, pale in the afternoon light, and in moments a hand-sized fire was burning on the gravel by the stone.

"He rode a wind of his own choosing," Bertaud said quietly, and stood gazing down at the fire for one more moment, and then turned away at last.

They walked back toward the house in silence. It looked just the same as it had a month ago, to a casual glance. But if one looked more closely, one would see the scars of battle on the doors and the shutters, and cut into the earth of the gardens...The real scars were invisible. For all of them. Mienthe broke the quiet at last to ask, "How did you leave Kes?"

Bertaud glanced down at her, smiling a little. "Well, I think. Or well enough. Grieving, of course. They do grieve for their losses. Busy. She is helping Gereint and Tehre rebuild the Wall. Now the law of the world is solidly in place, it seems quite unimaginable that the Wall ever broke, until you see the shards scattered all across the desert and the mountains."

"They're rebuilding it?" Mienthe was surprised.

"Fire and earth are still foreign to one another, if not inimical. Besides, Tehre said she couldn't bear to leave the Wall shattered and broken. But this time they are building it with a gate. When I left, Tehre was explaining all about the different ways there are of building gates and why arches are superior to architraves, or something of the sort. I confess I wasn't paying close attention."

Mienthe smiled.

"Kes is as beautiful as ever, and no more human. But...less unfamiliar, somehow. It's strange watching her with Gereint. They remember the antipathy, and yet they don't remember how it *felt*. I think they may even become friends, in time. She is the most powerful fire mage in the world now, I imagine."

Mienthe would have been astonished to find other-wise. She nodded.

"So she has become Lady of the Changing Winds. That would have pleased Kairaithin, I think. His humor was not like that of a man, but he would have appreciated the irony. And . . . I'll never like Tastairiane Apailika. Nor will he ever have much goodwill toward any creature of earth, I'm sure. But he is her *iskarianere*, you know. He is willing to please her, and so he is now willing to be . . . if not friendly, at least forbearing. I think Kairaithin would appreciate the irony in that, as well."

Mienthe nodded again. She paused as they reached the door, her hand on the splintered wood, and asked tentatively, "How is Jos?"

Her cousin glanced down at her. "I offered him a place here. I told him that the Delta is a good place for exiles, even those without full use of both their hands . . . I think he will come. He owes me something, and of course we all owe him everything, and why should he not live near those of us who know it? He no longer needs to live close to fire, not when Kes can so easily step from one country to the other. I think . . . I am certain that she will not forget him again."

"I'll be glad to see her again from time to time," Mienthe said seriously.

Bertaud nodded. He pushed open the door of the house, but turned to look once more back over the gardens. He still looked weary and grieved, and yet Mienthe thought there was a difference to the sorrow she saw in him now. It seemed deep as the earth, yet she thought this grief was not the same as the grief that had haunted him through the years. This one, she thought, might in time be assuaged.

He turned again, gesturing for Mienthe to precede him. "And your Tan? How does he do now?"

Mienthe shook her head. "The same. Kes told you? Nothing has changed. I have been sitting by him...Iaor made me leave him for the day, but I'm sure it's all right if I take *you* up. Will you come?"

Tan lay, very still and pale among the bed linens, in the same tower room Bertaud had given him when they had feared he was still pursued by his enemies. Before they had known who those enemies were, or why they pursued him...it seemed so long ago. How astonishing, Mienthe thought, that it had been so short a time.

The room contained little clutter. Only the bed, and a small fire in its brazier, and a single chair framed by two small tables. The first of these held a jug of water and an earthenware cup, and the other a single glass vase from which tumbled the fragrant ivory flowers of honeysuckle in full bloom.

Iriene occupied the chair. The healer-mage was looking at Tan, though the abstraction of her gaze suggested she might not be seeing him. A heavy cloth-bound book was propped open on her knee. Geroen was leaning on the back of her chair with a patient air that suggested he might have been there for rather a long time.

Iriene did not look up when the door opened, but Geroen straightened as he glanced around—then saw Bertaud and stiffened. "My lord—"

Bertaud held up a hand to check him. "Captain Geroen. How is he?"

"There has still been no change?" Mienthe asked anxiously. She slipped across the room and hovered over the still figure on the bed. He was not breathing—oh, of course he was, only slowly and shallowly. He was so pale—"Iriene, is he worse? He's worse, isn't he?"

"About the same, I should say," the healer-mage answered judiciously. She got to her feet, nodded absently to Bertaud, and said to Mienthe, "He's steady enough, you know. Don't you fret over the next few hours. I don't think there's much likely to change any time soon. Not that we exactly want this to go on, but it can, you know, for quite a long time. I'll just go down to the kitchens and have them warm up some broth, shall I?"

She was not really asking permission. Mienthe nodded anyway and perched on the edge of the chair, gazing down at Tan's still face.

Her cousin came to look over her shoulder, frowning. "Lord Beguchren looked very much like this, after he..." He did not complete the sentence.

"He said you could use yourself up," Mienthe said in a low voice.

"Gereint broke Beguchren out of his long sleep."

Mienthe nodded. "He told me. But he said it wasn't just that Gereint was a mage, but that he was also his friend." Tan had been away in Linularinum so long, and he was so private a man. Iriene might have healed his knee, but she didn't know him at all...no one knew him at all. "Beguchren said this might not be the same. He said we should just wait," Mienthe finished softly.

Tan was so thin and pale, and he looked so cold...She took one of his hands in both of hers. His fingers were cold as ice. She said over her shoulder, "Geroen, would you please build up the fire?"

The captain silently added a pine log to the fire, so

that its resinous scent blended with the fragrance of the honeysuckle. Then he said again, "My lord..."

Bertaud turned to him, raising his eyebrows.

"My lord," Geroen repeated more firmly. "I've prepared a full report for you. All the damage that was done—not much out in the town, not that that's to my credit, which I know very well. More to the house." He hesitated and then said, "I should never have let those Linularinan bastards get a foothold on this side of the river, as I know very well. All the harm we suffered— My lord, I acknowledge it's my fault and my failing—"

Mienthe looked up in astonishment, though she didn't let go of Tan's hand. "That's not true—"

"Certainly it seems unnecessarily simplistic," Bertaud said mildly. "Mie, you're well enough here? Will you send me word immediately in the case of any change, or tonight in any case? Captain Geroen, you must tell me all that happened in my absence." He took the captain's arm, turning him gently toward the door. "I shall assuredly be glad of your report. But let's not be too hasty in declaring where the fault lies, shall we?" He led the other man out, and the door swung gently shut behind them.

Mienthe immediately forgot them. She leaned forward, studying Tan's drawn face. He *was* still breathing. About the same, Iriene had said. Mienthe thought he was worse: more still, more fine-drawn, colder.

If this were an epic romance, she would sit by his bed until at last he wasted away—that was the phrase an epic would use: wasted away. *Wasted*, indeed. What a terrible waste Tan's death would be. Bertaud had said Jos had saved them all, and of course he had; and so had Kes, and Kairaithin; and the Arobern by his courage, and Iaor by his generosity; and so had she, and what a very strange thought that was. But most of all *Tan* had saved them all, by knowing at the last what law to use to bind the world *properly*.

In a romantic epic, she would have fallen in love with Tan, and now she would watch him slowly waste away, and then she would go fling herself to her death from the highest tower of the house. Not that even the highest tower of this house was very tall, and it was surrounded by gardens and not paving stones. Probably, even if she were such a fool, she would only break her leg or something. So the romances had every detail wrong.

Or nearly every detail.

A mage who was also a friend could break this stillness. Mienthe came closer to being a friend than anybody else, but she wasn't a mage. *I just did things that came to me to do*, she had said to Bertaud, and that was true. Nothing came to her now, though she would have welcomed an urge to draw a spiral, any sort of prompting toward anything that might help. But there was nothing, though she tried to clear her mind and heart invitingly. She had no idea how to coax Tan out of his deep silence.

She might find a quill, fold his fingers around it, and offer him a book with blank pages. The feel of a feather quill, the smell of paper—that might draw him out of himself. Except, not if he had burned out his gift. Mienthe thought; then the grief of realizing his loss might drive him further away into his silence rather than drawing him back into the world.

She leaned forward, reached out with one hand, and touched his cheek. "Tan," she said, and realized with a faint despair that she did not even know with any

certainty whether that was his name at all. He lied so easily about who he was...He lied with his words and his
voice and his face, and then told the truth with his own
blood, drawn out on the page...She said her own name
instead, because she knew that it, at least, was true.

His eyelashes fluttered.

Mienthe was too startled to move, or to speak again.

"Mienthe?" he whispered, in a voice as scraped and
raw as though he'd bound new law into the world by
shouting and not with a quill.

That broke her stillness. Mienthe laughed, and found
she was weeping. As weak as his voice was, the echo
behind it was very strong. In fact, the echo behind *him*
was suddenly very strong. She knew at once, though she
could not have said how, that he had not lost his legist
gift, that he had not lost anything. In every way that mattered, he was still himself, and she was suddenly glad
of the strange new perception that let her be certain of
that. She said through her tears, "Tan! I'm here—so are
you—we're safe, we've fixed everything, we're all done,
we're home— Do you remember everything? Do you
remember anything?"

Tan blinked, and blinked again, and turned his head
to look at her. A slight crease appeared between his
eyebrows, and he frowned. "Home?" he whispered. "Sil-
vered by the tears of fall, jeweled by the touch of winter,
quickened by the breath of spring, and nourished by the
generous summer...Am I come home?"

"Yes," said Mienthe. She touched his cheek again,
lightly, fearing to hurt him. "Oh, yes. Don't try to remember." Mienthe poured some water into the cup for him.
Then she was doubtful whether he could sit up—whether

she should try to coax him to sit up. Maybe she should shout down the stairs and send someone running for Iriene—

"I do remember," Tan said, in a hoarse but stronger voice. He moved vaguely to sit up. "Mienthe—"

"I was so frightened we'd lost you." She folded his hand around the cup, and added in a much lower voice, "That I'd lost you." She looked up quickly then, meeting his eyes.

Tan's mouth crooked, but he shook his head. "Your cousin—"

Mienthe was surprised. Then she smiled. "You saved us all," she said. "So did we all, but mostly you. Do you think my cousin doesn't know it?"

"That's not exactly as I remember it—"

"It's certainly how *I* remember it," Mienthe said firmly. "Tan—*is* that your name?"

He tilted his head a little to the side, but he did not look away. "That is my name. My mother's name is Emnidde. My father was, as they say, careless." He waited, seeming to hold his breath, though how she could tell she did not know, as shallowly as his breaths came.

"Tan," Mienthe said firmly. "Son of Emnidde. That will do, if you'll promise me to answer to it. I never again want to call you, and then realize I don't even know with certainty what name to call—"

Tan closed his eyes and leaned his head back against the pillows, and for a moment she was frightened. But he only whispered, "Whatever name you call, I'll answer to it."

"Will you?" Mienthe wanted to believe him. "Do you promise me you will?"

Tan barely smiled, his eyes still closed. "I promise you. I might lie to anyone else, Mienthe, but I'll always tell you the truth and I'll always answer when you call. Only promise you will call me."

He meant his promise, Mienthe realized. She could hear the deep, shadowy echo behind his voice, and she knew it was the shadow of truth. "Then sleep," she said gently. "Sleep. And when the dawn comes, I promise I'll call you." Then she sat quietly, very still and perfectly happy, her hand lying over his, and watched his breaths deepen again.

acknowledgments

Thanks to my agent, Caitlin Blasdell, whose insightful comments about my manuscripts always help me fix weaknesses that I should have spotted but missed; and to my editor, Devi Pillai, who not only tells me I'm "awesome," but also talked me into writing a trilogy when that wasn't initially what I had in mind.

extras

meet the author

Rachel Neumeier started writing fiction to relax when she was a graduate student and needed a hobby unrelated to her research. Prior to selling her first fantasy novel, she had published only a few articles in venues such as *The American Journal of Botany*. However, finding that her interests did not lie in research, Rachel left academia and began to let her hobbies take over her life instead. She now raises and shows dogs, gardens, cooks, and occasionally finds time to read. She works part-time for a tutoring program, though she tutors far more students in math and chemistry than in English composition. Find out more about Rachel Neumeier at www.rachelneumeier.com.

introducing

If you enjoyed LAW OF THE BROKEN EARTH,

look out for

HOUSE OF SHADOWS

by Rachel Neumeier

In a city of gray stone and mist, set between the steep rainswept mountains and the sea, there lived a merchant with his eight daughters. The merchant's wife had died bearing the eighth daughter and so the girls had raised one another, the elder ones looking after the younger. The merchant was not wealthy, having eight daughters to support, but neither was he poor. He had a tall narrow house at the edge of the city, near his stoneyard where he dealt in the blue slate and hard granite of the mountains and in imported white limestone and marble. His house had glass windows, tile floors, and a long gallery along the back where there was room for eight beds for his daughters.

The eldest of his daughters was named Ananda. Ananda was nineteen years old, with chestnut hair and pretty manners. She was not precisely engaged, but it was generally accepted that the second son of a merchant who dealt in fine cloth meant to offer for her soon, and it was also generally understood that she would assent. The youngest daughter, Liaska, was nine and as bright and impish as a puppy; she romped through her days and made her sisters and her father laugh with her mischief. In between were Karah and Enelle and Nemienne and Tana and Miande and Jehenne.

Gentle Karah, loveliest of all the sisters, mothered the younger girls. They adored her, and only Karah could calm Liaska on her more rambunctious days. Practical Enelle, with their father's broad cheekbones and their lost mother's gray eyes, kept the accounts for both the household and their father's business. Tana, serious and grave even as a child, made sure the house was always neat. Lighthearted Miande sang as she went about the kitchen tasks, and made delicate pastries filled with cream and smooth sauces that never had lumps. Jehenne learned her letters early and found, even when quite young, that she had a feel for the graceful phrase that could persuade a potential patron to invest or induce a legal advocate to rule on her father's behalf.

Nemienne, neither one of the eldest nor one of the youngest, neither the most beautiful nor the plainest of the daughters, drifted through her days. Her attention was likely to be caught at any moment by the sudden glancing of light across slate rooftops, or by the tangled whisper of the breeze that slid through the maze of city streets on its way to or from the sea. Though Nemienne baffled her father and puzzled her sisters, her quiet created a stillness otherwise rare in the heart of their crowded house.

For her part, Nemienne could not understand how her sisters did not see the strange slant into which light sometimes fell, as though it were falling into the world from a place not quite congruent. She didn't understand how they could fail to hear the way every drop of falling rain sometimes struck the cobbles with the pure ringing sound of a little bell, or the odd tones that sometimes echoed behind the sound of the wind to create a breathy, half-heard music pitched to the loneliness at the heart of the bustling city.

Even at home, Nemienne couldn't seem to keep her mind on letters of account or business—but then, Enelle was the one who was interested in the prices of stone. Nor could Nemienne be trusted to take bread out of the oven before it burned—and anyway, Miande made much better bread. And when Nemienne went to the market, she seldom came back with what she had been asked to buy, returning instead with a flowering sprig she'd found growing out of a crumbling wall, or humming over and over three notes of a song she'd heard a street musician play. When sent to even the nearest noodle-shop, just down the street and around the corner from the house, Nemienne sometimes got lost. She would find herself inexplicably walking down a street she'd no memory of entering with no idea where she might be, so she had to ask strangers for the way home. But then, Tana always struck the best bargains in the market and the shops, so there was seldom a need for Nemienne to go on such errands.

The merchant looked proudly at Ananda, who would surely be happily wed by the turning of the year. He treasured Karah and would not look for a possible match for her even though she was nearly seventeen, for she was his favorite daughter—but then Karah was so sweet and good that she was everyone's favorite sister and no one minded that she was their father's favorite, too. Practical Enelle was his greatest help in his business affairs; he called her his little business manager and joked that he should make his stoneyard over into a partnership with her.

The merchant depended on Tana and Miande when he had his business associates to his home for a dinner, and always the dinners ran smoothly and comfortably, so that even the wealthiest merchants, who had wives and *keimiso* and children of their own, said they wished they had such a houseful of pretty and accomplished daughters. The merchant beamed smugly. He never told them that the invitations that brought them to his house had usually been written by Jehenne, whose hand was smoother than his. And on quiet family evenings Liaska set her father and all her sisters laughing with her clever puppets, which she used in wickedly accurate mimicry of her father's associates.

Nemienne laughed at the puppets, too. But sometimes, especially on those evenings, she felt her father's puzzled gaze resting on her, as though he understood how each of his other daughters fit into his household, but did not quite understand where Nemienne might exactly fit. Sometimes Nemienne herself wondered what kind of puzzle it might be, that had a Nemienne-shaped piece missing out of its middle.

Then one spring the merchant died, collapsing suddenly in the midst of his work and leaving his eight daughters alone in a city they suddenly found far from friendly.

There were business assets, but these were tied up in the stoneyard and could not easily be freed. The assets could be sold in their entirety to the merchant's associates, but all of these men, whom the girls had thought were their father's friends, they now found had been his rivals. All the offers were very low. There were funeral expenses, and then there were the day-to-day expenses and the ordinary debts of business investments, which ought to have yielded eventual profits if only the merchant had lived, but promised nothing but losses after his death.

"Must we sell Father's business?" Ananda asked Enelle, after the cold edge of necessity had worn through the first horrid shock of their father's death.

Enelle glanced down at the papers between her hands. They were all seated along both sides of the long supper table. None of the girls had taken their father's place at the head. Enelle, who had always taken the place at their father's left hand, sat there still. She was pale. But her voice was as calm and precise as ever. "We can't run it ourselves. We can't even legally own it," she said. "Petris could. Legally, I mean." Petris was the cloth merchant's son who had been expected to marry Ananda. "And we could run it with his name on the papers. But that is supposing he would be willing to marry a pauper. The business could be an asset to build on, but it isn't a... a fortune to marry into." Even her steady voice failed a little.

"We aren't paupers!" Jehenne exclaimed, offended at the very idea.

Enelle looked down, then lifted her gaze again. "It's strange about business. While Father was alive we operated at a profit. But now that he is...gone...we own a net loss. We are, in fact, paupers. Unless one of us can very quickly find a man to marry, someone sensible who will let me run the stoneyard. Ananda?"

Ananda, across from Enelle, had her fingers laced tightly together on the polished wood of the table. She looked at her hands, not at her sisters. "Petris would still marry me. But his father won't permit the match if I don't have a dowry. A dowry up front, nothing tied up in future profit."

"We can't get you a dowry right now, without the stoneyard," said Enelle. Her voice fell flatly into the room and there was a silence after it.

"But what shall we do, then?" Tana asked, and looked at Enelle, who seemed, uncharacteristically, at a loss for words.

"We must all think together," said Ananda.

"You already have an idea," observed Karah, studying Enelle. Faint lines of concern appeared on Karah's forehead; not worry about the difficulties they faced, but concern because she saw Enelle was distressed. "What is it? Is it so terrible?"

"It can't be *that* terrible," declared Miande, always optimistic; but even she sounded like she didn't have much confidence in this statement. They all understood now that sometimes things *could* be that terrible.

Enelle drew a breath without lifting her gaze, started to speak, and stopped.

"Enelle, no," said Ananda firmly.

"We could sell parts of Father's business?" suggested Jehenne, but doubtfully. "Or the house?"

Enelle glanced up. "The business would be worth ten times less broken up than it is intact. And if we sold the house to get a dowry for Ananda, we would have nowhere to live until the business begins to yield a profit, which will take years, now, no matter what we do. None of our creditors will set favorable terms for us right now. They expect the business to fail quickly now that Father is...is gone. I...I would not like to live in the sort of house we would be able to afford, if we sold this house."

"But..." said Jehenne, her voice trailing off as she found nothing else to suggest.

Nemienne drew a spiral absently on the polished surface of the table with the tip of her finger: She drew the spiral going in, and then she drew it again opening out. Then she looked up and said, since Enelle clearly could not bring herself to say it even if Ananda would let her, "Some of us will have to be sold."

The silence this time was fraught, but it did not last long. It was broken by Liaska, who leaped to her feet and cried, "No!"

"Or have you thought of another way?" Nemienne asked Enelle. She might be wrong. Perhaps Enelle was thinking of something else. But, surely, if Enelle had thought of some other way, she wouldn't be so hesitant to explain it.

Enelle looked up, and then down again. She was only sixteen, just a year older than Nemienne herself. It was a horrible decision for her to have to make. But it was not, of course, her decision to make. Not really. It was only her responsibility to tell them all that it was going to have to be made. Nemienne could see she had talked about this idea only with Ananda, and it was obvious Ananda had forbidden her to suggest it. Poor Enelle.

"How many of us?" Nemienne asked.

"No," said Ananda sharply.

Enelle didn't look at Ananda. She didn't look at any of them. She said to her tight-laced fingers, "At least two. Maybe three. It depends on the price we'd get, you see."

"Who would we—who would—who would be sold?" asked Karah.

"No one will be sold!" Ananda exclaimed. "We'll think of another way."

"I don't think there's another way," said Enelle, still looking at her hands, which had now closed into fists on the table. "And there's not much time to think of one."

"There is another way!" Ananda said fiercely. "There must be!"

"Me," said Nemienne, since that was obvious. "But who else?" She looked around the table. Not the little girls. Not Enelle, who was needed to run the stoneyard and keep track of household expenses.

"No!" said Ananda. "No one will be sold."

"I am the most beautiful," Karah said simply, putting into plain words a truth they all knew. "A keiso House might be willing to give a large gift for me. That—that is an honorable life."

It wasn't that simple, of course. First Ananda and Miande and Jehenne had to argue bitterly that there had to be some other way. Enelle obviously couldn't bear to argue back, but her figures spoke for her. She had a whole long scroll of figures. She'd obviously tried very hard to find another way. It was equally clear that there wasn't another way to be found.

Jehenne looked at Enelle's figures and then ran out of the room in tears, because she knew Enelle was right but couldn't bring herself to argue for selling anybody. Liaska, who idolized the glamorous keiso and collected painted miniatures of all the most famous ones, was nevertheless outraged into a tantrum at the idea of losing Karah—and a little bit because she at least half wanted to be a keiso herself and knew none of her older sisters would consider selling *her*. In the end, Miande took the little girls away and the older ones looked at Enelle's papers.

Karah didn't examine Enelle's figures. She only believed them. She absolutely rejected any plan that involved selling the house. Nemienne saw that Karah's stubbornness surprised Ananda, though surely it should have been obvious that Karah would never agree to see the little girls forced to live in a violent, filthy part of the city.

Not that Karah argued. She simply continued to insist that she would do very well as a keiso, that it wasn't as if she were suggesting she might become an actress or an *aika* or anything disreputable. Then she announced that she would sell herself without Ananda's approval if she had to, and from this position she would not be budged. Ananda declared wildly that she herself could as well be sold as anybody, but of course that wasn't true. Nobody else had a merchant's son ready for a quick wedding and for the struggle that would follow to get the stoneyard back into profitability.

Nemienne didn't argue either. She waited. And two

days later she and Karah and Enelle took their father's small open carriage and drove to Cloisonné House, which all their cautious inquiries indicated was the very best keiso House in the candlelight district. Karah drove the carriage, with Enelle and Nemienne crowded close to either side of her on the high bench. None of them had wanted Tebbe, their father's driver, to accompany them on this particular errand.

Karah had cried. Then she had fixed her face and her hair very carefully. She was not crying now. Enelle was: a sheen across her gray eyes like the silvery mist before a storm. She looked out at the city streets, one hand gripping the seat against the jouncing from uneven cobblestones, but Nemienne doubted Enelle either saw the city through which they drove or felt the roughness of the cobbled streets.

Nemienne had not cried. She felt a low, tight sensation in her stomach, not like illness, but as though she had swallowed the icy mountain winter and it had crept through her body. The cold was uncertainty: She knew very well that Karah would make a wonderful keiso, but when Nemienne tried to picture *herself* learning to be charming and glamorous so that she might win honor and acclaim and eventually become a rich nobleman's flower wife, and wealthy in her own right...nothing about that future *fit*.

The wet cobbles of the street shone dimly in the diffuse light that came through the clouds. Lonne spread itself out around them, loud and busy: To Nemienne, she and her sisters seemed like ghosts, not nearly as solid and real as the streets through which they traveled. She lifted her gaze to the mountains, which loomed all around the northern and western edges of the city. The Laodd loomed among them; its stark white walls and thousand glass windows glittered in the light. Set into the rugged cliffs where the Nijiadde River plunged down from the heights to the sea, the king's fortress seemed from this distance no more a thing of men than were the mountains.